WRAITH
AND THE
REVOLUTION

Other Fiction by A.J. Calvin

THE RELICS OF WAR
The Moon's Eye
The Talisman of Delucha
War of the Nameless

The Ballad of Alchemy and Steel

Serpentus

THE CAEIN LEGACY
Exile
Guardian
Harbinger
Legend

WRAITH AND THE REVOLUTION

HUNTED

PRAISE FOR WRAITH AND THE REVOLUTION

"[The] worldbuilding is on point… But as good as the worldbuilding is, the character work far exceeds it. Calvin is a master craftsman of the character."

—Cat Bowser, author of *Mirrors & Ashes*

"*Wraith and the Revolution* has an electric energy, surrounding its unassuming protagonist with a charismatic, colourful cast. It's a rollicking adventure with great humour, some sobering moments and a steady stream of action."

—C.B. Lansdell, author of *Far Removed*

"[R]eal characters with depth who are then thrown in at the deep end into, well it says it in the title, into a revolution. But one at which they are at the crux and the action, intrigue and energy, take you on a roller-coaster ride of sci-fi promised by the title and that stunning cover."

—Nick Snape, author of *Weapons of Choice* and *The Wrecking Squad*

"[W]hen I reflect upon the story at large I can't help but think about what a fun adventure it was—not to mention all the little moments and decisions Calvin made to set this world and these characters apart."

—Adam Bassett, author of *Digital Extremities*

A.J. CALVIN

This one's for the dreamers,
the ones who want to fly amongst the stars
even if reality makes it all but impossible.

But who needs reality when you have imagination?

Wraith and the Revolution is a story that I tinkered with off and on for almost thirty years. I've lost count of how many times I started this book, only to set it aside for one reason or another. It has been a long time in coming, and the finished product is markedly different than my original drafts.

But some of the characters remained the same throughout, those like Sorin Johnston and Reginald Zylar. They've been haunting my writerly thoughts for most of my life. I just never had a story worthy of sharing until now.

My husband was the first person to read the final draft of this book, and he told me something that, in retrospect, isn't very surprising. He said there was more of *me* in this book than any of my previous works. Some of that was intentional, but other aspects just bled in from my personality. I have lived with some of these characters for decades, after all.

The intentional part, though? Our main character, Kye, has the same genetic condition that I have: sickle cell trait. It's often overlooked, because it can be completely asymptomatic... Until something triggers an attack. And most of the time, an attack can be deadly without swift medical intervention.

I was fortunate enough to be tested at birth, and given the time (1983), testing wasn't standard procedure at most hospitals. It is *now*, but not back then. Sickle cell trait has been a silent killer of many young athletes; there was a spate of news stories in the early 2000s about it, and most of the time, those athletes weren't even aware of their condition.

I decided to write Kye as I did because I feel sickle cell of any form isn't talked about enough. While the heterozygous condition of trait is manageable, the homozygous form of sickle cell disease is a serious ailment that afflicts a significant portion of the population.

But it's rarely mentioned, and that isn't *right*. More awareness should be given to this disease.

If you'd like to learn more about sickle cell or how you can help with research and awareness, please visit sicklecelldisease.org.

But back to Kye...

He also shared my dream of going into space, a dream that, because of my genetics, will never happen. Sickle cell of any form is an automatic disqualifier. Some studies indicate the G-forces required to leave Earth's atmosphere will trigger an attack in those with trait.

As a kid, I wanted to become an astronaut. I wanted to experience the weightlessness of zero-G, I wanted to see the Earth from above, I wanted to go to Mars. Imagine my disappointment when I learned it was not, and would never be, possible.

So I've done the next best thing. I've written a space opera that begins on a future Earth, with a character who knows exactly how I feel.

Will he reach the stars one day?

You'll have to read his story to find out... And I hope you enjoy his journey.

Thank you,
A.J. Calvin

GALACTIC AND OTHER ACRONYMS

AI	Artificial intelligence
ACTH	Adrenocorticotropic hormone
CVRT-BT	Camouflage, Visual Reflectance, and Tactile function Biomechanical Technology. A variety of stealth-based cybernetics reserved for ZIEG soldiers.
DFNR-BT	Defensive-shield, Fortified Neural-linked damage-Resistant Biomechanical Technology. A variety of defensive cybernetics reserved for ZIEG soldiers.
GEMS	Galactic Emergency Medical Services
GISA	Galactic Investigational Services Agency
GNN	Galactic News Network
GTS	Galactic Transportation Security
H/CR	Human/Cyborg Resources department
MSTI	Megatropolis Solar Tech Institute
NDA	Non-disclosure agreement
OMMA	Olympos Mons Military Academy
PTSD	Post-Traumatic Stress Disorder
R&D	Research and Development

SLTR-BT   Strength, Leverage, Tensor, and Rapid movement
            Biomechanical Technology. A new, state-of-the-art
            brand of cybernetics reserved for ZIEG soldiers.

ZIEG   Zylar Inc. Elite Guard

BOTANAARI TERMS

Botanaar	Both the name of the species (singular) and their home world. Botanaari is the plural form of the word.
Briia	An official unity ceremony, similar to human weddings.
Diivoraa	Botanaari promise bands signifying the pair's intent to join in *briia*.
Kiiru	A mammal-like creature native to Botanaar, prized by some as show animals.
Paavylaar	A word that directly translates into Standard as "seed father." In Botanaari couples, the *paavylaar* is the parent who gestates a new seedling child. The seedling inherits the *paavylaar's* surname.
Siindolaar	A word that directly translates into Standard as "pollen father."
Vynaas	The Botanaari term for their people's leader, who is essentially a monarch. The post of Vynaas is passed down through the *paavylaar* line.

CHAPTER ONE

ACCEPTING OUR FATES

**THE BAJA
EARTH, SOL SYSTEM**

Diablos rojos. Red devils. Humboldt squid.

They're a plague on our oceans, monsters no longer relegated to the fetid depths. They thrive, but they're the only creatures left that do.

Earth is a cesspit of toxic shit. It's our fault, but the all-knowing government turns a blind eye. Or retinal scanner. Whatever the hell an AI calls its optical interface. And the squid have become the apex predators in our polluted seas.

I do my best to ignore them as Pablo and I comb the beach for useful scrap. Some days we get lucky and find a working circuit board or a fuel cell with enough juice to net the credits required to buy our supper. On other days, we find nothing but useless detritus laced with radioactive sludge. Today is proving to be the latter.

As I said, Earth is a cesspit, and I'm doomed to die here. The AIs who run our government condemned Earth generations ago, and only those who can scrounge the means to get off-world live past thirty-five. The rest, like me, will waste away from radiation poisoning or cancer. I can't get off-world. I'm flagged as ineligible for space travel due to a genetic condition, one that can be cured for the right price. *Everything* in the galaxy has a price, but not everyone can pay it.

Case in point: I can't.

Did I mention we salvage scrap to pay for our damned food? I'll never afford the exorbitant fees the biotech companies demand for their treatment. And since my condition isn't typically life-threatening on its own, the treatment would be classified as *non-essential.* It's bullshit.

Pablo, on the other hand, could leave if he wanted. He's brilliant. I know he's been applying for scholarships at every engineering school the galaxy has to offer, and he'll land one eventually. I won't deny that I'm jealous of my best friend's fortune. I just hope he'll remember me as I fade away into obscurity here on our trash heap of a home world.

I glance at Pablo through my smudged goggles as he kicks at a mound of discarded plastic shards twenty feet up from the edge of the surf. He's closer to the water than we usually venture, but he's still within the safe zone. I can't see his face beneath the goggles and mask he wears, but his dark hair is tousled by the sea breeze and a sheen of sweat is visible on his tanned forehead. His hazard suit shows dark stains from boot to thigh, clear evidence we slogged through a mire only a few hours ago.

He notices my attention and backpedals away from the surf, then strides to my location.

"I got a bit close there, didn't I?" he asks with a nervous laugh, his voice tinny behind the mask's filters.

I frown, though he can't see it. "Yeah. The devils are active today."

"The devils are active *every* day, Kye." He shakes his head, then tears off his goggles and mask, revealing his dark eyes and ready smile. He studies me for a moment, then nods to a location behind me. "I don't think we'll find anything today. Not here, anyway. We should go."

I nod and remove my goggles and mask, then follow him back to our rickety hover truck. Pablo and I salvaged parts for two years to build the thing, and he managed to improvise and tweak its original design until he had an operational vehicle. It's a mishmash of seven different colors, and the engine compartment is held together with a roll of industrial tape and blind faith, but it *runs*. And on this blasted world, that by itself is a miracle.

We peel off our utility belts and hazard suits, our crud-encrusted protective boots, and toss them in the truck bed before climbing into the vehicle. I lean back into my seat with a weary sigh as Pablo slides behind the steering wheel. He always drives, and I don't argue. He built the damned truck, after all, and it's keyed to his genetic signature besides.

"Where to?" I ask.

He laughs as the engine hums to life. "I was thinking of our place."

Our place isn't a shared home, despite what you may have assumed. It's a hill overlooking one of the last relatively unspoiled sections of beach left on this planet, a place few people from our dwindling settlement have access to. It isn't easy to reach our place without a hover car of some form, and Pablo's is only one of two working vehicles we collectively possess.

I close my eyes and nod. "Yeah, our place is good. Let's go."

The hover truck lurches forward and is soon gliding swiftly between the scrap heaps littering the beach. In another time, the Baja was considered a prime vacation spot. I've seen the holovids from back then, from a time before humanity spread through the stars and promptly forgot their origins. The beaches had been pristine, the oceans a deep blue-turquoise, and there had been real palm trees growing in the sand. The only palm trees I've seen have been on holovids advertising the latest vacation destinations for the rich and influential—destinations light-years away from *here*.

Earth's soil has been poisoned and most of the vegetation that once grew has shriveled and died, along with our species' desire to protect it. Sure, *some* plant life survives, but in a mutated form that can withstand the toxic wasteland Earth has become. Humans are a shitty, self-centered species.

My thoughts drift to a question I've often pondered. "What would the Botanaari say if they visited Earth?" I ask aloud, not expecting Pablo to answer.

"They'd hate it," he replies. "Even their solar tech can't undo what we've done to this world. Why are you thinking of Botanaari?"

I shrug. "There used to be palm trees. They died."

He nods, though I notice the momentary unease that ripples through his expression. "Hmm. Perhaps I'll ask the next Botanaari I meet."

"They don't come here," I reply with a snort. "Unless you've met some in your net-dating endeavors?"

There's a tightness around his dark eyes that I don't like. He's uncomfortable with my questions, but I don't know why. We've been friends since childhood, even though I'm a few years older, and Pablo has a crush on me that he'll never let me forget about. I know him better than I know my damned sister. I'm certain he's hiding something.

"Pab, what the hell? Talk to me."

He shifts in his seat but doesn't look at me, his focus on the poisonous landscape outside. "I was hoping to wait until we reached our spot. I thought it would make the news easier."

I cross my arms and glare out the window, watching as the draft issuing from beneath the truck disturbs a colony of rats. Yeah, the rats survived the planet's corruption, just as the damned squid did. They're part of the reason we wear hazard suits while we scavenge.

"You're upset," he says. "Kye, I didn't mean for it to go this way. I'm sorry."

"How can I not be upset?" I demand. "You have news and you're withholding it. From *me*."

"Kye…" He releases a sigh filled with frustration. "You're my best friend. The man who, despite my better judgment, I fell in love with, even knowing you don't reciprocate. Please don't be like this."

I clench my jaw and continue to glare. "If you weren't my best friend, I wouldn't care so damned much. You're leaving, aren't you?"

He stiffens in his seat and stares ahead. Silence fills the cab like a plume of rancid smoke, so thick I think I'll choke. His refusal to respond only solidifies my theory; he's leaving Earth behind, and me with it. *Fuck.*

I shift my attention to the scenery beyond the truck's grimy windows. Mountains of garbage obscure the landscape ahead, tapering off as it nears the trash-laden waves of the polluted sea beyond. More rats scurry away from our exhaust to hide in the nearest pile of rusting starship engines and leaking fuel cells, cracked barrels of industrial waste, and the remnants of long-forgotten buildings. A few manchineel trees dot the shoreline, just as toxic as the rest of the landscape, and one of the few botanical survivors left on our world.

A splash in the water not far from the shore draws my attention, and I witness a red sucker-laden tentacle withdraw beneath the choppy surface, a large rat struggling in its grasp. At least the devils are good for something other than instilling terror.

Pablo Noriega has found his ticket off this forsaken rock. I should be happy for him, should be thrilled he's managed to escape, but I'm not. I'm frustrated, envious, and seriously pissed off. Not because he's leaving, but because I can't go with him. I'm trapped here in the noxious sludge with only the desperate souls of the colony for company. And their numbers have been in decline for generations.

No one lives on Earth by choice anymore.

I cross my arms and pretend to ignore Pablo as he fumbles for an apology. I should say something, but I'm too furious to form the words. He should have told me sooner, not after a day spent wading through the muck and sifting through who-knows-what in search of scrap to pay for our next meal. I know I'm acting like a petulant child rather than a mature twenty-six-year-old, but in this moment, I don't care.

"Kye," he says again, "you're right. I should have said something earlier. You deserve to know, and keeping it quiet all day has been difficult. But I thought it was better to make sure we could eat tonight before I told you."

"That didn't work out, did it?" I snap. "Today was a bust."

"Damn it."

He sighs and reaches across the cab to touch my arm. I would have jerked away from him if I wasn't already pressed against the door. I slide my furious gaze from the window to his face, hoping he'll take the hint and leave me to stew. We still have another twenty minutes before we reach our place, by my estimation. *Our place*, soon to be *my place, alone*.

He doesn't drop his hand. Instead, he guides the truck to a full stop and swivels in his seat to face me directly.

"I've been accepted into Megatropolis Solar Tech Institute," he says. "They've offered me a full scholarship. Now you know."

This has been his dream for years. I study his face, the pain he can't hide from his eyes, and realize he's struggling with the news just as much as I am. He knows what his scholarship means for *me*, and it's tearing him apart.

I look away and hope he doesn't see the guilt in my expression. I've been an asshole when I should have been excited for his future. I swallow the remnants of my fury and force a nod.

"It's what you've always wanted," I manage. "When do you leave?"

"In two months," he replies, finally dropping his hand. He knows my rage is spent.

"You weren't kidding when you mentioned the Botanaari." I force a laugh that sounds hollow to my own ears, but it's the best I can conjure at present. "And MSTI is the best of the best. They don't take just anyone."

"I haven't replied to the offer yet," he confesses, then turns to face forward again. The truck shudders and begins to move.

"What? Why not?"

I know the answer before he responds. He doesn't want to leave me, knowing he may never see me in person again once he does. Did I mention most people trapped on this hellhole don't live past thirty-five? By that average, I have less than a decade left, and my final months will likely be spent in agony. He knows this, knows why I can't go with him, but he's a damned idiot if he thinks I'll let him pass up this offer to waste away here with me. He deserves better.

"Kye, I don't want to lose you."

"You were always going to lose me some time," I reply, feigning nonchalance. "Don't worry. I still have that holoreceiver you installed in my flat, and you know my frequency without looking it up. You can always call me while I'm still around to breathe the toxic smog of our lovely home world."

He sighs, struggles to hold in a smile, then cuts a glance in my direction. "You aren't making this any easier."

"You've known me for how long, and you're still surprised when I choose the path of most difficulty?" I ask with a grin. "Seriously, Pab, you need to do this. You'll never get another opportunity like it, and if I find out you decline, I will do my damnedest to make your life hell."

He chuckles. "Then we're good?"

I roll my eyes dramatically. "Yes, you dumbass. We're always good. You're my best friend, even when I think you're being stupid."

"I still want to go to our spot."

"Then let's go. Maybe the devils will put on a show."

A half-hour later, we're sitting side by side on the crest of a dune, watching the surf's ebb and flow. The sun is low in the western sky, wreathed in our world's eternal haze, a mixture of toxic fumes and dangerous hydrocarbons trapped high in the atmosphere. Pale sunlight shimmers against the oily sheen of the surface waves, creating fleeting rainbow effects until the water breaks along the shore.

Some distance along the beach, a trio of people lug a steel vessel toward the water. They're here to fish, but I learned at a young age that it's safer to consume the bland protein cubes we trade for scrap than it is to ingest anything that comes out of these fetid depths. If the devils don't kill you, the translucent, malformed fish you eat will. It's just a matter of if you'd rather go swiftly and screaming, or slowly and spewing. I choose neither.

"I hope your prediction about the devils doesn't come true," Pablo says. "Those people shouldn't be out here."

I shrug, and he leans his head against my shoulder. I exhale loudly, but he doesn't budge, ignoring my unspoken complaint. Maybe he thinks he'll get one night with me after his news, a final farewell comprised of all the suppressed desire he's felt over the years. I don't have the heart to tell him no, that it will never happen. I'm not romantically interested in him—or anyone, for that matter.

Maybe he'll find someone new after he leaves for MSTI. Someone who can fill the void in his soul that he seeks to fill with me, someone who will love him *fully* and not just as a friend. I am not that person. He knows it. We've discussed it several times, yet he still clings to the hope that I'll change my mind.

I won't. I'm stubborn that way.

"Should we stop them?" I ask, though I know the sentiment is as useless as attempting to dissuade the fishermen from entering the water. They know the risks. At least their boat has a metal hull; it might prevent the squid from killing them.

He shifts his head slightly against my shoulder. "They won't listen to us. They never do."

I tilt my head up and stare at the gray-white expanse of smoggy sky. The old holovids show images of blue sky and puffy white clouds, but I've known nothing but the haze. Sometimes it's so thick the sun doesn't penetrate at all. I wonder what it would be like to see an unblemished sky, to behold a sunrise in all its glory, to witness the twinkle of stars overhead. Watching holovids is a sorry comparison to the real thing, or so I've been told.

I look back to the beach. The trio have maneuvered their craft to the water's edge, well beyond the safe zone, and are loading it with various supplies. I see greasy tangles of what I believe is netting, several metal cages, and at least a dozen plasma rifles, their tell-tale green charging lights giving away their presence. At least they're going in prepared, not that it'll help them if the devils are pissed off. They're far enough away that their features are blurry.

"Where did they get the guns?" I muse. "One of those is worth more than anything we've ever found scavenging."

Pablo lifts his head and stretches his arms behind him, his curiosity regarding the fishermen overriding his desire to invade my space any longer. "They're in sorry shape," he replies. "I'm not sure they're worth anything, Kye."

I nod. His eyesight has always been better than mine. That's yet another thing I can't get fixed; it's even more nonessential than correcting my blood condition. I've learned to live with my world being blurred at a distance, and my shoddy vision is one reason I don't mind sitting on the dune with Pablo as three people prepare to row out to their deaths. I'll see the tentacles rise from the water, see the vague shapes of the unfortunate souls as they're dragged from their vessel into the churning sea, but I won't see the gory details. The blood, the chunks of flesh, the severed limbs; those will be lost to my sight.

I will hear their screams, but not everyone cries out when the devils find them. I wonder which these fishermen will be.

The sun dips toward the horizon, turning the haze a sickly yellow-green as the fishermen push their boat into the surf. I watch for sign of the squid, but they're quiet. Two of the fishermen pull oars from the bottom of their craft and begin to row toward deeper waters, while the third fusses with the nets. I don't think they'll get far, but maybe today the devils will prove me wrong and they'll return unscathed.

"I'll send my official acceptance letter once we're back in the colony," Pablo says, his eyes on the sinking image of the sun.

"Good," I reply with a grin. "You wouldn't want me to harass you into a premature grave, and I'd do it too."

He chuckles and slides a hand across the sand to place it over mine. "I know you would. I just hope you don't hate me for leaving."

I turn to look at him, nonplussed. "I could never hate you, Pab. This is your dream. Get off this rock before it kills you."

Screams pierce the air, answering my previous unspoken question. I turn toward the sea, an ingrained reaction to the sound of someone in distress, then immediately regret the decision. The water is roiling beneath the fishing vessel, seething and frothing as the devils converge on their victims. Tentacles lash the boat's metal hull, but they're long enough to reach the people cowering inside. I note there are only two now; the third is missing. His must have been the screams that drew my attention.

"Shit," I hiss and avert my gaze. I don't want to see this.

"We should go," Pablo says. He rises and offers me a hand.

I accept and allow him to pull me to my feet, then quickly break contact. I won't lead him on.

We walk back to the truck and I climb inside as the whine-pop of a plasma rifle fires behind us. Relief floods through me as the door closes and the noise of the fishermen's desperate battle with the Humboldt squid is blocked from my ears. Pablo stands outside for several moments, watching the spectacle. I fix my eyes on him, unwilling to watch my fellow humans be torn apart and dragged into the rancid depths. His expression is a mixture of a dozen emotions.

Finally, he climbs into the driver's seat and shakes his head. "I won't miss the devils when I leave."

I nod an acknowledgment as the truck lurches forward and Pablo guides it toward the colony. *No one* misses the devils when they leave.

"I will miss you though," he says after a time. "And I'll call as often as I can."

"I know. I'll be here, waiting to hear about all of your new adventures."

"Kye…"

I force a strained laugh. "I can live vicariously through you, can't I?"

"I wish you didn't have to."

"I wish that too, but there's nothing I can do about it." I shrug. "I've accepted my fate, Pab. It's time you do the same. You deserve better than what this shit heap has to offer, and now's your chance to escape. Don't give it up for me. I'm not worth the trouble."

He exhales loudly, an indication I've struck a nerve. "You're wrong. You *are* worth it."

"I'm not worth giving up your life for," I reply stubbornly. "Don't back out on that offer, or I swear I'll feed you to the damned devils myself."

He laughs at my hollow threat. "I won't back out, but I *will* keep in contact. And we both know you'd never go near enough to the water to make good on that promise."

I shrug, and we fall silent for a time. He's not wrong; the red devils terrify me and I'd never stray beyond the safe zone, even if the payout would set me up for the rest of my dwindling days. I value my life, such as it is, and the squid are a sure way to end it. I also don't like the thought of being eaten.

He flicks the truck's forward lights on, and I realize belatedly that it's almost fully dark. Even if we had scored in the scrap piles today, it'd be too late to trade it in by the time we reach the colony.

Ignoring the fiery pangs in my stomach, I release a sigh. I finished the last of my protein cubes at breakfast.

Pablo studies me in the dim glow of the truck's display. "I have a small stockpile in my flat," he says as if reading my mind. "You're welcome to some of it, if you'd like."

I nod, certain he's hoping for more than mere conversation after we eat our meager suppers, but I'll have to disappoint him on that front. I may be stubborn, but I won't pass up a free meal.

"Good," he says. "I'll even let you watch me send my acceptance letter."

"Then it's a non-date," I reply with a smirk.

He hides his disappointment well, but I spy a fleeting glimpse of it in his eyes before he smiles. "Anything to make you happy, Kye."

CHAPTER TWO

BORN TO A DEATH SENTENCE

**THE BAJA
EARTH, SOL SYSTEM**

I'm awakened by the blaring sound of an incoming call on my holoreceiver station at three a.m. I rub my eyes blearily and scowl; there's only one person in the whole fucking universe who would be calling me at this hour, and she won't care that I was soundly asleep. She'll laugh and dismiss my surliness, then regale me with an update of her life since we last spoke.

With Pablo's news to darken my previous evening, I had forgotten tonight was our scheduled call. Unfortunately, my sister never forgets *anything*, and she accepts no excuses on my part.

I groan and force myself off my mat, then stumble into the other room of my flat. The holoreceiver hanging on the opposite wall flashes between white and red, and the hideous alarm blares again. I make a mental note to have Pablo change the sound to something less abrasive before he leaves for Megatropolis.

I locate the device's remote on my makeshift table—a pair of overturned crates topped with a rusting sheet of hammered steel we found on the remains of a wrecked starship three years ago. I press the button to accept the call, and the deafening racket stops.

The screen ceases flashing, and a moment later, Kelsey's face appears on the screen. Behind her is a shelf crammed with books on strategy and combat tactics; I know what it holds because she's told me, but I can't see the titles clearly enough to read them. Next to the bookshelf is a window overlooking a bleak expanse of rocky red terrain, the only glimpse I'll ever have of the summit of Olympus

Mons. She sits behind a desk, immaculate and ordered, a nameplate reading "K. Verex" displayed prominently before her.

Kelsey smiles and brushes a lock of dark hair away from her brown eyes. "You look pissed, little brother."

I cross my arms and glare. "You woke me up, Kels."

Her eyebrows lift and she fixes me with a no-nonsense expression, one I've grown used to receiving when she thinks I'm being particularly difficult. "I call you every month at the same time."

I pull my flat's only stool—if you can call an overturned metal cylinder a stool—toward the center of the room and perch on top of it. "Tell me about the academy then," I say. "What's new?"

She sighs for dramatic effect. "The latest batch of recruits arrived last week. I have my work cut out for me this term."

"You didn't have to take the combat instructor post," I remind her.

"Maybe not, but it put me closer to you." She flashes a grin. "OMMA is only a day trip from the Baja colony. Speaking of which, I'd like to see you in person when my leave comes up in three weeks."

I nod, both thrilled and horrified by the prospect. Kelsey hasn't returned since she left to join the military when I was eleven. She's been granted periodic leaves, but never once has she decided to pay me a visit in person, even after she took up residence as an instructor at the Olympus Mons Military Academy two years ago.

I eye her image with unconcealed suspicion. "You haven't visited me in fifteen years, Kels. What changed?"

"Isn't it enough that I want to see you?" She feigns a pout that rapidly dissolves into a laugh. "You're right, though. Something's come up, but I can't talk about it over an open channel."

My eyebrows rise of their own volition. My sister's whole career has centered around the military, and she's never once risked her position to divulge classified information to me, even when I've begged for details of her missions.

"Don't stare at me like that, Kye," she admonishes playfully. "This thing involves you. I'll give you details when I arrive, but not before."

"I hate when you keep secrets from me."

She smirks. "You'll get over it, trust me. How's Pablo?"

A groan escapes my throat, and I tell her of our conversation from the previous evening.

She smiles, despite my obvious distress. "Good for him. Give him my congratulations. MSTI is the best solar engineering school in the galaxy."

"I will."

"Hey," she says, "cheer up. I think you'll be even more pleased with *my* news when I arrive, now that I've heard this story."

I try to push away the sudden hope that surges in my core. I've grasped at blind hope before, when Kelsey first left with the promise she'd one day secure my ticket off this world, and again when she claimed she was close. But it has been years since then, and I no longer believe she'll succeed. There were too many letters from biotech companies declining my case for one reason or another, too many rejected scholarships because I was unable to secure the funds for the gene therapy required to grant me eligibility for space travel.

"I wish you'd tell me more," I reply sullenly.

"Three weeks," she promises. "Now go back to bed. You clearly need your beauty rest."

I flip her off, and she laughs before terminating our connection. Despite everything I know she's seen during her tenure, Kelsey hasn't changed. And maybe, if I'm lucky, she hasn't given up on me yet.

I skip breakfast the next day and meet Pablo outside my flat at our usual time. The wind is blowing, kicking up dust that adds another layer to the perpetual haze. I slide into his hover truck after tossing my gear in the back, and he drives off.

I rub my eyes and yawn expansively as my body fails to recover from Kelsey's early morning call. It's going to be a rough day, but I need to work. We need to find useful salvage today, or I'll be relegated to death by toxic mutant fish by the week's end.

"Long night?" Pablo inquires with an uneasy glance in my direction.

I know he thinks my fatigue is his fault, and I'm eager to prove him wrong. "Kelsey called. She sends her congratulations."

Relief pours off him in waves, and he grins. "I'm surprised you told her."

"She asked how you were. It was bound to come up." I shrug. "She's coming to visit."

He turns his head to peer at me for a moment, startled by the revelation. "Why?"

I snort. "She wouldn't say."

"Do you think—"

"Don't go there, Pab. If it isn't that, I'm not sure I can live with the disappointment this time around."

He knows of her unfulfilled promises to me, knows she wouldn't pay me a visit unless something very good or very bad has happened. Based on her cheery demeanor at three a.m., I'm inclined to bet on the former, but without details, I fear putting too much faith in it. Unbridled optimism has burned me before. I won't let it happen again.

He nods, then turns the truck northeast. "We'll head inland today. I heard they were dumping fifty miles from the colony yesterday."

I grimace. New refuse holds the most promise, but it's often the most dangerous to sift through. And I need the damned money. I console myself with the knowledge there shouldn't be many rats—yet.

"I was thinking," Pablo says after a time. "When I leave, I won't have any use for this truck."

"And?"

"And I think I'll rekey the DNA signature to yours before I go." He smirks, mischief in his eyes. "Which means you'll have to learn to drive him."

I lift an eyebrow. "Him? Since when was your truck masculine?"

"You wound me, Kye. He's always been masculine. I happen to like men."

"I'm aware," I say with a laugh. "You rarely go a day without reminding me, but please tell me you haven't *named* your truck too."

He focuses on the path ahead and refuses to make eye contact, though his lips twitch as he attempts to conceal a smile.

"You have named it." I shake my head. "Unbelievable."

"*Him*, not *it*. And people name starships all the time," he replies with a grin. "Why not trucks too?"

"Because it's ridiculous."

"Then you'll be pleased to learn I've exceeded your expectations." His grin widens and his dark eyes sparkle with amusement. "His name is Rusty."

I groan melodramatically, sending him into a peal of laughter. I'm going to miss these moments with him.

It takes another hour before we reach the new dump site. It's obvious even to my shoddy distance vision that the rumor he heard was true; uncorroded metal gleams in the sun's muted rays, and bright colors are visible between hunks of garbage. Without time and the elements to erode paint and bleach labels, it's a sure indicator this trash heap is *new*.

My empty belly grumbles in response. New means the potential for better scrap, which means I won't have to beg for more of Pablo's stash tonight. I'll need to get better at learning about new sites and finding the worthwhile amidst the junk before he leaves for MSTI. I've always relied on him… And I don't want to take my chances with the local seafood.

"Your intel was good," I state as he guides the truck up an incline built from centuries of trash.

He grins. "Better than yesterday's, that's for sure."

He parks the truck—I refuse to call *it* Rusty—along the perimeter of the new dump site, and we clamber outside to don our gear. Hazard suits, knee-high boots, air-filtering masks, utility belts, and scratched goggles go on over our ratty clothes. We've been using the same set of gear for five years, but it still has some life left in it. And we don't have the funds to replace any of it, so we make do.

Pablo nods in my direction once we're attired in our safety gear. "Ready?"

"Always."

I follow Pablo, watching my step as we near the new deposit. It hasn't had time to settle properly, and one wrong move could send us careening through an avalanche of trash and toxic waste. It's why few people take up scavenging, and those who do spend their hard-earned cash on gear to survive the damned endeavor. It's still better than taking my chances on catching fish from the shore.

Pablo makes his way to a gleaming hunk of metal that looks like it once belonged to a planet-bound aircraft. A row of windows reflects the haze-shrouded sunlight, and beyond, I spy cushioned seats. The rim of the wreckage is jagged with torn metal and wires, but that's what drew his eye. Wires mean circuitry. Circuitry means supper.

I grin and increase my pace to loop around it, careful to avoid tearing my suit on the exposed sharp edges. If I can't afford my food on a regular basis, I sure as hell can't afford to replace my hazard suit.

Debris slides precariously beneath my feet for a moment and I pause, arms outstretched to maintain my balance. The unstable garbage settles and I move on, my steps moving in time to the thundering of my heart.

"That was close, Kye," Pablo calls from my right.

I nod but don't respond, focused on the gray, polymer-coated foam panels that line what had once been the wreck's inner hull. They're held in place by a series of rivets, but they're nothing the flat-head screwdriver attached to my belt can't handle. We make short work of several panels and toss them aside to reveal a network of coated wires and the prize we made the journey for: Undamaged circuit boards.

I grin at Pablo behind my mask. I think he shares my excitement; his eyes gleam with triumph. Our moment of unspoken celebration is interrupted by a low roar overhead, and I peer skyward to see the squat body of a refuse barge sailing through the haze. Its trajectory is taking it farther inland, likely beyond our reach.

We spend several hours prying circuitry from the aircraft wreckage, then another toting our loot back to the hover truck. We don't talk as we work; it's a distraction we can't afford, given our precarious footing. I manage to avoid any further near-slides down the garbage heap, and we finish our work by noon. The truck's bed is crammed with our finds, our best haul in months.

We strip off our gear and stow it, and I climb into the cab in search of my canteen. It isn't a hot day by any stretch, but the work made me sweaty and the mask's filters left me thirsty. I down half my water and release a contented sigh as Pablo starts the truck.

"I'm glad you remembered to hydrate on your own today," he says with a smirk, though I see the worry in his eyes.

Dehydration is more dangerous for me than it is for most people. To risk an attack out here, an hour from the colony where there's no hope of receiving treatment, is plain stupid. I may not be the smartest guy in the galaxy, but I take self-preservation seriously.

"I'm trying to do better," I reply. "I have to."

I don't voice what we're both thinking. I'm a liability to *myself* without Pablo around to watch out for me. I'm forgetful and sometimes so focused on what I'm doing that I neglect my body's needs. It's a bad combination, considering an attack of my blood could kill me. I have a condition known as sickle cell trait, one that is largely asymptomatic, but it can be deadly under certain conditions.

Dehydration isn't the only thing that might trigger it. Too much exertion at altitude can do the same. So can excess pressure or prolonged exposure to zero gravity—which is why I'm flagged as ineligible for space travel. Despite all our technology, we still haven't managed to eliminate the G-forces involved in leaving a planet's atmosphere, and there's always a small risk something will go wrong during a routine flight, rendering the craft's gravity generators useless. Most interplanetary shuttles don't feature a med bay equipped for emergency blood transfusions.

Kelsey used to remind me it could be worse. I only possess *one* bad copy of the hemoglobin gene, so most of the time, my blood is fine. There was a time, generations ago, when my condition was more prevalent, when people were still born with *two* bad copies and dealt with complications daily. As Earth's native population dwindled, fewer humans were born with either condition, and now there are only a handful of us left. We were born on Earth—and doomed to die here amongst the toxic shit and galactic garbage.

Unless Kelsey's visit turns out to be my salvation. I fear to put my hope into words; I may jinx myself and wind up depressed and alone in two months' time.

Pablo nods, eases the truck into a wide turn, then we're speeding toward the colony once more. I glance through the truck's back window and smile; we haven't had a haul this good in months, and yesterday should have been shipment day. Hans will be well-stocked on protein cubes, and I'll be set for weeks, provided he's in a good mood. He has a reputation for being stingy with his trades when he's not feeling well, which has become a frequent occurrence.

"You think Hans will be happy with our haul?" I ask.

Pablo chuckles. "He should be. Just let me do the talking. You always seem to piss him off."

I shrug. "It's not my fault he shorted me—*twice*—when we traded. I only brought it up last time because—"

"Because you were desperate and hungry," Pablo finishes with a wry grin.

"That wasn't what I was going to say." I cross my arms and feign annoyance.

"I know, but my version is *nicer*."

I snort. "Funny, Pab. Hans is a fucking miser at the best of times, and we all know it."

He shoots me a knowing look. "As I said, I'm nicer. You just happen to be cuter."

I roll my eyes and shift my attention forward. "It's still not going to work, Pab."

He laughs. "You can't blame a man for trying. And it's true, Kye. If we weren't *here*, you'd be a heartbreaker throughout the galaxy."

"Well, I *am* here, and I'll take your word for it."

I don't own a mirror, and I can't afford the accessory program for my holoreceiver that doubles as one. The most I've seen of myself in years is the faint reflection in the truck's grimy window glass; dark hair, olive skin, hazel eyes, and a frame that's too damned thin to be attractive. I didn't shave this morning, and there's stubble on my cheeks, felt more than seen as I consider the watery version of me looking back from the glass.

If I've learned anything during my twenty-six years, it's that nothing is free, and most people don't give a fuck about those trapped on cesspits like Earth. My situation isn't theirs, so why should they care?

Their apathy is a plague. The AI government is bound by the whims of the greater population, and when the humans can't be bothered to help members of their own species, the bots ignore us too. People like me suffer.

"Hey, I was only teasing."

Pablo's voice breaks me from my dark thoughts and elicits a smile from me. His optimism has kept me going through some of the worst days of my life. His concern is genuine, and I don't know what I'll fucking do when he leaves. He's the best friend I'll ever have.

"I know," I manage. "I was just thinking."

"That's dangerous." He flashes a grin. "Don't worry about Hans. I'll talk to him, get your half of the cubes, and be done. You won't even have to leave the cab."

"Deal."

We drive in silence until we near the colony's western outskirts. The trash heaps and slag piles fade, replaced by parched earth and dilapidated structures, many on the brink of collapse. We pass our flats and many others, receiving a few nods and waves from the locals as we continue toward the gleaming structure on the eastern perimeter. The spaceport's signal towers rise high above the landscape, its domed roof of shining glass and brightly painted nanosteel a stark contrast to the bleak desperation and poverty surrounding it.

I hate coming here, but it's where Hans has set up shop. The trip is a necessary evil if I plan to eat tonight.

Pablo pulls the truck around the spaceport's northern side, to a dusty lot where Hans works out of an empty hangar. Hans is hunched over a crate as we approach, but peers up when he hears the truck's exhaust.

He's a tall man, nearing seven feet, and would have been intimidating if he wasn't wasting away from some form of cancer. He's stick-thin, his pale skin tinged yellow, but he still manages to glare when he spies me. I turn my face away, refusing to engage in a silent battle of wills, a battle I'll likely lose.

"I'll be right back," Pablo promises, then hops out of the truck. He slams the door behind him.

I watch as he walks into the hangar, speaks with Hans, and the cantankerous bastard smirks. A moment later they return, and Hans begins to assess our haul. I can hear the murmur of their conversation beyond the window, but I can't make out their words. Pablo's tone is calm, even, steady. Hans' vacillates between argumentative and thoughtful. Several minutes pass, then I hear the squeal of rusting hinges as the tailgate is pried open.

I peer over my shoulder and make eye contact with Pablo. He shakes his head while Hans strides toward the hangar. I nod and slump back in my seat; he doesn't need me outside, where I'll likely spoil whatever passes for a good mood from Hans. The big man returns a minute later, driving a battered forklift, an enormous crate on its tines. He positions the crate so its top is even with the tailgate, and Pablo begins shoving circuitry inside. Hans watches him with a sneer, then flicks a gaze at me. His expression sours into something akin to a grimace.

I don't know exactly what I did to earn his disfavor, but he's treated me like this since I began salvaging a decade ago. When I've attempted to initiate our trades, things always devolve into heated arguments and I wind up with half the protein cubes I should have been allotted. I'm content to let Pablo broker our payment today.

Hans drives the forklift back inside the hangar and returns with four cases of protein cubes. I note the peeling orange labels as they're shoved into the truck bed. Plain again. I don't complain; on the rare occasions when Hans receives the flavored varieties, they're usually so old they taste as bland as the plain ones. And I need the food.

The tailgate squeals in protest again as it's raised. Pablo pauses to say something to Hans, who shrugs, glowers, and drives away. He slips into the truck a moment later.

"This is enough to last you for six months," he says with a grin.

"What about you?" I ask. "You still have two months."

He nods. "My stash will last that long. From here on, I say we stockpile that flat of yours with as many cubes as we can get. I don't like the thought of you salvaging solo."

"I can manage," I reply defensively. "I'm not helpless."

"Think of it as my parting gift to you, Kye. I…" He averts his gaze with a shake of his head and starts up the truck. "I'd do anything to see you free of this place. You know that, right?"

"Yeah." I release a sigh. "I wish you didn't feel obligated."

"I don't. I just want to do what's right. For *you*."

I nod and look down at my hands. I don't deserve his friendship. I'm a lost cause, a man doomed to die on this forsaken planet because of politics and corporate greed, a fluke of genetics, and the apathy of our species.

I hope he finds the means to move on, to forget me and the misplaced love he bears once he's off world.

He deserves better than a man born to death sentence.

21

PABLO NORIEGA

CHAPTER THREE

ZIEG

THE BAJA
EARTH, SOL SYSTEM

The blare of an incoming holovid call rings through my flat as I open the door nineteen days later. I'm grimy and coated in sweat from another day spent scavenging, a half-case of protein cubes cradled in my arms. I kick my door shut with the heel of my boot, drop the cubes on the overturned crate that doubles as my table, then fumble with the holoreceiver's remote to accept the call.

Kelsey's image appears on my screen. She's not in her office at OMMA this time, but in what looks to be her apartment. Behind her is an unmade bed, the sheets twisted and rumpled in one corner. Above the bed is a small window overlooking another dusty red Martian plain. She never calls me from her home, and I wonder at the change.

"Kye!" She beams, her eyes scanning me through the connection. "I tried calling you earlier, but you didn't pick up."

I gesture at my sweat-soaked clothing. "We were working. Besides, you never call me this early."

"My leave officially started this morning," she says, still grinning. "I've made arrangements to be at Baja Spaceport at noon your time tomorrow. Do you think Pablo's willing to give me a lift to your place?"

"I don't think he'll mind, and we can use a break."

I didn't tell her we'd been scavenging daily since my last call to her. I knew she'd be furious if she learned, concern for my condition overriding the necessity of acquiring food. And Pablo is leaving in five weeks.

She lifts her eyebrows. "I hope you haven't been working *too* hard, Kye. I need you alive and coherent to listen to my proposal."

"I wish you'd just tell me now," I whine, acting for all the galaxy like her kid-brother, if only for a moment.

She laughs. "I will tell you everything tomorrow, but as I said before, I can't do it over an open channel. And this one's more open than the one in my office. Less encryption, smaller firewall, and all that."

"Your news isn't going to get you in trouble, is it?" I ask.

She waves a hand dismissively. "Don't worry, little brother. Everything is by the books, and I won't risk losing my job over it. I've just been told—*very* firmly—that what I have to share is between you and me alone. It's…unusual, to say the least."

My interested is piqued, but I know she won't elaborate. I'm just relieved she won't lose her job over…whatever she's planning. I've already drained enough of her limited resources over the years, though I've tried to be more self-sufficient the last few.

"Is it good news, at least?" I ask, both hoping and dreading her answer.

She nods. "It is, but it doesn't come without a few conditions."

I resist the urge to roll my eyes. *Of course* it will come with conditions. Nothing in this damned galaxy is free, and charity isn't fashionable.

"So why all the secrecy?" I ask.

Her smile falters and she chews her lower lip in thought. "The *benefactor* of this proposal doesn't want news of the offer they're making you to get out. As I said, it's unusual, and they wouldn't have made it if not for me."

"You're not giving me warm fuzzies, Kels."

She laughs, but this time, there's a nervous edge to the sound. "Just know I wouldn't suggest this if I hadn't exhausted all other options. I can't watch you waste away there, Kye. Maybe you're too young to remember how mom went, but I will *not* let the same happen to you."

I shift uneasily and avert my gaze. We don't speak of our parents often, and it's always more painful for Kelsey than it is for me. She remembers in detail how our mother battled to stay alive, determined to protect us despite the tumors riddling her body. They ruled her death was the result of prolonged radiation exposure coupled with breathing toxic smog for the entirety of her life.

I was only seven years old. Kelsey was sixteen, and she'd found herself unexpectedly thrust into the role of surrogate mother. She postponed her plans for the military for four years to ensure I was old enough to understand our situation, then left me in the care of Pablo's father, who subsequently died while fishing two years later. Pablo and I have been on our own since—and memories of his father spur our desire to keep a healthy distance from the devils in the sea.

As for my father… I have no memory of him. He died when I was an infant as the result of an accident while salvaging scrap. Kelsey was nine at the time, but has often commented that I remind her in many ways of him. I wouldn't know.

But Kelsey's words stir that spark of hope, the one I've been trying to ignore since our last call. She's determined to get me out of this shit hole, and if I'm lucky, she has a real plan. The mysterious benefactor is a good sign. It's better news than any she's shared in years.

I want to ask her more, but I hold my tongue. She'll likely evade my questions until she arrives tomorrow anyway. Unsecured connection and all.

"I'll talk to Pablo," I offer instead. "Can I share your news with him after you finally tell me what's going on?"

She grimaces. "I should say no, but I told our benefactor I'd need two NDAs. One is for him. I know you can't keep secrets from that boy." She shakes her head, seemingly exasperated. "The NDA will ensure he keeps quiet, and if he doesn't, there will be hell to pay."

I scowl. "What sort of benefactor is this, Kels?"

She crosses her arms. "I'll tell you tomorrow. I'll be in the spaceport at noon. Don't be late."

"We'll be there," I promise a moment before she disconnects.

I release a sigh and wander into the other room of my flat, peeling off my shirt as I do so. I fling it into the open maw of the laundry bot Pablo rigged for me, then kick off my boots. I move past the mat that serves as my bed to the little alcove containing the shower and toilet. I start up the shower, setting it to a warmer temperature than usual, desperate to wash the grime from my skin.

I strip and enter the jet of water with a contented groan. The heat and the steam force my muscles to relax and eases the tension in my limbs, something I've desperately needed for hours. If I didn't have to ration my water stores, I would have stayed in that little alcove for an hour. But I can't afford the luxury, so I cut my time short once I've cleared the day's residue from my body.

I grab a ragged towel from the rack, dry off, then wander back to my tiny bedroom to seek clean clothes, depositing the remainder of my soiled ones in the laundry bot's capable innards. Five minutes later, I feel markedly better about my day, Kelsey's strange news, and myself. I'm ready to call Pablo and tell him of our change in plans.

On my way to the holoreceiver's remote, I swipe two protein cubes from the crate I left on the table earlier. Today's haul claims they're coconut-flavored.

Palm trees died out on Earth long ago. I don't know what coconut is *supposed* to taste like, but the cubes are a touch sweeter than what we usually get from Hans. It's a minor improvement over the completely tasteless plain variety. I munch on the first cube as I turn on the holoreceiver and scroll through the menu to Pablo's personal line.

It rings once before he answers. He waves cheerily, but I note the confusion in his eyes. I rarely call him, since we spend nearly every day together sifting through the galaxy's waste.

"Hey, Pab."

He nods. "Is everything okay over there?"

"Kelsey will be at the spaceport tomorrow."

I can't keep the grin from forming on my face. It has been fourteen years since I've seen my sister in person. I was only a kid when she left, and though we've spoken often, holovid calls aren't the same. My stomach does a somersault, and I realize I'm *excited,* despite her cryptic hints at whatever she has planned.

Pablo's relief is palpable through the screen, and I stifle a laugh. "I'm glad you're okay. I was worried… But it's great she'll be here to see you. Finally," he adds with undisguised bitterness.

"She'll be here at noon. I told her we'd pick her up," I reply, ignoring his dark look.

He nods. "I guess this means you get the day off from scavenging. Is she ever going to tell you what the hell this is all about? She's been gone forever, Kye. I gave up hoping she'd come back for you years ago."

It's the same argument we've had dozens of times. Pablo believes Kelsey abandoned me while she went off to tour the galaxy. I've tried to explain her situation, defend her motives, but it always comes back to this. Maybe when she explains her plan—to *both* of us—he'll finally listen.

"I don't know the details," I remind him. "She won't say over an open channel, but she mentioned something about NDAs. She has one for you too, so you can listen to whatever she tells me."

Pablo smirks. "You've never been able to keep secrets from me."

I groan dramatically. "She said the same."

He laughs. "I hope for your sake it's good news. The news we've been waiting for."

I nod, uncertainty clawing at my gut and squeezing my heart. I want to believe that's why she's visiting. I want it so damned bad I can taste it, but I've been let down before. I temper my hopes with the knowledge that this isn't the first scheme she's tried, and all the other times have failed.

"We'll find out tomorrow," I reply.

"If she's stringing you along with another round of false hopes and empty promises, I will throw her into the sea myself." Pablo crosses his arms, his posture rigid with rage. "She's broken your soul too many times, Kye. I don't give a damn if she's your sister. It's not right, and I won't stand for it again. The devils can take her."

I bite my lower lip and look away. He has every right to be pissed with Kelsey. She *has* made promises before, and she *has* led me to believe I'd be free of this hellhole time and again. But this is the first time she's scheduled a trip to Earth. This time feels different.

Pablo exhales loudly. I look up to find he's slumped forward, his momentary anger spent. "I shouldn't have said that. I'm sorry."

"Don't worry about it."

A twitch of a smile tugs at the corners of his lips. "I won't, but I will worry about *you.*"

"You shouldn't. I've known what my future holds since I was a kid. I've accepted it, and for the record, I think Kelsey *has* been trying."

"Hmm." Pablo scratches his jaw thoughtfully, then says, "I hope she's prepared to answer all of our questions, because there's no way in hell I'm letting her go otherwise. You deserve better from her, Kye. You deserve better than this semblance of a life."

Deserving or not, this is the life I have.

Pablo bangs on my door three hours before we're supposed to meet Kelsey at the spaceport. I'm not surprised he's early, but I am irked by the intrusion. It was a rare morning; I didn't have any salvaging to prepare for, and I had planned to relax. I'm in the middle of reading one of the four battered paperbacks I own, the newest one, when he arrives.

With an exasperated sigh, I set the book aside and stomp to the door, flinging it wide. Pablo grins, ignoring my scowl, and pushes past me into the flat. He perches atop my makeshift stool and picks up the book I'd been reading from the table, scanning the cover with amusement.

"What?" I ask, a touch defensively.

"I know books are hard to come by, but this?" He grimaces. "How much gore is in this story?"

"No more than what we've witnessed from the devils," I reply with a frown. "It's the one I found last month in that old cache. It's something new, and I was tired of reading the same three books over and over."

He replaces the book with an exaggerated shudder. "I'll never understand why people like reading horror. Life is difficult enough without imagining it'll get worse."

I crack a mischievous grin. "It's fiction, Pab. None of it is true."

"And that won't make me like it," he replies, then glances at the holoreceiver. "I should have called you before I showed up at your door, but I've been thinking."

I sit cross-legged on the floor and peer up at him. "About Kelsey?"

"Yeah." He scratches his jaw as he considers his next words. "Maybe I was too harsh last night. She's never come back with news before."

I nod. "I've thought the same. This time is different. And damn it, I've missed her."

"How long has it been?" he asks. "Fourteen years?"

"Yeah."

Fourteen years ago, I was still a kid. I've grown seven inches since then, though I know I'm too thin. It can't be helped, and I'm not going to gorge myself on protein cubes just because I have them. Kelsey has always called me once a month, even when she was deployed to the far corners of the civilized galaxy, and she's watched me grow up from a distance. But meeting in person still may come as a shock. I'm not the little brother she affectionately refers to me as. Not any longer.

She'll recognize my face, but little else. And Pablo hasn't made an appearance in any of my calls since we procured our own flats almost a decade ago. She won't know the gangly twenty-three-year-old with the dark hair and eyes, the chiseled jaw, and the hopeful grin. I suspect she still remembers Pablo as he was the day she left, a hesitant eight-year-old, half hiding behind his father as she asked them to look after me.

"Kye?"

I startle and look up. "Yeah?"

"I lost you for a minute. I asked what time you think we should leave."

"She said she'll be there at noon. It doesn't take that long to drive there, but it can't hurt to be a little early."

"So we'd have time to make a trip to our place?" he asks hopefully.

"Sure. Let me grab my boots."

I sense he wants to talk, and our place has always been the location of choice. I hope there aren't any fishermen to ruin the fragile serenity today. I don't want to overhear their screams as the devils drag them into the depths, or the thrashing of tentacles striking a boat's hull. The book I was reading before Pablo arrived isn't half as horrific as the reality of Earth's damaged oceans. I doubt the author has experienced what we do every damned day.

Minutes later, we're in his hover truck, speeding away from the colony. The day appears overcast, but maybe the perpetual haze is just thicker than usual. Sometimes it's impossible to tell. He doesn't speak during the trip, and I'm content to stare out the window at the mounds of refuse, the choppy shoreline dotted with its noxious trees, the refuse barges streaking through the gray-white sky. The squid don't appear active this morning; I consider it a good sign.

The truck stops at the base of the dune we always sit along, and I scramble out of the truck in Pablo's wake. He sits down, a pensive expression on his face, and studies the incoming tide. I pause a moment too long before joining him, and he turns, his look morphing into one of concern.

"I'm fine," I assure him as I sit down, "but I don't know if you are."

He forces a smile, then leans back, stretching his arms behind him. "If Kelsey's visit isn't what I hope it is, what will you do?"

"The same thing I was planning to do before I knew she was coming." I draw my knees into my chest and rest my forearms across them. "I'll continue salvaging to survive, and I'll make sure I'm home when you plan to call. What more can I do?"

He sighs. "I wish I could take you with me."

I want that too, but there's no use pining for an outcome that can never be. He doesn't have the cash to pay for gene therapy, and without it, I won't survive the trip through Earth's poisonous atmosphere. We've been over the details time and again, and I'm in no mood to repeat myself.

Instead, I shift the conversation toward something more upbeat. "And if her visit *is* what you hope?"

"I will throw a party. A *real* party." A smile tugs at his lips as he gazes toward the ocean, but his eyes are distant, lost in the workings of his imagination. "Between the two of us, we have enough protein cubes to act the proper hosts. And Diego has a new batch of his homebrew ready for sampling."

I grimace and make a noise of disgust. Diego's homebrew tastes like used astrofuel and burns worse than acid. I could do without that addition to Pablo's plans.

Pablo laughs. "I don't think we'll scrounge up any other drinks besides water."

"What does he make that shit from? It's awful."

"A secret recipe, or so he claims." Pablo shrugs, undeterred. "I'll rig up my holoreceiver for music. We'll have a great time."

"I'll hold you to it."

He grins and loops an arm around my shoulders. "I always follow through, Kye."

He releases me a moment later, and we stare toward the water. Wind tousles our hair, and I begin to wonder if we shouldn't be bracing for a storm. The sky looks ominous beyond the haze, and there's no pale glimmer from Earth's yellow sun.

We don't leave the dune immediately, but continue to talk side by side as the tide inches closer to our location. We're well within the safe zone, even at high tide, and the devils haven't made an appearance yet. I just want to enjoy what might be the last relaxing day I have with my best friend, a day without a hazard suit and mask to interfere with our conversations.

An hour before noon, we reluctantly leave our place and head toward the spaceport to meet my sister. We fall silent during the drive as fingers of worry begin to worm their way through my gut. I don't know what Kelsey plans, and her vague insinuations haven't eased my mind, but I'm more anxious about how she'll receive me. Fourteen years is a long time.

He parks the hover truck near the main entrance of the spaceport, and I exit the cab to lean against the front fender. Lights sparkle beyond the windows, shifting in hue as the advertising holopanels cycle through their fleeting features. I've never been inside the spaceport, but I imagine it's clean and free of dust or debris.

Pablo walks around the truck to stand at my side. He crosses his arms and peers up at the sky with a frown. "She's coming on the regular shuttle?"

"I assume so."

"Then we should see it coming."

I glance around the cracked and pitted parking area. There's a small group of people clustered in one corner, their anticipation of the shuttle's arrival almost palpable from afar. I can't make out faces from this distance, but I believe most of them are still children based on their heights. Nearer to our location, a lone woman lounges on the steps next to the spaceport's entrance, her expression wistful as she stares inside. There is no one else waiting. We all appear desperate, clinging to the hope someone we love will step through the doors to greet us, despite the forsaken world we inhabit.

Minutes later, a boom reverberates overhead. I peer up to see the sleek lines of a passenger shuttle arrowing toward the spaceport. As it nears, the roar of its propulsion system quiets, and the craft stills. It hovers in the sky above for several minutes, then begins to descend noiselessly toward a hangar on the opposite side of the entrance.

I shift uncomfortably and cross my arms to keep from fidgeting. I shouldn't be this nervous to see my sister, but I'm pretty sure I know the first thing she'll say once she sees me. The knowing sets me on edge.

"Hey, it's okay," Pablo says after a time. "No matter what happens, I'm here for you."

I nod, but my response catches in my throat and lodges there. I swallow it, my eyes fixed on the entrance doors as they slide open. A man exits and races toward the lone woman, his arms wide. They embrace, then begin to walk away. Will Kelsey drop her military persona for a few moments to hug me when she arrives? I don't know.

The next time the door slides open, two women exit. Both are blond and wear filtering masks that obscure their faces. They walk toward the group in the corner of the lot without a glance in our direction. There are no hugs for the children, and I sense the pair aren't familiar with the group that awaits them.

I turn back to the door in time to see a lone figure in matte black combat armor striding toward us, a plasma rifle across her back and a military-issue pack slung over one shoulder. She's almost to our location before the glare on her face shield dissolves enough that I can make out the smiling face beneath. I grin and push away from the hover truck as she breaks into a run. A moment later, I'm pulled into a firm embrace, then she steps back to look up at me.

"Damn, Kye. I didn't realize how tall you were."

I laugh. It wasn't the first response I'd expected from her, but I'll take it. It's better than, "You're too thin," or "You don't look well." I've heard both from her often enough over the holoreceiver.

"It's good to see you too, Kels."

She grins and peers past me, then her eyes widen in stunned surprise. "Pablo Noriega?"

I turn and lead her toward the truck while Pablo nods a greeting. She breaks away from me to offer him a hug too, which he accepts awkwardly.

"Kye told me of your scholarship acceptance," she says. "Congratulations."

Pablo flicks an uncertain glance in my direction, then scratches his jaw. "Thanks."

"Is there somewhere we can talk?" Kelsey asks, her demeanor shifting abruptly to business. "Preferably where there's filtered air and I can take off this damned suit?"

Pablo nods. "My flat has a working filtration unit."

I climb into the truck's cab, taking the middle seat. Kelsey's armor is bulky, and I suspect I'd take up less space even if she was unsuited. She has the luxury of real food at OMMA.

She drops her pack in the truck bed but keeps the rifle with her when she enters the cab. The weapon is expensive and would draw unwanted attention to her visit if anyone outside were to see it. The people trapped here aren't above thievery when it's convenient.

"So," Kelsey says as we begin to drive away from the spaceport, "I'll have you both sign the NDAs when we arrive, then I'll share my news. I know I've been vague, but it's necessary. You'll understand once I can finally tell you."

"I hope so," I reply. Pablo releases a low growl of frustration.

"Is he always so protective of you, little brother?" Kelsey teases.

I laugh uneasily. "Yes. If the reason you're here is what I think it is, you'll have to get used to it."

She studies us in turn, her dark eyes narrowing in thought. "Why do you live apart?"

The question catches me off guard. I stare at her, uncomprehending. It's Pablo who answers.

"We're friends, Kelsey. Your brother isn't interested in romance of any sort. Please don't press the issue."

She blinks, then nods, her face flushing beneath the dome of her face shield. "I'm sorry. I didn't know, and I shouldn't have assumed."

Pablo snorts. "It was a valid assumption given how much time we spend together. But our relationship isn't like that. I tease him on occasion, but he's not—"

"I'm right here," I growl, cutting him off.

He shrugs. "You weren't speaking for yourself."

Kelsey's gauntleted hand squeezes my forearm. "It's okay. It was my mistake, and it isn't something we ever discussed. And everyone in this truck knows Pablo is right on his last point. You never speak up for yourself, little brother." She cracks a tentative grin. "I should amend that to not-so-little brother."

I manage a smile. "It's fine, Kels. *I'm* fine."

Pablo parks on the curb outside his flat, and I'm forced to wait as Kelsey eases out of the cab before I can exit. Pablo grasps my hand as I slide toward the door and gives it a squeeze.

"I meant what I said, Kye."

"Which part?" I ask.

"All of it. Do you trust her?"

I nod. "She's my sister."

His skeptical frown indicates his disbelief, but he accepts my answer. "Okay. Let's see what she has to say."

Once inside Pablo's flat, which is furnished about as well as mine, Kelsey nods, then pulls off her helmet. Her dark hair is plastered to her forehead, and she expels a relieved breath.

"I was explicitly told not to breathe the atmosphere without filtration," she says as she presses a button on her left forearm. The armor encasing her body splits open from top to bottom.

I gape as she frees herself from the contraption, enthralled by the technology on display. Her armor would set me up for the rest of my dwindling life. I can't begin to comprehend how much it must have cost to fabricate and tailor it to fit her frame.

Outside of the armor's protective embrace, Kelsey is muscular. She could easily overpower us both if she wanted to, but I don't think it's a possibility. I trust her, even if Pablo doesn't.

She grabs her pack from the floor and rummages inside, withdrawing a tablet a moment later. She moves toward the table where we're gathered and places it on the surface, tapping the screen several times. She spins the tablet to face me.

"Here's your NDA."

I nod and stare at the logo on display, the bold script decorating the top of the document. Zylar Inc, the galaxy's premier weapons manufacturer and technology broker.

Beneath the logo is a second, smaller design. Zylar Inc. Elite Guard.

"Fuck," I breathe, gaping for the second time in as many minutes. "You know people from ZIEG?"

CHAPTER FOUR

THE PRICE OF LIVING

"Not only do I *know* people from ZIEG, but Commander Patil owes me several favors." Kelsey folds her arms and smirks at me, a gleam of mischief in her eyes. "It helps immensely that I saved his son's life during the uprising on Chavez-2, and again with the pirate fiasco two years ago. Once you've both signed the NDA, I'll explain further."

I shake my head, trying to collect my thoughts. Her words raise even more questions. ZIEG soldiers are the best of the best, elite fighters known even *here* for their combat prowess. What the hell did they want with someone like me?

I force my eyes to focus on the rest of the document. It's a standard non-disclosure agreement; don't share anything you're told, don't make copies of any documentation without prior approval, don't take photos of anything you may see in Zylar Inc. facilities...

"Wait," I say, confused. "This mentions Zylar Inc. as if I'll be going there."

Kelsey's self-satisfied grin widens. "Yep. Keep reading."

I skim the remainder, too excited by the hope her confirmation brings to care what else it says. When I scroll to the bottom of the document, a signature line appears. I scrawl my name with my index finger.

"Good," she says, spinning the tablet away from me and tapping it a few more times. She pushes it across the table to Pablo, who eyes both it and her warily before he begins to read.

"Mine isn't as in-depth," he says after a moment. "There's nothing about their facilities on here."

"That's because you're only covered for the conversation we're about to have," Kelsey replies. "If Kye agrees to this scheme, he's getting the hell off this world. You'll be leaving for Megatropolis anyway, and I may be able to arrange for you to go on the same shuttle. We'll see. It depends on if he's willing to meet their conditions, and if so, how long it'll take them to arrange for his treatment."

My heart stutters in my chest and tears prick my eyes. "They're willing to do that?"

She nods and tilts her head in my direction. There must be something in my expression that tugs at her heartstrings, because she envelops me in a fierce hug. I'm overwhelmed with emotion by her insinuations, her proximity, the *hope* she's given me. Until this moment, I hadn't realized I'd given up, but the truth was, I had. I never once entertained the notion I'd be leaving Earth behind, even when she'd promised time and again that she'd find a way. I thought she was only humoring me, her kid-brother, doomed to share the same fate as our parents due to a quirk of genetics.

I open my mouth to speak, but a strangled sob escapes, and I burrow my face into her shoulder. She came through. She never gave up on me. Damn it, I have the best sister in the galaxy, and I never appreciated her until now.

"Oh, Kye," she says softly. "I wish I could have done this for you sooner."

I sniffle and lean back, wiping my eyes. "But you did," I manage, my voice raw. "You did."

Pablo clears his throat and slides the tablet across to Kelsey. "I signed it. Now will you tell us everything?"

"Two openings came up for ZIEG recruits," she says and begins pacing. "Patil promised if this happened, he'd reserve a spot for you. As I said, he owes me."

"Why me?" I ask, still unable to fit all the pieces together.

Kelsey laughs. "Your OMMA scores, for one. You excelled on the exams seven years ago. I thought they'd accept you based on that alone, but fucking politics got in the way. I was furious when they denied you entry because of your condition. They had the funds to cure it, but *no*, they had to go and spend it on a fancy transport ship for a blasted diplomat who hasn't even used it!"

I blink, startled by Kelsey's rage, and exchange a look with Pablo. His eyes are wide as he shrugs helplessly. Kelsey continues a moment later in a calmer tone.

"Anyway, your scores plus your history *here* make you an ideal candidate for ZIEG. You're a survivor, Kye, and they acknowledge that." She smiles and we lock eyes. "They're willing to fund the gene therapy you need to get off world if you accept their proposal."

"And their conditions?" Pablo asks. There's an edge to his tone, a nearly imperceptible tremor that I recognize as fear.

"All ZIEG soldiers are enhanced with cybernetics. *Heavily* enhanced," Kelsey replies. "I hear the process is incredibly painful, and about ten percent of those who enter the program don't survive the process."

Some of my previous elation evaporates. "If I survive, I won't be fully human anymore."

She nods. "ZIEG requires more from its soldiers than any other military organization in the galaxy. What they'll expect from you requires those enhancements. You'll be half machine, but you'll *live*."

I look away, unable to meet her eyes. Was escaping our ruined home world worth sacrificing my humanity? There were rumors about ZIEG soldiers, and she'd confirmed some of what I'd heard. They were faster, stronger, and more resilient than the average human. They were immune to illness, poison, radiation, and every noxious facet of Earth's desolate surface. But their enhancements were said to come with a price.

"Is it true they erase a cyborg's ability to feel emotion?" I ask, my tone accusatory in the wake of my fear. I couldn't imagine a life where I was unable to *feel*, to *connect* with others.

Kelsey's laugh eases my anxiety. "No, that's a fabrication if I've ever heard one. Do you remember Tariq?"

I frown, unsure why she's bringing up her ex. "Yeah."

"Tariq is ZIEG," she replies with emphasis.

"What?" I splutter, stunned. "He looked like he'd break in half if the wind picked up."

Kelsey rolls her eyes. "I wasn't referring to his physicality, Kye. You met him over the holovid a few times. You even told me you liked him."

"I did. He was good for you. He's really ZIEG? You're not fucking with me?"

Kelsey smiles patiently. "He really is ZIEG. You thought he was human."

"Yeah."

She lifts her hands, palm-up. "There you have it. You won't lose your emotions, little brother."

"ZIEG soldiers are required to serve for life," Pablo cuts in. "Is that what you want?"

I gnaw at my lower lip. Was a lifetime serving the galaxy's most loved and loathed corporation worth the risk? At best, I'll have another ten years if I stay here. It's possible there are already tumors growing in my body that I'm unaware of and my time will be cut short. Do I want to stay here with the garbage and the fumes, the dangerous seafood and tasteless protein cubes? Do I want to be left behind when Pablo leaves?

The answers are simple. No, and no. I don't want to stay. I don't want to be left behind.

I meet Pablo's eyes, and he offers me a small smile. He knows what I'm going to say, but I still have one question for Kelsey first.

"Their conditions are that I enlist for life and agree to the cybernetics. What else?"

She grins. "There is nothing else, Kye. That's it."

"I don't understand the secrecy," Pablo complains. "It makes no sense."

Kelsey's good cheer falters. "Yes, that. Apparently, it doesn't paint the 'appropriate' image for Zylar Inc.'s executives if it comes to light that they've taken on what they deem a 'charity case.' They fear if word of our arrangement leaks, they'll be forced to take on every desperate soul seeking to better themselves." She slams a fist into the table, and it rocks precariously. "I fucking hate politics!"

"It doesn't matter," I cut in before she rages on. "We signed the NDA. We're legally obligated to keep it quiet, and I've heard what Zylar Inc. does to people who cross them. I won't be one of them, Kels."

Pablo nods his agreement, and after a moment, Kelsey composes herself.

"I'm sorry. I've worked so damned hard for so damned long to see this happen," she says. "I won't bore you with every roadblock I've encountered, but suffice it to say, there have been a few. This though… It's a guarantee. You'll just need to sign their contract, and then we can schedule your treatment."

"Read it carefully," Pablo advises with a frown. "And be *absolutely certain* this is what you want."

"Can I think it over tonight?" I ask Kelsey.

She smiles affectionately. "Of course, little brother. In fact, I insist on it."

By the time I return home, Kelsey has sent a copy of the contract to my holoreceiver terminal. She's staying with Pablo and his filtered air environment, so I have the evening to myself.

The contract is straightforward. I agree to work for ZIEG until they deem it necessary to terminate our partnership or I fall in the line of duty. I agree to keep all intellectual property I may encounter a secret. I agree to their training regimen, which includes the addition of cybernetic and/or bionic enhancements. I acknowledge the fact that there's a probability I may not survive the training period.

In return, Zylar Inc. will pay for any future upgrades to my person they deem necessary, and they will cover any medical and/or mechanical healthcare I may require. They will pay for any training costs, my gene therapy, and any other health-related maladies that may be uncovered during my initial scans. They state my personality will remain intact.

They offer a signing bonus of fifty thousand credits, and an annual salary of two hundred thousand.

I stare at the promised credits and salivate. I've never seen so many zeroes, never dreamed they'd be offered as payment to *me*. I'm lucky if I scrape together one hundred credits a month with my salvage work.

I continue to read. Zylar Inc. promises six weeks of leave every year, and I'm given the freedom to choose when it is. They offer apartments to all ZIEG soldiers, and meals will be provided while I'm on duty.

There's some italicized print below the signature line that I assume is legalese stating my signature is binding. I don't read the fine print, and close the document.

It all sounds too good to be true. They're offering more than I could have hoped for, and seeking my service in return. The only snag is the cybernetics. The thought of losing half my humanity makes me queasy, but what choice do I really have? If I don't accept this offer, I'm signing my own death sentence and damning myself to this toxic shit hole.

I don't want to die here. And I will if I refuse to join ZIEG.

I pace through my flat as my mind races, grappling with the dilemma. For most people, there wouldn't be one, and I acknowledge that. But something nags at the base of my brain, urging caution. If I go through with this, I may not be *me* anymore.

Fuck.

Either I die a slow death, or become half machine.

What should I do?

I struggle with my indecision well into the night. I reread sections of the contract until the words are burned into my brain. I don't want to waste away on this forsaken planet, but the prospect of losing part of who I am terrifies me. I want to speak to Pablo alone, but it's impossible with my sister staying in his tiny flat. I don't think Kelsey will understand my hesitation, but he will.

I forget to eat my allotted two protein cubes that night as my anxiety mounts. I'm restless, fidgety, and my mind whirls with possible outcomes, few of them happy. When I lay down to sleep, I can't relax. I stare at the dark ceiling for hours before finally giving up on the endeavor. A decision eludes me.

I shower and shave the stubble from my cheeks, then prepare for the day. I remember to eat breakfast, though my stomach rumbles its complaints at being neglected the night before. When I arrive at Pablo's door, I still don't know what I plan to do.

Concern etches his brow as he swings the door open. "Kye, what's wrong?"

He doesn't wish me a good morning or ask how I'm feeling. He doesn't have to. My troubled night is written in my features, burned into my soul. He knows.

"Didn't sleep," I confess, then peer past him. "I need to talk, but not with an audience. Is she…?"

He nods in understanding and pauses to place a hand on my shoulder. "I'll let her know we're going to our place for a while."

I loiter at the threshold while Pablo speaks with Kelsey in low tones. I can't make out their words, but her tone conveys she understands. He steps outside a minute later, and we walk to his truck. The familiarity of the cab, of the drive along the coast, of his presence, is a salve to my frayed nerves. Even the thrashing of the squid in the waters beyond is strangely comforting. Despite its poisonous atmosphere and decimated landscape, Earth is *home*.

I can't wrangle my thoughts into words, though I want to. My voice lodges in my throat like a stone, and I'm rendered mute as the hover truck speeds toward our place and its strangely pristine dunes.

Pablo senses my internal conflict and doesn't pry. His expression is pensive as he parks and we exit the cab. He's never been one to press me when I'm tangled in a mental snare like this one. I'm grateful for his patience, his friendship, his *love*.

We settle atop the dune and watch as several brave rats scurry along the water's edge. I don't know what the creatures hope to find, or if they're merely drifting, drawn by an unnamed biological imperative toward the ocean. As I watch, a tentacle lashes across the damp sand and wraps around the largest rat. The terrified creature squeals once as it's pulled into the water and disappears.

I draw my knees into my chest and wrap my arms around them. "I don't know what to do," I confess, breaking our long silence. "I read the contract more than once. It looks legitimate."

Pablo shifts closer and rests his hand on my shoulder. "No matter what you decide, I'll support you. And I spoke with your sister last night. She told me everything. The loopholes she tried to exploit, how she's tried to save up the money for your treatment since she left, but hasn't managed to make it. Every time she was close, they increased the prices. Fewer people need gene therapy in the galaxy, meaning there's less demand."

"Less demand means higher prices," I reply with a nod. "I know."

"She honestly believes this is your last shot at leaving Earth," Pablo continues, "and after our conversation, I'm in agreement. But it's your life, Kye. This is a decision *you* have to make."

I draw a shaky breath and exhale through my nose. I've never been any good at making decisions, and this one is potentially life-altering. For the first time in my life, I can't rely on Kelsey or Pablo to come up with a plan for me. He's right; this is something I have to do alone.

I chew my lower lip and watch as the devils thrash in the water, fighting amongst themselves. When food is scarce, they often resort to cannibalism. I shudder and look away, meeting Pablo's gaze.

"I'm afraid of what the cybernetics will do to me."

He nods in understanding. "Would you like to hear my thoughts as a prospective engineer?"

Relief floods my veins, washing away some of my doubts. "Please."

"First, the cybernetics ZIEG uses are state of the art. They've been tested thoroughly for safety and efficacy. I asked Kelsey for schematics, and she agreed since I signed the NDA." He pauses to study me, his dark eyes unreadable. "She wasn't exaggerating when she said people die during the enhancement process. Most don't, but there is significant risk involved. They'll be threading machinery through your muscles and bones. They'll replace most of your organs with more efficient constructs. You have every right to be terrified."

The notion makes me squirm. "Is giving up my humanity worth leaving this shitty planet?"

Pablo drops his hand to his side and shrugs. "That's the question you need to answer. I can't do it for you."

"Will I still be *me?*" I ask. "That's what I fear most, Pab. Will I lose myself to the machine?"

He chuckles then, and I look up in surprise. "You read too damned much science-fiction, Kye. The contract explicitly states they won't tamper with your personality. You'll still be Kye Verex, my best friend and Kelsey's not-so-little brother."

I nod and know then what I'll do. "Thanks, Pab."

He smiles. "Any time. You're going to sign it, aren't you?"

"Yeah."

His smile stretches into a grin. "Then it's time I start planning your *bon voyage* party."

"No, Pab. It's *our* party."

When we return to Pablo's flat, my sister is sitting at his table, the sleek tablet in front of her. She's watching a holodrama, but pauses the show immediately when we walk in. She looks between us expectantly, sensing I've come to a decision.

I sit down across from her and meet her eyes, unflinching. I'm ready for this.

"I want to sign the contract."

She beams and begins tapping on her screen. "I know this couldn't have been easy. I'm asking so much of you… But you'll *live*, Kye."

Tears sparkle in her eyes, and I'm rendered speechless. I've never once witnessed my sister cry. She has always been the strong one, my anchor. Seeing her rush of emotion uncorks a wellspring of my own, and I blink rapidly as tears threaten. I never realized how much saving me meant to her.

"I have to get through the training first," I manage, my voice rough.

She grins. "You're my brother. I have no doubts you'll survive."

She spins the tablet to face me and pushes it across the table. "Sign whenever you're ready."

I glance at Pablo, hovering behind my right shoulder. He nods in silent encouragement.

I scroll to the bottom of the contract and scrawl my name with my index finger. Kelsey taps the screen again, and a confirmation of receipt appears in its place.

"Now we wait," she says. "Scheduling will be forwarded next."

"For the gene therapy?" I ask hopefully.

She nods. "That will be the first piece. Then you'll—" She stops to study her tablet as a new message flashes across the screen. Her eyebrows lift in surprise. "That was fast."

"It's happening?" Pablo slides into the vacant seat between us, peering at her tablet.

"Someone will arrive next week to initiate the gene therapy. You've been granted clearance to enter the spaceport for treatments. It's cleaner there," she adds pointedly. "ZIEG has agreed to allow Pablo to visit you while you're there, and my military clearance is sufficient for me."

I grin uncertainly, elation warring with terror within my core. Nerves flutter through my stomach, and I realize my hands are shaking. "I can't believe this is actually happening."

Kelsey reaches across the table to grasp my hand. "There's more, if you'd like to hear it." When I nod, she continues. "The treatment will take approximately two weeks. Once it's confirmed your hemoglobin-S mutation has been eradicated, you'll be cleared for space flight. They've scheduled your transport to Megatropolis on the same date Pablo leaves."

"What's the shuttle number?" Pablo asks.

"UGE-8719."

He grins and nudges me with an elbow. "We're on the same transport, Kye. That means I have time to plan our party. I can iron out the logistics while you're being patched up. We'll say our goodbyes to the colony, then we'll be on our way."

"Party?" Kelsey asks with a smirk.

"Before you landed, I promised Kye I'd throw him a party if you finally followed through."

She grimaces. "If I could have arranged for this sooner, I would have. You know that, right?" she asks me.

I nod. "I know, Kels. What matters is you never gave up."

"I'm too damned stubborn to give up," she replies. "You should know that by now."

"Will you be here to see us off?" I ask.

"Of course. I'm granted six weeks of leave every year, and I'm using it all now. I hope you'll invite me to your party."

I grin. "If Pablo's plans get too extravagant, we may need a bouncer."

She tips her head back and laughs. "I can work security detail for you, little brother."

CHAPTER FIVE

OKAY

I stand nervously at the doors to the spaceport eight days later, flanked by Pablo on one side and an armored Kelsey on the other. I have a battered backpack slung over my shoulders containing several changes of clothing and the handful of personal items I need to see me through my treatment; a razor, my newest paperback, a comb, and the beaded bracelet that had once belonged to my mother. I don't wear the bracelet, but it's the only memento I have of hers. It gives me comfort when I most need it, and the others won't be there every hour.

We provide our information to the kiosk outside the spaceport doors, then wait for our clearance to be verified by the AI barring the way. The AI isn't much to look at. It's just a black box with a screen, the paint cracked and chipped from years of exposure to Earth's toxic fumes. The screen has clouded over time, making the AI's virtual face difficult to focus on. I squint at the androgynous profile and hope I won't be reduced to lip-reading when it speaks. Given the state of the AI's exterior, I'm not sure its voice box will work properly.

A loud squeal erupts from the speakers and I jump, startled. The AI's face crumples in a frown, and a moment later a hiss of static issues from the voice box.

"Apologies," it says in a carefully modulated tone. "My speakers don't see frequent use."

"It's fine," Kelsey says briskly. "Are we cleared to go in?"

"Yes. One, Kye Verex, is scheduled to meet with Dr. Rana Malhotra in the medical bay in thirty-three minutes," the AI replies.

"Guests Kelsey Verex and Pablo Noriega are permitted to visit at will for the duration of his stay. One moment while I open the doors."

Several seconds tick by, then the entrance doors slide open. "Enjoy your visit to Baja Spaceport!" The AI's cheery tone is at odds with our bleak surroundings, but I'm excited to learn what awaits beyond the doors. This is a realm I've been denied access to for the entirety of my life, though it has always been nearby.

I step inside and pause, taking in the dozens of colorful advertisements scrolling by on the holographic screens. Beyond the panel of screens is a tiled corridor leading to a security checkpoint. There's a single GTS agent at the checkpoint, his uniform rumpled and his expression bored. I doubt he's seen anyone pass through his station since his shift started today.

Kelsey removes her helmet and breathes a sigh of relief. "I hate wearing this damned thing, but I can't risk the outside air. Not anymore."

I follow Kelsey's lead as she moves into the security checkpoint. The bored agent nods and presses a button on his console. Green laser lights form a grid pattern across Kelsey's matte black armor, and a vertical wash of red scans her face from right to left.

"Identity confirmed. Lieutenant Verex is cleared to proceed with weapons in possession by galactic military decree," a tinny voice drones from the console. The guard waves her through.

I step in after she exits and endure my own laser scans.

"Identity confirmed. Citizen K. Verex is cleared to proceed. No weapons detected."

The guard motions for me to pass, and I move to stand beside Kelsey as Pablo is scanned. He came into the spaceport with nothing but his clothing, and he's allowed through in moments.

"Let's get you to the medical bay," Kelsey says, taking the lead once more.

I follow her with Pablo at my side as we move to the end of the corridor. It bends at a right angle and opens abruptly into an artificially lit space. Rows of cushioned benches fill the center, while the perimeter is ringed by an assortment of vending machines. At intervals throughout the room, live plants are growing from raised beds.

Skylights are cut into the room's vaulted ceiling between rows of cool white lights.

"Those are real plants," Pablo whispers. "They're unlike anything outside."

Kelsey nods and points to one with tall fronds made up of many leaf blades. "That's a form of palm," she says. "They once grew here in abundance." She motions to an even larger plant, one with a woody stem and a purplish sheen to its leaves. Yellow flowers peek from beneath its glossy foliage. "That one is native to Botanaar."

"Have you been to Botanaar?" Pablo asks as I continue to stare wide-eyed at our surroundings.

Kelsey laughs. "No. The Botanaari are notoriously selective about who they allow on their home world. It seems they don't trust us, given the state we left our own home world in." She pauses thoughtfully, then says, "Since you'll be earning a degree from MSTI, there's a chance you might be welcomed there one day, Pablo. You'll certainly meet plenty of Botanaari amongst the faculty."

Kelsey motions for us to follow as she makes a right turn. "This way."

I don't know how she navigates the sprawling spaceport interior until we make another three turns and pass through several other open spaces. Only then do I realize there are signs indicating the direction of its various features; departures, arrivals, baggage claim, entertainment venues, and the medical bay. The signage was nearly lost amongst the more brilliant advertisements and colorful vending displays.

We turn a final corner, and glaring red and white lights shine from above a series of sleek glass doors. We aren't near enough for them to coalesce into the letters they represent for my waning distance vision, but I know we've found the medical bay when Kelsey announces, "We're here."

More cushioned benches line the walls along the corridor, but there's no one present. The spaceport has been almost vacant beyond the regular staff we've passed, and it seems none of them require a doctor. Or if they do, they don't have any friends or family to wait for them outside.

As we walk closer, the red lights above the doors crystallize into the words "Medical Bay," while the white ones read, "Galactic Emergency Medical Services Welcomes You," beneath. The doors slide soundlessly open at our approach, and we enter a small lobby. There are no chairs inside, but a woman dressed in a crisp gray uniform with "GEMS" printed along the sleeves stands behind a desk. Several holovid screens and a tablet decorate the desktop. A white nametag pinned to her top reads "Olivia, Patient Processing."

Olivia plasters a smile on her face, though it fails to reach her eyes. "How may I help you today? We only have one scheduled appointment on the books, and—"

"I'm Kye Verex," I interrupt, receiving a disapproving frown in response. "I *have* an appointment. With Dr. Malhotra."

Recognition blooms in her eyes alongside suspicion. "I will confirm with the doctor that she is expecting you. She is not a resident here, but she is using our facilities. I'm afraid I don't have your name in our register."

Kelsey steps forward. "Please speak with the doctor. She is here for Kye."

Olivia glares at Kelsey but nods tersely. "I will call her now."

I turn to Kelsey while Olivia taps one of her screens. "Why isn't my name in her fucking register?" I hiss. "This was supposed to be scheduled."

Kelsey holds up a hand, seeking patience. "Your name isn't in the books because of the secrecy your benefactors are attempting to maintain. She'll see you, little brother. Don't worry."

I cross my arms and glare at the gleaming tile floor. "I hope so."

"Hey," Pablo says gently, "this will work out. You've done everything they've asked, and they won't renege on their contract. It's bad for business."

"Ah, Mr. Verex?" Olivia asks uncertainly.

I turn to face her, fearful she'll tell me Dr. Malhotra doesn't know who I am, that I'll be sent packing and must resume my life as a scavenger, eking out an existence amongst the toxic debris, the rats, and the inhospitable seas.

"Dr. Malhotra is expecting you. You and your companions may follow me."

I exhale audibly, relieved beyond measure. Zylar Inc. is willing to fulfill their first promise to me.

Olivia leads us through a door behind her desk and along a brightly lit hall. Doors line the walls, each closed for patient privacy, until she arrives at one standing ajar. She motions for us to go inside, but it's clear she has no intention of following.

I chew my lip and hesitate. This is the point of no return.

"We're here for you," Pablo says.

I nod once and pull the door fully open. The room is furnished with a single bed adorned in white hospital linens, and a padded bench lines one wall. A variety of medical apparatuses line the wall behind the bed, each with a different display. Some are illuminated, others are blank. A dark-skinned woman in a pale blue lab coat stands in the center of the room wearing a friendly smile, but the room and its doctor aren't the cause of my sudden panic.

Three soldiers occupy the space between her and the door. Each wears dark blue armor similar to Kelsey's, though where hers displays her name and rank, theirs is marked with the ZIEG logo. Two are women; the third is androgynous. They stand at ease, their weapons stowed at their belts and across their backs. One of the women, a blond, offers me a knowing smile. The other, whose hair is dyed in a rainbow of colors, winks and flashes a grin. Their companion remains stoic, though I see a glimmer of curiosity in the depths of their startlingly blue eyes.

Despite their seemingly friendly demeanor, I'm eclipsed by fear. The itinerary I was given didn't mention there would be three ZIEG soldiers present for my treatment. Are they here to ensure Kelsey and Pablo don't talk about what they might see? Or are they here to keep tabs on me, to make sure I don't run once my blood condition is cured?

The rainbow-haired woman steps forward and offers her hand. "I'm Luna," she says as I tentatively grasp her fingers. "You must be Kye."

I nod, and she grins. "I'm sure you have a thousand questions. We can answer them once the doctor is finished setting you up." She jerks a thumb at the other woman. "That's Jen, my second-in-command. And this one is Vee."

Jen smiles in greeting but makes no move to step forward. Vee offers their hand, and we shake.

"You'll have your work cut out with this one," Vee says to Luna. "He's in worse shape than Patil led us to believe."

I look away, abruptly aware of every inadequacy I possess. Kelsey steps in to introduce herself and Pablo while I grapple with self-loathing.

"Don't worry," Luna says, placing a hand on my shoulder. "We don't see many people from Earth, and those we come across are often much younger when they flee. We knew you'd be in poor physical shape, but your OMMA scores were quite impressive."

She turns to the doctor. "This is Dr. Malhotra, one of our ZIEG medical specialists. She'll assess you, then you'll begin treatment."

"Please, call me Rana," the doctor says in a motherly tone.

I'm ushered to the bed and asked to remove my shirt. I peel it off and refuse to meet Kelsey's gaze, certain she's busy counting every rib she sees. They're all starkly visible beneath my taut skin, as are my collarbones. The litany of muttered curses that fly from her lips confirms her reaction. I know I'm malnourished, but I'm in better shape now than I was before we located the starship wreckage full of circuitry.

"Please lie back," Rana says softly. "The scans will take approximately an hour to complete, so make yourself comfortable."

I nod and glance at the others in the room. Luna is speaking with Vee and Kelsey in hushed tones. Jen leans against the wall next to the door, her eyes on Rana as the doctor begins to tap at a panel beside my bed. Pablo moves to sit on the unoccupied bench and offers me a nervous grin.

"Are you ready to begin?" Rana asks.

I draw a breath and close my eyes, hoping to calm my anxiety. I don't know what else the scans will uncover, and I'm not sure I want to be confronted with the full extent of what this planet has done to me over time. But I can't back out now. I'm here, and if Luna's team is any indication, I won't be slipping from ZIEG's grasp. I'm committed to this path.

"Yeah," I reply. "Let's do this."

"Scans complete. Data analysis pending," a monitor behind my bed chimes an hour later.

The room falls silent. I glance at Pablo where he perches on the bench, his expression betraying his fear. He doesn't look at me, focusing on the readouts on the wall instead. I shift my gaze to Kelsey, who walks to the foot of my bed. She offers a strained smile, and I know the results appearing on the display can't be good. The trio of ZIEG soldiers exits the room, giving us privacy.

"Data analysis complete. Results incoming."

Dr. Malhotra focuses on her tablet and taps it several times, her features carefully composed. She nods as she scans the data, glances at the monitors behind me, and taps a manicured fingernail against her lower lip.

"What does it say?" I ask, scanning each face in turn.

Pablo still won't look at me, Kelsey's smile is strained, and Dr. Malhotra continues to muse thoughtfully for several seconds. I know the scans have uncovered something more than the sickle cell trait, something that may disqualify me from this entire endeavor judging by Kelsey's reaction alone.

The silence drags on. I want to scream, but I bottle my fear inside and clench my fists as my impatience grows. Damn it, tell me already. I can't take the suspense.

Finally, the doctor sets the tablet aside and her dark eyes meet mine. "The scans uncovered multiple tumors."

I swallow and force a nod, certain of what will come next. I'll be sent home to waste away, another casualty of humanity's wanton destruction of our home world.

"We'll need to treat the cancer first," she continues. "It will delay your gene therapy a few days, but this was not unexpected. I'm surprised there weren't more, and that they weren't farther along the malignancy scale."

I stare at her, uncomprehending. "What?"

She smiles compassionately. "We will treat your cancer first, then proceed with the gene therapy as planned."

I still don't understand. "But…why? I thought—"

"When you signed your contract with ZIEG, Zylar Inc. was legally bound to oversee your medical costs," she replies. "Cancer treatments are a part of that."

I look to Kelsey. She's grinning while tears spill from her eyes.

Holy shit, this is actually happening.

"Once an individual is earmarked for ZIEG, we do not refuse them treatment of any kind," the doctor continues. "Your scans revealed one more item of concern, but it can be addressed later. Your teeth show signs of multiple cavities. Again, this was expected. You've subsisted on protein cubes for most of your life, correct?"

I clear my throat. "Yeah."

"You see, protein cubes provide necessary nutrition, but their consistency isn't ideal for healthy teeth. I suspect your captain will ensure you're eating very well before you leave here."

"Captain?"

Dr. Malhotra smiles. "Yes. Luna Zeta is your unit's captain. She and the others will be your guides as you go through ZIEG training. It's why they're here."

"Oh."

I don't know what else to say. My assumptions were so completely off that I'm left reeling.

"We'll begin the cancer treatments once the tailored formula is ready." She lays a hand on my bare shoulder. "I would prefer that you change into proper hospital attire before we begin. It will be easier on us both." She points to a cabinet near the door that I'd missed previously. "You'll find garments in there." To Kelsey and Pablo, she says, "We should give him a few minutes of privacy."

Kelsey nods. "We'll be in the hall, little brother."

Pablo lingers after they leave and walks to the cabinet as I climb from the bed. He pulls out a shapeless top and baggy pants made of a thin blue fabric, and hands them to me when I reach his location.

"I'll be scanned when I reach Megatropolis," he says quietly. "I'm sure they'll find tumors. We've always been together..."

His face crumples with emotion as a sob rips from his throat. I drop the garments and pull him into my arms. He's been my anchor for years; it's time I reciprocate. He needs comfort, and unlike me, he doesn't have a sister to offer it.

"Pab, it's okay. We'll get through this."

"What if they send me home?"

I shake my head. "They won't. Your scholarship covers healthcare, once you arrive on Megatropolis. You didn't have to jump through hoops to be cleared for space travel like I did."

He sniffles but doesn't push away. I suspect he's secretly enjoying our proximity, but he'll never admit it. And I don't mind this time; I understand his fears all too well.

"You'll be okay," I promise. "And for the first time in my life, I think I will be too."

His arms tighten around my torso for a moment, then he steps away. He wipes his eyes with the heels of his hands and forces a smile. "Sorry, Kye. I just needed a hug."

"I know, Pab. Don't worry about it."

He moves to the door as I bend to retrieve the hospital garb. "Kye?"

"Yeah?"

"I think you're right. I think we *will* be okay."

I spend the next three and a half weeks in the spaceport's medical bay. Kelsey and Pablo visit daily, but they don't stay beyond the posted visitor hours. The ZIEG crew keeps a watchful distance as I undergo multiple rounds of cancer treatments, followed by the gene therapy. I suspect they'll talk to me more after I'm officially cleared to leave Earth. Jen and Vee are more distant than Luna, who stops in for brief chats every evening.

Dr. Malhotra oversees every aspect of my care, and I find myself in conversation with her most often when Kelsey and Pablo aren't here. We discuss topics ranging from my education to my time spent scavenging to my aspirations for the future, and everything in between. I tell her about my past, Kelsey's decades-long struggle to see me cured, and Pablo's acceptance into MSTI. She's a patient listener and only asks questions when it seems I've come to a natural endpoint in my tale.

She monitors my progress carefully. I'm scanned each day, and serum samples are collected for analysis. She tailors my diet to gaining lean muscle, and I'm introduced to a wild variety of foods I never imagined possible. Food—*real* food—contains an explosion of flavors. I begin to enjoy meals for the first time in my life.

By the end of the second week, I'm cancer-free and have gained almost ten pounds. It's not enough, and she increases my caloric intake.

By the end of the third week, she's pleased with the results of the gene therapy, and I've gained another seven pounds. My ribs are no longer visible and she claims my face is no longer gaunt. The medical bay doesn't have mirrors in its rooms for safety reasons, so I take her word for it.

By day twenty-six, I'm officially cleared for space flight, and she places me on an exercise regimen to build muscle mass now that overexertion is no longer life-threatening. Several exercise machines are moved into my room, and it falls to Vee to instruct me on their use. Vee doesn't mince words, but I find their company strangely comforting. There is acceptance in Vee's faint smiles, and I begin to feel like part of the team.

Pablo is never able to make good on his promised party. I'm not allowed to leave the spaceport even after my treatment is complete, but I am granted the freedom to wander its nearly empty corridors. I learn all I can about the plants growing inside, how to operate the vending machines, and I ask a thousand questions of Kelsey during her visits. What should I expect when I reach Megatropolis? How many people live on our galaxy's capital world? What is that planet like?

I bombard Vee with even more questions during our workouts. I want to learn as much about ZIEG and Zylar Inc. as I can, but Vee is unwilling to answer many of them.

"You'll see when you get there," is Vee's favorite response.

After four weeks, I'm given a blue uniform with the ZIEG logo on its back. Dr. Malhotra—Rana, as she insists I call her—wishes me good luck and departs. The trio of ZIEG soldiers meets me in the corridor after I change, and we walk to the departures area of the spaceport. Kelsey and Pablo are already there.

Pablo flashes a grin and points through the window to a sleek black spacecraft. "By this time tomorrow, we'll be on Megatropolis."

I nod. "I'm ready. Are you?"

"Always."

A chime echoes overhead, and a toneless voice follows. "Shuttle UGE-8719 for Megatropolis is now boarding."

A flutter of anticipation ripples through me, and I glance at the spacecraft once more as our group moves toward the AI kiosk. We're scanned, much as we were at the security checkpoint on our arrival, then allowed to enter the passenger boarding bridge. We're greeted by a man in a red and white uniform as we step into the shuttle.

"You may sit anywhere you wish," he says with a gesture toward the interior.

It's lined with faux-leather couches, and each seat features both a headrest and a recliner. At the rear of the passenger cabin is an L-shaped bar, where another man in red and white waits expectantly. The holoscreen behind him displays a menu featuring both food and drink items, followed by their costs. Several polished machines line the counter behind him, lights blinking in anticipation.

I ignore the refreshments and take a seat next to a window. I want to watch every moment of our departure from Earth. Pablo follows me and perches at my side, leaning forward to peer around my bulkier frame.

The others find seats as well, and soon the pilot's voice issues from speakers overhead. "I'm Akira, your pilot. Please fasten your safety harnesses as we prepare for launch and accelerate to escape velocity. You will experience heavy gravitational forces as we exit the atmosphere. Once in true space, the grav-generators will turn on, and you will be free to move about the passenger cabin."

I pull the safety harness from the seat back and secure it around my body while my heart pounds a frantic cadence. This is the moment I've dreamed of since I was a child. This is the moment I believed would never happen only two months ago.

The shuttle glides gently upward until we're peering down at the spaceport. Moments later, the pilot applies a burst of speed and we're streaking through Earth's hazy skies. I'm pressed into my seat by the force of the blast, and the pressure doesn't relent as the ravaged landscape disappears beneath the noxious smog. We continue to ascend through layers of gray-brown clouds, then suddenly, we're racing through an impossibly blue sky.

I gape at the color, at the yellow rays of the sun cascading through our window, my words stolen from me by the sheer wonder beyond. The stories we grew up hearing were true; Earth really *does* have a blue sky.

Pablo laces his fingers through mine, and I don't pull away, too stunned to register the act.

The cerulean sky darkens to navy, then black dotted with innumerable stars. It's the most beautiful sight I've ever beheld. The shuttle slows and the forces pinning my body to the seat abate and disappear. For a few seconds, I'm weightless, and I understand the necessity of the safety harness.

Pablo squeezes my hand, then disentangles his fingers as I hear the hum of the grav-generators kicking on. Gravity returns to Earth-standard, and I unbuckle the harness, but I can't look away from the expanse of space beyond my window. It's more incredible than I imagined possible.

I shift slightly to peer back the way we came, to take in the view of Earth from space. Most of the planet is wreathed in gray-brown clouds, but I spy hazy patches of blue. Despite its devastation, our home world still possesses a dangerous and ethereal beauty all its own.

"You were right, Kye," Pablo says after a time. "We're going to be okay."

CHAPTER SIX

MATRIX PROCESSING

MEGATROPOLIS, TRAPPIST-1 SYSTEM

I freeze the moment I step off the shuttle, confronted with the sheer volume of people crammed into Spaceport 7's corridors. I've never seen so many in one place. There are more in the waiting area just beyond the passenger boarding bridge than there were in all of Baja Colony. The press of humanity overwhelms me, makes my skin crawl, sets my nerves on fire.

"Kye?" Luna asks over her shoulder.

I shake my head and force my feet to move forward. I focus on keeping pace with her and the rest of the ZIEG unit, and my mind begins to relax. One thing at a time. That's all I need to focus on.

Pablo's reaction is less extreme. He doesn't shut down as I almost did. He stares in wonder at the sea of faces occupying the benches and roaming the corridors. He walks on my left side and begins to point out every fascinating bit of technology on display. Vee glides along on my right, their movements graceful in a predatory way. I note with a measure of unease that Vee's hand rests on the grip of the pistol holstered at their hip.

"Are you expecting trouble?" I ask.

Vee chuckles darkly. "You're on Megatropolis now, friend. We must *always* be prepared for trouble."

I can't fathom what Vee's concerned about. Despite the thousands of people inside the spaceport, it's immaculate. Pristine. It provides a sense of security, something the Baja Spaceport lacked with its empty corridors and endless silence.

Luna halts our group as we reach a junction in the corridors. She gestures to a security checkpoint along one. "This is where we part ways," she says to Kelsey and Pablo. "Our route goes through the Zylar Inc. private wing. Your group from the university will be waiting in the main atrium, and you," she says with a meaningful smile for Kelsey, "have another shuttle to catch."

The ZIEG soldiers stand aside as I stumble over my goodbyes. Kelsey embraces me firmly, then holds me at arm's length.

"You'll do great, little brother."

"I hope so."

"Hey," she says with a tilt of her head, "you take after me in that regard. You're a fighter. A survivor. They recognize that, even if you don't. Call me when you're through with your upgrades."

I force a smile and nod, the reminder tying my stomach in knots.

As she steps away, Pablo offers me a grin laced with sadness. We haven't spent a day apart since I moved into his father's flat fourteen years ago, and I'm going to miss his gentle brand of companionship.

"Good luck at MSTI," I say.

"Good luck with ZIEG," he replies. "I'll be okay, Kye. Call me when you can. *Please.*"

"I will," I promise. "And… I'll ask Luna to call you if I can't."

His smile dissolves as he battles to hold back tears, but he doesn't reach for me.

"Need a hug?"

He nods, and I wrap him in my arms for what may be the last time. "Kye," he says after a moment, his words muffled by my shoulder and warped by emotion, "please don't die."

A nervous laugh bursts from my throat. "I don't plan to, Pab. Focus on your scans, then your studies. I'll be here."

He nods, then pushes away, wiping at his eyes. "I didn't realize leaving you would be so hard. I…" He shakes his head, then backpedals to Kelsey's location. "I'll be waiting for your call."

I watch them go, disappearing into the crush of humanity clogging the spaceport's corridors. I don't know what he was planning to say before he stopped himself, but our parting tears at my heart with a savagery I wasn't prepared for. I'm walking away from my best friend and may never see him again.

I shove my emotions aside, burying them in a dark corner of my mind where I can revisit them in private. I won't break down in the middle of one of the galaxy's busiest spaceports.

When I turn around, Vee is studying me closely. Luna and Jen are gone.

"Saying goodbye is never easy," Vee says as we begin walking toward the checkpoint. "Pablo adores you. This was harder for him than it was for you."

I chew my lower lip and nod. "I hope he finds someone to share his life with. He deserves to be happy, and I can't give him what he wants."

Vee lifts an eyebrow. "Can't, or won't?"

"Can't," I reply, irritated. "I'm not interested. In *anyone*."

Vee flashes a rare smile. "I thought so. You and me—we're alike in that respect. And in our line of work, it's easier that way. No one to sit at home worrying when you're deployed, no messy breakups when work demands extended time away, no children to potentially leave fatherless." Vee shrugs. "Does he know?"

"Yeah. It doesn't stop him from flirting, though."

"He will move on," Vee says with certainty. "MSTI will be good for him in that regard. I suspect he fell for you because there weren't many eligible bachelors on Earth to choose from."

"Maybe."

We stop outside the checkpoint, and Vee gestures that I should go through first. I step into the checkpoint, endure my scan, and am cleared to move on. Luna and Jen wait for me on the opposite side, and we move on once Vee is through.

The crowds thin to a bare trickle in this section of the spaceport, and I breathe a sigh of relief. It's quiet, almost peaceful without the dull roar of conversation filling the air.

"A private shuttle will take us from here to ZIEG headquarters," Vee says as we follow the two women through a skylit atrium.

The sky above the clear panes is a dusky blue-purple dotted with puffy white clouds. I spy a glimpse of this system's sun, a bloated, reddish orb that is easily twice the size of Sol.

"HQ is where we'll part ways for a time," Luna says over her shoulder. "It takes several weeks to implant all the required cybernetics. Once you're cleared for duty, one of us will return for you."

I nod but don't reply as my thoughts careen through the reality of what I'm about to do. I read through the specs several times while I was in Baja Spaceport, and I'm aware of what the ZIEG doctors will do once I'm in their hands. I know it will be painful; they don't administer painkillers during parts of the process because I need to be coherent enough to answer questions and alert them if something feels wrong. But the notion of pain isn't what causes my insides to squirm.

I'm giving up half of my humanity, maybe more. Luna has assured me I'll still be *me*, and I believe her, but it's a difficult pill to swallow. My whole damned life will be different.

But I'll *live*, as Kelsey told me. It's a hell of a lot better than the alternative.

There is no departure queue in the Zylar Inc. wing of the spaceport, only a series of passenger boarding bridges with illuminated kiosks indicating destinations. Luna leads us to one reserved for ZIEG headquarters, and the AI swiftly confirms our identities. We board, and Luna taps at a console just inside the door. Unlike the shuttle that carried us from Earth, this one doesn't have a crew.

"Most planetary shuttles are automated," Jen says when she notes my confusion. "You select your destination from a pre-programmed list, and the shuttle's system takes over from there."

Vee pats the plush seat next to theirs, then points at the adjacent window. "Sit. Enjoy your first views of Megatropolis while we fly."

Settling into the offered seat, I peer through the window. Skyscrapers dominate the view, rising to impossible heights all around us. The sun's crimson light reflects from countless windows, shimmers across glossy exteriors, sparkles from the nanosteel arrays and metal sculptures. Every building is unique in form and color, and most are adorned with artistic flourishes I've never imagined possible. Holoscreens glare from the lower stories, advertising everything from Megatropolis' best restaurants to the latest Zylar Inc. tech to the galaxy's premier vacation destinations.

Plant life is everywhere. Trees spring from the ground across the spaceport's tarmac, encircled by colorful flowers. Vines and trailing plants hang from balconies in a cascade of green, softening the sharp lines and industrial components of the architecture. Creatures flit between the nearest trees, unlike anything I've encountered before, though I recognize their form from holovids.

"Are those birds?" I ask in wonder as the shuttle begins to slide forward.

Vee chuckles. "Yes. They are the descendants of the finches and wrens that once thrived on Earth. Someone had enough foresight to relocate them before our home world became uninhabitable."

"They have evolved since coming here," Luna adds, taking the seat facing mine. "Their beaks have changed to better forage from the local flora."

The shuttle rises vertically for a time, and soon we're flying between the upper levels of the skyscrapers. Other shuttles speed by in a constant stream.

"How many people live here?" I ask, overwhelmed once more by the volume of traffic I'm immersed in.

"About six billion live here full-time," Luna replies. "There are another one million in the rings, and there are *always* tourists."

"Rings?" I echo.

She smiles. "Megatropolis hosts eight concentric ring colonies. You can access them by shuttle or one of the planetary elevators, though some have restricted access."

I nod in understanding.

"Most of ZIEG is housed on Ring Five," Vee adds. "You'll be set up there too, if I'm not mistaken."

"Lodging won't be assigned until after he's finished with the next phase," Jen cuts in. She shoots a hard glare at Vee, who seems unfazed by her reaction.

I turn to the window once more, taking in all that Megatropolis has to offer from the air. This sector of the planet is stunning. I wonder if the rest will be the same.

The shuttle banks gently, then begins to descend. Brilliant holoscreens fill my vision, each a different advertisement for a Zylar Inc. product or service. As we near the ground floor, the corporate logo is displayed in vibrant blue, spanning the width of the skyscraper's base. The shuttle doesn't stop at what appears to be the main entrance, but arcs around the building to a narrower thoroughfare. At the end is a set of gleaming nanosteel doors, the ZIEG insignia printed across them in white.

"Welcome to HQ," Luna says brightly as the shuttle doors slide open.

I'm led through a nondescript lobby furnished in sterile shades of white and gray. There's a desk inside with a holoscreen behind it, but no one is there to greet us and the screen displays only the ZIEG logo. Tall potted plants flank the entrance door.

Luna takes us past the desk to an elevator and presses a button. Moments later, a chime sounds. The doors slide open to reveal a sparkling nanosteel interior. She hits a sequence of buttons on the panel inside as we file in, then we're accelerating skyward at a breakneck speed. I stumble and nearly lose my balance, unaccustomed to travel of this variety.

Vee nods at a handrail behind me with a flicker of amusement. I flush and grasp it with both hands.

"First time?" Luna asks, as if it wasn't obvious.

"Yeah."

"You'll get used to it."

I snort and roll my eyes. I doubt I'll ever become used to *half* of the tech I've been confronted with in the past hour, and the elevator is no exception.

"If you think this one's bad, take the planetary elevator to the rings," Jen says with a smirk.

Luna chuckles. "One step at a time. He's going to need a slower pace."

Jen crosses her arms and taps one foot impatiently. "Then why were we—"

"Enough," Luna interrupts. "Our next mission can still go off as scheduled while he's here. We don't need a fourth for this one."

I glance at Vee, hoping they'll clue me in on what the women are discussing. Vee winks and silently mouths, "Later." I nod and suppress a grin. I think I've gained a potential friend and ally.

When the doors slide open moments later, we're greeted with a reception area eerily reminiscent of the medical bay at Baja Spaceport. There is no Olivia peering at our group from behind the desk, but there is a middle-aged man with a shaved head and an auburn goatee wearing a Zylar Inc. uniform.

He rises and beams as he scans our group. "Captain Zeta! It's always a pleasure to see you, though it's always better when I'm not tasked with patching you up."

"Good to see you too, Mat." Luna gestures to me. "Kye is our newest recruit. I'm sure you've been informed that your particular brand of magic will be required."

Mat nods and his eyes fall on me, scrutinizing every detail of my person. "Magic isn't necessary when you have science and the galaxy's best tech on your side. You're the one from Earth?"

"Yeah." I chew my lower lip, anticipating his next words.

"I've read your file. You're lucky the commander selected you, or you'd be dead by this time next year." There's compassion and sympathy in his gaze, but his words irk me.

I don't need his fucking pity, and I don't want to be treated as a charity case. I stiffen and clench my jaw against the heated words that threaten to spill from my lips. I didn't survive for twenty-six years on that ruined shithole of a planet to be treated as fragile.

Vee must sense the shift in my mood. They step in. "Mat, he's here for the full package. Can it."

Mat blinks in surprise, then manages a nod. "Yes, of course. I only meant—"

"It doesn't matter what you meant," Vee cuts him off. "Just do your damned job."

Luna raises her eyebrows in question, but Vee merely shrugs, unrepentant. I think I'm going to like working with Vee.

Mat sighs and runs a hand over his scalp. "Fine, fine. No more questions. If you're ready to begin, follow me."

Luna smiles as I step forward. "We'll be back to visit you in a few days. Until then, do as Mat says." She grasps my shoulder firmly. "You'll get through this."

I nod and receive a pat on my other arm from Vee, the only display of encouragement they'll likely give.

"And don't die," Jen says from behind me. "Our unit needs a fourth."

"Jen!" Luna admonishes her as I follow Mat through a door. It slides shut before I can hear any more of their exchange, but I have the distinct impression that Jen isn't overly fond of me.

"Don't mind the sergeant," Mat says as I take in the room. "She's like that with everyone."

We're in a round chamber with a hospital bed at its heart. Dozens of machines encircle it, each with its own tactile display. Tubes and wires hang from the ceiling, robotic arms protrude from the walls, and a glass tank is nestled in the space behind the bed, filled halfway with a blue-green liquid. The overhead lights are brilliantly white, casting deep shadows beneath each apparatus, the bed, and the two humans invading this sterile environment.

"This will be your home until the enhancements are complete," Mat says when I don't respond to his remark. "I'll explain each step of the process as we move forward. And don't worry—I do no work without an AI to oversee my calculations. You're in good hands."

He points to the bed. "Hop on, and remove your shirt. We'll begin with a scan, and then Zymedica will help me pinpoint the best place to begin working on you."

"Zymedica?" I echo as I peel off the blue ZIEG top.

"She's our best medical AI," Mat says with unabashed pride. "I've spent the past eight years working with her. I trust her more than I do most human doctors."

"Thank you for the compliment, Mat," a feminine voice croons from somewhere in the room. I can't pinpoint her location, but I'm certain she's contained in one of the blinking displays.

I lay back on the bed as Mat begins to work, my eyes on the bright ceiling as Zymedica completes her scans. It takes only seconds before the AI begins to rattle off her assessment of me. Half of her words are meaningless; it's medical jargon without context, but Mat seems to understand what she's found hidden within my biochemistry.

"As I suspected, we'll work on your bones first. They'll be reinforced with a matrix of carbon nanotubes, making them nearly unbreakable." He taps a screen and several of the tubes hanging from the ceiling uncoil and position themselves ominously above me. Mat clears his throat and fixes me with an anxious look. "This is going to hurt, but I need you to tell me the moment you feel any sort of burning sensation."

I clench my hands involuntarily. "I'm ready."

"Zymedica?" Mat calls. "Initiate the matrix processing."

The tubes plunge toward me and pin me against the mattress. Something sharp pierces my skin as each makes contact, then my veins shriek in agony. Cold deeper than anything I've felt previously lances through my body, making my bones ache and tendons scream.

I buck against the apparatus, but I can't move. It's skewered me like the insects I've seen on display though the holovids. My ears ring. My blood pulses furiously, while splinters of ice slice through my muscles. Pain doesn't begin to describe the sensation. I'm in agony.

I scream wordlessly. I roar. Tears leak from my eyes as every synapse in my body fires its fury and anguish simultaneously.

I want to die. I cling to life.

Finally, the tubes disengage and I sag against the mattress, muscles quaking. My breaths are ragged gasps, each one scratching painfully along my ravaged vocal cords. I've screamed myself hoarse.

Mat's face appears above mine. He says something, but I can't make out his words over the persistent ringing in my ears. I don't possess the energy to respond anyway; my body is spent. I close my eyes, seeking release.

A sharp pinch on my bicep drags me from the merciful arms of slumber. I snap my eyes open to find Mat holding an empty syringe.

"Stay with me, Kye. We're not finished yet." His words float through the air to hang like a storm cloud between us, his tone guarded.

I shake my head. I can't do this again.

I try to sit up using my elbows, but my limbs refuse to move. Did he just inject me with a paralytic? Panic seizes my heart and my eyes seek his, desperate for answers to the questions my lips refuse to form.

He ignores my reaction and turns to assess one of his many displays. There's one showing my pulse and blood pressure levels; both are dangerously high. Another displays a list of my current biochemical values; blood glucose levels, renal and hepatic markers, dissolved oxygen, and more. Mat taps at a display that's blocked from my view by his torso, then nods to himself.

"Zymedica, initiate phase two. He's looking good so far."

I stare helplessly as a new set of tubes descends from the ceiling. Terror grips my mind in its dark claws, but my body refuses to brace itself for the next assault. I'm trapped in my own skin, forced to watch as a madman inflicts horrors on my being. Needles pierce my skin and more frigid hell pours through my veins.

What the fuck have I signed up for?

CHAPTER SEVEN

RING FIVE

ZIEG HEADQUARTERS
MEGATROPOLIS, TRAPPIST-1 SYSTEM

The pain ebbs and flows, waxes and wanes, with Mat's ministrations. I'm allowed to rest after each stage of the process is complete, a few days to recover and rebuild under Zymedica's watchful gaze. I'm not permitted to leave what I've come to think of as Mat's laboratory. It's my haven and my prison, my salvation from the ravages of Earth's fetid embrace, and my own personal hell.

Days bleed together, and I lose track of time. When I'm not resting, I'm strapped to the bed as my body is reworked and improved. Most of my internal organs are replaced with nearly indestructible versions that are more efficient and easier to repair. Data chips smaller than my cells are implanted in my brain. Some are required to maintain and operate my new organs, others enhance my reflexes and reaction times, and another set is part of a vast data repository that I now have access to.

My muscles, tendons, and ligaments are subjected to a process similar to what my bones went through at the onset. When that phase is complete, I collapse into a deep and dreamless sleep, only to wake days later to a body I'm no longer familiar with. Gone is the wraith-like Kye Verex with gaunt cheeks and too little flesh on his bones. My muscles are defined. I'm *ripped*.

I don't know how to process this new version of myself. I laugh, then cry, then merely stare at my bare torso and arms, corded with muscle that I've never possessed, let alone imagined belonging there. It feels impossible. *Unreal.*

Mat renders me unconscious for the final phase, where he plans to replace my eyes. He shows me the replicas Zymedica has created before he puts me under; the hazel irises are identical to my natural ones, and he assures me no one will realize they're cybernetic under normal circumstances.

When I awake from that phase, I can see clearly across the laboratory for the first time. I can read the displays on every monitor, and even make out the tiny print declaring each machine's manufacturing information. I can shift from normal vision to infrared to night vision. I can overlay schematics across my field of view, the chips implanted in my brain working seamlessly with my new optical interface to display Mat's identity, vital signs, and history as he taps at his various screens. With a thought, I can adjust it to display Zymedica's information, or show the building schematics of ZIEG headquarters and my precise location inside.

The stream of data is nearly overwhelming. Mat patiently guides me through each aspect of my new physiology and runs a battery of tests. Then he drops a bombshell.

"While you were unconscious, I installed the final piece of your programming," he says. "Let me plug it in to make sure it works as intended. Then you're finished."

I frown at him. "What do you mean by 'plug it in,' Mat?"

He moves behind me, and before I understand what's going on, something clicks into place at the base of my neck. My world immediately goes dark.

When I reactivate—I'm not sure what else to call it—I'm in a different room and Mat is nowhere to be seen. I'm sitting on an uncomfortably hard chair, my back to a wall. Across from me is a middle-aged blond man I don't recognize, though he wears a blue Zylar Inc. lab coat. His arms are crossed as he studies me from behind a pair of glasses with iridescent blue lenses.

"What the fuck did he do to me? And who are you?" I demand, rising to my feet. Anger propels me, and if given sufficient reason, I'll lash out.

The man lifts his hands in a gesture of surrender. "Mat had you brought here for final evaluation," he says.

I frown and activate my internal display. If he won't tell me who he is, I'll scrape the information from my connection to ZIEG's database. Fear worms its way into my core when the word "classified" flashes across my vision. His heart rate and breathing indicate he's calm, but I'll learn nothing about him unless he deigns to tell me himself.

What the hell is going on?

"Your enhancements are complete," he continues, unperturbed by my rising frustration. "You're the first of your series, an SLTR-BT designation cyborg. As for what he did, Mat tested your final bit of programming. It was a success."

I cross my arms and fix him with the glare. "I'm not a fucking machine. I'd like details."

"I'm afraid that's classified and well above your galactic security clearance."

"What the fuck?!" I roar. "This wasn't part of my contract—"

The man chuckles. "I'm afraid it *was*, Kye. Did you not read the fine print beneath the signature line?"

The fine print. I read and reread that damned contract from start to finish, but I never bothered with the small text at the very end. It was after the signature line. What sort of asshole includes important details like security clearances *after* the signature line?

"Allow me to explain," he says, his vitals still at ease. "There are aspects of your new physiology that you will *never* be granted clearance to fully explore or understand. This final bit of programming is one such item."

"Why?" I demand.

He shakes his head. "You know I can't answer that. But as to your second question, know that I am not your enemy, and we will meet again. I'll share my name with you then, but I can't do so now."

He turns to pick up a tablet from the chair behind him and taps its screen a few times. "There. You're all set. Your enhancements are complete and the final diagnostics look good. I'll inform Mat." He turns to the door, tablet in hand, then pauses to offer me an enigmatic smile. "Welcome to ZIEG, Mr. Verex."

"This is bullshit!" I roar as the door clicks shut behind him.

I want answers. I didn't join ZIEG to become a corporate pawn. I joined to be cured, to leave Earth, to have a future…

I release a groan and rake a hand through my hair, pacing the length of the room. I want to hit something, but I know it won't help my situation. I should have read the blasted fine print. Maybe I'd understand what the hell just happened, why I blacked out, and who the fuck the man with the blue glasses is.

When the door opens several minutes later and Mat steps inside, I don't hesitate to give him a piece of my mind.

"What the fuck did you do to me? You put something in my neck and I blacked out. What the hell? And who was that blond prick that just left?"

Mat stares at me with wide eyes. I watch as his heart rate spikes and sweat beads across his brow. He's *afraid* of me. Good.

"Kye, please relax," he says, holding up his hands to placate me. "I can explain."

"I hope so," I growl.

"Zylar Inc. technology must be tested thoroughly before our cybernetic soldiers are cleared for duty. I was testing the final piece, and—"

"What *is* the final piece?" I demand. "He wouldn't tell me."

Mat draws an uneasy breath. "That's classified. The man who visited you was one of our software engineers. He ran your system diagnostics after the final test was complete."

I cross my arms and glare. Part of me wishes they had installed lasers when they upgraded my eyes. I would have fried him on the spot.

"Your diagnostics came back clean," Mat continues in a wavering tone. "I asked the engineering team to run an extra set since you're the first of your series. I just placed a call to Captain Zeta. She's sending Vee to collect you."

I suspect Vee can provide me with the insight my torturer refuses to share. I'll get nothing from this cowering asshole but excuses and an urge to smash something. And after the hell he put me through during the past five weeks, his face is a prime candidate.

"Kye, you need to calm down," he says again. "I'm not your enemy."

With a glower, I force my hands to unclench and my posture to relax. Taking my frustration out on him is a stupid idea, even if it will make me feel better. We're in the heart of ZIEG's headquarters, and we're on surveillance every second of every damned day. The company will send in reinforcements if I act out. Even with my new strength and speed, I'd be outmatched by the veteran cyborgs that are sure to arrive in seconds.

And I won't waste the years of work Kelsey put in to free me from Earth's ruined clutches.

"Fine," I concede, "but I don't like secrets."

"No one does, but it was in the fine print."

"Fuck your fine print. It should have been part of the main contract, not an afterthought."

Mat shrugs uneasily. "I don't write the documents. I'm just here to do my job and hope a pissed off cyborg doesn't kill me in the process."

I smirk, then begin to laugh. "I wasn't going to hurt you, but the thought may have crossed my mind."

"You aren't the first to react…adversely…to the news," Mat replies. "I doubt you'll be the last." He shifts from foot to foot. "Which engineer assisted you?"

"I don't know. He didn't give me his name, and I didn't think to ask."

Mat sighs and shakes his head, exasperated. "You didn't run his profile?"

"I did. It was classified."

Mat's face scrunches in confusion. "Damn it. They haven't updated your access, have they? You should have…" He trails off and pulls a tablet from his pocket, tapping furiously on his screen. "That's odd. It says you have… Oh, I see. Your access was only granted three minutes ago. Our H/CR department must have been a bit slow in processing your new status."

Rather than ask him what the latest acronym means, I query the database. Human/Cyborg Resources. I look up my personnel file to find I'm officially classified as "Cyborg, human origin" now.

I swallow my unease. I signed up for this, and I've since learned my sister was right—this *was* my last shot at being cured and leaving

Earth. I can't change my mind now anyway. The process of becoming a cyborg is irreversible.

"Does this happen often?" I ask in an effort to focus on something other than what I've become.

Mat rolls his eyes. "More often than it should. Your clearance is now active, so I don't believe there is any reason to be concerned. It's annoying, but H/CR isn't staffed by bots. AIs, I mean."

I narrow my eyes and frown at the designation. "Do you consider someone like me to be a bot?"

He laughs nervously and wrings his hands. "No. Cyborgs are a different breed all their own. Bots are mindless machines. They can't think for themselves and require intelligent input—whether it comes from one of us or an AI. And you're no AI. Your brain wasn't altered during the enhancement process. It's against policy."

He fidgets and won't meet my gaze. His heart rate spikes and I detect sweat emanating from his pores. The bastard is lying—or at the very least, not sharing the whole truth. And I'm keenly aware *he* plugged something into the base of my neck the instant before I blacked out. I don't believe for one damned nanosecond that my brain survived the process unscathed.

I cross my arms and do my best to look menacing. It isn't as hard as it used to be now that I have the musculature to bulk up my frame.

Mat squirms beneath my glare. "You don't believe me. But I swear to you, everything was done according to protocol. I would never risk my position here."

I still don't believe him, but I can't do anything about whatever he may have done to me while I was unconscious. Or whatever the mysterious engineer may have done while Mat was away.

Biting back the heated words that dance on the tip of my tongue, I force myself to look away. Picking a fight with Mat won't change anything, and Vee should be arriving to rescue me from the situation soon, regardless of what transpires between us. I release a sigh and sit down heavily in the room's only chair.

"How long does it usually take for new recruits to…adjust?" I ask, hoping my suspicions and rage are misplaced.

He shrugs. "Some take only a few hours, others take months. Given your past, I suspect you fall into the latter category. I'm sorry, but there isn't anything I can do to help you cope. It's what your unit is for. Captain Zeta and the others will guide you. They know what you've gone through better than I do anyway."

"You're the one who *changed* me, Mat. You know damned well what I've been through."

He shakes his head. "I know the physical process, yes. I *don't* know the psychological toll it takes on a person to give up the core of who they are. And in cases like yours, the stakes are higher still. I read your file. You exhausted all of your other prospects. ZIEG was your last hope of escaping that rock."

I nod and stare at the tiled floor as an unexpected weariness descends over my body. I'm tired of this conversation and want nothing more than Vee to stride through the door and deliver me from Mat's hollow sympathy. He'll never understand the enormity of what I endured on Earth, nor can he comprehend the obstacles Kelsey and I had to overcome just to get me here. If ZIEG's commander hadn't owed Kelsey a favor, I'd be wasting away from the cancer I hadn't been aware of, scraping up a shadow of a living amongst the galaxy's garbage heaps.

The door slides open and I snap my head up at the sound. Vee steps inside and nods in silent greeting to me before flicking their gaze toward Mat in question.

"He's cleared to go," Mat says with a shrug.

Vee motions to me and I rise, every fiber of my being relieved that I don't have to endure any more awkward conversation. And I'm silently grateful that it's Vee who was assigned to escort me away from Mat's laboratory rather than Jen with her judgmental stares and acerbic tongue.

Once we've left Mat behind, Vee pauses to appraise me. "How do you feel?"

"I…" I shake my head, uncertain how to articulate what I experienced over the course of the past month. "I'm still me, but I'm different. I've never felt this healthy before."

Vee's eyes narrow imperceptibly, a small frown tugging at the corner of their mouth. "Luna asked me to escort you to your new apartment on Ring Five. You'll be free to do as you please until morning." We begin walking again, moving toward the same elevator that first delivered me to Mat's chamber of technological horrors. "We will speak more of your experience once there. Unlike this building, private residences are not under constant surveillance. I know the process to become what we are can be traumatic, and most don't want their words recorded."

I nod, once again grateful Vee is here. "Thanks."

We enter the elevator and Vee presses the button for the roof. "Don't mention it."

I consider what I'll tell them once we're away from the watchful eyes of Zylar Inc. I don't know if it's safe to share my mistrust of Mat and his motives or the strange encounter with the nameless engineer, but it might do me good to recount the rest of my experience with someone. Vee isn't Pablo, but I trust them.

"When we're finished, am I cleared to make holocalls?" I ask.

Vee smiles faintly. "As I said, you have the rest of tonight to do as you please. That includes holocalls. There should be a holoreceiver in your apartment, if you don't want to place a call from your head." They tap their forehead meaningfully.

Despite the reminder that I have tech lodged inside my skull, I grin. I haven't spoken to Pablo since we parted ways at the spaceport, and I'm eager to learn how he fares at MSTI. I'm sure he's been dying to hear from me too. I should call my sister as well, but I don't know if she'll pick up. It isn't our usual date, and her schedule is almost impossible to pin down.

A thought occurs to me then. I query my database for information on Kelsey Verex, and her file appears on one side of my vision. I sift through it briefly and find her current instructor schedule. She's on duty tonight; our call will have to wait.

The elevator door slides open, revealing the rooftop. Garden plots line the perimeter, but the center is clear of vegetation. A white shuttle with the Zylar Inc. logo is parked and waiting for us.

"It seems you're adjusting to the data streams well enough," Vee says as we walk toward the shuttle. "What were you looking up just now?"

I chew my lower lip uneasily. "My sister's schedule. How did you know?"

"Your eyes weren't focused for a few seconds. It's the only outward sign of a cyborg accessing information that isn't stored in their biological memory." Vee pauses to point at an access panel on the outside of the shuttle. "Let's see if your clearance has been issued. It's keyed to your body's signature. Place your hand on the blue pad."

I follow Vee's instructions, and a heartbeat later, the panel's tiny screen displays "Access Granted. Kye Verex, ZIEG." The shuttle door irises open and we step inside.

"All of the shuttles we use for transport between HQ and the Rings are keyed to our signatures," Vee explains as they slide into the pilot seat. "It's the same for the long-haul transports we use on critical missions."

With a nod, I sit on the cushioned bench behind Vee. "It's more than just our DNA they've coded it to recognize, isn't it?"

Vee deftly taps several panels on the shuttle's interface, and we noiselessly lift off from the rooftop. "Yes. For our kind, it's a combination of DNA, the unique bone matrix we possess, and the singular network of wire filaments running through our muscles. Each of us has a slightly different combination, and it's impossible to replicate. The filaments stop responding if severed too, so if someone gets the brilliant idea that taking a cyborg's hand is going to grant them access to our toys, they're mistaken."

I lift my eyebrows in surprise. "Has someone tried that?"

Vee nods. "Jen lost her left arm on one of our first missions together. Pirates are ruthless bastards—you'll learn that soon enough. They tried to steal our shuttle with the arm, but as I said, it doesn't work that way. Mat patched her up afterward."

"How, exactly?" I ask, trying to imagine what Mat might have done to restore Jen's arm.

"Mat uses stem cells to regenerate the biological portions of our bodies that need replacement, then replicates the cybernetics based on our individual schematics. Once that's done, they're attached and connected to the rest of the body. You'll get used to it after a few scrapes." Vee shrugs but doesn't turn away from the shuttle's window, their eyes fixed on the streams of traffic ahead. "Don't worry. They start everyone off on a slow progression. Our unit will be stationed here for a few standard months while you go through combat and vehicle training modules. Luna said we're on security detail for the corporate office until you're finished."

I stare through the windshield, grappling with the new information as our shuttle weaves between buildings and private vehicles. What the hell have I landed myself in with ZIEG? I expected the training modules, but I wasn't prepared to learn I might require replacement limbs on a regular basis.

"I assume corporate security isn't as…exciting as your typical missions."

"It's not. It's *safe*, and that's what you'll need until you've fully adjusted to your new life." Vee glances over their shoulder and studies me for a moment before refocusing on Megatropolis' traffic. "Combat training can be a bitch, Kye. Just be thankful Luna assigned that to me rather than Jen. She doesn't like you."

"Why?"

"You're unproven, untested. Learn to operate to the best of your capacity, and she'll come around." Vee shakes their head, exasperated. "Jen thinks you were chosen for ZIEG due to your sister's involvement with Tariq."

"That's not how I—"

"I know," Vee says evenly, cutting off my protest. "The directive to bring you in came from Commander Patil himself, and Tariq Osirious had nothing to do with it."

"Kels broke up with him four years ago." I cross my arms, frustrated. "I don't know what happened between them, and it wasn't my business to ask."

"If Jen had read your file, she would know that," Vee says with a frown. "But she hasn't, and likely won't until she gets to know you better."

The shuttle arcs abruptly skyward. Within moments, we're streaking through Megatropolis' atmosphere. The reddish glow of the system's star transitions from diffuse and warm to piercing and brilliant as we enter space. A series of concentric rings crisscross the view ahead, each adorned with an array of colorful lights. As we pass the first ring, I note the lights are illuminated windows. I can see people within.

Vee guides the shuttle past several rings, then begins to decelerate toward a docking bay rimmed in blue lights.

"Zylar Inc. identities verified," the shuttle's AI chimes as we approach. "ZIEG status verified. Bay doors opening."

Vee twists in their seat and smirks. "This is ZIEG's private hangar. Welcome to Ring Five, Kye."

CHAPTER EIGHT

PABLO'S WINGMAN

My new apartment is located in the section of Ring Five reserved for ZIEG personnel, a thirty-minute walk from the hangar along the ring's central corridor. It's easily four times the size of the flat I lived in on Earth, fully furnished, with expansive views of the interior rings and Megatropolis' blue-green surface set to a backdrop of twinkling stars. I have a bedroom with an ensuite bath; a room set up as an office replete with a desk, several holoreceivers, and a VR cubicle which I assume will be used for some of my training; a living room with several plush gray sofas and a minibar; and a small kitchenette with an array of food preparation devices.

This apartment probably costs more than all of Baja Colony's wealth combined.

I wander through the rooms, taking stock of my new home as Vee points out a few features I may have otherwise missed. The drink mixer seems to be one of Vee's favorite devices, and they demonstrate its capabilities by requesting an Old Fashioned. The device's menu is extensive, and I'm unfamiliar with almost every ingredient featured. Vee studies me for a moment, then orders a gin and tonic for me.

"If you don't like it, try something else," Vee says with a faint smile as a glass is filled and pushed toward me.

I take a tentative sip, then nod. It's not bad. It's better than the shit Diego served back home, and I don't think *this* could double as engine degreaser.

Vee gestures to the plush sofas. "Let's sit. We should talk now that we're away from HQ."

I sit carefully on the end of one sofa as Vee perches on the one across from me. They sip their drink and study me thoughtfully, as if deciding where to begin. I wait, unsure of what they hope to learn from me and unwilling to share some of what I endured while in Mat's custody.

"I knew when we met that you'd survive the process," Vee says after a time. "Your life was hell, and you're a survivor. I don't want details of what you experienced unless you're willing to share them, but I need to know how you are coping right now."

I stare at the drink in my hand. I'm overwhelmed, overstimulated. There's so much I don't know about the wider galaxy and its workings. I was thrown into this with very little information beyond what Zylar Inc. provided regarding my cybernetics. I don't know what ZIEG's purpose is other than protecting corporate secrets, but I haven't forgotten Vee mentioned pirates.

In my younger years, my education included galactic history, basic math and science, and I was encouraged to read anything and everything I could get my hands on. Kelsey oversaw my studies from a distance, and under her guidance, I scored in the top tier of candidates when I applied to OMMA. I know enough to get by, but not enough to blend in. I'm an outsider, masquerading as a ZIEG soldier until my training is complete.

"I'm floundering," I admit. "There's so much information. I don't know where to begin."

Vee nods and offers a smile. "I understand. It's a lot to take in, and we haven't started testing your enhancements yet. I will not push you too far too fast, Kye. We will move at a pace that's comfortable for *you*."

"Thanks. But what exactly will we be testing?"

"Your combat abilities, for starters." Vee sits back and crosses one leg over the other. "Once I'm confident you can hold your own in a fight, we'll progress to weapons training and piloting courses. You'll be expected to work security detail three days per week once I sign off on your basic weapons training. All security officers are armed with multi-grade pistols—we call them handcannons. They have a variety of ammunition, but we'll cover the details once we get there."

"And you said we'll start tomorrow?" I ask.

Vee nods again. "I sent you a schedule before I arrived at Mat's lab. It'll be in your personal inbox. You can access it from your desk or through your implant."

I down half my drink and stare at Vee. "I can do that?"

"It's no different than accessing your sister's file," Vee says with a sly grin. "Try it."

My inbox appears overlaid across my vision, and I gape in response. There are dozens of messages from Zylar Inc., welcoming me to the company and detailing various benefits I can expect to receive. There are a handful from Luna Zeta and two from Vee Domineaux. There are forty-three from Pablo—he's sent a message every day since we parted ways. There are three from Kelsey, the last providing a link to her latest OMMA schedule.

With a thought, I organize the messages into something resembling order, prioritizing those I deem most important. I'll read Pablo's once Vee leaves for the night, then I'll call him.

"Holy shit," I breathe. "This is… I didn't know this was possible."

Vee chuckles and drains the last of their drink. "It isn't for most people. Welcome to the life of a cyborg, Kye. Infinite information at your fingertips and galactic connectivity in the blink of an eye." They stand and move to the kitchenette, placing the empty glass in a machine meant for cleaning dishes. "I'll be back at 0900 Galactic Standard Time to begin your training. The rest of the evening is yours."

"Thanks," I say as Vee moves toward the door. "I'll be ready."

As soon as the door closes, I begin skimming through Pablo's messages. Most are brief, sharing scant details about his life at the university and his studies, but all of them end with the statement, "Call me when you can." The last few end with a distinct note of desperation. He's worried, and rightfully so.

I deposit my empty glass in the cleaning contraption and wander to my new office. The holoreceiver on the wall is both larger and newer than the one we salvaged on Earth. It doesn't have a remote, and it takes me several minutes of searching before I realize I'm supposed to activate it through my implants. I'm not sure I'll ever get used to *being* the remote for my personal devices.

I input Pablo's new frequency from his MSTI file and pace while I wait for him to accept the call. His image appears on the screen seconds later, his eyes wide.

"Hey, Pab."

"Kye? Holy shit. It's really you."

He continues to stare in disbelief, and I begin to wonder how much I've changed. There was a mirror in my bathroom, but I didn't go inside when I was exploring earlier.

"It's really me," I say, forcing an uneasy grin. "They set me up with an apartment on Ring Five. That's where I am now."

"So you're…ZIEG now?" he asks.

"I'm still in training, but the enhancements are finished." I look away, uncertain of what more I should say. I want to tell him everything. He's my best friend, and he'll understand, but for the second time this evening, I don't know where to begin.

"The muscles suit you," he says with a mischievous grin. "You were attractive before, but now… *Damn.*"

I shrug. "I haven't looked in a mirror yet."

He rolls his eyes. "Which means you haven't properly looked at yourself since you were ten years old. You should fix that, Kye."

I sit down in the room's only chair and cross my arms. "How is MSTI? I read your messages, but you didn't say much."

"It's great here," he says with a smile. "You were right, you know. When I went for my health screening, they fixed me up. I was right too. There were tumors."

My biomechanical heart squeezes painfully with emotion. "I'm sorry."

"Don't be. They're gone now, and I'm perfectly healthy. My classes so far haven't been terribly interesting. It's introductory stuff, and I already know most of it. But next term, I'll be in some real engineering classes." His eyes light up with excitement. "Almost all of the faculty is Botanaari. They're fascinating, and their tech is top-notch."

"What are they like?" I ask. I haven't seen anyone but humans and ZIEG cyborgs since coming to Megatropolis.

"You know the basics. They're photosynthetic, so naturally, they're very *green*. But they do eat meat on occasion. I didn't realize they were carnivorous too." He shrugs. "Other than their coloration, they aren't so different from us, apart from the monogender thing."

I nod, recalling from my history lessons years ago that the Botanaari species had confounded humanity when we first made contact. A dual-gendered species with multiple subsets based on personal identifiers was wholly alien to the Botanaari, just as a monogendered people was to us.

"Is it true they refer to themselves as male?" I ask.

"Yeah. They all consider themselves 'male' in terms of human pronouns since they look the part," he replies. "The Botanaari language has other terms, but I've been told they don't translate well. And Kye, the Botanaari are *beautiful*. Their features are more…refined than ours, a bit…sharper, but…" He shakes his head, his eyes distant, his expression wistful.

"I think someone has a crush," I tease.

Pablo flushes. "I won't deny my attraction."

"Is there someone in particular?"

He shakes his head. "No. There's a policy against faculty dating students, and most of the Botanaari students keep to themselves."

"Give it time, Pab. You'll find someone."

His lips quirk into a lopsided grin. "I hope so."

We talk for another hour, and I divulge my experience in Mat's laboratory. Pablo is horrified when I describe the pain I endured, but I shrug it off. I survived, I'm past it, and I'm *alive*. That's the only thing that matters.

He stifles a yawn at the end of my tale and shakes his head. "I'm sorry, Kye. Unlike you, I require a full night's sleep, and I have class at seven a.m."

I smile. "I'll call you when I can, Pab. Have a good night."

He nods. "You too. I'm glad you're okay."

He signs off, and I remain where I am for several minutes. I've missed our conversations, and I'm thrilled he's happy and enjoying his first term at MSTI. Somehow, we both made it off Earth and on to better lives, despite the odds laid against us.

Finally, I rise and walk to my bedroom. I'm not tired yet; part of my enhancements included a reduced need for sleep, but I am curious to see my face in the mirror. Pablo's reaction had been unexpected, almost as though he didn't recognize me at first glance. I've gained weight and muscle mass, but I assumed my face was still the same. None of the other cyborgs looked anything but human, after all.

But would I know if I looked different? I haven't seen a clear reflection of myself since I was a child, and I only have a vague impression from the windows of Pablo's hover truck.

I pause at the threshold between the bedroom and bath, unsure of what I'll find. Will I like the face staring back at me from the silvered glass?

The overhead light turns on as I step inside. There's a shower stall large enough for five, a wide tub set into the floor, and a toilet cubicle with its own door. Along one wall is a pair of sinks set into a wide vanity, and above that, a mirror runs the length of the room.

I stare at the man reflected in the glass and move toward him, drawn inexplicably to the tall, muscular figure with his angular jaw, high cheekbones, and sharp nose. My dark hair is cut short, and dark stubble is visible along my chin. I haven't shaved since entering Mat's laboratory, and in all that time, my beard never filled in. The same is true for my hair; it was last trimmed at Baja Spaceport the day before our departure. I query my databanks for answers and learn I can alter the length and growth rate of my hair at any time. It's currently paused, and I decide to leave it as-is.

I study the reflection with my cybernetic eyes, eyes that appear human in every way, while I maintain standard vision mode. They're hazel, just like my biological ones had been, and the right iris has two darker brown spots the left one lacks. I remember that was true of my natural eyes; Mat did an excellent job of replicating them.

On a whim, I switch my vision to night mode. I can still see clearly, though the overhead light is almost blinding. My eyes are overlaid with an iridescent green sheen, a telltale sign that I'm not fully human. I switch to infrared with one eye and return to normal with the other. Infrared mode makes my eye glow faintly crimson.

I shudder and revert to standard vision in both eyes. The visible evidence of my cybernetics is unsettling, but I remind myself why I'm here.

Earth had been killing me. I needed to do this.

I fall into a routine over the next three weeks. Vee arrives every morning at the same time. We move the sofas in the living room to clear the space, then spar for several hours. I'm slow at first, hesitant, but rapidly gain confidence as I begin to understand my capabilities and limitations. Vee is relentless in their determination to see me succeed, harsh in their criticism of my technique, and sparing with praise—but when praise comes, it's meaningful.

Vee doesn't hold back, and during the first two weeks, I'm left battered and bruised after each session, but my body heals after a few hours' rest, and I'm ready to begin again.

When I'm not sparring, I'm tasked to complete an array of virtual training modules designed to help me adapt to my new technological abilities. Some I stumbled upon by accident, like accessing personnel files, while others are brand new. I learn how to infiltrate databases, override encryptions, and break through firewalls using the cybernetic filaments embedded in my fingertips. I'm taught how to recognize electronic viruses designed to cripple my own systems and how to neutralize them or protect against them. I begin to understand my own biomechanics and the myriad ways I can repair myself if I sustain too much damage. Mat's laboratory is still the best place for critical repairs, but I know how to manage on my own if I can't reach him for a time.

I'm given the evenings to do as I wish, and I often call Pablo. It isn't until the end of my third week that my schedule aligns with Kelsey's, and I finally give her a call. She picks up on the second ping.

"Kye!" She shouts as her image fills my screen. "I've been waiting to hear from you, little brother."

I grin. "It's good to see you too, Kels."

"I know my schedule doesn't allow for many calls, but you could have sent me a message." She crosses her arms and frowns. "I had to learn how you were from Pablo."

My expression falters and shifts to a grimace. "Shit. I'm sorry."

She laughs then. "Don't worry. I'm familiar with your habits, and he's been keeping me informed. So how is ZIEG?"

I share what I can of my experience so far; she doesn't have the clearance to learn everything, but she's still impressed with what I tell her. It hasn't been an easy road, but it's better than the alternative, and for the first time in my life, I'm content with my situation. I'm not eking out an existence and struggling to secure my next meal. I have a purpose, a future.

Kelsey listens as I speak, then smiles. "I'm glad this worked out for you. I wasn't sure it would, but we had to try."

I nod. "I owe you, Kels."

"Nonsense. You would have done the same for me if our roles had been reversed."

She pauses to study me, her expression unreadable. And over the holovid, I can't read her vitals to guess what she may be feeling.

Finally, she says, "You look good, little brother. I used to worry about you constantly before. You were too thin. Now you're…" She waves a hand vaguely at me and laughs. "You're built like a professional boxer. Even if I didn't know you've been enhanced, I'd think twice about crossing you."

I snort. "You know I'd never hurt anyone without cause, and I do my best to keep my temper under control."

"That you do. When will you be placed on active duty?"

"I don't know. Vee isn't satisfied with my combat skills yet, and I still need weapons training after that."

She nods her understanding. "I doubt it will be long. ZIEG soldiers are the best in the galaxy, and you're one of them now."

The holoreceiver beeps, indicating I have another call. It's Pablo.

"You're popular tonight," Kelsey says with a laugh. "Should I let you go?"

I shrug. "It's Pablo."

"Ah. I'll call you on our regular schedule, little brother. I won't keep you from him." She winks and signs off before I can form a response.

With a frown, I accept Pablo's call.

"Hey, Kye! I have a question. And I hope you say yes."

I laugh in spite of myself. "What's the question?"

Pablo draws a breath. His every movement conveys unabashed enthusiasm, but he's hesitant to ask. Whatever he wants from me is something important to him, something he fears I won't agree to.

"Pab?"

He looks at me hopefully. "I've been invited to a party on Ring Eight tomorrow night. It's hosted by a Botanaari tech broker I met yesterday."

I lift my eyebrows. Rings Seven and Eight house some of Megatropolis' wealthiest residents. "Ring Eight? Damn."

Pablo laughs nervously. "I know."

"How did you meet him?" I ask, feigning casual interest.

"I went to the singles bar near MSTI campus last night, and he was there." Pablo flushes crimson, but continues. "We talked for a while, then he invited me to his party. He gave me a passcode to the rings and his apartment. He said I could bring a friend, and I was hoping you could go? I can't go to Ring Eight alone. I don't even know what I should wear!"

I laugh; it's typical for Pablo to fixate on minor details. "If he invited you and knows you're a student, I doubt he cares what you're wearing, Pab."

"I want to make a good impression. Kye, he's *gorgeous*. And I think he's interested."

"You aren't really looking for a friend, are you? You're hoping I'll be your wingman."

"Yes. Will you?"

"Tell me about this mystery Botanaari tech broker, and maybe I'll decide to help."

I'm teasing him; I've already made the decision to go, but it's fun to rile him up a bit.

Pablo groans. "Please, Kye? I need this."

"What's his name? I can look him up, since you won't spill the details."

"Daaros," Pablo says grudgingly. "Daaros Syl'Vaasis."

I access his public file. Daaros isn't just any Botanaari tech broker; he's the owner of one of the galaxy's most profitable solar technology firms. He was born into money and has a reputation for throwing extravagant parties and lavishing gifts on his friends. He's also a bachelor, which explains his presence in the singles bar. Daaros has more assets to his name than most *planets* can claim, and he's only thirty standard years old.

I study the image attached to his file and understand immediately why he piqued Pablo's interest. He's peering over his shoulder at the photographer, a mischievous grin on his near-perfect, green-hued features. The dark fringe on his head that resembles hair is tousled artfully, his sharp white teeth are pristine, and his dark eyes gleam. The black button-down shirt he wears has the collar pulled up and the sleeves rolled to his elbows, but even my untrained eye can see the quality of the fabric is exquisite. His shirt probably cost more than all my cybernetic implants combined.

"Holy fuck," I whisper. "Do you know who he *is*, Pablo?"

Pablo is silent for a moment, then nods. "He's one of the richest men in the galaxy. But did you *look* at him, Kye? How can I say no to a face like that?"

"I can see why you're interested," I concede. "Fine, I'll go with you."

He beams. "You're the best."

I snort and shake my head. "You're just lucky I have evenings free right now."

"Which is why I need you to go with me *tomorrow*." He rises from his chair and bounces on his feet, unable to contain his excitement any longer. "Can you meet me at the space elevator landing? On Megatropolis?"

"What time?"

"Six. I can get us to Ring Eight from there." He flashes a grin. "You're the best friend in the universe, Kye!"

I laugh, thrilled to see him so happy about a prospective date, and secretly pleased that he's finally set his sights on someone who might reciprocate his desires.

"I'll see you at six, Pab. Enjoy your night."

KYE VEREX

CHAPTER NINE

THE BOTANAARI PLAYBOY

**RING EIGHT
MEGATROPOLIS, TRAPPIST-1 SYSTEM**

The ride from Ring Five to Megatropolis' surface takes twenty-eight minutes, and though I know the descent is rapid, I don't notice the speed at which the elevator plummets through space or the planet's atmosphere. I'm the only one riding the car from Ring Five.

When I emerge onto the paved plaza a handful of city blocks from MSTI, the planet's reddish sun is obscured by a thin veil of clouds. I thread my way through the throng of people awaiting their respective elevator cars; Rings One through Four appear to be the most sought-after as the world's populace evacuates their workplaces for the day to return home. Only a handful of people await the cars for Rings Seven and Eight, and I spy Pablo within moments.

Now that I can see him in person, I notice the subtle changes since our arrival on this world. He's still thin, but no longer dangerously so, and the lines of worry that once constantly marred his forehead have been erased. He's dressed in what I assume is his nicest outfit; a pale yellow collared shirt beneath a gray vest, paired with gray slacks and black boots he's polished to a shine. He looks up as I approach and flashes a grin, then darts forward to envelop me in a hug.

He stands back and holds me at arm's length, then squeezes my right bicep experimentally.

"I thought you had a date with someone else tonight, Pab," I tease.

He blushes furiously and drops his hands. "I do. Kind of. But I had to see if they were…real. You've never had muscles before."

"They're real. And Vee has been kicking my ass daily to make sure I don't lose them," I add with a grimace.

My body heals rapidly as long as I keep hydrated and eat regularly, but I'm still feeling the remnants of today's training session. Vee was in a singular mood when they arrived, and there was nothing I could do to please them. But I didn't complain; the combat training is necessary for my role, and I'm determined to succeed after everything I've been through just to get here.

Pablo studies me head to toe, silently appraising me with his dark eyes. "You look good. I don't know how I feel about the outfit, but I suppose it will have to do."

"What's wrong with my outfit?" I ask, feigning hurt.

I wore what constitutes as my best, but it isn't as nice as Pablo's. My apartment was stocked with an array of clothing tailored to my size, but for all the money Zylar Inc. put into my cybernetics, they didn't waste a cent on my wardrobe. I'm wearing dark-washed denim pants, a white tank, and a white button-down shirt. Most of what I own is branded with the Zylar Inc. logo or ZIEG's, and I didn't want to draw attention to my affiliations at this party.

Pablo crosses his arms. "When we meet up next, I'm taking you shopping. I *know* you have a regular salary now. I will accept no excuses."

The arrival of the elevator spares me from further discourse regarding my wardrobe. The passengers heading to Ring Eight are required to input a passcode before they're allowed to enter, and Pablo's code is sufficient to grant us both entry. The elevator's controlling AI pings me through my implant a moment after the doors slide shut.

It is a rare honor to host a member of ZIEG on Ring Eight. I hope your presence here does not indicate trouble on the horizon.

I struggle to keep a straight face, amused by the AI's misplaced concern. *I'm attending a party,* I reply. *Nothing more.*

Pablo nudges me with an elbow. "What's so funny?"

"We were scanned on our way inside," I reply quietly, hoping the other three passengers won't overhear my words. "The AI in charge of this elevator was concerned I might be going to Ring Eight on business."

Pablo rolls his eyes. "Because cyborgs aren't allowed to have fun? That's ridiculous." He pauses to study me, his head tilted to one side. "How did you know the AI scanned us?"

I draw a breath and shift uncomfortably. "I have implants in my brain. The AI can link directly to one of them. We spoke."

Pablo stares at me, incredulous, then shakes his head. "That's insane. You can link directly with an AI? What else can you do?"

I smirk and decide to have a little fun with Pablo. "That's classified."

"Liar."

"Maybe, but how will you know?"

He groans. "So that's how it's going to be? You're the owner of fabulous technology. I'm an engineer *and* your best friend, but you choose to keep it secret?"

I grin. "Yep."

"I need to find a new best friend."

"You wouldn't know what to do without me."

His laughter echoes through the elevator, drawing curious glances from the others. "That's true. And I wouldn't want to."

It's damned good to hear him laugh. A *real* laugh, not the half-hearted approximation I've grown accustomed to during our years together on Earth. He's thriving on Megatropolis, and I'm once more grateful to my sister that I'm here with him. He would have been devastated knowing I was left behind in the cesspit we called home.

As the elevator begins to rise past the inner rings, Pablo adjusts the cuffs of his shirt and straightens his collar. His heartbeat speeds along at a nervous gallop. I can't recall a time when I've ever seen him this anxious.

"Relax," I whisper as he brushes imaginary dust from his vest. "He invited you to his party, which means he has more than a passing interest in you. Just be your charming self, and everything will be fine."

Pablo fixes me with a skeptical look. "And how would you know, Mr. I-don't-bother-with-romance?"

"I read," I reply with a smirk. "And I know *you*, Pab. He's stupid if he lets you get away."

Pablo blushes and averts his gaze. "That means a lot, Kye."

"And if he hurts you, he'll have a pissed off cyborg to deal with." I cross my arms and lean against the wall. "I hear I can be intimidating."

Pablo snorts. "Doubtful."

I shrug, thinking of my final conversation with Mat. "I'll always have your back, Pab. And I won't let anyone break your heart and get away with it."

He smiles, and I note the undercurrent of anxiety he was attempting to hide has ebbed. "This is why you're my best friend."

When the elevator stops at Ring Eight, Pablo leads me along the main corridor for some time. This ring is quiet, the door to each private residence spaced much farther apart than the ones on Ring Five. I suspect the apartments are much larger too, though no doors stand ajar to let me peer inside. By the time we arrive at a security barrier, curiosity is nagging me relentlessly.

Pablo inputs a code into the kiosk and we're allowed through. The others who rode the elevator with us have long since disappeared from our wake.

"Are we early or late?" I ask Pablo as the corridor arcs directly toward a single door.

He chuckles nervously. "Late, but I don't think he invited many people tonight. He said it would be low-key."

I nod and gesture for him to enter first. This was his invitation after all, and his potential date. I'm only here to provide moral support.

He straightens his garments a final time, draws a breath, and opens the door. Music spills into the corridor, a loud and brazen beat underlying a mix of electronic instruments. The room we enter is dark, illuminated by pulsing lights in a dozen colors that change in time to the music's throbbing rhythm. Groups of people dance throughout the room, and on the far side is a sleek bar tended by a trio of robots. A few guests linger at the bar, while others cluster along a window, watching TRAPPIST-1 disappear in a blaze of crimson beyond the planet's rim.

Most of the guests are human, though I spy several Botanaari on the dance floor. They're even more captivating in person; their features are both more refined and more feral than a human's, accentuated by the emerald tones of their skin and the sharper quality of their starkly white teeth. I take note of their ears for the first time as we wander toward the bar. They're pointed and curl at the tip, not unlike a leaf beginning to unfurl in spring.

"I don't see him," Pablo murmurs, dejected.

I take the lead and guide him to the bar. We order drinks, then turn to study the others in the intermittent flashes of light.

"It's his party and his place," I remind Pablo. "He'll turn up."

"I didn't know the elevator would take so long. I thought we'd be here sooner. What if he's not interested?"

"Your drinks," the robot behind us interrupts. "Refills are free until ten p.m."

I pick up my gin and tonic while Pablo grasps his cocktail, staring glumly into its depths. I don't know how to cheer him up—he's usually the one bolstering *my* spirits, not the other way around.

I scan the room and notice a door opening across from us. Daaros emerges alone, his dark eyes unreadable in the pulsing light.

"Pab—"

"What if he's given up on me because we were late, Kye?" Pablo asks.

I glance at him to find he's still staring into his glass, his drink untouched.

"Pab, he's—"

"I was hoping this would work out. I felt a spark last night."

I draw a sharp breath. "Damn it, Pablo, *look*."

I point toward the middle of the room, where Daaros maneuvers through the dancers. He's walking toward the bar, toward *us*, and my preoccupied best friend is oblivious, despite the phosphorescent stripes on the Botanaari's attire.

Pablo glances up, then freezes, his eyes wide. I think I could have heard his heartbeat stutter without my enhancements to tell me it did.

Daaros flashes a knowing grin, then slides onto the stool next to Pablo's. "I was hoping you'd come, Mr. Noriega." His voice is smooth, seductive, and I sense Pablo's heart rate skyrocket.

"I wouldn't miss it," Pablo manages in a strangled whisper.

"Who's your friend?"

Pablo blinks, then glances at me guiltily. "Ah, this is Kye."

Daaros nods and rakes a hand through the dark green fringe on his head. It looks so much like human hair I wouldn't have known it was something else if I hadn't studied Botanaari biology briefly while preparing for my OMMA exams.

Daaros' dark eyes slide away from me to land on Pablo, a playful smile quirking the corners of his mouth. "You mentioned Kye was your friend from Earth. You failed to prepare me for his singular *presence.*"

I down my drink and hope Pablo comes up with a response, because I sure as hell don't know what to say. I turn to the robot behind the counter and gesture for a refill.

"Kye isn't interested," Pablo says, his voice almost lost in the swell of music as the song changes. "You don't have to worry about that."

I struggle to control the blush heating my face and focus on the robot pouring my drink. Fucking hell, I didn't realize Botanaari were so forward. Or was it just Daaros?

Daaros laughs. "It seems I've made him uncomfortable. I apologize, but I needed to be sure you weren't already attached. I rather enjoyed last evening. I was hoping for more."

The robot slides my glass across the bar and I drain half of it. Maybe I should try my luck on the dance floor, or seek conversation elsewhere. I'm merely an intrusion into Pablo's date—and I'm pretty damned sure that's what this is turning out to be. Daaros is making his intentions blatantly obvious.

"I was too," Pablo says.

"Shall we dance, then?"

Relief washes through me as Pablo accepts the invitation and I'm left alone at the bar. He's my best friend and I'd do anything in the galaxy he asked of me, but overhearing his conversation with Daaros was awkward. I exhale and turn my back to the bar, watching as Pablo follows the taller Botanaari into the throng. He smiles shyly as Daaros takes his hands, and moments later, they disappear into the crowd.

I want to be happy for him, but I don't trust the Botanaari yet. What drew him to Pablo, and why is he seeking the company of a human over one of his own people? Why is he interested in a poor kid from Earth when he has the galaxy at his fingertips? What does he want from my best friend?

The song ends, and some of the crowd disperses. Pablo becomes visible again. He's beaming, enthralled by the green-skinned man and his seductive smile. The next track begins to play; it's slower, with a depth of musicality the previous songs lacked. More people clear the floor until it's only Pablo and Daaros. A spotlight shines from above to illuminate them in stark contrast to their darkened surroundings. Daaros pulls Pablo into an elegant dance, flowing smoothly from step to step, while Pablo follows his lead with ease.

I don't know when Pablo learned to dance, but he's a natural. And paired with Daaros, his movements are fluid and graceful. The two are stunning. They complement one another in a way I never would have believed possible.

I push my suspicions aside. Pablo is clearly enjoying himself, and I won't ruin his moment. He's been longing for meaningful romance for years, something I'm incapable of giving to him, but that Daaros is willing to provide. I'll watch from the sidelines and intervene if I think Pablo will be hurt, but I won't interfere otherwise.

Pablo deserves this chance. I've held him back long enough.

I loiter at the bar until my internal clock reads almost midnight. Most of the other guests have gone, but a few linger on the dance floor. Pablo stands at the window with his back to the room, Daaros' arm around his waist, holding him close. Since their first dance, the two have been inseparable.

Unfortunately, I have no choice but to interrupt; I need to leave for Ring Five. I don't know what Pablo's plans for the rest of the night are—whether he'll return to his room at MSTI or remain here with his new beau—but I won't leave without saying goodbye.

I push away from the bar and move toward them. Daaros peers over his shoulder and offers me a content smile. He whispers to Pablo as I approach, but Pablo doesn't disentangle himself from the Botanaari's easy embrace. He merely turns in my direction, his eyes alight.

"Hey, Kye."

"Hey, Pab." I lean against the window and study the pair. "I didn't want to leave without saying something, but I need to go. Vee will be at my place at seven."

Pablo laughs softly. "I know. Even cyborgs need to sleep sometimes."

Daaros narrows his eyes and studies me anew. "You must be the one flagged as ZIEG," he says quietly. "My security system alerted me that one of your kind was here."

"Is that a problem?" I ask.

"No. I find it a relief our dear Pablo has such capable friends. Megatropolis isn't the safe haven your government touts it as." Daaros shakes his head, then smiles fondly at Pablo. "Does this mean you'll be leaving too?"

"Only if you want me to."

Daaros chuckles. "As much as I wish you would stay, I think it's best we get to know one another a bit better before you spend the night here. I'm not in the habit of one-night stands, and I want to be *certain*."

I lift my eyebrows, surprised that Daaros is the one urging caution. Maybe I assumed his motives incorrectly after all.

Pablo grins, then raises up onto his toes to plant a kiss on the Botanaari's lips. Daaros' eyes widen for an instant before he closes them to better enjoy the moment. I look away, taking in the view of space from the window while the pair say their final goodbye for the evening. I look back only when I hear Pablo's mischievous laughter.

"I'll see you on Friday," Pablo says. "If you're still up for another date, that is."

Daaros hooks a finger beneath Pablo's chin and nods. "I've already made reservations. But your friend is right—it's late, and you have class in the morning. I've kept you too long as it is."

We make our way to the door, and Pablo looks back a final time before we depart. Daaros' gaze lingers on his, and I begin to suspect this is something more profound than mere attraction.

We walk in silence until we've cleared the security barrier, then Pablo releases a contented sigh. "He's incredible. I would have stayed if he asked."

"I know. And he knows it too." I eye him with a smirk. "So you have another date planned?"

Pablo beams. "We do. Tonight went so much better than I hoped it would, but I'm sorry I left you behind at the bar. I dragged you to this party thinking I needed to catch his attention and that I'd need your help to get it, but I already had it."

"That you did."

"What do you think of him, Kye? Be honest. I need to know."

I chew my lip as I consider what to tell him. "He's not what I expected. From the outside, he looks like any rich playboy with too many credits and too little sense. But he's more than that. I don't know why he's interested in you, and I hope he isn't using you in some way, but... You seem so natural together. I don't know what else to say, other than I haven't fully formed an opinion yet."

"You need time to get to know him."

"That would help."

"I think I can arrange something." Pablo flashes a grin. "I was afraid you wouldn't approve. I like him, Kye. *A lot.*"

I laugh. "I noticed. You can't keep your eyes off him."

"Did you know he owns the company that makes the solar tech in your optics?"

"What?" I ask, unsettled by the abrupt change in topics.

Pablo nods. "VaasTek makes all the solar enhancements in the ZIEG optics package. It's why he was interested when I let it slip that you're a cyborg."

"I hope he knows how to be discreet," I grumble. "I'm still not used to referring to myself as a cyborg, and I'm not ready to draw attention to it publicly."

"Don't worry. He's not in the habit of sharing trade secrets."

I lift my eyebrows, amused. "You sound awfully certain, Pab. This was only your first date."

"And I trust him. I think you will too, given time."

CHAPTER TEN

ZIEG REPUTATION

MEGATROPOLIS, TRAPPIST-1 SYSTEM

I follow Vee through the expansive glass doors that enclose the lobby of Zylar Inc.'s main office. Vee hasn't told me why they've deviated from our usual routine this morning, and I hope I won't be reprimanded for attending Daaros' party the night before. I was scanned at least twice that I know of while Pablo and I traveled between Megatropolis and Ring Eight, and I know my employer likes to keep apprised of its assets' movements.

Rather than dwell on the what-ifs, I surveil my surroundings. The lobby is glassed in on all sides, and an abundance of exotic plants decorate the space, each housed in a separate blue pot emblazoned with the company's logo. Blue cushioned benches line the outer walls. A triangular desk occupies the heart of the lobby, staffed by several humans, two AI kiosks, and a plethora of small robots that zoom about the desk's surface. At the far point of the triangle is a glass elevator shaft.

Dozens of visitors congregate around the desk. I watch as several are granted visitor's badges and pointed toward the elevator, while others are sent to wait at the benches for further assistance. Vee ignores the desk and moves straight toward the elevator.

"Where are we going?" I ask for the fifth time since we left my apartment.

Vee tilts their head and smiles enigmatically. "You'll see."

I cross my arms and lean against the glass as Vee presses a button for the ninety-eighth floor. "I hate secrets."

"This isn't a secret. It's a *surprise*."

I roll my eyes. "I fail to see the difference."

"You're cranky this morning. It spoils my fun."

I groan and stare out the glass as we pass floor after floor packed with cubicles. The people beyond the panes take little notice of our passage, used to the elevator's movements throughout the day. Most are busy at desks, flicking through tablets and holoscreens or taking calls. I don't know how they manage; I would die of boredom in minutes if I was trapped in a corporate job like theirs.

"I went to a party last night," I admit after a time.

"I'm aware. What I'd like to know is how you met Daaros Syl'Vaasis, the most eligible bachelor in the galaxy and a man who isn't easy to befriend. Or so I hear." Vee tosses their head and fixes me with a knowing smirk.

"Pablo got the invite. I was just…his wingman." I laugh uneasily. "He didn't need my help to catch Daaros' attention." I pause to stare outside the elevator car for a moment, then blurt, "Am I in some kind of trouble?"

Vee tips their head back and laughs. "No. Our visit to the corporate office has nothing to do with your extracurricular activities."

"Then why are we here?"

Vee shakes their head. "That's not going to work on me. As I said, it's a surprise."

I glower and turn away. I hate surprises.

"I amend my previous assessment. You're not cranky. You're fucking surly."

I glare at Vee, who grins unabashedly in return.

"I'm not wrong, Kye. Just relax. You'll like what I have planned today."

The elevator ascends to a level where the glass is blocked by opaque white panels, then chimes. The door slides open to reveal a security barricade staffed by an AI kiosk and two burly men in form-fitting body armor stamped with the ZIEG logo. I glance at Vee uncertainly as we exit the car.

"Vee Domineaux," one of the men says in greeting, his blue eyes crinkling with his smile. "It's been a while."

Vee nods, then gestures to me. "Kye Verex is our newest recruit. I signed off on his combat training yesterday. Kye, this is Ivon Trex and Chadwick Cleary. They report to Captain Osirius."

I stare at Vee, startled that I'm finished with combat training. Vee kicked my ass yesterday, and I was preparing for another grueling morning of punishment.

"And we're staffing the corporate office until the captain's back on his feet," Ivon, the blue-eyed man, says. "Welcome aboard, Kye. Today begins the fun portion of your training."

I eye him skeptically. "Fun?"

"Weapons training," Chadwick answers. "I take it Vee didn't tell you?"

I shake my head, both irritated and elated, causing both men to laugh.

"That's cruel, Vee," Ivon says as he waves us through the barricade. "But typical."

Vee shrugs and saunters past them. "I have a reputation to maintain."

I follow Vee through a set of nondescript doors into a vast open space. Weapon racks line two walls, holding everything from small caliber pistols to plasma rifles to nanosteel swords and everything in between. The wall opposite the entrance flickers to life as the doors close behind us, and I realize it's a giant holoscreen. Icons appear on its surface for programs relating to target practice, basic weapons training, posture assessments, and more. I turn in place, taking in every facet of the room, speechless.

"This is our weapons lab," Vee says with a grin. "I thought you'd like the surprise."

"Why didn't you tell me you signed off on my combat training?" I ask after a time. "You kicked my ass yesterday—harder than usual."

Vee chuckles. "I almost didn't. If I had been anyone but a cyborg, you would have won every match in seconds. The only reason you didn't best me is that I have the advantage of experience, and you're still a bit hesitant to utilize your full strength."

"I didn't want to hurt you."

Vee smirks knowingly. "There's nothing you can do to me that Mat can't repair. But you're ready for the next phase, which is this."

Vee walks to one of the weapon racks and I follow, intrigued. They pick up an old-style projectile pistol and a box of ammunition from the cubby beneath it.

"We'll start with the basics," Vee says. "Have you used one of these before?"

I shake my head. "Not a real one. Kelsey ran me through several low-quality simulators before I tested for OMMA."

I feel my face flush at the admission. With the abundance of tech present in the everyday lives of Megatropolis' citizens, the simulator Kelsey employed long-distance feels like a shadow, the barest essence of what could have been if I hadn't been trapped on Earth.

And I'll never confess that I used two blocks of potentially radioactive steel, welded into a crude shape vaguely resembling the pistol in Vee's hand for my initial training. OMMA was only concerned with reaction times and basic aim; firing the makeshift weapon wasn't part of the testing regimen.

Vee studies me, then nods. "We're aware of your history, Kye. There's no need to be ashamed of it. I'll demonstrate how to load and operate each weapon here as we progress through your training, but if you ever require a refresher, Mat should have installed the user manuals in your personal databanks. They're set to update automatically when new weapons are added to the Zylar Inc. catalog."

"I…What? I have manuals for all of this in my head?" I splutter.

Vee rolls their eyes, but appears amused. "I've told you to explore the databanks in your free time. There are more than weapon specs stored in that thick skull of yours."

Vee has told me numerous times to look at my databanks, but with all of my other required tasks and training modules, I haven't bothered. My free time is usually occupied by calls with Pablo or reading, now that I have access to an unlimited number of novels. Scrolling through a list of what Mat had stored in my mechanized memory didn't appeal to me before now.

"I'll look through them tonight," I promise.

Vee proceeds to demonstrate how to load ammunition into the pistol and the proper stance for firing the weapon, then swivels smoothly to face the screen at the far end of the room. Before I'm able to frame another question, Vee fires three shots directly at the holoscreen. The noise is deafening. I wince, stunned that they possess the audacity to intentionally destroy a piece of incredibly expensive technology while we're in the midst of company headquarters.

"What the fuck?"

Vee laughs at my reaction and points at the screen as I open my eyes. It's undamaged, and three of the targets that were present moments before are gone.

"It's protected by impenetrable polymer-coated glass three inches thick," Vee explains. "I didn't think you'd believe me when I told you to fire at it, so I saved you the trouble."

Vee unloads the pistol's chamber, then hands it and the ammunition to me. "Your turn. Let's see how well your simulators have taught you."

We spend the morning cycling through various weapons and how to operate them. My aim is solid, thanks to the countless hours I spent with Kelsey years ago, though it takes me a few shots with each to anticipate the recoil. That was an element my welded facsimile had failed to account for.

While I practice, dozens of pings flood my personal inbox, but I ignore them. I can read them when we're finished, and I'm doubtful their contents are important. My focus remains solely on training, while Vee stands by, amused.

It's almost noon when Vee holds up a hand for me to stop. "Lunch is in order. We'll return tomorrow. You're doing okay so far."

I frown as I stow the plasma rifle I had been working with in its rack. I thought today's session had gone better than *okay*.

"You disagree?" Vee asks as we walk toward the exit.

"I didn't miss a single target, and—"

"Your aim is excellent, yes," Vee interrupts. "Your reaction times are passable, but you're capable of moving faster. You overthink your compensation for recoil, and you haven't read through any of the weapon specs stored in your databanks. It's my job to push you to your limits, and you have yet to reach them. Until you do, my assessment is that you're okay, but you require further improvement before we proceed."

I resist the urge to argue. "I'll read the damned specs tonight."

I trudge after them as we pass the security barricade and reenter the elevator. Another internal ping warns me I have yet another new message, and I grudgingly access my inbox. Eleven new messages, all of them from Pablo. I frown, immediately concerned, and open the first.

Have you checked GNN this morning?

I roll my eyes. The Galactic News Network is the last thing I check on any given morning, and he knows that. I open the second message, which is a link to a GNN holovid. I groan aloud, drawing a curious glance from Vee, and open the video.

A smiling reporter appears on my retinal screen, with the words "No Longer Single?" floating on her right. The ticker tape beneath her scrolls by offering brief highlights of other breaking stories. She begins to speak in a carefully modulated tone, her bright smile unwavering.

"This just in from Megatropolis' elite Ring Eight district. It's no secret the galaxy's most eligible bachelor, owner of VaasTek and heir to the Syl'Vaasis Dynasty, has been covertly seeking romance, but a sighting last night may end the debate once and for all."

The image morphs into a darkened video of relatively poor quality, showing the interior of Daaros' expansive apartment. It's focused on the long window beyond the dance floor and displays a three second clip of Daaros and Pablo locked in their kiss. I see myself from behind, turned to face away from them.

Shit. No wonder Pablo has been sending me messages all morning.

The video flashes back to the reporter. "That, my friends, was the wealthy Botanaari playboy, Daaros Syl'Vaasis, and what appears to be his very *human* partner."

I'm laughing as I close the link and scroll through Pablo's remaining messages. He's shocked to find himself the object of a GNN story, horrified someone at the party took a video of his bold and intimate moment with Daaros, but relishing the attention he's receiving from his classmates.

"What's so funny?" Vee wears a mischievous smile, and I suspect they already know.

"Pablo," I reply as I send him a brief response.

"Your friend has become a minor celebrity." Vee chuckles. "Anyone affiliated with *that* Botanaari will be a target of the galaxy's paparazzi. Including you."

My good humor flees like a desperate rat escaping one of Earth's deadly hurricanes. "Why me?"

"You're a friend of Pablo's, and he's the object of Daaros' affection," Vee replies patiently. "The gossipmongers will stop at nothing to sink their teeth into a juicy story, and theirs is bound to become one. It's not forbidden for a Botanaari to seek human companionship, but it's very rare. And he has more money than all of Zylar Inc. combined. Think about it."

"They'll try to learn more about Pablo from me."

"Exactly." Vee crosses their arms. "I hope you're prepared to fend off a few obnoxious reporters. They're bound to seek you out—and you *were* on that video too."

"You watched it."

It's not a question, and my heart sinks like a stone. Now I understand why Vee knew about the party. They weren't following my movements as I had suspected; they were merely watching GNN.

Vee nods. "I think most of the galaxy watched it, Kye. But this may be good for you. Flex your ZIEG muscles a bit. The reporters will back off, and more rumors will swirl around your friend and his Botanaari beau. Reporters are irritating, but they're not stupid. They know when not to pursue a topic, and ZIEG is one they'd rather avoid. They'll likely leave Pablo alone when you're with him too."

"And by flexing my muscles, you mean I should tell them I'm ZIEG?" I don't like the idea. I don't want the attention, and I'm still uncomfortable with what I've become. There has to be a better way.

Vee shrugs. "You can tell them, or you can just give them your name. They can look up your redacted file easily enough. The choice is yours."

"I'd rather they don't know at all."

Vee's expression softens. "I understand, but eventually, they'll find out who you are. It's best for you *and* Pablo if they learn sooner rather than later."

I'm still grappling with my decision when the elevator opens several minutes later and we emerge on the ground floor. Vee hasn't said anything more, and I'm not sure what the hell I plan to do. But I'd do anything to help Pablo, and if speaking to a damned reporter about who and what I am will give him some semblance of privacy, I'll do it. It's *how* to do it that I'm uncertain of.

I receive another message from Pablo as we walk through Zylar Inc.'s main doors into the early afternoon light. He asks if we can meet later that day after he's finished with classes and I'm released from Vee's smirking custody. I readily agree; we have too much to discuss, I have questions, and maybe if I'm lucky, the paparazzi conundrum will resolve itself while I'm with him.

We should meet somewhere public, I add to my response. *I'd like to have a word with your new followers.*

His response pings in my head seconds later. *I was hoping you might help with that. Daar said your status should scare most of them off. He'll join us, if you don't mind. I'll send a location once we decide on one.*

I chuckle to myself, unsurprised he's been chatting with the Botanaari while I've been otherwise occupied. I'm also amused that he's started to refer to Daaros by a nickname already, and I wonder if *Daar* knows about it yet. Knowing Pablo as I do, Daaros doesn't.

Ahead, Vee pauses outside the ZIEG shuttle we used to travel here and crosses their arms. Impatience is written in their expression, and I increase my pace.

"Your friend again?" Vee asks as we climb inside.

I nod. "Yeah. He wants to meet later."

"And the Botanaari?"

"Him too." I collapse into a seat with a sigh. "What do you think is best, Vee? Should I tell the reporters what I am, or just give them my name? Apparently Daaros thinks as you do, and my presence should be enough to deter the paparazzi."

A small smile creases Vee's features. "ZIEG has a reputation. It serves us well in many situations." They tap several screens, and the shuttle rises from the landing pad. "We'll eat lunch near the base of the space elevator. There's an excellent taco shop there. As for how you should approach the gossip hounds, I suggest bluntly. Tell them you're with ZIEG, give them your name, and say nothing else. Act the part of a bodyguard for your friend, and they'll believe your words before they verify your identity."

"Have you been through something like this before?" I ask.

Vee laughs softly. "On occasion. One more bit of advice: Change into something with our logo on it before you join them. Intimidation can be your greatest ally. Use it to your advantage."

I follow Vee's advice and return to my apartment after we eat lunch to change. I opt for a t-shirt with the ZIEG logo emblazoned on the front. It's a bit more form-fitting than my usual attire, and my new muscles bulge beneath the thin fabric. I grimace, snag a looser t-shirt, and change a second time. I'm imposing enough that I don't need my attire to accentuate it any further. I wonder, and not for the first time, who stocked my wardrobe before I arrived at my apartment.

Maybe I *should* take Pablo up on his offer of a shopping trip.

Pablo sends me another message as I contemplate changing my pants too.

Daar made reservations at Sileca's near the Government District for three p.m.

I check my internal clock and note it's almost one-thirty, then look up the location of Sileca's. It's a forty-minute shuttle ride from the space elevator's landing. I should leave now. My present attire will have to suffice.

I'm on my way, I send to Pablo. *Any chance your boyfriend can arrange a shuttle from the space elevator? I'll be planet side in thirty.*

I'm halfway to the elevator before Pablo responds. *A VaasTek shuttle will be waiting for you. Thanks, Kye.*

The line for the elevator is lengthy when I arrive at the descent pad, but I'm given priority access when I pass through security and bypass most of the line. I'm learning there are certain perks to being employed by ZIEG.

The elevator is crammed by the time the doors close and we're cleared for descent. I stare out the windows, enjoying the view of the rings as they speed by. The backdrop of stars is stunning. I'll never grow tired of this view that was once an impossible dream.

The stars are rapidly replaced by haze as we enter the planet's atmosphere, then it clears as we plummet through filmy clouds and open sky. I look down at the rapidly approaching spires of Megatropolis' skyscrapers and watch as they come into sharp relief as the ground nears. Despite the crowded elevator car, the trip is pleasant enough.

And the other passengers give me a wide berth. I suspect it's the t-shirt.

When the car stops and the doors slide open, I wait for most of the crowd to disperse before I exit. The plaza is buzzing with activity, but I've come to expect it from Megatropolis. It's rare when somewhere *isn't* busy.

I scan the perimeter and locate a white shuttle bearing a vibrant green VaasTek logo across its broad side. There isn't another, so I assume it's my ride. The passenger door slides open as I approach, and I note a slender Botanaari sits behind the console. He's dressed in a crisp white suit and matching fedora, which sits tilted in a roguish fashion atop his head. He nods as I slip inside and take the unoccupied copilot's seat, eyes the shade of emeralds raking across my form.

"The boss described you in detail, but he didn't mention you were ZIEG," he says as the door closes and we lift off. "I'm Araan, personal assistant to Mr. Syl'Vaasis."

I nod in greeting. "Kye Verex. I'm a friend of Pablo's."

Araan chuckles. "He's sweet, from what I hear. Daaros is quite taken with him. I haven't seen him this interested in anyone for years."

I lift my eyebrows in question, but Araan doesn't oblige me. I suspect it's history Daaros isn't keen to discuss. Based on what I've learned from Kelsey, ending a relationship can be a messy affair. I'm glad I have no need for one.

We pass the remainder of the ride in relative silence. I'm not the best conversationalist, and Araan doesn't seem interested in small talk. I gaze out the window at the buildings as we speed by, following TRAPPIST-1 across the sky until we've traveled almost halfway around the planet. The Government District suddenly looms ahead, its towers and monoliths rising to dwarf every structure I've encountered so far. I'm no engineer, but the scale and height of the buildings seem impossible. Some appear to brush the stratosphere.

"Holy shit."

Araan laughs good-naturedly. "You haven't been to this part of Megatropolis before."

"No. How do they stay upright?"

"Clever engineering. It's impressive, isn't it?"

I nod, unable to tear my eyes from the sight.

"Sileca's isn't within the district, but it has a stellar view of it. We're almost there."

He lands the shuttle on what appears to be a private pad attached to one of the smaller skyscrapers at the fringe of the Government District. There's a glass door leading inside the building, but it's unmarked.

"This is the VIP entrance to Sileca's," Araan says. "The staff will be expecting you."

"Thanks for the ride."

He smiles. "What Daaros requests of me, Daaros receives."

The shuttle departs moments after I exit, and I'm left with no choice but to step inside the building. A pretty woman in a flashy gown of silver greets me within, her platinum hair twisted into a severe knot at the base of her skull. Her makeup is immaculate, her nails are manicured in brilliant cerulean, and she wears enough diamond-encrusted jewelry to out-dazzle the brightest of suns.

My eyes dart past her, and I note all of the staff is similarly attired. *Shit.* I'm beyond underdressed.

"Mr. Verex, I presume?" the woman purrs.

I swallow my discomfort and manage a nod.

"Right this way."

She beckons me to follow with a bejeweled hand, but it doesn't take me long to realize where we're headed. A throng of reporters crowd a doorway leading to what should have been a private balcony. Lights flash as they vie for the best photograph of their quarry, while voices raise in question. I have no doubt Daaros is present, though I can't yet see beyond the crowd.

The woman leads me through a separate doorway and along a narrow corridor that empties onto the balcony a short distance from the rabid gossipmongers. They shout over one another in desperation, voices blending together into an unrecognizable deluge of sound. I adjust my aural implants to reduce the volume of the crowd and follow the woman across the balcony.

A circular table is set for three at its center. Daaros lounges in one chair, smirking mischievously at the crowd, while Pablo occupies the seat to his left. He breaks into a grin when he sees me, then bounds to his feet and waves me over.

The throng gasps collectively and begins to fall quiet as my presence is noted. I suppress my unease and shoot a glare in their direction. Vee encouraged me to intimidate, so that's what I'll do. If nothing else, I can at least hear myself think now.

Daaros stands and makes a point of welcoming me as well. "It's always an honor to have you join us, Kye."

One brave reporter breaks the relative silence that follows in the wake of his words. "Who is he?"

I turn slowly, ensuring the ZIEG logo across my tee is visible. "Kye Verex, ZIEG operative."

I don't technically have a title or a rank yet, but it sounds impressive, and they take the hint. Most of Daaros' unwanted guests rapidly disappear inside Sileca's and don't return. The woman who escorted me from the entrance silently moves toward the door and secures it from the outside, then assures us someone will arrive to take our drink orders soon.

Daaros sighs and pinches the bridge of his nose as she departs. "Your arrival was timely. The noise was giving me a blasted headache."

"Is it always like this?" I ask.

He shakes his head, drops his hand, and looks at Pablo, his expression pained. "No. I do my best to keep out of the spotlight, but sometimes it finds me no matter what I do. I didn't want the media circus, particularly not so soon after our first meeting."

Pablo smiles in understanding. "I don't blame you for this. But our plan worked." He glances toward the door, where not one reporter remains. "They're gone. We can talk in peace."

"Thank the suns for that," Daaros growls. "It's not enough that they invade my corporate lobby and arrive unannounced at my apartments on occasion, but they insist on ruining my dates too. Blazing nuisances."

He turns to study me. His dark eyes aren't black as I first believed, but a deep green much like the silken fringe on his head that passes for hair. In the daylight, the subtle differences in his humanoid features mark him as distinctly *alien*, but he's no less attractive for it. I understand why Pablo is so fascinated with his species.

"I must thank you, Kye. I wasn't sure you'd agree to assist."

I grin and glance at Pablo. "He's my best friend. I'd do anything for him. Just know it's in your best interests to keep him happy, because if you hurt him—"

"Kye!" Pablo cuts in sharply. "Don't."

I shrug and lean back in my chair, but Daaros takes the hint.

"Believe me when I say harming Pablo is the farthest thing from my mind."

CHAPTER ELEVEN

A FUNDAMENTAL BREACH

MEGATROPOLIS, TRAPPIST-1 SYSTEM

Luna Zeta turns toward the door as we enter the weapons lab on our now-routine schedule. Beside me, Vee crosses their arms, their expression neutral as we approach our rainbow-haired captain. I suspect Vee wasn't aware we'd have an audience today. I certainly wasn't prepared for it.

"How are you progressing?" Luna asks.

I shrug, suddenly self-conscious. "Vee says I still need some work."

"You've passed combat training," Luna replies breezily. "That's the more difficult portion, if you ask me. Weapons training will go swiftly."

I shift uncomfortably but don't respond. We've been working in the lab daily for almost three weeks, and while I've grown used to the arsenal at ZIEG's disposal and have read the weapon specs stored in my databanks, Vee still isn't satisfied. I need to be faster, bolder, unafraid to fire when presented with a threat. The last point has been the most difficult to overcome.

"Why are you here?" Vee demands, an edge of surliness to their tone.

Luna's smile falters, and her eyes grow hard. "Isn't it enough that I'd like to keep tabs on my unit?"

Vee's head tilts to the side as they glower. "No. You can 'keep tabs' on him through the reports I place daily, as you've done in the past. I know you well enough to realize you aren't here for a damned checkup."

Luna nods. "Fine. I've been told Kye may be transferred elsewhere, and that it might occur before his training with you is complete." She turns to me with a disapproving frown. "The damned Botanaari you've been fraternizing with has made a bid to purchase your contract. The Executive Committee is meeting later today to discuss the possibility."

I'm unable to hide the stunned surprise on my face. I gape at her. "What?"

"I'm not in the habit of repeating myself," Luna replies. "Daaros Syl'Vaasis is one of only a handful of people in the galaxy with the resources to buy out a ZIEG contract. And he wants yours."

"But why?"

The question escapes my lips, though I suspect I know the answer. I dealt with his reporter problem at Sileca's simply by appearing at his table, and after the news leaked that Daaros and Pablo had enlisted ZIEG, they haven't returned to ruin any more dinner dates.

Luna rolls her eyes. "I think you know why. I came to tell you the news before you're whisked away to one of the quadrillionaire's many estates."

"You think they'll vote to allow the sale, even though he's part of the new series?" Vee asks.

"Zylar Inc. is a business, Vee. This will net them more money than he's worth, and Daaros has agreed to sign any and all NDAs relating to Kye's upkeep." Luna shakes her head and moves past us toward the door. "I hope for your sake they'll let you stay with us until your first year in ZIEG is complete. There's so much you still need to learn."

I stare at the floor, dumbfounded, frustrated, and uneasy. They refer to me as if I'm a piece of equipment, a mere asset rather than a living being. Maybe I am; I signed the damned contract in my desperation to leave Earth, and it binds me to Zylar Inc. in ways I'm still uncovering. And Daaros wants to *purchase* me, as though I'm a shiny bauble to decorate his apartment.

Fuck. I hate this.

I need to call Pablo. I need to know what his boyfriend is attempting to do.

A hand falls on my shoulder. I look up to find Vee staring into my eyes, concern etching their brow. I don't know what to say. I can't manage a smile or even a shrug. I merely stare back at Vee and hope they understand something of my emotional turmoil.

"I think your training can wait for another day," Vee says gently. "You need time to process."

I nod and avert my gaze.

"I'll take you somewhere else. Somewhere peaceful, away from corporate oversight, where you can let loose and just *be* for a time."

I nod again. "Okay."

"Don't call Pablo until you've had time to think over what you want to say," Vee advises as we leave the weapons lab and make for the elevator. "In your current state, you're liable to say something you'll regret later. He's a good friend to you, and I don't believe he'd agree to Daaros' plan if it was meant to harm you."

I sigh and lean against the elevator's glass wall as we enter. Vee's right. I need to wait, to sort through my thoughts before I call Pablo. I'll only make a mess of things if I call him now.

"How do you stand this shit?" I ask as we descend toward the ground floor.

Vee's expression is solemn. "We all signed a contract giving our lives to Zylar Inc. Most of the time, they treat us fairly. In this instance, we're little more than corporate assets, and for the right price, they'll alter the original terms. This isn't the first time a ZIEG soldier has been slated for purchase by a private party."

"And because of the contract, I won't get a say in any of it." I cross my arms and stare through the glass over my shoulder, watching as office workers move between desks and manipulate holoscreens, oblivious to our passage and my current plight.

"I'm sorry, Kye."

"Does Zylar Inc. always prey on those who are as desperate as I was? If I didn't join this unit, I would have *died*. You were there when Dr. Malhotra found the tumors. Earth was fucking killing me. No one else would pay for my gene therapy… This was my only shot!"

I slam my fist into the glass in my frustration, but the elevator must be constructed of the same polymer-coated material that protects the holoscreen in the weapons lab. I'm denied the satisfaction of a moment's destruction, and it stokes my simmering temper further.

"It's difficult to find willing recruits of any kind," Vee replies quietly. "It's no secret that becoming a cyborg can kill the recipient, and most people aren't willing to sell their soul to a corporate overlord."

It's as much of an admission as I'm likely to receive, and I wonder for the first time what led Vee and the others down this path. Vee's body language conveys their own hurt and vulnerability, their unspoken resentment of the situation.

"You know why I joined," I state sullenly. "Why did you?"

Vee shakes their head. "We'll discuss my reasons once we're away from here."

The elevator door slides open, and I have no choice but to follow Vee through the lobby and outside to our shuttle. I don't think Vee will say anything more until we arrive at their promised peaceful locale, and I'm content with silence.

Vee guides the shuttle to a sector of Megatropolis that I haven't visited before. Gone are the multitudes of skyscrapers clamoring for visibility along the crowded skyline. A dense, forested expanse speeds by beneath our shuttle. I stare in wonder at the sight; I've never seen so many trees in one place before.

Winged creatures flit gracefully between leafy branches, and I query my database to learn what they are. *Dragonflies.* A species that was rescued from Earth generations ago has found its home on Megatropolis, in this inexplicable expanse of verdant landscape encircled by steel and glass monstrosities.

Vee lands in a clearing designated for shuttle parking and we exit. I stare at the trees towering over us, nature's version of skyscrapers. They're all the same species; smooth gray bark sporting few blemishes covers the trunks in a protective layer, while branches lace and intertwine in a tangled network above. Glossy leaves of deep green, the same green as Daaros' eyes, I realize with some irritation, create a lush canopy and dappled shade. The forest is beautiful.

Vee motions for me to follow, and we exit the parking area to a narrow track paved with what appears to be natural stone. A black dragonfly with green spots zips past us without a care, its wings humming in an iridescent blur.

"I come here when I need time alone," Vee says after a while. "The trees invoke serenity. There's peace here that can't be found in the heart of this city-planet."

"Where are we?" I ask.

Vee offers me an uncertain smile. "Syl'Vaasis Gardens. One of Daaros' grandfathers founded it as a place of refuge on a planet that is nearly overtaken by corporate buildings. The Botanaari value and preserve nature, where we often fail to do so."

The majesty of the forest is tempered by the knowledge that it's part of Daaros' legacy. I can't seem to escape him today.

"Your situation isn't unique," Vee says. "It's a risk we all faced when we signed the ZIEG contracts, but it happens only rarely. I wish I had some bit of advice to give you, but with this, I have nothing. You are bound by that contract, and if Zylar Inc. decides to sell it to Daaros, there is nothing we can do to stop it."

I don't reply. Instead, I focus on the trees around us, the humming of insects, and the strange, hooting calls that emanate from the shadows. I detect the sound of running water somewhere ahead. I won't deny Syl'Vaasis gardens is both beautiful and calming, but its association with the man who seeks to *buy* me sours the effect.

"I joined ZIEG to escape the uranium mines of Yellow Hell. The planet is aptly named."

I'm not familiar with the world Vee refers to, but I know enough about uranium and its side effects to understand their life was likely not so different from mine.

Vee pushes up their left sleeve to reveal a faded tattoo. It's a series of numbers and letters. I recognize it as a slave mark.

"Vee…"

They shake their head with a sad smile. "I was born into a society that follows a caste system, and the lowest ranks are branded as property. I was slated to work the mines from the day I could walk, and I did. In exchange, my family was given a home, food, and education. We were denied access to credits, however. And the work was brutal. Yellow Hell has more sulfur on its surface than entire star systems claim to possess. But it was the uranium that made the overseers wealthy."

"You really do understand what it was like for me."

Vee nods. "Better than the others, though I didn't have to scrounge for food as you did. In many ways, I think your situation was worse."

I shrug. I can't imagine what it must have been like for Vee, forced to labor in an environment that was, in my mind, more hostile than Earth has become. But I'm no stranger to the hazards of radioactive material; that part of Vee's story I fully understand.

"Zylar Inc. seeks those desperate to leave their current situations," Vee says after a moment. "If we die during the enhancement process, they have nothing to lose. We signed the contracts knowing well that we were giving our lives over to a soulless corporate entity, one often without conscience, but in return, they promised a better life. A future. It's something neither of us would have had without them."

"I'm struggling to be grateful today," I growl. "They want to sell me like I'm some kind of...tool!"

"To the company, you *are* a tool." Vee sighs and shakes their head. "But the contract is legally binding. There is no one in the galaxy brave or stupid enough to take Zylar Inc. to court, not when the company is responsible for the coding that runs our AI government. They'll tweak the code and change the laws to suit their interests. They've done it before."

"You're saying I have to accept it."

Vee draws a breath, then says, "No. I'm saying there's no way to change it, but you *are* fortunate, Kye. I believe Daaros will treat you better than Zylar Inc. has."

Helplessness and despair sit like weights in my gut. There's nothing I can do. I signed the fucking contract, and now I'm enduring the consequences.

It's bullshit.

I want to scream, to cry, to lash out at something, but I'm paralyzed by the sheer hopelessness of my situation.

"I wish Pablo or Daaros would have said something to me beforehand."

"I think I understand why they didn't," Vee replies. "If you had known, and Daaros' proposition to buy your contract came to light too soon, the Executive Committee would likely have denied his request outright. They would have seen it as collusion on your friend's part to see you freed from your contract. Your ignorance in this matter is to your benefit."

I glower at the trees. It makes sense, but I don't like it. I'll *never* like it.

"I need to call Pablo."

Vee nods. "I'll be just ahead. Find me when you're finished, and we can talk further. Or not, if that's your choice."

I wait until Vee disappears around the bend in the path, then dial Pablo's frequency. I haven't called him from my implants before, and I'm not sure how he'll respond—or what he'll see on his end, if anything. But I'm desperate to talk with him after my conversations with Vee. I need to know what Daaros plans if the corporate executives agree to accept his offer.

"Hello?" Pablo's voice resonates within my ears, uncertain and edgy.

"Pab, it's me."

"Kye! Where are you calling from? There's nothing on my screen and the frequency is encrypted."

I laugh uneasily. "I'm calling from my implants. My head? I wasn't sure what you'd see on your display."

"Oh." His tone conveys awe. "I didn't know you could do that."

"There's a lot I can do now. Listen, I—"

"I know why you called," Pablo says, cutting me off. "Please don't be mad, Kye. I wanted to tell you two weeks ago when we first made the plans, but Daar said it wasn't a good idea."

"You were in on this?" I demand, trying and failing to keep the anguish from my voice. "Fucking hell."

I collapse into a sitting position in the middle of the path and stare skyward, furious with Pablo, with Daaros, with Zylar Inc., with *everyone.*

My impulse is to end the call, but I don't. Pablo has never done anything to hurt me before, and I don't believe he's intentionally doing so now, but my present reality stings. I need answers.

"Why?" I demand.

"Daar knows the terms of your contract. Even the fine print." Pablo sighs heavily, and I can hear the unspoken pain in his voice. "It never sat well with me, but I also didn't want to watch as you wasted away on Earth. I supported your decision, even if I didn't like what Zylar Inc. planned for you."

"You put him up to this."

Pablo is silent for several seconds. "Yes," he admits. "He has the resources to free you from that company. I couldn't sit back and do nothing, knowing you're little more than a pawn to them. You're my *best friend.*"

"What if things don't work out between you? He'll still own my contract, and I'll be stuck with him." I groan aloud and rake a hand through my hair. "I don't even know if I can trust him."

"Then don't. But you should trust me."

"They won't share the details until the transaction is finished," I reply sullenly. "Do you understand how this makes me feel, Pab? I'm being *sold* to your fucking *boyfriend* to do with as he pleases."

"It's not like that," Pablo says defensively. "We're under a new NDA, and I can't tell you what Daar has proposed, but trust me when I say it's a better arrangement than what you have now."

A bitter laugh escapes my lips. "What other choices do I have?"

"Kye…"

"Don't, Pab. I can't stomach an apology right now."

He sighs. "Fine. Just trust me, okay? This will work out."

"I hope you're right, because I don't have a say in any of it." I slam my fist into the stone path and feel it crumble on impact.

I feel better, even if my hand screams in momentary protest. Sometimes venting rage is necessary.

"Give this a chance. *Please.*"

"I'll call you later. I can't do this right now."

I disconnect before he can respond.

I need time for my temper to cool, and depending on what I learn about Daaros' proposal, it may never drop below the boiling point. I hope Pablo is right, but I can't bring myself to trust him any longer. This breach has shattered something fundamental between us, something I'm not sure can be repaired.

I ask myself a hard question. Is Pablo acting to help me, or to please his new beau?

From my perspective, either is possible.

CHAPTER TWELVE

NEW TERMS, EXISTING OBLIGATIONS

MEGATROPOLIS, TRAPPIST-1 SYSTEM

I face Luna across her desk on the top floor of our headquarters, while Mat paces the length of the room behind me. I know why I've been summoned. I've been waiting for this moment since I first learned the Executive Committee was voting on Daaros' damned offer, but I never imagined it would take this long to receive formal news.

I'm learning that megacorps like Zylar Inc. move slower than congealed astrofuel on an ice field.

"The terms of your contract with Zylar Inc. have been amended," Luna says evenly as she taps on a tablet. "You will remain with us for another four months while you complete your training modules, but no longer. Your contract has been transferred to one, Daaros Syl'Vaasis. You will retain your status as a cybernetically-enhanced elite soldier, but as of now, you are no longer in the employ of Zylar Inc. Your status and security clearances with ZIEG are void. In effect, you are on loan to us until your training is finished."

I manage a nod. "Can I read the final contract?"

Luna spins the tablet and pushes it across her desk. "Of course."

"I need to modify your automatic updating," Mat says as I begin to read. "With your clearances gone, you can't have access to our preliminary files or the R&D network."

I shrug, more interested in the document than Mat's words. "Fine."

"You'll keep all of the files for our products that are commercially available, of course," Mat continues.

I shoot him a glare. "Can this wait five minutes? I'm trying to read."

He nods, and I return to the document on the tablet.

Daaros paid a sum with more zeroes than I care to count for my contract. I skim past the financial data to the portion of the agreement pertaining to me.

I'm to be employed as his personal bodyguard, and I'm expected to travel where he does at all times, unless specified otherwise. He promises to pay me a higher rate than ZIEG has done so far and matches their other benefits packages. He agrees to maintain my cybernetics and upgrade them as required.

There is no mention of lifetime service, only a statement that the contract will remain in place as long as it is mutually beneficial to both parties. I reread that section to be sure I didn't miss anything, then check for the fine print. There is no fine print, no footnotes claiming ownership of my very soul.

The contract is signed by twelve Zylar Inc. executives, Commander Patil of ZIEG, and Daaros Syl'Vaasis.

I owe Pablo another call. And an apology. I should have trusted him to do the right thing.

I look up to find Luna staring at a point in space, her expression distant. "Captain?"

She blinks once, then focuses on me. "I hope the terms are satisfactory. Vee had high hopes for your future with our unit. It's a shame to see you leave so soon. You haven't seen any real action yet."

"It's not like I was given any voice in this matter."

She nods, then motions to Mat. "Make your updates. He's scheduled to meet with Vee in an hour."

Mat nods and approaches me cautiously. He withdraws a device from his pocket and connects one end to his tablet. The other he holds up for me to inspect.

"I need to plug this into your, ah, neck."

"Am I going to black out again?" I growl, recalling the last time this man plugged something into my body.

"No, but you'll sense the deletion of certain files in your databanks. Enough time has passed that you should be attuned to that by now."

I scowl at him while Luna studies us silently from behind her desk. Mat shifts uncomfortably, but doesn't move forward with his task.

"Stop stalling," Luna says with a laugh. "He's not going to bite you."

Mat nods and reaches forward to plug his device into the port at the base of my neck. I feel it slide into place and sense the connection to his tablet almost immediately. The data streams between my implants and his tablet are too swift for me to decipher their contents, but I *can* sense each classified file as it's erased from my mechanized memory. It's surreal.

After several minutes, he nods. "That's everything, and your access to the R&D network has been revoked. I'll unplug you now."

I stand once I'm free of Mat's device and nod to Luna. "For what it's worth, thank you for everything."

"This isn't goodbye yet," she says and rises to offer her hand. "You're with us for another four months, Kye. We'll make the most of it before you run off to play babysitter to a rich Botanaari."

We shake hands, and I walk to the door wearing a smile. Things are looking up.

I call Pablo after I board the automated shuttle to Zylar Inc. HQ. He picks up on the first ring, even though it's a Tuesday and he should be in class.

"Kye? Is that you?"

"Yeah, Pab. It's me."

"Look, I'm sorry about what happened. I know you didn't want to hear it when we talked last, but I really felt bad. I didn't want to leave things hanging between us. I was afraid I would make it worse. I'm sorry, Kye. I'm so damned sorry."

"It's okay," I reply with a grin. "They finally let me read the contract. I should have trusted you."

He breathes a sigh of relief. "Finally! Now we can discuss the details. Daar was going to make arrangements for your personal items to be transferred to his place on Ring Eight. He has a suite ready for you." He pauses, then adds, "Zylar Inc. reassigned your lease as soon as the contract was signed this morning, so your apartment on Ring Five belongs to someone else now."

"Hmm." The contract hadn't mentioned lodging, but at least Daaros is keeping up his end of the agreement so far. I won't be a homeless cyborg while off-duty.

"You don't sound very happy."

A nervous laugh escapes me. "Honestly, I don't know what to think. Are you okay with me living in your boyfriend's apartment, Pab?"

Pablo snorts. "You're the head of his security team, and you have no interest in romance besides. I have nothing to worry about." He pauses, then blurts, "I'll be moving in with him at the end of this term."

"So it's serious then."

"Yes. He's everything I've dreamed of, Kye. I… I spent the night with him."

Curiosity takes root, and I utter a question I should have left unasked. I regret it immediately. "How exactly does it work?"

Pablo bursts out laughing. "I didn't think you'd want specifics."

My face burns crimson as he describes their first sexual encounter. Apparently, Botanaari possess an opening to what they refer to as a "seed chamber" where a "pollinator" can be inserted. Pablo doesn't have a pollinator, but he has the human male equivalent, which serves a similar function in our species. A Botanaari's pollinator is retractable, a fact I can't wrap my head around.

Heat pours from my face as he continues, and I finally manage to speak the words to make him stop. I wasn't prepared for this level of detail regarding my best friend and his paramour.

"Pab, no more. I get it."

He laughs again. "You *asked*."

"I wish I hadn't."

"Anyway, I need to head to my next class. I'll see you tonight."

He's still laughing when he disconnects, and I'm still blushing furiously. I'm not sure I'll be able to look him or Daaros in the eye after that conversation.

I'm no less flustered when the shuttle stops outside Zylar Inc. headquarters, and Vee lifts an eyebrow quizzically as I join them in the lobby.

"Is it done?" Vee asks.

I nod, grateful for a topic other than Pablo's love life.

"I thought so. Luna sent an official memo to us regarding your change in status. They took your clearance away."

"Yeah. I'm technically a visitor now, I guess."

"But you're freer, aren't you?"

I chew my lower lip guiltily, then nod again. "The new terms aren't as overbearing."

"Good. I'm happy for you."

I adjust to my new role better than I did with ZIEG. The suite Daaros has given me in his expansive apartment is spacious enough for a whole family, and he ensures I have every amenity. It's comfortable, and I see much more of Pablo, though he's often distracted by Daaros' presence.

I don't mind being ignored on occasion; the pair are clearly enamored with one another, and I've never seen Pablo look so content. Daaros is proving good for him, and my previous uncertainty regarding the Botanaari's motives rapidly dissolves. I think he genuinely *cares*— and that's sufficient to ease my concerns.

Araan visits often too. He's cordial, but distant, and always seems to be wearing a fedora to match his array of tailored suits. I learn he runs errands for Daaros, and often for Pablo as well. What his function is beyond that remains a mystery.

I meet with Vee each morning, and after another six weeks, they deem me finished with weapons training. I'm placed on a rotation at several security desks throughout Zylar Inc.'s headquarters, often paired with Vee. We spend an hour each afternoon after our shift is over in the flight simulation lab, where I learn to pilot an array of commercially-available spacecraft, shuttles, and civilian vehicles. With my reduced access to what Vee deems the "fun stuff," my training progresses rapidly.

I have twenty-eight days left of my four-month stint with ZIEG when a blanket command is issued by Commander Patil. All ZIEG operatives and temporary active soldiers like myself are summoned to ZIEG headquarters for a meeting. The date is a week from today at eight a.m.

"What's this about?" I ask Vee as I watch business people stroll through Zylar Inc.'s main lobby from our vantage point behind the security kiosk.

Vee shakes their head. "I don't know, but usually when orders of this nature are issued, it means something or someone important requires our collective services."

Our security details are uneventful. I'm bored, so I'm eager to learn what the summons has in store. It would be nice to have a bit of excitement before I leave ZIEG for good and move onto the relatively tame life of protecting Daaros from the paparazzi hordes.

I know what you're thinking: I should be careful what I wish for.

Speculation swirls amongst the other ZIEG soldiers for the next week, but no one, not even Luna, has been informed of why we've been summoned. When the date finally arrives, I'm at ZIEG headquarters twenty minutes early, but I'm forced to loiter at the entrance until someone from my unit arrives to escort me inside. Without my previous clearance, I'm not allowed through the doors alone.

Luna appears from within after five minutes, and I follow her inside and up two flights of stairs to a conference room packed with other cyborg soldiers. I know only a handful of them; some by reputation only, others in passing, but there is only one I consider a friend. Vee.

We move through the crowd to the vacant seats next to Vee and spend the next ten minutes listening to the conversations of others and chatting amongst ourselves. The atmosphere is thick with anticipation, and I'm certain something big will be revealed.

Voices fall silent as a broad man with a dark complexion stalks to the front of the room. He wears a full set of nanosteel body armor and is armed with a bristling array of weapons. I recognize his squarish features and steely gaze from my training modules. This is Commander Patil.

He crosses his arms and surveys the room for several seconds, his expression unreadable. After a time, he nods to himself, glances at someone near the back of the room, then clears his throat.

"We've been called upon to ensure corporate security is well in hand at headquarters from now through tomorrow night. A number of VIPs will be arriving throughout the day to engage in trade negotiations and investment discussions with Zylar Inc. Human and Botanaari business leaders will be present, as well as our CEO, Reginald Zylar, and his heiress, Marim."

A few whispers echo across the room, and Commander Patil scowls as he waits for them to dissipate. "Our purpose is singular. We are to provide the utmost protection to our esteemed guests and this company's leadership during the negotiations. Those of you with higher levels of clearance will be stationed at strategic positions throughout the building. You are to report any and all suspicious activity and conversations immediately. Assignments have been sent to each unit's captain. Regroup and move out within the hour. Dismissed."

Luna says nothing until Jen appears from somewhere near the back of the room. I haven't spoken to Jen in weeks, and she fixes me with a cold stare before forcing a smile for Luna's benefit. She likes me even less now that I'm no longer ZIEG. I ignore her hostility and focus on Luna's orders.

"We've been assigned to the executive suites on the top floor," Luna says with a note of surprise. "Even Kye."

I frown in confusion. "It has to be a mistake. My clearance—"

"I know. I'll verify with the commander." Her expression blanks for several seconds, then she shakes her head. "He says it's no mistake. *My* clearance is higher than most of the others in this room, which flagged me for the executives. Since you're part of my unit, you've been assigned there with the rest of us. It's contradictory to what he said to the group, but orders are orders."

Jen eyes me with unconcealed suspicion. "He's a liability."

"He isn't," Vee replies firmly. "He can handle this assignment."

"Doubtful," Jen scoffs. "He isn't even one of us now. Couldn't cut it with ZIEG, so he found a rich playboy to rescue him."

"Fucking hell—" I growl and clench my fists, only to be cut off by Luna's furious glare.

"*Enough.* Both of you." She jabs a finger at me. "You're untested, but I trust Vee's judgment when it comes to your training. Keep your damned temper in check." She whirls to face a smirking Jen. "And you need to stop provoking him. You don't know what occurred with the blasted Botanaari. Stop spreading baseless lies, or I will have you court-martialed myself."

Jen's smirk dissolves. She nods tersely, but her eyes stare daggers at me. What the hell have I ever done to earn her unmitigated ire?

"We're assigned to the CEO's corridor," Luna continues. "We are to set up security checkpoints at each end of the hall. Both checkpoints will be staffed by two of us at all times, along with the building's security AI. We've been given schematics of the checkpoints, along with blueprints of the floor, the corridor, and all three suites. Given the contentious mood between you this morning, Kye will be working with Vee. Jen, you're with me—and don't make me regret it."

"I won't," Jen replies coldly. "It's him you should be worried about."

"What did I say two minutes ago?" Luna snaps. *"Stop fucking provoking him."*

When Jen says nothing more, Luna nods. "Our first stop will be the ZIEG arsenal. We're to gear up for combat." She looks to Vee. "Kye will need to be fitted for armor. Make sure he carries the appropriate weapons."

By appropriate, she means only those weapons that are commercially available and not above my clearance to touch, despite my training. I'm not upset; I understand she has to follow her orders to the letter, and the VIPs we're protecting are some of the most powerful figures in the galaxy. One defect in our plans could spell disaster for ZIEG.

I nod my acknowledgment as Vee says, "Will do, Captain."

Jen rolls her eyes but mercifully says nothing.

Luna points at the exit. "We'll regroup at the arsenal. Move out."

I trail behind Vee as we move toward the elevator, then clench my jaw as Jen continues to glare in my direction once we're inside. I remind myself I have eighteen more days with Luna's unit, and afterwards I'll never see Jen again. I can endure another eighteen days.

The elevator conveys us to the twentieth floor. I follow Vee and the others through a security checkpoint and into a room reminiscent of the weapons lab at the company's HQ. Vee draws me across the room and through a door, where several bots lay in wait behind an AI kiosk. Vee activates the kiosk, and a moment later, an androgynous face appears on the screen.

"Welcome to the armor depot. I am Zydress. How may I assist you today?"

Vee points at me. "Kye needs fitted for combat armor."

The AI's image nods. "Scanning. Clearance for commercial grade equipment approved." Its digital eyes find mine. "Please move to the yellow circle at the center of the room and remove your clothing."

I shoot a questioning look at Vee.

They shrug, the smirk I've grown accustomed to twisting their lips in amusement. "I'll wait outside while you're scanned."

With a nod, I walk to the yellow circle imprinted on the floor as Vee disappears into the armory and the door to this room slides shut. I remove my boots and belt, then scowl at the AI kiosk. The screen is facing away from me, but I know its inhabitant can see me.

"Is this really necessary?"

"Yes," Zydress replies. "In order to perform an accurate scan of your physical exterior, all clothing and jewelry must be removed."

I groan and pull off my shirt. "Fine."

Moments later, I'm naked, and the AI begins its scans. "Ah," it says after a few seconds. "You have the new series of enhancements. The SLTR-BT series was specifically designed for combat, but I'm certain you already knew that."

I did; the information was stored in my databanks, and I'd skimmed through it during my initial weapons training with Vee. The long acronym stands for Strength, Leverage, Tensor, and Rapid-motion Biomechanical Technology. The enhancements explain the muscle mass I came away from Mat's tinkering with, among some of the other features I now possess.

"Do my enhancements affect the armor you're supposed to be making?"

"Oh, yes," the AI replies. "SLTR-BT enhancements allow you to link to your armor's offensive mechanisms directly. Even unarmed, you will be a deadly weapon against any opponent." The AI pauses, then says, "Scans complete. You may dress."

As I pull on my clothing, I refresh myself on how my specific enhancements are supposed to link with the armor. It looks straightforward enough. I move toward the exit once I'm decent, and pull open the door. Vee is outside, but they now wear a set of navy body armor with the ZIEG logo in electric blue across the torso.

"Please don't leave yet," Zydress says from behind us. "Your armor will be ready in approximately four minutes and fifty-two seconds."

"We'll wait," Vee assures the AI.

More ZIEG soldiers have filed into the arsenal and group according to unit, I assume. They browse the weapon racks, many of which are now off-limits to me, though I haven't forgotten the training I received prior to my change in status. I still know how to use some of them; the deletion of their schematics from my databanks doesn't affect my biological memory.

But Luna is playing this task by the books, so I'll follow orders. In eighteen days, none of the imposed hierarchy within ZIEG will matter anyway.

"Your new armor is complete. Please enter the yellow circle for fitting."

Turning from the door, I find the bots encircling Zydress each holds a new piece of armor. I should have paid attention to the manufacturing process, because I know Pablo will ask me for details when I return to Daaros' apartment.

I make a mental note to call my new boss after we're finished at the arsenal. Daaros will need to know I've been commandeered by ZIEG for the evening and all of tomorrow.

I move back into the yellow ring, and the AI demands that I disrobe again. I glower at it; what was the point of telling me to dress for less than five minutes? I could have saved myself the trouble and not bothered to open the door at all. Vee remains outside, and the door slides closed once more.

I strip a second time, and the bots' long arms move toward me. I step backward inadvertently, startled by their advance.

"Please remain within the yellow circle," Zydress states placidly, though I detect a hint of irritation in its tone.

I recenter myself in the damned circle and wait while the AI's bot minions fit the armor over my body. It's lighter than I expected and moves seamlessly with my joints when I'm asked to test it for fit. It's not navy blue like the ZIEG soldiers wear, nor is it branded with their logo. It's sleek and black, with vibrant orange highlights at the joints and seams. The boots are sturdy with a thick sole and good tread, and the gauntlets fit my hands like a second skin.

"Are you satisfied with the fitting, Mr. Verex?" Zydress inquires.

"Yeah. It's great."

"Good. Now link your enhancements to the armor. We must assess the connection before you depart."

This is when shit gets *weird*.

I link at the AI's request, and am immediately bombarded with sensory input from every square-inch of my new armor. A list of attachment points begins to scroll behind my eyes with detailed specs on every joint, nerve ending, pore, and orifice I possess. The list continues, and I *feel* the armor physically attach to my skin at every location.

I freeze, panicked by the overstimulation of my struggling brain.

As abruptly as the onslaught begins, it mercifully stops. If my heart wasn't mechanical, it would have been close to bursting. At some point during the process, I fell to my knees.

"Fuck," I breathe as I rise to my feet.

"Your armor's connection to your implants has been determined," Zydress says in a serene tone. "Links are stable. Do you have any questions before you depart?"

"Just one. Will it be like that every time I put this on?"

"No, Mr. Verex. The first time requires that you establish the connection. Once complete, there is no need to repeat the process."

"Good. That was…unexpected."

"You are free to go. Have a pleasant day."

I pick up my discarded clothing and boots and stride to the door. I can sense the air around me *through* the nanosteel plating. That's going to take some time to get used to.

Vee is still outside the door when I emerge. They appraise me with a nod. "How was it?"

"Fucking weird."

They tip their head back and laugh. "The first time is always unsettling. The orange highlights are a nice touch."

"That was the AI's choice, not mine."

"Not a fan of orange?" Vee teases as they begin to move across the crowded arsenal.

"Orange is fine. It just stands out more than seems necessary."

"That is to your benefit," Vee replies. "If people notice *you*, they'll be more likely to leave your new employer alone. And by proxy, Pablo."

I nod; I hadn't considered that. "You're right."

Vee smirks. "I usually am. Now, for weapons…"

Five minutes later, I'm armed with a plasma rifle across my back, two pistols at my hips, and several nanosteel daggers placed strategically about my person. We regroup with Luna and Jen, who sport some of the more sophisticated weapons I'm no longer allowed to handle.

"Now that we're all ready, it's time to move out," Luna says. "We have a lot to do before the CEO and his daughter arrive."

CHAPTER THIRTEEN

ROOKIE MISTAKES

"Is this your personal frequency, Kye?" Daaros' smooth voice filters through my aural implants as I assist Vee with the setup of the security checkpoint which will be our responsibility to manage.

"Yeah. I don't exactly have access to a holoreceiver at the moment."

"Pablo mentioned you can place calls without one. Interesting." He pauses, then says, "Why are you calling me, rather than him?"

"I work for you now," I reply. "Something's come up, and I've been assigned to assist ZIEG tonight and all day tomorrow."

"Ah, the Zylar Inc. annual open house for investors and prospective trading partners," Daaros replies. "Yes, I should have known they'd include you amongst the security teams."

I'm surprised he knows of the event, but when I stop to consider *who* he is, it makes sense. "Will you be attending?"

Vee shoots me a questioning glance. I shrug and silently mouth his name. They nod in understanding and go back to adjusting the scanners we'll attach to the AI kiosk.

Daaros laughs. "No. VaasTek's dealings with Zylar Inc. are secure. There is no reason for me to make an appearance, and the meetings are always dull. It's better to spend my time on worthwhile pursuits than on shallow pretenses."

"You mean Pablo."

I grimace as the words leave my mouth. Sometimes I can't avoid making an ass of myself.

"He is certainly a pursuit worthy of my time." He pauses, then says, "Other than your change in schedule, was there anything you needed from me? I have another meeting in three minutes."

"No, that was it."

"Good. Then I will see you tomorrow evening. May the suns grant that you don't die of boredom in the meantime."

I chuckle as I disconnect. "What's with the Botanaari obsession over the suns?" I ask Vee as I finish programming the security feed for our checkpoint.

"Botanaar is in a binary star system. There's a now-defunct religion that worshipped the two suns as gods, much as humans did with Helios, Surya, or Ra." Vee shrugs and steps back to assess their work. "The Botanaari don't believe in their mythology any longer, but they are still heavily dependent on the galaxy's many suns."

"Hmm." I pause as the holoscreen before me blinks to life and an image of the corridor ahead fills the screen. "The video feed is working. What's next?"

"I just connected the AI to our system. That was the last item. Now we sit back and wait for visitors to arrive." Vee collapses into the chair next to mine with a laugh. "Don't worry, I doubt we'll see anyone until Zylar himself shows up."

"Daaros said he hopes I don't die of boredom."

"I'll hope for that as well. The annual meetings are usually uneventful. We're called here to put on a display and ensure the rich and powerful assholes of the galaxy play nice with one another." Vee shrugs. "They usually do."

"And when they don't?" I ask.

Vee grins. "Things can get interesting."

No one arrives at our kiosk for several hours, and nobody appears on the camera feeds. We're in periodic contact with Luna and Jen, who fare the same. I'm tempted to access the 'net and my intergalactic library account to interrupt the boredom, but I fear I'll be skewered if I'm caught reading on the job. Vee and I chat to pass the time, our eyes fixed on the unchanging video feed.

I might die of boredom, after all.

My internal clock reads ten forty-one p.m. when movement on the screen draws my attention. The elevator doors at the end of the corridor slide open, and a contingent of five emerge. Three wear ZIEG body armor akin to Vee's. Their weapons are stowed and they appear relaxed. A good sign.

The other two are clearly civilians. A tall, imposing man with gray streaking his brown hair frowns imperiously at the ZIEG soldiers ahead of him. He wears a charcoal suit worthy of Daaros' expensive collection.

A younger woman is with him. I estimate she's in her mid-thirties, and she bears the same brown hair and striking features as the man. She wears a form-fitting jumpsuit in red patent faux-leather so shiny it reflects the overhead lights.

"Is that them?" I whisper.

Vee nods. "Reginald and Marim Zylar. The CEO and heiress to this corporation."

"And him?" I ask, pointing at the ZIEG soldier at the front of the group. He's wiry and lithe, and sports a goatee dyed the same shade of garish yellow as his mohawk.

Vee lifts their eyebrows, exasperated, but quickly relents. "I keep forgetting you no longer have access to classified personnel files. That's Warrick Waxman. Captain Wax, to most."

I snort a laugh. "Seriously?"

"Look at him. The ridiculous nickname is fitting, isn't it?"

The group begins to move down the corridor toward the bend, and I force my expression into neutral. They'll be around the corner in moments, and I won't be caught smirking at a ZIEG captain with questionable tastes in hair color.

We stand as the CEO and his entourage appear. The trio of cyborgs fan out behind them as one of the most powerful men in the galaxy steps up to our AI kiosk for a security scan. Up close, I note that Reginald Zylar's eyes are a deep blue, but his daughter's are a soft brown. He doesn't make eye contact. He merely strides past once the AI confirms his identity, then walks directly to the door leading to the centermost suite.

Marim's expression tightens as she watches him leave, an undertone of frustration in her posture. She steps forward for her own scan and forces a tired smile.

"I must apologize for my father's lackluster greeting," she says. "He's had a trying day."

Vee murmurs a bland reassurance on our behalf, while I nod mutely.

When the AI clears her, she says, "I'll be in the first room. I'm certain everything is in hand?"

Vee nods, and Marim's eyes lock with mine. "You're the one on loan from Mr. Syl'Vaasis, aren't you?"

I swallow awkwardly. "Yeah."

"I thought so. Your face was all over GNN for a few days when you appeared at Sileca's." She smiles enigmatically. "You're taller than I expected. And better looking in person. Find me later if the mood suits you. We'll have some fun."

I feel heat rush into my face, but she whirls away and strides toward her room without another glance. How the hell do you tell one of the most influential women in the galaxy that you're not interested in her overt suggestion? *Fuck.*

"Looks like our temp has caught the eye of the next CEO."

I startle and spin around to find the ZIEG soldiers have approached the barricade. Captain Wax grins wolfishly behind his glaring yellow goatee.

"I..." The words die in my throat. I don't know what to say, and why is he making this his business anyway?

"Kye is a lot like me," Vee cuts in. "There won't be any sordid gossip about a liaison come morning."

"Too bad. I hear she's wild beneath the sheets." Waxman shrugs, then signals to his unit. "We're on rooftop duty tonight. We'll be back in the morning for our executive charges."

I slump into my chair as soon as they're gone and release a groan.

"Hey, don't mind Waxman. It's rare that he *isn't* being an ass." Vee crosses their legs and leans back in their seat. "And Marim does this every year, you know. She has a penchant for male cyborgs."

"Why didn't she hit on Wax-face then?"

Vee laughs. "Wax-face. That's funny. She probably realized he's an ass the moment she laid eyes on him. And *he* wasn't on GNN with Daaros Syl'Vaasis."

Damn Daaros. He's done nothing but complicate my life since the moment Pablo met him. It's not his fault the rumormongers of the galaxy seek him out, but I have no one else to blame for my current predicament.

A half hour passes, and I'm forced to manually adjust my body's cortisol and melatonin levels to keep awake. Vee stifles a yawn and shakes their head.

"We won't get a break until morning, will we?" I ask.

"No. You'll need to adjust your biochemistry a few times."

I nod, then stand up to stretch. Sitting isn't helping me stay alert.

Moments later, the overhead lights go dark. The ever-present hum of electronics imbedded in the walls falls silent.

"Vee?" I ask.

"Switch to night vision. Arm yourself."

I follow their instructions. If anyone is lurking in the dark, we'll see them, but they'll also see our eyes. I crouch behind the security desk and peer over the rim. The monitor is dark, and the AI kiosk is unlit.

"What happened?" I whisper.

Vee shakes their head and clicks the safety off their plasma-core handcannon. It's a weapon I never got to test in the lab, the size of a large pistol, but packing heat-seeking plasma-filled projectile rounds meant to shatter on contact. The plasma will punch through any target, while its casing produces wicked shrapnel. Their choice of weapon alone tells me the blackout is not routine.

Shouts erupt behind us from the direction of Luna's checkpoint. I glance at Vee in question.

"We stay here," Vee says firmly. "We follow protocol."

"Even if they're—"

"Luna is a ZIEG captain for a reason," Vee cuts me off. "She can handle any attackers, and Jen is just as capable."

I nod, both relieved and concerned. I don't like sitting on the sidelines, but I'm not sure I'm prepared to test the limits of my training yet. Simulations are one matter, but actual combat with potentially armed assailants is another entirely.

Vee hisses. "Damn it, our internal comms are down too."

I attempt to ping Luna, only to find my access to the 'net and all external databases are completely offline.

"How is this possible? We have our own frequency, separate from the building and—"

Brilliant blue light blazes across the corridor in streaks from the direction of Luna's checkpoint. I know the plasma signature; it's from ZIEG weaponry.

I draw a breath and click the safety off my rifle. My heart rate is steady and my breathing is easy thanks to my mechanized organs, but nerves still manage to rattle my core.

More shouts echo along the corridor. I glance at Vee as an explosion rocks our floor. I turn toward the noise in time to see the door of the center suite—Reginald Zylar's—fly across the corridor to splinter against the opposite wall. A gout of fire issues from within the room, but my enhancements tell me it's a weapon's emission and not a result of the explosion.

"Stay here and hold this position," Vee growls. They rise and move swiftly toward the open doorway.

I swallow and stare down the hall in time to see Jen's slender figure soar through space and crash into the wall with a sickening thud. ZIEG soldiers can take a lot of damage, but she doesn't rise to fight again. Her body slumps against the wall, her neck twisted at an unnatural angle. It's an injury even Mat can't repair.

I lift my rifle in preparation for an assailant to appear, focused on what I learn too late is the wrong damned direction.

More blue plasma bolts lance through the air. They sizzle as they strike the hallway's painted façade. The walls melt around the impact sites.

There's weapons fire in the CEO's suite, and I hope Vee has the upper hand. They've always seemed capable and confident. And damn it, I like them. They've become a good friend.

Marim exits her room and gapes at the destruction in the corridor for several seconds. She turns toward me, then freezes. In the greenish glow of my night vision, her eyes widen and her lips part. She stares at something behind me.

I turn slowly to peer over my shoulder, only to find the barrel of a plasma rifle inches from my face. "Shit!"

A dark chuckle issues from my assailant. He's a muscular bald man with a network of twisted scars marring the right half of his face. "Don't move a muscle, kid, or your face will look worse than mine."

There's a flurry of footsteps, then a door slams. I hope Marim had the sense to retreat into her suite and utilize the safe room hidden in its expansive closet. I don't turn to find out; I'm afraid to look away from this asshole.

"Drop the gun," scar-face orders.

I hesitate. I can move faster than him, and maybe I'll catch him off guard, if I—

A rustle issues from beside the bald man, and too late, I realize he isn't alone. Six others suddenly materialize out of the shadows. They weren't there seconds ago.

Shit, they *were*, but my sensors had failed to pick them up. I recognize the traces of stealth-inducing energy fields as they dissipate in the air. All of them point weapons in my direction. I'm outnumbered and alone, our internal comms are still down, and I can hear nothing from the CEO's suite behind me.

"I said, drop the fucking gun." The plasma rifle inches closer to my skin.

I swallow and comply. Maybe if I cooperate, they won't kill me. I lift my hands in a display of surrender and slowly stand up from my crouch.

"Kye!"

Vee's voice roars through the corridor as my rifle is kicked away from my reach. I spin around, hopeful Vee can extract me from this situation. They stand frozen in the center of the corridor, unarmed, dark blood running in thick ribbons down their face from a laceration on their forehead.

Vee's hurt, their weapons are gone, and I'm surrounded by scar-face and his minions. Vee shakes their head, a look of frustration twisting their features, then bolts down the hall toward Jen's broken corpse.

Vee recognizes an impossible scenario when they see one, and I've just been left on my own. Again.

Fuck.

"Do it," I hear the bald man order.

I begin to turn toward him when something hard and cold is pressed into the port at the base of my neck, and I'm falling face-first toward the carpeted floor.

My senses are shutting down, just as they did that day in Mat's lab. Whoever our attackers are, they've used the same device, and I'm rendered helpless. Immobile. The world goes dark in a flash as my optics turn off, and my aural enhancements are rendered mute.

I hope Vee survives.

I sure as hell won't, all because I've made the worst of rookie mistakes. I should have watched my damned back.

CHAPTER FOURTEEN

OVERRIDE CODES

LOCATION UNKNOWN

The sensation of the device being extracted from my neck jerks me awake. My abrupt forward movement is halted instantly, and I realize I'm shackled to a chair. My arms and legs arc strapped securely, and another band wraps around my torso. With my enhancements back online, I recognize the restraints are made of polymer-coated nanosteel as indestructible as the holoscreen in the weapons lab. I'm not going anywhere.

I'm still wearing my armor, but all of my remaining weapons have been taken.

I look up to scan my surroundings. I'm in a cargo bay or warehouse of some sort. Dozens of crates are stacked against the walls, and several others are scattered across the floor. The room has no windows, and a single light shines overhead from directly above my chair. The light is painfully bright, and I realize belatedly that I'm still in night vision mode. I switch to normal, but it's only a marginal improvement.

There's movement behind me. I crane my neck to find scar-face's leering and twisted countenance. He lumbers around my chair and comes to stand in front of me, fists on his wide hips. He's wearing scuffed and battered body armor that might have looked new a decade ago. A handcannon identical to the one Vee had before running into Zylar's suite hangs from his belt.

In the light, his scars are even more pronounced. His skin puckers and twists, pulling the right corner of his mouth up into a perpetual sneer. The overhead light reflects off his bald head as his dark eyes study me for several seconds.

I clench my jaw and glare at him defiantly. I have a thousand questions, but it would be a mistake to voice even one until I understand what's going on. I've made enough mistakes for one night already.

"So, you're the latest and greatest of Zylar Inc.'s elite cyborg soldiers."

I follow him with my eyes as he begins to pace, arms crossed before him. What does he expect me to say? I can't deny what I am, and I'm pretty sure he's already studied my system's specs. I don't know how long I was unconscious, and with that *thing* in my neck, I had no way of tracking the passage of time. He could have done any number of "updates" to my system while I was at his fucking mercy.

"My employer was keen to get his hands on you," scar-face continues. "He provided us with this."

The same device Mat had plugged into my neck in the lab appears in his hand. He holds it up for my inspection. I still don't know what it is, only that it makes me black out.

"What is it?" I blurt.

He pauses midstride and swivels to face me. "A bit of tech Zylar has tried to keep classified. Obviously, they've failed." His face twists into a leer. "If my boss wants you to know the details, he'll share them when he arrives. Until then, sit tight."

He cackles at his own joke as I bristle beneath my restraints. There has to be some way to get out of this mess, but I'll be damned if I can figure it out right now.

I scan his face and query my databanks for information now that my systems seem to be functioning again. His file comes up, and I clench my jaw tighter as I scroll through his information to keep myself from gaping.

His name is Van Duval, and he has a rap sheet at least a parsec long. Theft, assault, kidnapping, murder, attempted murder, racketeering, possession of illegal firearms, breach of intergalactic treaties… The list of his alleged crimes is daunting. His file claims he's the leader of the mercenary group known as Omega Prime, and *their* list of galactic infractions tallies even higher.

I'm beginning to understand why he was in Zylar Inc.'s headquarters, but why has he abducted me? How do I fit into this scheme?

"Why am I here?"

He smirks and holds the device up again. "We have this, and it only works on *you*. That you happened to be assigned to security detail when we struck was a bonus. You were our secondary objective."

I clench my fists and strain against my bonds. I can't escape, but I'll make damned sure he knows how pissed off I am. "You didn't answer my fucking question."

"And you're in no fucking position to receive answers," he snarls. "My employer wanted you brought here unharmed, but he didn't say anything about keeping you that way. Don't push your luck, kid." He turns away and begins to walk toward the room's only exit. "I'll return when the boss arrives, and don't try calling for help. I have signal jammers installed throughout every inch of this station. Don't go anywhere."

"Fuck you."

He chuckles and disappears, leaving me alone beneath the spotlight with only my muddled thoughts for company.

I replay the scene in the corridor in my mind. Vee went into the CEO's suite after the explosion, but someone had attacked Luna's checkpoint first. The attack had been a distraction to draw our attention away from Reginald's room. No one had slipped past us throughout the day, but what if someone had been inside his suite before we arrived?

Our orders had included an inspection of the executive suites before we set up the checkpoints. Jen and Vee had conducted the inspections and found nothing unusual. But the mercs had stealth technology. Was it possible someone had managed to avoid our searches, then lain in wait for hours until the CEO finally arrived? Or had they been less subtle? Maybe the explosion hadn't come from within the room after all, but from outside, as Duval's crew blasted through the walls.

The only certainty I have is that the attack targeted Reginald Zylar, the galaxy's most powerful corporate executive and the man responsible for the tech running our AI government. Hell, he *is* the government, when I stop to think about it. Is he a prisoner as I am, or is he dead?

Either scenario would throw the galaxy into chaos.

No one enters the room again for more than two hours. I check my internal clock to find only twelve hours have passed since the attack on Zylar Inc.'s HQ. Wherever I am, it can't be far from Megatropolis, unless the mercs who abducted me have access to interstellar tech far superior to what I've experienced in my limited travels so far. And based on their seamless infiltration of Zylar Inc., it's a distinct possibility.

I test my bonds periodically, but they're designed to restrain people like me. I scan the materials several times, checking for weak points, but find nothing. Even with my enhanced strength and the boost I'm granted by my new armor, I can't break free.

The fruitless exertion only pisses me off further, but I'm forced to stop as time crawls past the two-hour mark. My internal monitors warn that I'll require food soon, or I'll risk the breakdown of some of my muscle mass. I realize I haven't eaten since before my summons to the ZIEG command center. Struggling further will only expedite the onset of my body's encoded response to running on empty.

I slump in the chair and bide my time, hoping Van Duval isn't planning to let me waste away under his watch. He wasn't forthcoming with his plans.

I attempt to place a call despite Duval's claim. I'm met with another warning message: "Signal blocked. Jamming equipment detected in your area." The same text appears when I try to send a standard message.

Okay, he wasn't bluffing. Damn.

A little more than two hours later, the door opens, but it isn't the mercenary leader who enters. It's a middle-aged blond man with a pair of unusual glasses propped atop his head. They're iridescent and blue, and I recognize them instantly. I recognize *him*.

I was too disoriented and irritated on our first meeting to notice much beyond his hair and those damned glasses, which at that time had masked his pale blue eyes. He's clean-shaven, and his hair is trimmed in a stylishly short fashion. He wears a blue jumpsuit with white stripes running the length of its arms.

He crosses the room with a confidence borne of someone wielding significant power. Or delusions of grandeur. I'm not certain yet which it will be.

He stops a few steps away from my chair, crosses his arms, and studies me for a moment. "It's nice to see you again, Kye."

I clench my jaw and look away. I won't give him the satisfaction of a cordial greeting. How the fuck did a Zylar Inc. engineer wind up working with a ruthless mercenary crew?

He sighs. When I refuse to look at him, he says, "We never had the opportunity for proper introductions, and I'm sure you have questions. My name is Sorin Johnston."

I run his name through my databanks. After scrolling through candidates, I spy a picture matching the man standing in front of me. Sorin Johnston was one of Zylar Inc.'s chief engineers until five years ago, when he unexpectedly quit his position and summarily disappeared from galactic records. He has no listed criminal history.

"You won't find any of my recent history on the 'net, I'm afraid. I'm willing to share my story with you later, but right now, I owe you an explanation."

I turn my face slightly to scowl at him. "You owe me more than that."

He forces a tight smile. "Perhaps."

When he doesn't speak again, I say, "Why am I here?"

He produces that damned device. "When I learned Zylar Inc. was preparing to launch its latest line of elite cybernetic soldiers, the SLTR-BT series, it presented a unique opportunity for my current organization. You see, I'm the man responsible for designing all of your combat enhancements. The project was scrapped months before I resigned as chief engineer, and I never believed they'd resurrect it. I know what you're capable of far better than any of your ZIEG counterparts."

"So?"

"I require your assistance. In exchange, you are freed of the corporation's binding contract."

I glare at him. "I would have been freed in eighteen fucking days! Seventeen, now. My contract was purchased by a private party."

Surprise flits through his eyes. He didn't know about Daaros' involvement in my life.

"Hmm. This may present an unforeseen complication."

"If you don't believe me, it's in my personnel file." I glare a challenge at him.

He nods, slips the device into a pocket, and withdraws a tablet. He taps on the screen several times with a frown, then his expression brightens. "Maybe this will work out after all."

I continue to glare as he tucks the tablet into his pocket once more.

"Daaros is an acquaintance of mine. I will speak with him. In the meantime, do you require anything? Food? Water?"

"Yes. Both."

"I'll have one of my people bring you something."

And I'm left alone again, though not for long. A few minutes after Sorin leaves, a young woman enters carrying two glasses. One's filled with clear liquid—water, I assume—and the other contains a thick brownish slurry that looks wholly unappetizing. She wears a jumpsuit much like Sorin's that compliments her dark skin, and her black hair is pulled up in a long ponytail. She chews her lower lip as she approaches, then stops a few feet away. Her dark eyes are filled with unspoken questions.

"Sorin said you were hungry."

I nod, but opt to remain silent, as wary of her as she is of me.

She lifts up the glass containing the brown slurry. "It's a protein shake. Sorin said it contains everything you require." She sets both glasses on the ground near her feet, then produces a straw in a sterile package from one of her pockets. "Um, you'll probably need this."

While she fiddles with the packaging, I scan the contents of both glasses. Water, and as she said, a nutritional compound containing all the sustenance my biological parts require to continue functioning with an added bonus of chocolate flavoring. It isn't poisoned. I'll take that as a sign my captors don't want me dead.

She slips the unpackaged straw into the protein shake, lifts both glasses, and takes a tentative step forward.

I stifle the laughter that threatens to burst forth. "I can't hurt you. Believe me, I've tried to break free. I can't."

She nods. "Sorin said he engineered your restraints. I know you can't do anything…"

"But?"

"I've never met a cyborg before. You don't have lasers in your eyes, do you? You're not going to burn me to ash?"

I can't contain my laughter any longer. "You've been watching too many holovids. They don't equip us with lasers. I doubt my limited clearance even allows me to *touch* one."

She continues to hesitate, grappling with indecision.

"If I had lasers in my eyes, don't you think I would have blasted my way out of here by now?" I ask, hoping logic will overrule her fear. As unappealing as that shake looks, I need it. I'm running on fumes.

A small smile appears on her lips. "You're right. I'm being ridiculous."

She mercifully crosses the distance between us and holds the glass toward my face. I take a tentative sip, expecting it to be as tasteless as the protein cubes I was used to from Earth. It's not. It's mildly sweet, with an edge of bitterness to offset it, and a rich flavor I've never experienced before. I drink more, and my internal warning markers swiftly disappear.

When I pause for a breath, I ask, "Is this really what chocolate tastes like?"

She stares at me, uncomprehending. "You've never had chocolate before?"

I shake my head. "Can I have some water?"

She switches the glasses and lifts the water to my lips. It's cooler than I'd expected.

"How is it possible you've never had chocolate?" she asks as she switches glasses again.

"I lived on expired protein cubes most of my life. I've *heard* of chocolate but never tasted it." I take a few more sips and grin. "This is fucking fantastic."

She laughs nervously. "Where are you from that you've never had chocolate?"

I pause to peer at her directly. "Earth."

"Oh." She looks down as I finish the remainder of the shake. "I didn't think anyone lived there anymore. It's a garbage heap, according to the holovids."

With the glass empty, I tilt my head back and sigh. "It is, but there are still some people there. People like I was, who can't escape for one reason or another."

"But you did escape." She offers me the half-empty water glass, and I drain it.

"Yeah. But after the last few hours, I'm beginning to think leaving was a mistake. I would have died there. Maybe I'd be better off."

She visibly bristles. "Sorin brought you here to *help* him. He's not a killer."

I fix her with my most skeptical frown. "He hired Van Duval."

"He hired Van for another purpose. That he came across *you* was a pleasant surprise. Sorin has been meaning to remove you from Zylar Inc. for some time."

"Why?" I demand.

"He stole your override codes."

I narrow my eyes. "My what?" But I think I already know.

"It's what allowed Van to deactivate your system and transport you here without a fight. Didn't you know?"

I shake my head as the pieces fall into place, and dread grips my soul. I knew Mat had been hiding something from me when I asked him what happened that day in his lab. And I now understand why Sorin was there, why his personnel file was marked as "classified," and why he promised he'd see me again. Fucking hell, I'm nothing but a pawn in his game, whatever it might be.

She sighs. "I'm not surprised. Why would ZIEG tell you they manipulated your brain in that manner? I don't know everything the codes can do to you, but you've experienced the deactivation."

I swallow uneasily. "There's more?"

She nods. "Sorin can tell you. They were his design." She pauses, a look of sympathy on her face. "I'm sorry they did this to you. It's why he wanted to save you."

"That merc has the same device as your boss does."

"I know. It was part of their agreement." She shifts uncomfortably, then says, "Do you want another protein shake? I can get one if you're still hungry."

I shake my head. "I'm fine for now, but I would like to speak with Sorin."

"I'll tell him."

"Hey," I call as she turns to leave, "what's your name?"

"Quiara," she says, glancing over her shoulder with a tentative smile. "Quiara Jaide."

"I'm Kye."

"I know. I'll talk to Sorin."

Sorin returns fifteen minutes later. He looks weary, as though the past half-hour has drained him. I remain silent, watching as he paces and gathers his thoughts. His heart rate is higher than it was before and spikes further as he begins to talk.

"I spoke with Daaros. He's glad you survived the attack, but he's livid."

"He invested a lot of money in my contract."

"Yes. He did what I never thought to do, but it doesn't matter. What's done is done." Sorin runs a hand through his hair and expels a heavy sigh. "I think I've found a way for him to recoup some of his financial losses. He's filing a lawsuit against Zylar Inc. for damages in the case of your 'death,' since you were on loan to them during the attack."

"I'm not dead, and you just said—"

He holds up a hand for silence. "I know, but we're utilizing your disappearance to further our cause. And I reminded Daaros I have this." He withdraws the device—the override codes—from his pocket and holds it up for my benefit.

I clench my jaw. "So, what? You're forcing him to cooperate with your plans, or you'll deactivate me again?"

Sorin winces. "This can do more than shut down your systems, Kye. Part of my bargain with Omega Prime was that they'd receive the secondary copy of your codes. Duval needs someone of your…caliber for his next mission, which I am funding. If you don't follow orders, he won't hesitate to enforce an override."

"I'm not much good to anyone unconscious," I sneer.

"The codes can do more than shut you down," he says again.

I freeze as dread runs icy fingers along my spine. "What the fuck did you do to me?" I whisper, terrified of the answer but unable to proceed without knowing the truth.

"*I* didn't do anything," Sorin replies evenly. "When Zylar Inc. first funded the SLTR-BT enhancement program, I was enthusiastic. I was the lead engineer on all of your unique enhancements, and was responsible for designing a cybernetic system that was superior to the previous models. They shut down the program when the first three volunteers died during the transition."

"Then why do I have them?"

"They corrected the flaws in the process after I resigned my position five years ago."

"Why did you leave?" I'm certain my inquiries are headed toward the answer I desperately seek, the answer I dread to hear.

"The company was forced to eradicate several ZIEG soldiers after a minor uprising. My team was tasked to design an 'upgrade package' for the remaining members of ZIEG, each tailored to their unique biomechanical physiology. It allowed the cyborgs to be shut down in emergency situations, or they could be controlled remotely so long as the override codes were plugged in."

Sorin won't meet my furious gaze, but I know where he's headed. This shit was *not* included in the fine print of my contract.

"In essence, any member of ZIEG can have their conscious control torn away from them at any moment, with this plugged into their data port." He holds up the device again and shakes his head. "I didn't agree with their decision. To rip away someone's free will is abhorrent. I resigned, hoping the work wouldn't progress without me to oversee it. I was wrong."

"No one in ZIEG knows, do they?" I ask, swallowing a bitter wave of bile.

Mat *had* reduced me to the level of a common robot. No wonder the cowering bastard had been so terrified of me.

He shakes his head. "It's strictly confidential. Even your commander is in the dark. They sent assassins after me when I resigned, which is why I was forced to disappear. But I haven't been idle during that time."

"Quiara told me you stole my codes."

Sorin chuckles softly. "I did. I borrowed the identity of another Zylar Inc. engineer and bypassed their security system. I had a very narrow window of time between Mat's initial plug-in and the activation of your security clearances in which to work. I falsified the records of your override protocols. For all they know, your codes are stored in the company's secure vault along with the rest of ZIEG's."

"So, what now? Are you going to force me to help Duval under threat of my brain being hijacked?"

He grimaces. "In essence, yes. Which is why I was forced to endure not one, but two of Daaros' tirades."

I glare at him. "Good."

"As I said, he should recoup some of his financial losses, and I've promised to return you when we've accomplished our goals."

"And what would those be?" I demand, my patience evaporating as my rage intensifies.

"Look up the Resistance Coalition in your spare time," he replies. "Everything you need to know is there."

"Am I allowed to talk with Daaros?" I demand. "Forgive me if I don't trust your bullshit."

He nods. "I'll arrange a call. For what it's worth, I'm sorry. For everything."

"I doubt it. Assholes like you always take advantage of those they deem expendable. And I've been classified as expendable since birth." I pause to glare at him a final time. "Until I talk to Daaros, I'm finished talking with you."

SORIN JOHNSTON

CHAPTER FIFTEEN

A DEAL AND AN EXOSKELETON

Sorin returns an hour later with a dozen armed mercenaries, Van amongst them. I clench my jaw and tense, prepared to endure whatever this band of bastards has in store. I can't exactly do anything to defend myself.

"Daaros will speak with you, but only under the condition that you are freed," Sorin says.

He moves forward while the mercenaries fan out across the room at a signal from their leader. Weapons are trained on me from every side.

"And you're agreeing to his request?" I ask, mildly surprised.

"He has threatened to cut off funding if I don't," Sorin replies. "Your friend is more involved with my organization than you realize."

The Resistance Coalition. I scan the 'net for information and locate a wealth of minor GNN stories mentioning the name. The wider galaxy believes they're pranksters lacking a real agenda, but when I locate a data repository with a full list of deeds they've claimed responsibility for, I understand it's much more than petty political tricks they're aspiring to. They started a movement to disband the AI government, then transfer the rule to the people, and they've made a good start on making it reality. A draft of their "constitution" outlines their plans for rule by biological entities.

It's all beginning to make sense. Sorin left Zylar Inc. for ethical reasons, and now he's spearheading the effort to bring them—and their AI-controlled government—down. Some of my previous fury with him dissipates, but I still don't like the man.

He's in possession of those fucking override codes, after all. I will never trust him.

Sorin withdraws a tablet from his pocket and taps the screen several times. After a moment, all of my bonds snap open. I study him warily as I rise to my feet. The sound of safeties clicking off echoes through the room as the mercenaries prepare to defend the blond menace who steps in front of me.

I'm not in the mood to fight them. I know when I'm outnumbered.

I remain still, awaiting Sorin's next directive.

He nods to Van, and most of the mercenaries holster their weapons. Two break away from the rest, guns drawn as they approach to flank me. I roll my eyes and lift my hands in a show of surrender.

Seemingly satisfied, Sorin motions for us to follow as Van and the others disperse. "This way."

I access public records for the pair of mercs who accompany us. The tall woman on my left sports a mohawk dyed a bright flamingo pink and wears battle-scarred armor that was once lavender, but is now so scuffed it appears more white-gray than its original color. Gray eyes gleam with mischief above a smirking, crimson mouth as she holds a pistol inches away from my temple. Beneath the armor, she appears almost as muscular as I am. A tattoo of a skull with a snake slithering through its eye sockets marks the right side of her neck.

Her name is Zinn Jarek. She's the second-in-command of Omega Prime, behind Van. Her rap sheet isn't as extensive as her boss's, but it's damned close.

The man on my right is wiry and dark-skinned. A deep scar runs across his forehead, forming a crevice among the creases there. Gray mixes with black in his dark curls. He appears weary, though his plasma rifle is aimed unwaveringly at my gut. I don't know how well my armor will withstand a plasma round, and I'm not keen to find out. His name is Felix Shuraji, and like the other mercs I've profiled, his list of criminal endeavors is lengthy.

I'm led out of what I learn is a cargo hold and through a wide corridor lined with windows. The starry expanse of space is visible on both sides, but it's immediately apparent we're nowhere near a star. It's too dark, too *empty*.

"Where are we?" I ask.

"Haven," Zinn replies. "As for the coordinates, those are classified."

"We are in uncharted space," Sorin adds. "Until I'm certain you can be trusted, that's all you will learn."

I snort. "I'm not the one with trust issues, asshole. You're the one who keeps waving those fucking codes in my face."

Sorin expels an exasperated sigh but makes no response. Felix edges the barrel of his weapon nearer, but Zinn laughs.

"I think I'm going to like this one," she says with a grin. "He's feisty."

"You would," Felix growls.

Sorin enters a door at the end of the corridor that opens into a disorganized mess hall. Several mercs loiter around a table, drinks and empty dishes scattered around them while they laugh raucously at something one of their number said. A handful of people in blue jumpsuits cluster around a countertop, peering down at someone's tablet display. None of them pay us any mind.

On the far side of the room is a square of countertops littered with various devices. I recognize the same model of drink mixer I had in my apartment on Ring Five, crammed alongside a machine with "Protein Cubes" scrawled across its surface and something that looks vaguely like the coffee maker Pablo is so fond of. A lone mercenary presses buttons on the surface of an unrecognizable rectangular device. He glances at us in mild curiosity, then returns to manufacturing whatever food item has captured his attention.

Beyond the mess hall is a smaller room with three more doors, each leading to a different corridor. Sorin leads us through the center one, down a short hall, and into a room with an impressively large holoscreen. A handful of battered chairs are strewn about the room. Felix secures the door behind us as Sorin withdraws his tablet and activates the screen. Zinn keeps the barrel of her pistol aimed at my head.

Sorin glances at us as the screen flickers to life. "Holster your weapons. It will only make matters worse if Daaros believes our cyborg is under duress."

Zinn frowns, then slides her pistol into her belt. "Don't try anything stupid, Slaughter Bot," she says with a smirk. "I won't hesitate to fill your insides with more lead than even your purge systems can handle."

"Slaughter Bot?" I echo, incredulous. "What the fuck…"

She shrugs. "SLTR-BT. Slaughter Bot. Fitting, yeah?"

"Oh, hell no," I growl as Sorin clears his throat meaningfully.

I turn to find the screen flashing "outgoing communication, pending response." I'll continue my debate with Zinn later, but I'm not going to be known by the Resistance or Omega Prime as a damned bot. Despite what the override codes can do to me, I'm more than a bot, aren't I?

I'm yanked out of my dark musings as Daaros' green countenance appears on the screen. I recognize the room in the background; he's in his apartment on Ring Eight, seated at the desk inside his security terminal. I've never seen Daaros look angry before, but right now, he's *pissed*. His deep green eyes narrow into slits as he stares daggers at Sorin.

"You kept me waiting long enough."

"I had to take precautions," Sorin replies. "I know better than anyone what he's capable of."

I cross my arms. "Did you tell him I was strapped to a fucking chair?"

Daaros' expression darkens further. He's a storm cloud in botanical form, and I'm certain Sorin is about to receive an earful.

"You agreed he would be treated fairly," Daaros seethes. "If you thought your scheme to appease my financial losses earlier was sufficient, think again. You will treat him as an individual possessing free will, or I will pull every last credit of funding away from your Resistance. I could use a new vacation home. Or five."

Sorin nods tersely. "I have already apologized for our mistake, and we're willing to work with him on your terms as long as he doesn't prove a threat to *our* interests."

Daaros frowns, but some of his fury abates. "I'd like to speak with Kye privately."

Sorin motions to the mercs, who retreat toward the door. "I'll be in the corridor," he says to me. "When you're finished and ready to speak with me, I'll be waiting."

Once the door is shut and we're alone, Daaros slumps forward in his chair and runs his hands through his artfully mussed hair. "I never intended to have you or Pablo entangled in this game."

"I'm not sure I understand half of what is going on," I admit. "Sorin's with the Resistance Coalition, and Omega Prime works for him, but beyond that, I'm running blind."

"The Coalition approached the Botanaari government three years ago seeking an alliance. My fathers are both high-ranking officials, as you know. They didn't want to risk an open partnership with a faction the AIs consider a minor terrorist group, but agreed to funnel resources and personnel through back channels. Due to my connections, I was tasked to oversee the financial interests between Botanaar and Sorin's Coalition."

"And how do I fit into this?"

"Sorin truly believed he was doing you a favor," Daaros replies with a shake of his head. "The misguided fool never thought to check your personnel records after he stole your codes. Your capture by Omega Prime was unfortunate, but it presents a unique opportunity for the Coalition. I will not order you to assist them, but it would make both our lives simpler if you willingly agree. Sorin is close to obtaining the final piece he requires to overthrow the AI systems Zylar Inc. has put in place."

"And he needs me because of something I've been upgraded with."

"Yes."

I shift uneasily. "I don't trust him."

"You should. He has made a mistake, one he regrets, but he has the best interests of the galaxy at heart." Daaros leans back and pauses to stare up at the ceiling. "The Botanaari support his cause with good reason. The AI government has been increasingly bold with its edicts regarding the educational levels and research activities acceptable for what they deem biologics. They seek to hamper galactic progress for their own gains by subverting our brightest minds. Zylar Inc. is responsible for the coding of every AI currently in the system—and after what they've done to *you*, I suspect you'd like to see them fail just as much as we do."

"I do, but…" I glance over my shoulder at the door. "He's threatened me multiple times with those damned override codes. I don't want to be anyone's fucking puppet!"

"Then agree to go along with his schemes," Daaros replies wearily. "You are beyond my reach right now, and I can do nothing if he decides to use those damned codes. My credits may speak volumes to Sorin, but I can't fully protect you until this is finished. Cooperation is in your best interests."

"Will he agree to treat me fairly if I do?" I ask. "And will he honor that agreement?"

Daaros nods. "Sorin is not known for breaking promises."

"Good. Does Pablo know what happened?"

"He has been in class all day, and I didn't want this to distract him. He knows of the attack on Zylar HQ and of your disappearance, but nothing more. He was…distraught." Daaros runs a hand through his hair again. "As I said, I didn't want either of you to become caught up in this business, but I will not keep this secret from him. When he returns, I will tell him everything."

"Thank you. I don't want him to think I'm missing."

"I understand. You were very close before you arrived on Megatropolis." He manages a tired smile. "Please recall Sorin. I would like to speak with him a final time before I sign off."

When I open the door to the corridor, the mercs are gone, and only Sorin remains. He lifts a blond eyebrow in question but makes no move to reenter the room.

"Daaros wants to talk to you."

He nods, and I follow him back inside the room, then close the door. Daaros frowns imperiously at the Coalition's leader, an expression that seems at home on his sharp features. I bite the inside of my cheek to keep from laughing; it's clearly an act, and one Daaros is eager to perform.

"You will treat Kye as you would any other member of your organization," Daaros says in an unyielding tone. "You will think of him as an ally on loan from *me*. And may the suns help you if I learn he is mistreated in any way."

"I would never jeopardize our alliance with such an act," Sorin assures him.

Daaros looks down his nose at the other man. "Nevertheless, I have sent you an official contract regarding my personal bodyguard's involvement in your affairs. You will sign it, or I will pull all of Botanaar's funding."

Sorin glances over his shoulder, concern and exasperation warring for dominance across his expression. He withdraws his tablet and turns to face Daaros while he pulls up the contract and skims it.

"Your final demand is a point of contention."

Daaros folds his arms and stares at Sorin for several moments. I sense Sorin's heart rate accelerate to double time; he knows he's pushing my employer too far.

"My final demand is non-negotiable," Daaros replies.

Sorin grimaces, then sighs. "Fine. I'll allow him to visit you and your partner on occasion until our mission is done. Do you realize how difficult it is to manufacture a verifiable false identity for a *cyborg*, Daaros?"

Daaros' smile is feral. "Yes, but I also know the scope of your coding talents. I'm certain you'll find a way to make it happen before I grow impatient."

Daaros shifts his gaze to meet mine, then grins as he disconnects from the call. I've found an unexpected ally in Pablo's boyfriend.

Sorin stares at the ceiling for several seconds, then shakes his head. "He's impossible."

He turns to me, tablet in hand, and holds it up for me to read.

Daaros' demands are straightforward. I am to be treated as a human being and an ally on loan from the Botanaari government and specifically, their liaison, Daaros Syl'Vaasis. Sorin is to ensure my needs are adequately met, and I will not be forced to operate under duress while the contract remains in place. The contract will be deemed fulfilled when Sorin succeeds in his mission, and I'm to be allowed visits with Daaros and Pablo periodically.

While I watch, Sorin scrawls his signature on the document and hits send.

"It's going to be a challenge to manufacture identities for you, but I'm capable of doing so. He isn't giving me a choice."

"Just how much is Daaros paying you?" I ask.

Sorin scowls. "Let's just say that without his government's backing, the Resistance Coalition would be dead on its feet."

I nod, biting back a self-satisfied grin. Maybe this will work out for me, after all. "What now?"

"Now, I find you a bunk in the crew quarters and something to wear other than your armor." He shakes his head, nearly dislodging the odd blue glasses still perched there. "Afterwards, I'll ask one of the mercs to give you the grand tour, since Haven is *their* base of operations. My crew is only visiting."

An hour later, I've been given a bunk in the same section of the space station as Sorin's crew, and I've been allowed to change out of my imposing body armor and into a light blue jumpsuit that is only slightly too short for my frame. The well-worn boots I'm loaned cover the gaps, and although they're used, they're still comfortable. I'll make do.

Zinn reappears not long after, grinning from the doorway of my temporary home. "The boss said you need a tour, and things have been sorted between Johnston and the Botanaari."

"I'm reporting to Sorin now."

Her grin widens. "Good. I hate playing babysitter. Let's go."

She shows me the shared restroom area first. "I don't know if you actually need the facilities here, but this is them. Toilets, showers, and a vaporized decontamination system are all inside. I suppose you still have to shower, yeah?"

"Yeah. And I do require a toilet sometimes."

Her eyebrows lift. "Is that so? I thought your systems were supposed to be ultra-efficient at processing everything you consume."

I shrug uncomfortably. "They are, but I like a drink every now and then. I still have to purge the alcohol."

She brightens at the mention of drinks. "What's your poison, Mr. Cyborg?"

I clench my jaw in irritation, but this term is better than *Slaughter Bot*. "Gin, usually. You like nicknames, don't you?"

She laughs. "Gin's good. And yeah. Makes our line of work a bit easier. We use code names in the field. Fake IDs and all that." She shrugs and points out the mess hall as we enter. "We have a drink mixer there, protein cube coder if that's your preference, or an actual food distributor if you'd rather. Sometimes the menu's limited. It depends on when our supply shipments come in and if there are any snags in customs."

"Do you choose your nicknames?" I ask as we cross the mess hall.

"Nah, the boss does that. And if you're working with us—which I assume you will be—he'll pick one for you too. Lately, mine's been Pink, for obvious reasons." She gestures to her mohawk in all its garish glory. "I doubt he'll use *Mr. Cyborg* for yours. It's too obvious, and we don't need Big AI to figure out who you are."

She leads me to a lounge next. Several holoscreens are affixed to the walls, and there's a bookcase with actual paperbacks, many of them worn, their pages dog-eared and crumpled. In the center is a glass-topped gaming table. Several mercs sit around the table, engaged in a game involving rotating maps and dice.

Zinn notes my interest in the bookcase. "Are you a reader, Circuit Boy?"

I snort a laugh at her latest name for me. "Yeah."

"Interesting." She falls silent as we wind through another corridor to a room equipped with a variety of weight-training bots. "Not sure if you need this stuff either. From what Sorin says, your muscles are more machinery than honest human cells."

"Yeah."

She tilts her head to one side and fixes me with a perplexed frown. "Why'd you do it? Why become ZIEG?"

I chew my lower lip, surprised Sorin hadn't told Omega Prime everything about my past. "I was born on Earth. You can figure out the rest."

A gleam of something—respect, maybe?—shines in her eyes. "Yeah, I think I can. Come on, I'll show you the arsenal and the docking bays."

"You're going to show me your arsenal?" I ask, surprised.

"If you're working with us, you'll need to know where your weapons are stored," she replies with a smirk. "I hear your armor is something else, but it's damned stupid to run into a gunfight with only your fists for company."

"I haven't tested my armor yet," I admit, feeling a flush rise in my cheeks.

"Why the hell not?"

"Your boss abducted me before I went through that part of my training."

She crosses her arms. "We'll need to remedy that. And I know just the thing. Quick detour. I'll show you."

Zinn leads me to a small cargo bay different from the one they used as my makeshift prison cell. Beyond the standard crates and barrels sits a mechanized exoskeleton comprised of a polymer-coated alloy.

"We filched this beauty from a mining operation in Sol's Oort cloud," she says with pride. "The frame's almost indestructible. So's the shield that protects the operator. I've been itching to test it out, but the boss said it's too valuable to 'play' with."

She feigns a pout, and I can't help but grin.

"We'll make a deal, Metal Man," she says. "Agree to let me train you."

"That's not exactly a deal," I point out, amused.

"I teach you what you need to know before we run off on our next mission for Mr. Blue-eyes, and in exchange, the boss will let me use that." She jerks a thumb at the exoskeleton. "It *is* a deal, and it benefits us both."

"You just want to use the fancy equipment."

"Guilty. And you're giving me the excuse I've been looking for." She grins. "Come on, Pretty Boy. What do you say?"

I cross my arms and decide to play difficult. "That sort of flattery doesn't work on me."

"Fine, you're ugly. What's your answer now?"

I laugh. It's the first real laughter I've produced since waking up in Haven's cargo bay. "I think we have a deal."

CHAPTER SIXTEEN

A BARTENDER FROM THE ALOHA MOON

"Come on, Baby Bot. Hit me!" Zinn's maniacal laughter fills the cargo hold, echoing off the protective shield she sits behind.

She knows by now I hate being referred to as a damned bot, and her words have the desired effect. I'm immediately *pissed*.

I allow my armor to augment my speed and charge toward her exoskeleton in a blur. I'm not just going to hit her; I'm going to tear her and that damned contraption apart. My armor responds to my desire for destruction, and I sense it amplify my existing musculature. I'm a whirlwind of devastation aimed at an insane mercenary with a penchant for horrible nicknames.

I crash into the exoskeleton, my right shoulder taking the brunt of the impact. It shudders and staggers, but its specialized arms remain undented. I release a roar and strike with my left elbow, followed by a solid kick. My limbs are jarred by the impacts, but I haven't taken any damage.

Neither has the damned exoskeleton.

I glare at Zinn. She winks suggestively and blows me a kiss from behind her shield before she swings the machine's arms in tandem toward my head.

I duck and kick at a leg, amused she thinks her overt attempt at distraction will actually work. Zinn maneuvers deftly away, then aims a punch at my face. I side-step, then grab the exoskeleton's forearm and begin squeezing.

The pressure I exert is tremendous, but it doesn't have any effect. She warned me the damned thing was almost indestructible.

She tries to pull away, but I don't release my grip. An idea forms, one that might land me in trouble with both Sorin and Van, but we've been at this for three hours, and it's more aggravating than fun now. I shift my weight subtly, adjust my center of gravity, and heave as I release my hold.

The exoskeleton tilts precariously to one side. Zinn's eyes widen almost comically with surprise a moment before the contraption crashes to the floor on its side. I'm grinning, high on adrenaline and victory, as she begins to unbuckle her harness.

I saunter toward her, and she returns my smug look with an amused smirk. "Took you long enough," she says.

I extend a hand to help her out of the operator's seat, but she refuses the offer.

"No, Brutus, I'm not stupid enough to fall for *that* trick. I'm fond of my hands remaining intact." She hauls herself out of the seat and slides to the floor.

"I wasn't going to hurt you."

"And I'm not willing to risk it." She flashes a grin. "Now that we've established what you can do, it's time to put your ridiculous strength to another use." She jerks her chin at the toppled exoskeleton. "Pick up your toys. Playtime's over."

"Seriously?"

"Hey, you're the one who had the brilliant idea of pushing me over. Not my fault you chose to act on it." She shrugs. "Besides, we can't let the bosses see how rough you are on their equipment. They won't let us do this again."

I groan. "Fine."

I move past her and around the metal monstrosity toward its shoulder. With a gentler shove than my previous one, I tip it upright and onto its legs.

"Happy?"

"For now. And look who's here."

I turn to find Sorin watching us from the door, his eyes obscured behind those ever-present blue glasses. He points at me and indicates I should follow.

"Busted," Zinn drawls before erupting into a gale of irreverent laughter.

I suppress a sigh and trudge after Sorin. I doubt he cares what we did to Van's exoskeleton, and it's in one piece anyway. I'm pretty sure it's still functional after I knocked it over too.

Sorin doesn't speak until we're well away from the cargo hold, and it's clear Zinn hasn't decided to follow us. "I'm glad you've decided to test the limits of your capabilities. We received critical intel that provides the Coalition with an opportunity I won't squander."

"Okay…" I don't know why he's confiding in me, but I suspect he's about to call in my contractual obligations.

"I don't like repeating myself, so I've summoned everyone on my crew," Sorin continues. "That includes *you*."

Time's up. No more fun and games with Pink in the cargo hold for this guy.

"When we're finished with the briefing, I'll install your new identity on the 'net, but it will also require a bit of backend coding to your biometrics."

I swivel my head to face him as I fight a wave of panic. Daaros said I should trust him, and there's no way I can bypass even a standard security system flagged as a former ZIEG soldier. I adjust my biochemistry, pushing my dread to an annoying background buzz that I can ignore.

"What exactly does that entail?" I ask.

"Your biometrics are hard-coded to your identity as Kye Verex," he replies. "That includes your unique cybernetic signature, your optics, and your DNA. I can't change your genetic profile, but I can update the coding for the rest, tying it to your biological imprint as…someone else."

"And?"

"It requires that I plug into your system with a standard tablet configuration. No override codes," he adds pointedly.

I'll trust Daaros' judgment and hope I don't regret it later.

Sorin leads me to the room with the single holoscreen. A dozen people in blue jumpsuits are already inside. Sorin moves to the front of the room, and I take an open chair near the exit. I've been at Haven four days, but I haven't met most of them. Quiara offers me a timid smile from across the room, and I nod in acknowledgment. The others either ignore me or sneak curious looks when they think I'm not watching. Typical.

Sorin scans the room, then motions to me. "Kye, the door, please."

I rise to close the door and return to my seat as Sorin pulls up a GNN clip on the holoscreen. I stifle a groan, hoping my Botanaari benefactor hasn't been accosted by reporters again.

"This is the latest from Megatropolis," Sorin says as he starts the video.

A thin man in a suit appears on the screen. He stands in front of the entrance to Zylar Inc.'s headquarters while a steady stream of people move in and out of the glass entry doors. "Breaking news from Zylar HQ. The death toll has been confirmed at fourteen from the recent attack on our galaxy's greatest megacorporation. Ten were members of ZIEG, two were members of the notorious gang of mercenaries known as Omega Prime, one was the personal assistant to SolarFleet's CEO, Tiimar Vy'naaris, and the last and greatest casualty of this unfortunate event was none other than Zylar Inc.'s CEO, Reginald Zylar."

The image switches to a conglomeration of photos of those confirmed dead in the attack. I scan the faces and recognize Jen, but Vee is nowhere on the list. I'm relieved, until I see the last picture in the group of ZIEG soldiers. It's *my* face staring back from the screen.

Sorin pauses the video as I gape at the screen. "They think I'm *dead?*"

He nods. "An unexpected consequence of our operation, but a fortunate one. You can move freely with a new identity and assist our cause without drawing any unwanted suspicion when you pass through standard security."

"You were ZIEG?" one of Sorin's people asks. "I thought you were human."

"They all look human," someone else replies. "They're meant to."

Sorin holds his hands up for silence. "You'll have time enough to become acquainted with Kye later. But I wanted you to be aware of who he is, who he *was*, and that he's working with us from now on."

I nod, grateful for Sorin's interruption. I'm not eager to rehash my story.

"There is more to the report," he says. "Listen."

The video resumes, the screen flashing back to the reporter's false, camera-ready smile. "In the wake of this tragedy, the Executive Committee of Zylar Inc. has reconvened in an emergency session that finished only moments ago. We have been given the following statement: 'Zylar Inc., in tandem with our galaxy's renowned AI government and the Galactic Investigational Services Agency, will locate the perpetrators of this heinous crime. They will be tried in a court of law and punished accordingly for their role in these terrible events once apprehended. To maintain order during these trying times, the Executive Committee has voted to promote one, Marim Zylar, to the rank of CEO.'"

Sorin closes the video. "With GISA focused on Megatropolis, we can proceed with the next phase of our plans."

He taps his tablet, and the holoscreen refreshes to display a series of maps. The first is a map of Sol System, with all major inhabited locations labeled. The second is a topographical map of Saturn's moon, Titan. The third is a detailed blueprint of what appears to be a shielded military installation labeled Titan Base.

I frown in confusion. "Titan isn't inhabited. Is it?"

Sorin gives me a quizzical look. "Remind me to reactivate your security clearances," he says. "You'll need the information stored in the classified sections of the 'net. And *we'll* need your remote access capabilities to said information."

"You can do that?"

Sorin chuckles, but it's Quiara who answers. "Sorin can bypass any firewall there is and engineer any manner of electronic data. Yes, he can do that."

"Mat said he deleted those files."

Sorin rolls his eyes. "Mat is a bumbling fool. He may have deleted the files giving you access to classified materials, but there's nothing stopping me from providing you with replicates. And I can do one better. I'll give you access equivalent to Zylar's new CEO, with an encryption that prevents deletion of the new files."

I nod thoughtfully, but I still have questions. They can wait for when Sorin and I are alone.

When I remain silent, Sorin returns to his briefing. "Titan Base is the clandestine headquarters of GISA. I have it on good authority that the base holds information on the AI-contrived firewalls that protect Zylar Inc. and its puppet government, as well as the location of the AI mainframe. For all of Kye's 'net access, this bit of data isn't available online. It's currently stored in a secure bunker beneath the base, shielded by Zylar's best security systems and firewalls. It's staffed by several top ZIEG operatives."

Most of the eyes in the room turn to me, and I begin to understand why Sorin believes I'm so important to the success of this mission. I was ZIEG, even if I wasn't fully trained. I can give them a rundown of what they might be facing while simultaneously giving them the edge they desperately need to see this through.

Fuck.

Why did I sign that damned contract again? Right, so I wouldn't *die.* And this looks like it might be a suicide mission.

Sorin proceeds to explain the base's schematics and security systems in detail. I was trained to hack electronic systems and breach AI defenses, but only on a rudimentary level. Sorin assigns me to the strike team, where I'll remain in constant contact with him during the operation. It will be my responsibility to bypass the security systems, but I'm also expected to provide combat support. He promises to guide me through the more delicate code, an assurance that does nothing to alleviate my concerns.

"Once through security, the primary strike team will descend to the bunker," Sorin says, tapping the map of the base. "The secondary and tertiary teams will cover their progress and protect the rear. Another team will remain behind at the landing site. I will be with them."

"Sorin, no," a woman interrupts. "You can't place yourself in that kind of danger."

"I can't maintain an encrypted connection with Kye from off-world," Sorin replies. "Titan's atmosphere is dense. It's frequently a source of comm interference. We need to remain in contact, and there is no one else who can maintain it."

When there are no further arguments, Sorin details his plans for the strike. He expects we will face the ZIEG soldiers in the bunker, and it will be my job to distract them while the remainder of the team secures the data package.

"I will call upon Omega Prime for further combat support. Every team will be bolstered by several mercs," Sorin adds. "I'll brief each team individually once I have a full roster. Are there any questions?"

Again, I hold my tongue. I have questions, but none of them are strictly pertinent to Sorin's madcap operation.

The questions that arise have to do with minor details, and Sorin answers them all smoothly. When the room falls silent, he dismisses his crew, then his eyes meet mine.

"Kye, a moment."

He waits until the others are gone, then closes the door.

"I understand why you need a cyborg for this, but why me?" I demand.

His smile is weary, the strain of his role as the Coalition's leader clearly evident as he collapses in a chair across from me. "At first, it was a matter of convenience. ZIEG doesn't bring in new recruits very often, and I'd been waiting for the opportunity to sneak into Mat's lab while he installed his final…upgrade. It was purely coincidence that you happened to be selected as one of their new recruits at a time I was seeking to reappropriate a member of ZIEG for my own cause."

His words force me to recall the conversation I had with Kelsey back on Earth. There had been *two* openings for ZIEG, but I don't recall meeting any other new recruits during my time with them. And after the torture I endured in Mat's lab, that minor detail had slipped my mind.

"What happened to the other?" I ask.

Sorin looks away. "She died during phase one of the enhancement process."

"How do you know all of this?"

Sorin chuckles. "I was Zylar Inc.'s chief engineer, and before I worked for them, I was the galaxy's most legendary hacker. Have you heard of the Blue Ghost?"

Everyone has heard of the Blue Ghost, even poor scum like me, who were trapped on Earth at the time. The Blue Ghost was supposedly responsible for bringing down the AI network servicing Megatropolis for an entire standard week, only restoring services after they were paid several million credits. Speculation had run rampant over the Blue Ghost's true identity and where they'd acquired their skills, because despite Zylar Inc.'s best and brightest, no one could infiltrate the hacker's brilliant firewalls.

"*You're* the Blue Ghost?"

He holds his hands up with a sheepish grin. "Guilty."

"Why is everything blue with you?"

He taps the glasses perched atop his head. "I designed these myself. They allow me to see the wiring and circuitry in any mechanical or biomechanical system when activated. They're blue and the color seemed fitting for everything else."

I stare at him, unease prickling along my spine. "You were wearing them in the cargo bay earlier."

"Yes. I was assessing your performance against the exoskeleton. The network of cybernetics in your system is truly remarkable. You're the first SLTR-BT series cyborg who has survived the enhancement process."

I frown. "You didn't fully answer my question earlier. How do you know all of this?"

"The Blue Ghost is still active," he replies with a grin. "I'm in Zylar Inc.'s most secure files on a daily basis, and I've been keeping a close watch on ZIEG's."

"If you were the Blue Ghost, how did you wind up *with* Zylar Inc.?"

His smile falters. "Someone I trusted let it slip that I was the Blue Ghost. GISA arrived on my doorstep unannounced and I was apprehended. I sat in a solitary cell on Primordia-1 for a week before Reginald Zylar himself paid me a visit. He offered me a choice. I could be prosecuted and left to rot in prison for the rest of my life, or he could make my criminal history disappear if I agreed to work for him."

I pause to access information on Primordia-1. It's classified.

"I don't know anything about Primordia-1."

"After I restore your clearance, look it up. You'll understand why I opted to work for Zylar." He sighs and rises to his feet. "If you're ready, I'll do that while I install your new identity."

I nod, shoving aside my unease. I don't like the fact that I have to be manipulated in this manner, but it's the life I ultimately chose. It's *a life*, not the shadow of existence I would have maintained on Earth. Damn it, I need to get used to this.

Sorin narrows his eyes in concern. "Kye?"

I force a smile. "I'm still adjusting to…everything."

There's compassion in his gaze, something I hadn't expected to see. Not from the same man who has threatened me several times with using the override codes, anyway.

"I watched many ZIEG soldiers go through training. Some handle it better than others. Some don't adjust at all. I doubt this will mean much, but if you ever need to talk, I'm here."

I shrug and avert my gaze. "I'm fine. Let's get this over with."

He produces a connector cable from one of his pockets, inserts one end in his tablet, and holds the other out to me.

It's a peace offering of sorts. He's allowing me to plug it in myself, allowing me to decide if I want to go through with this. He's giving me the freedom to trust him—or not.

I stare at the cable for a moment, then choose to take the plunge. The cable slides seamlessly into the port at the base of my neck, and seconds later, I can sense an influx of information.

"I'm replacing your clearance," he says. "Are you okay?"

A loaded question. On many levels, *yes,* I'm okay. I'm alive, I'm aware, I'm operating under my own control. I have Daaros and Pablo to back me up, and Kelsey—once I'm allowed to call her.

But on the flip side, I'm plugged into this man's tablet like a fucking machine, expected to help him with his insane plot to overthrow Zylar Inc. and the AI government. If I refuse, he'll force me, and I'm not eager to learn what it's like to be operated by someone else like an overgrown marionette. The invasion of my being each time someone jabs a device into my neck is something I'll never get used to.

Instead of answering, I merely shrug. Let him figure out the complicated mix of emotions I'm experiencing. I don't want to talk about it. Not with him.

"Try accessing a file Mat deleted when your clearance was revoked," Sorin says after a time.

I seek the section of my databanks where the classified weapons specs were stored. They're back—and there are even more to choose from than there were previously. It seems Zylar Inc. didn't stock ZIEG's arsenal with every toy they had to offer.

"It's working," I reply.

"Good, now on to step two."

I frown as I feel a tug in my electronic system, then shake my head. It's not a physical sensation; rather, it's embedded in the circuitry of my implants. I lack the words to describe it, but I know he's tweaking some fundamental aspect of my cybernetic half.

"That's fucking weird," I whisper as I suppress a shudder.

"I'm sorry. The sensation can't be helped." He pauses, and a moment later, the odd tug inside my head disappears. "I'm finished. You can disconnect if you like."

I don't hesitate to pull the cable from my neck. I rub my fingers over the port with my free hand as I hand it back to him.

"Pull up your personal file," Sorin says with a faint smile.

My image is the same, but everything else has been changed. I'm listed as human—not cyborg of human origin, just *human*. He's given me the name Jerome Ells, and I'm supposedly a bartender turned commodities broker from the Aloha Moon. There's a description of the location; it's a terrestrial moon with a tropical climate orbiting a rosy gas giant in the Teegarden's Star system, known for its singular brand of rum.

A bubble of laughter erupts from my throat. "I'm a rum salesman? Daaros will expect me to bartend for his next party."

"Which is why no one will question your business at the security checkpoints when you visit him." Sorin chuckles and leans back in his chair. "It's only temporary. After this mission, it would be best to alter your files again."

"Will you let me visit before this mission?" I ask. "I'd like to see Pablo."

Sorin nods. "I assumed you would. I'll accompany you."

"And Kelsey?" I press, uncertain if he'll agree.

"We'll visit her if I can make the proper arrangements. I'm sure she'll be thrilled to know you're alive, and you'll be headed to Sol System anyway."

Part of me wants to thank him, but the other part doesn't dare. I know why he wants to accompany me personally. He's not going to let me escape his grasp.

CHAPTER SEVENTEEN

THE BLUE GHOST AND HIS SUPPRESSOR

RING EIGHT
MEGATROPOLIS, TRAPPIST-1 SYSTEM

"We're here, boys. Don't have too much fun without me." Zinn turns to flash a roguish grin over her shoulder and winks as she taps the shuttle's console.

I peer out the window at the jagged and spire-filled skyline of Megatropolis. We've landed on the top of a nondescript building in the Financial District that's half the size of its towering brethren. Part of the roof is occupied by a flourishing garden, while the rest accommodates Omega Prime's dented and scarred shuttle. Zinn wouldn't answer when I asked, but I'm pretty sure the vehicle she drives is stolen.

"We'll call you directly when we're on our way back," Sorin says.

He's ditched his blue jumpsuit and wears denim pants, a plain white tee, and a gray vest with at least a dozen zippered pockets. I'm in a stolen black uniform with "Aloha Rum" stitched in metallic gold across the back. The outfit is supposed to be accompanied by a black Panama-style hat, but I haven't put it on. It lays on the empty seat next to the shuttle's exit door.

Zinn laughs. "Don't worry, Baby Blues, I'm not going anywhere. The identity you forged for me is great, but I tend to stand out in a crowd." She points at her garish pink crest of hair and smirks.

Sorin appears unimpressed. "Good, we don't need any unnecessary trouble." He motions to me and exits.

I grab the damned hat—which I maintain makes me look ridiculous—and follow him outside. TRAPPIST-1 is setting to the west in a blaze of crimson. The world is coated in fiery hues while the automatic lights on the nearby buildings begin to wink on.

"I'll call Daaros' private frequency," I mutter as Sorin leads me toward the door leading inside. "He should be home."

Sorin nods. "Enact all of your firewalls. We can't risk anyone learning who you really are."

I clench my jaw at the reminder. I'm supposed to be Jerome Ells, rum salesman and bartender, not Kye Verex, ex-ZIEG cyborg with illegal security clearances floating around in his skull. I'm supposed to be human, and most security checkpoints are capable of reading my cybernetics if I'm not shielding them properly. I go through the tedious process of enabling all of my biomechanical safeguards, and my head is immediately filled with an irritating hum.

Sorin made me practice this exercise several times before we left Haven, and though I've come to expect the nerve-jangling buzz that accompanies my internal firewalls, I'll never find it pleasant. Unfortunately, it's necessary.

We're in a windowless elevator before I place the call. I'm surprised when Pablo picks up the call rather than Daaros. Maybe the Botanaari hasn't returned home from the office yet.

"Hello? Who is this?"

"Hey, Pab. It's me."

Silence falls between us for several heartbeats, then he begins to laugh. "Kye? Why does it say you're a commodities broker?"

I groan audibly. "It's a cover. Daaros said he'd tell you what happened—"

"He did. He told me everything." Pablo's voice falters and cracks. "When I heard about the attack, and you were labeled as missing, I…" His words dissolve as he chokes back a sob.

"Hey, it's okay. I'm okay. I didn't plan for any of this to happen."

"Daar said you'd visit today." His tone is hollow. "Is that why you're calling?"

"Yeah. Is he home?"

Another pause. "He is. He's in the security terminal. Did you want to talk to him?"

Sorin points to the elevator's control screen. We're almost to the ground floor, and my time to chat is limited.

"Nah, I'll talk to him when I get there. We're…" I pause to calculate the time it will take to reach Ring Eight from our current location. "…seventy-three minutes out."

"We?" Pablo asks, suspicious.

"I'm not alone. Daaros knows."

"Okay. I'll be waiting."

I disconnect the call as the elevator doors slide open and we emerge into a dusty lobby. Metal chairs are pushed against one wall, none of which appear to have been used recently. The welcome desk sits empty, its holoscreens dark.

"This is the office of Diego Sandoval, an alias of our mutual acquaintance, Van Duval," Sorin says as we move toward the exit. "He has safehouses strewn throughout the galaxy. It's useful."

We move through the exit toward a wall adjacent to the main entrance. Sorin slips on his blue glasses, studies the wall for a moment, then presses his hand against it. I can see nothing different about the location, but then a hidden door slides up to reveal a parking garage filled with everything from standard shuttles to personal hoverbikes to luxury hovercars.

Sorin moves toward a sleek red car with room for two, withdraws a tool from one of his pockets, and inserts it in the car's locking mechanism. The doors rotate open a second later to reveal a plush interior designed for comfort. I run the specs for the vehicle and gape. This car costs more than my cybernetics did.

"If we're going to Ring Eight, we may as well go in style," Sorin says as he slides into the driver's seat. "I'll be your chauffeur, Mr. Ells."

I roll my eyes and enter the passenger side. "The specs say it's rated for spaceflight?"

He cycles the doors closed and nods. "It is. Not long-term, but it can withstand the journey to the rings and back. And Daaros has a private docking bay. We can bypass most of the security checkpoints this way. Besides, Duval won't mind if I borrow this for one night. He's being compensated very well for his time."

He guides the car forward and the hidden door closes behind us. Moments later, we're streaking upward at a rate far beyond the regulated speed limits, pressed into our seats by the acceleration.

"I thought you were trying to maintain our cover." I cross my arms and point toward the console.

Sorin laughs. "Duval has signal jammers installed on this vehicle. We're effectively invisible."

"Until you misjudge a gap and crash into someone," I point out. "You should have let me drive. I have better reflexes."

"We're keeping up appearances," Sorin says with a dismissive wave. "And I've been dying to fly this thing since he mentioned it. It's faster than I realized!"

Sorin darts and weaves between streams of traffic, laughing as horns blare in our wake. He's loving every moment, and I'm grudgingly forced to admit he's a damned good pilot. There are no crashes, and even the near-misses feel orchestrated for my benefit. I begin to relax as he nears the upper limit of terrestrial traffic and accelerates further.

"She handles beautifully, doesn't she?" Sorin asks as he engages radiation shields in preparation to enter space.

I groan. "Please don't tell me you've named the car."

"Of course not. She belongs to Duval. *He* named her Scarlet."

"I don't understand why people insist on naming their vehicles. Pablo rebuilt a hover truck on Earth. He named it Rusty."

I wonder who he gifted the truck to when we left. I haven't thought about Rusty since the day I entered Baja Spaceport to begin my treatment. I haven't thought about *anyone* from Baja Colony since I left, but I was never close to any of them, either. Only Pablo.

I've been a self-centered ass, haven't I?

I chew my lower lip as I consider my options. When I'm finally allowed to live my life freely, maybe I can go back to Earth. Maybe I can help some of those people escape as I did. I browse my internal specs, seeking information on the levels of toxins and radiation I'm designed to withstand. There are numbers attached, but they're meaningless to me without context. I'll need to research it further.

Then again, the man sitting next to me has the answers. I don't know if he'll tell me the truth—he's in possession of my override codes after all, and I'm not sure he's willing to part with them. But I decide to ask.

"Can I withstand high levels of radiation and industrial pollution?"

His grin falters and twists into a frown. "Why do you ask?"

I shrug. "Earth."

He's silent for a moment, but his expression softens. "I think I understand. I didn't look at those files when I was in your system, but while I worked for Zylar, ZIEG soldiers were modified to endure harsher conditions than we mere humans can. I doubt that has changed." He pauses as we glide past Ring One. "Earth's conditions should be well within your limits of tolerance, but if you'd like me to verify that, I will."

"I don't understand you," I growl. "You keep offering to help me, then at every possible turn, you throw those fucking codes in my face."

He winces and stares forward at the starfield broken up by the silhouettes of Megatropolis' engineered rings. "We desperately need your help, and I'm afraid you'll run at the first opportunity."

"You're an asshole." I cross my arms and glare out the side window. If I continue looking at him, I'll do something stupid that I'll regret.

"Your employer shares the same sentiment." He sighs wearily. "I want to help you, Kye, but until I'm convinced you won't disappear, leaving my people and our plans hanging, I can't risk destroying those codes. This is bigger than you or me."

I roll my eyes. "The greater good and all that bullshit."

"Exactly."

"I don't like being used as a fucking pawn!" I raise my fist, but stop myself short of striking the window. Even cyborgs aren't designed to withstand vacuum.

"You're no pawn, Kye." His tone is somber, deflated. "If we're using chess as a metaphor, you're more like a hidden queen. You're the most powerful piece on the damned board. Without you, the Coalition's objectives will never grow to fruition."

"And like the fucking queen, I'm forced to bow to the near-useless king and hope his plans don't land me in line for deactivation."

"Trust me, this will—"

"How can I trust you if you don't trust me?" I roar. "Trust goes both ways, asshole."

"So it does."

We fall silent. I continue to glare into space as we pass rings two through six, my eyes barely registering our progress as my thoughts whirl. I'm livid, but at least he knows how I feel about my present situation. I won't be made a puppet—the fear of that outweighs my desire to break free and flee—and he knows it. I doubt he'll relinquish his hold and the power it gives him any time soon, no matter what I do to "prove" myself.

If I really was the queen on the galactic chessboard, I wouldn't feel so trapped.

"Say you succeed with this suicide mission," I say without looking at him. "What happens to me then?"

He's silent for several seconds. I swivel to face him, determined to lash out again, but my heated words die in my throat when I take note of his expression. It's haunted, etched with unspoken turmoil, pained beyond comprehension.

"Everything I've done was to uphold the belief that no one should be made to live in servitude," he says quietly. "And what have I done? Forced you into obedience with the same tech I hated Zylar for creating. I'm no better than he was, no better than his corporation is."

I don't know what to say in response. I never expected him to admit his wrongs, but I remain unconvinced that he'll do anything to remedy the situation.

He draws a breath, shakes his head, and squeezes his eyes shut for a moment. "I can't allow myself to be like him. I've fought too damned hard to be labeled as a tyrant." He turns his head to look at me directly. "You may not accept an apology, but there *is* something I can do. As a show of good will. But we'll need to land first and ask Daaros if we can borrow his bathtub."

I lift my eyebrows. "I don't know what you have planned, but I'm not—"

He begins to laugh. It's weak at first, then builds in volume and mirth. "It's the best place to destroy electronics in a home. The tub will contain the sparks, and we shouldn't be forced to evacuate half of Ring Eight while I do what must be done."

Some of my anger fades as I begin to understand. I want to believe he's going to do the right thing. I want to hope for this impossible outcome, but I fear he's setting me up for a harsh lesson in reality. I'm afraid to speak my thoughts aloud, only to have them shattered. My disappointment will be less if I don't voice my burgeoning hope.

I nod and look away. Ring Eight nears, and with it, the blinking navigational lights that will guide us to the security checkpoint outside Daaros' private hangar. The car glides to a stop, and a blue-white light pulses from the AI terminal.

A moment later, the AI's voice issues from the car's interior speakers. "Identities confirmed. Contacting the hangar's owner for permission to enter."

"I'm your associate from the Aloha Moon," Sorin says as we wait. "Clark Kennedy."

"I know how you implemented my ID, but how does yours work?"

"I manipulated my public record to display a new name, occupation, and home world. I did the same for you, but since your cybernetics show up on security scans, I had to recode your internal profile as well." He shrugs. "There aren't many hackers who can bypass a cyborg's internal defenses without triggering undesirable results."

I cross my arms. "Such as?"

"It would have fried my tablet and given me a nasty shock," he replies. "You would have been fine."

"Permission to enter hangar granted. Please wait while I cycle the airlock," the AI interrupts.

Sorin taps his fingers against the steering controls impatiently, but we aren't made to wait long.

"Opening airlock door. Please proceed when the light flashes green."

I watch as a door irises open behind the AI terminal, and a green light shines from within. Sorin eases the car forward until we're inside the airlock, and the door closes behind us once more.

"Please wait while the airlock repressurizes. Do not attempt to leave your vehicle at this time."

The interior light switches from green to a harsh orange, and the hum of generators surrounds us, drowning out the incessant buzz from maintaining the firewalls that fills my head. I hope it will be safe enough in Daaros' apartment to lower my defenses for a while. I'm starting to develop a headache.

Finally, the interior door slides open and the light switches to green. "You may now proceed," the AI states cheerily. "Enjoy your visit to Ring Eight."

Sorin steers the car into a spacious hangar occupied by several other luxury vehicles, one VaasTek corporate shuttle, and a shielded hoverbike. I shouldn't be surprised by the wealth on display—it's Daaros' hangar, after all—but I'm not sure I'll ever become used to it. Every craft parked here puts Pablo's abandoned hover truck to shame.

Sorin parks between the shuttle and the bike, and I exit the car without prompting. I'm eager to see Pablo, but I'm also keen to find out what Sorin has in mind with Daaros' bathtub.

The door to the apartment flies open moments later. Pablo races toward me, his expression torn between elation and grief. I'm dragged into an emotional hug, and he clings to me. We don't speak. A sob bursts from his throat as he buries his face in my shoulder. Despite Daaros' assurances and my previous call, I suspect he still doubted I was alive until now.

I glance up to find Daaros leaning in the doorway. For a moment, his expression is filled with yearning, but he quickly masks it behind a haughty facade as Sorin steps around the car. They both disappear inside, leaving me alone with my best friend.

"Hey, I told you I was okay."

He pushes away reluctantly and wipes at his eyes. "I know, but I couldn't see you. And with everything that happened, I didn't trust myself to believe you were really alive."

"I'm here. And we should go inside. I'd hate to make your boyfriend jealous."

Pablo manages a laugh. "He knows you aren't a threat, Kye. And he understands how much seeing you means to me." He pauses as we begin moving toward the door, then says, "Was that him? The Coalition's leader?"

My smile morphs into a grimace. "Yeah. That's Sorin."

"You don't like him."

I shrug. "That may change depending on what he does next. But right now, no, I don't like him."

"Daaros told me…everything. I think I understand."

When we enter, Sorin is speaking animatedly with our Botanaari host, and I hear the word bathtub mentioned several times. Daaros maintains a carefully neutral expression, but flicks a glance in our direction as Pablo closes the door. There's a glimmer of mischief in his eyes that disappears as he faces Sorin once more. They stand amidst an array of elegant sofas, but neither man appears interested in sitting down.

Sorin falls silent and taps one foot restlessly as he waits for a response. He offers me a tense smile as we approach their location. In the ensuing silence, the hum in my head is nearly deafening.

"Am I safe to drop the firewalls?" I ask.

Sorin blinks, then flushes slightly. "Yes. I'm sorry. I should have mentioned it, but I had other thoughts on my mind."

I disengage my internal defenses and sigh with relief. The building headache immediately begins to dissipate, and I'm left with blessed, beautiful silence until Daaros speaks up.

"You may use the tub, but if you damage it, I will charge it against your future funding."

"It shouldn't cause any damage," Sorin replies. "But it's better the tub than risking a fire in your apartment."

"I will accompany you," Daaros says pointedly. "As will Kye and Pablo. I want to be *certain* you follow through on your proposal. Kye deserves to witness the act, and I will not keep secrets from Pablo."

"Of course. Lead the way." Sorin gestures to Daaros, who turns on his heel and beckons us to follow in his wake.

"What do you think of all this?" I whisper to Pablo as we're led through a corridor toward the apartment's spacious bedrooms.

"Do you mean the Coalition and Daaros' involvement in it, or yours?"

"All of it."

He draws a breath and frowns in thought. "I don't like what they've done to you, and I've made my opinion very clear to Daar. He didn't like it either, but after we spoke, he's determined to see that you're freed. As for the movement against Zylar Inc., that's more difficult. Some of what they've done for the galaxy is incredible, but some is downright horrible. And Daar has mentioned the AIs running the government are showing signs of... How did he phrase it?"

"They show signs they are overcoming their programming," Sorin says over his shoulder. "If they break free of their encoded restrictions, we can't be certain what they'll do."

"Did Zylar Inc. fail to create overrides for their AIs, because only *cyborgs* are a threat if left to their own devices?" I snarl.

Pablo's hand brushes my arm in warning. "Kye…"

Sorin chuckles. "It's a fair question. The answer is no. There are override codes for the AI government's mainframe, and we're going to obtain them."

Daaros pauses at the threshold of his bedroom. The door is closed, and I've rarely seen it more than ajar. I've never been inside, but I've had no reason to enter previously.

"I don't often allow outsiders into my private space," he says. "Unfortunately, the only tub in my apartment is in the adjacent bath. Know that by entering, I am granting you a measure of trust few humans have ever earned."

Pablo nudges me with his elbow as Daaros opens the door. "It's Sorin he's concerned with. Not you," he whispers.

"I understand, and I'm grateful you'll grant me the use of this space." Sorin shifts and adjusts his glasses. He's clearly nervous, something I haven't seen from him previously.

Daaros nods and opens the door, leading us inside. His bedroom isn't much different than the one he loaned me; there's a bed flanked by nightstands, a closet on either side, a mirror opposite the bed with a small table beneath, and a pair of comfortable chairs tucked in one corner. I note with amusement that Pablo's clothing hangs inside one of the closets. Behind the bed is a window that looks toward the system's ruddy star. The walls are painted in soft shades of lemon yellow and jade green, the different hues creating an undulating pattern that reminds me of ocean waves. Artwork in contrasting shades of violet and burnt orange decorates the walls.

The only items that seem unusual are the enormous sunlamps in each corner of the room and an odd contraption with a seat that I can't begin to understand the purpose of. The lamps are off, and the room is lit only by the dim glow of an overhead fixture that winds sinuously across the ceiling.

I query the 'net and learn the strange contraption is something gestating Botanaari use in the final stages before giving birth to a seedling. I shut down the query in a flash as my face grows hot. That's a detail I don't need to know about Daaros. Or Pablo. Or their potential plans for the future.

Is it even possible for a human and a Botanaari—? I shake my head. I don't need to learn about this aspect of my best friend's love life. He'll tell me when he's ready to share.

Between what I assume is Daaros' closet—it's closed, unlike Pablo's—and the wall with the mirror is another door. Daaros steps inside and a light blazes on within. Another sunlamp, based on the brilliance emanating from within.

"The bathtub is here," Daaros says with a sweep of his hands.

I file inside behind Sorin. The bathroom is as large as the bedroom. Across from the door are a pair of glassed-in showers, and on the adjacent wall is another long mirror with a pair of sinks beneath it. A massive bathtub with room for four occupies most of the remaining space, the sunlamp perched in the corner behind it. A small door opposite the sinks leads to what I assume must be a toilet cubicle. The bathroom is painted in pearlescent gray. More artwork adorns the walls in shades of black and white.

I return my focus to Sorin. A flurry of anticipation ripples through my core as he withdraws the device holding my override codes from one of his pockets.

Holy shit, he's actually going to do it.

But my elation is short-lived. I recall Sorin made a copy and gave it to Duval. *Fuck.* But that can be dealt with later. I hope. This is a start, a sign he took my words seriously.

Sorin kneels on the polished marble floor and places the device in the center of the tub's broad basin, then withdraws his tablet and what appears to be a screwdriver with an oddly-shaped tip. He adjusts his glasses, taps several times on his tablet, then twists the handle of the screwdriver several times.

He looks at each of us in turn. "Stand back. When I apply this to the device, there will be sparks."

"Is that a cybernetic suppressor?" Pablo asks, backing away to stand against the door.

Sorin nods. "I may have borrowed it permanently when I left Zylar Inc."

"But those are illegal."

Sorin lifts an eyebrow, amused. "Very little I have done in my life is legal. And I worked for the only company in the galaxy capable of successfully producing cyborgs."

"But that doesn't have any use in *building*," Pablo continues, appalled.

"Will one of you tell me why this is so important?" I ask when Sorin says nothing in response.

"It's a device used to destroy cybernetic implants or tech coded to respond to cyborgs," Pablo says with a shake of his head.

"And I'm planning to use it to destroy his override codes," Sorin replies with a scowl. "It can't be done without this tool. Would you rather I turn in my suppressor to the very people we're fighting against and allow his codes to remain viable?"

Daaros moves across the room to stand next to Pablo and slides an arm around his shoulders. "Don't worry. I have made it very clear that should any harm come to Kye, I will pull every cent of funding this man receives from the Botanaari government and buy us several extravagant vacation homes instead."

Pablo relaxes against Daaros' side and nods. "Okay. I guess we have to trust him. It's hard, knowing what that thing can do to my best friend."

I can't take the tension in the room any longer. "Just do it."

With a nod, Sorin aims the suppressor at the center of the device. When the tip makes contact, metal shards spring outward from the suppressor and dig into its target. Sorin rises and backs away as the shards begin to push outward from the center. Hissing and crackling fills the air. Sparks erupt at intervals, and the scent of burnt electronics permeates the room.

I stare at Sorin, unable to hide my fear. The override codes were bad enough, but the suppressor could fry my insides in an instant. I'd be nothing more than smoldering wreckage if someone were to drive a suppressor into my mechanical heart or through my wired skull. Sorin possesses the power to kill me, and his tool wasn't covered during my combat training. I wonder if ZIEG is even aware it exists.

Cloying bluish smoke begins to rise from within the tub, and I force myself to look away from the man who could end me if I piss him off. The device holding my override codes lies in six jagged pieces. Wires and bits of circuitry protrude from within, but every fragment is charred beyond repair.

"Will you destroy the copy too?" I ask.

Sorin nods. "It's simply a matter of extracting it from Duval's safe."

Daaros groans. "You made a copy?"

"It was the only way to sell Omega Prime on my plans for Zylar HQ," he replies with a wave of his hand. "Copies can only be made from the original device, which is now destroyed. I only made one copy, and cracking his safe is child's play."

"But you can do it?" I ask, desperate to have this chapter of my life behind me.

He flashes a grin. "Of course. I am the Blue Ghost, after all."

Daaros orders in supper, and afterwards I'm allowed to use his holoreceiver to place a call to Kelsey. When she accepts the call, she appears disheveled. Her eyes are rimmed in red, and dark circles mar the flesh beneath her eyes. She's in her private apartment, and I'm grateful my unscheduled call found her there, rather than behind her desk at OMMA.

She stares at me for several seconds, her dark eyes wide with disbelief. "Kye? It's really you?"

I force a grin. "Yeah, Kels. It's me."

"Oh, fucking hell, you damned piece of shit!" There's no fire behind her words, and she rapidly dissolves into tears. Her hands rise to obscure her face as she struggles to compose herself.

I'm stunned by her reaction, though I understand. I'm more shocked by her tears.

"Kels, I'm sorry. I couldn't contact you."

After a moment, she straightens and wipes her eyes with the heels of her hands. "I thought you were *dead*, little brother. You'd best have a damned good explanation, or I swear to every star in the fucking sky that I will become your worst nightmare."

I glance across the room at Sorin, who nods his consent. "It's a long story."

"I'm waiting."

"Okay."

I draw a breath and proceed to tell Kelsey everything from the moment ZIEG was summoned to protect Zylar Inc.'s headquarters until I arrived in Daaros' apartment two hours before. Her rage evaporates when I tell her of the override codes, and she begins to tear up again.

"Damn it, I thought I was *saving* you when I told you about the ZIEG position."

"You couldn't have known, Kels. *I'm* not even supposed to know."

"And the man who destroyed them is with you now?" When I nod, she says, "I want to speak with him. He deserves a piece of my mind—and my thanks."

CHAPTER EIGHTEEN

MEMORY WIPE OR DEATH

TITAN, SOL SYSTEM

I peer out the shuttle's window at a jagged landscape of rock spires, cliffs, and valleys that taper off into a nearby sea. The waves lapping at the shore move in a smoother fashion than those I'm used to seeing on Earth. It's not water that fills this sea; it's liquid methane. I look up into the hazy, black expanse of sky. Titan's atmosphere is so dense it obscures the stars, but we're so far away from our system's star that it's perpetually dark.

Titan's gravity is higher than Earth's or Megatropolis'. I've adjusted my cybernetics to mitigate the effects, but the rest of Sorin's crew and the hired mercs grumble about aching joints and slow reaction times. Two-thirds of our group is in the process of pulling on hazard suits and helmets. They're slated to infiltrate Titan Base first, establish visuals on those Duval calls "the locals," then provide backup as the second group sneaks in.

The second group is the strike team. My group.

"See anything interesting out there, Metal Man?" Zinn sidles up to me wearing her trademark smirk, and I shake my head.

"How are you going to fit your hair into a helmet?" I ask.

She laughs. "It'll flatten. Just don't make a scene when I take my helmet *off*. I've killed men for lesser offenses." She winks and strolls away, seeking her next victim.

I'm sure she has. She's Omega Prime's number two, after all.

I glance toward the shuttle's cockpit, where Sorin, Van, and a trio of others are deep in discussion. Both leaders feel our plan is solid, but we still don't know the scope of resistance we might face. Titan Base is a GISA black site, and we've pored over the list of personnel stationed here. Some are ex-military, others are GISA agents, and three are ZIEG soldiers. All have impressive records, and I'm hesitant to face any of them.

But we have surprise on our side and a cache of weapons to rival ZIEG's armory, not to mention one very determined Coalition leader with the galaxy's greatest knack for hacking.

And me. Sorin's damned hidden queen.

Sorin looks away from their discussion as I watch. Our eyes lock, and he beckons me over.

"We're having difficulty with the comms," he says. "This damned atmosphere creates too much interference."

"It's why they don't post sentries," Van replies with what I hope is a smile. The scarred half of his face turns every expression he makes into something of a snarl. "They don't think anyone is stupid enough to attempt an attack. Time to prove those bastards wrong."

Sorin pinches the bridge of his nose and grimaces. "Yes, but that's not why we need to speak with Kye." He drops his hand and looks up at me. "You'll need to be the primary contact for the strike team. I can pinpoint your frequency better than I can someone's helmet comm."

"Got it." I begin to turn away, but stop when Van speaks.

"I've determined your call sign for this mission," he says, mirth in his tone.

"Yeah?"

"Slaughter Bot."

It takes every ounce of restraint I have not to spin around and lunge at him, and another dose not to storm toward Zinn and throw her through the fucking airlock. I remain still, my body rigid and my fists clenched as I seethe. She planted this damned idea in her boss's ugly skull, and I will never forgive her for it.

"I think a different call sign is in order," Sorin says evenly.

I don't dare turn around to face the pair. Sorin knows how I feel about the label, and I recognize that he's not responsible for this bullshit. But if I turn my head, I'll see Van's cratered countenance, and I'll lose the tenuous hold I have on my temper. The urge to destroy him, to rip his scarred head from his body, is so powerful I can taste it.

"I've already briefed my people," Van replies. I can hear the condescension in his tone. "Call signs are set for this operation."

"Fuck you," I growl between clenched teeth.

He has the audacity to laugh. "Didn't think you were the type. Go suit up. Team one's in the airlock."

I stalk across the shuttle toward my gear. Zinn approaches, but when I shoot her a murderous glare, her eyes widen with surprise and she veers away to harass someone else. I collect my armor and head to the cargo bay in the shuttle's rear. I'm not going to strip in front of the mercs after their boss's latest incursion.

The cargo bay isn't empty, but there are fewer people inside and crates to hide behind while I change and endure the bizarre connection process between my body and my armor. Sorin has engineered a helmet that connects to the neckpiece of my armor, complete with comms, air circulation, and temperature control. I only require the air circulation, but he added the additional features out of sheer boredom during the long flight here. He's an engineer, what more can I say?

Five minutes later, I'm in my black-and-orange armor, my helmet tucked under one arm. I'm still pissed, but I'm no longer contemplating murder. When I return to the shuttle's seating area, Van is nowhere to be seen. Some of my tension eases, then Sorin waves me over.

I close my eyes for a second and exhale through my nose to ease my irritation before I oblige him.

"I spoke to Duval."

I shrug. "I doubt the bald bastard cared."

"He didn't, until I told him his 'joke' just jeopardized our entire mission. If you aren't clear-headed out there..." He expels a sigh and rakes a hand through his hair, dislodging the blue glasses perched atop his head. They clatter to the floor. "Damn it. That's the fourth time since we landed." He bends to retrieve them, then proceeds to fidget with them while he continues. "Kye, we can't do this without you, but I won't send you out there in this state. Rage makes us all stupid."

"I can deal with it. Just don't make me talk to him over comms."

"You're sure?"

"Yeah. I'll adjust my biochems. I'm okay."

"He's relegated to the cockpit until the strike team moves out," Sorin adds. "You have time to calm down. Naturally, if that's your preference."

"Thanks."

He nods. "He's monitoring the first team. I'll be your contact during the mission."

"I know." We discussed this as we prepared to land on Titan, and as far as I know, nothing has changed since we touched down.

"Let's run through your mission checklist," he says and gestures to the open chair next to him. "Yours is more technical than anyone else's."

I frown at him. "Why are you doing this?"

"Honestly? I want to make sure you're really okay."

I cross my arms but offer him a nod. "Fine."

He slips his glasses on, and almost immediately, his blond eyebrows arc skyward. "They didn't give you ZIEG armor, but the connections you've made with this brand are impressive."

I stare at the ceiling and its pale overhead lights. He can't stop being an engineer for five minutes, and it grates on my nerves. "Sorin. Checklist?"

"Right." He withdraws his tablet and affixes a comm unit to his ear. "Your frequency is verified. Comms working?"

I grimace as his voice issues from his seat beside me *and* my aural implants at the same time. "Yeah. That's weird."

We proceed through the rest of his checklist until he's satisfied I'm ready to move out. While we talk, I down a chocolate protein shake. I think Quiara has me hooked on them.

The exercise eases his concerns, but it has the unexpected side-effect of distracting me. I'm focused, my anger's spent, and I'm ready to do this shit. I didn't need to adjust my biochems after all.

Van emerges from the cockpit only seconds after we've finished. I glare at him, but it's not the same white-hot fury that possessed me earlier. He's in no immediate danger from the cyborg he pissed off—for now.

"Team one's at the rendezvous point," Van bellows across the shuttle. "Strike team is cleared to move out."

I rise and snap my helmet in place, then seal the reflective faceplate. That's my cue.

There's a mile and change between the shuttle's landing zone and the rendezvous point. The terrain is rocky but not steep, though with the increased atmospheric pressure, the others are prone to stumbling. We move in relative silence, the only sounds the crunch of rock beneath our boots and the occasional splatter of rain against our helmets. My sensors indicate the drops are a mix of methane and ethane.

Sorin's voice breaks the silence periodically as he speaks directly into my aural implants. He seeks status updates and provides information on team one's location. They're holding out at a control panel adjacent to Titan Base's protective habitat bubble and can't move forward until I arrive to override the controls. It looks like my hours spent in ZIEG's training simulations will actually be put to use today.

I wipe rain from my face shield and peer ahead. Titan's visibility is lower than Earth's on a good day, and the weather is only making it worse. I switch my vision to infrared and spy faint specks of color a quarter-mile ahead.

"I see them," I tell Sorin. "We're close."

Zinn peers over her shoulder with a frown. "I can't see shit."

I tap my helmet. "IR."

"I knew you were handy, Cyber Dude."

Since the unfortunate assignment of my call sign, I've learned it wasn't Zinn who put the idea in Van's head, but Felix, the other merc who had escorted me through Haven that day. Felix isn't part of this operation, which is probably for the best. I'm not sure he would have survived my temper.

"Team one reports no activity in their vicinity," Sorin replies, his voice clear despite the distance between us and Titan's propensity for interference. "You're go for rendezvous."

I motion to the others that we're to move forward. The strike team consists of me, Zinn, and four others. Yao and Elise are Coalition soldiers, both veterans of galactic campaigns and a number of Sorin's operations. Hammerfist and Streak I know only by their mercenary call signs, and I haven't bothered to look up their profiles on the 'net. I'm sure they both have rap sheets at least as long as Zinn's. They're each armed with a small arsenal of weapons.

Another three minutes pass before the others glimpse team one ahead, and by then, we're almost upon them.

"Team one confirms visuals," Sorin calls.

"Affirmative."

"Are you ready to hack the console?"

"I think so. But I can share visuals with you if I get tripped up."

Sorin is silent for a moment, then says, "I know, but that's an added strain on your system. You're already running selective firewalls."

He doesn't need to remind me that additional strain will deplete my energy reserves too rapidly. We've been over that aspect of what I am time and again, and they need me in top form when we storm the bunker. Sorin seems confident we'll meet resistance, likely in the form of Titan Base's resident ZIEG members, and it will be my job to hold them off while Yao and Elise steal the data we're here for.

"Okay."

A few steps ahead, Zinn waves to the members of team one visible to us. Their instructions are to disperse through the area and alert those of us at the console if trouble is coming. Another IR scan shows several more hiding amongst the rocky outcroppings not far from the dome of the base's habitat bubble.

Sorin sighs over the comm. "Van says it's all clear. You're go to manipulate the console."

One of the mercs from team one snickers within his helmet as I stride past. I'm sure it's the call sign.

"Something funny?" I growl.

His grin vanishes, then he shakes his head. Yep, it was the damned call sign.

I swallow my anger and move toward the tiny shelter made to look like natural rock that butts against the habitat bubble. Even without scanning, I can tell it's human-made; the color is a bit off from the rest of the landscape, the contours are too rigid and precise, and the shelter's surface is etched by years spent in Titan's hostile atmosphere. The door is made to look like a natural crevice. Inside is a small room housing nothing more than a nanosteel box affixed to the wall.

I kneel before the box and pry off the casing to reveal the console within. I should be able to interface with it through my armor, but this is something I've never tried before. I can't risk removing my gauntlets; Titan is fucking *frigid*. Even my cybernetics can't handle the outside temperature, and my biological parts would immediately freeze.

"I'm at the console," I tell Sorin. "And I have a question."

"Go ahead."

"All of the simulations I did for ZIEG were done without armor. Does it interface the same?"

"Your armor is designed to be an extension of *you*," he says. I can hear the smile in his tone. "But it's a valid question. Yes, it will interface exactly as your bare hand would."

"Okay. Here goes nothing."

Or everything, depending on your perspective.

I place my hand on the console's security readout and establish a connection. The system demands identification and credentials, but I evade its automated queries and bypass the safeguards easily.

That wasn't so bad. Now for step two.

I locate the command to open the habitat bubble at our location. "Preparing to open the dome."

"Copy that. Standby."

I wait, deflecting the console's continued attempts to eject me from its system while Sorin and Van coordinate with the others.

"Team one and our strike team are in position," Sorin says. "Open the dome and set a two-minute passage sequence."

We have two minutes from the time I open the bubble to move both teams through, myself included.

"Copy that. Dome opening… Now."

I input the command and withdraw from the console. By the time I emerge outside, most of team one is through the gap. We have ninety seconds. I race toward them and find a place to stand between Zinn and Yao.

"We're up," Zinn says as the last of team one scurries through. "Streak and Hacks, you're first."

Elise rolls her eyes and follows the thin merc named Streak through the bubble, where they join the others at the rear of what appears to be a warehouse.

"Hammerfist and Slaughter, you're next."

I nod in appreciation that she omitted the "Bot" half of the call sign. At least one of the damned mercs understands.

Hammerfist is built like a professional wrestler. He grins behind his faceplate as we step through the dome. Thirty-five seconds left. As we join the others, Zinn and Yao pass through the dome.

"We're through," I relay to Sorin.

"Strike team, you are clear to move out. Team one splits here. The half designated as team two will provide a distraction. The other half, team three, will cover the bunker's exit while you're inside."

I nod and signal to Zinn.

She flashes a grin. "Time to have some fun."

Hammerfist and Streak take point, while Zinn and I take the rearguard. Sorin's people are the only ones who know how to extract the data from its secure prison, so they make up the middle of our group. Team three follows at a discreet distance.

Beneath the dome, the hazard suits and helmets aren't necessary, and the mercs lift their face shields. I leave mine down; it's tinted and reflective, making it more difficult for others to identify me. If we encounter ZIEG soldiers, I don't want to risk being visually identified.

I'm supposed to be dead, and I'd like to keep it that way where Zylar Inc. is concerned.

We slink past several storage units, following the path Sorin had mapped for us previously. There are only two security cameras along this route, and so far, we've seen no movement of personnel. As we approach the location of the first camera, Streak holds up one hand. We stop. Hammerfist withdraws a plasma pistol from his belt, takes aim, and fires. A single yellow-green bolt sizzles through the air and strikes its target. The camera pops once, then gray smoke issues from its melting exterior.

"Camera one down," I whisper to Sorin.

"Copy that. Team two is approaching the well tower."

I relay the update to Zinn, who nods. "It's a good choice. If they shut down the deep well, the base is cut off from water."

Titan's interior is the primary reason it was chosen for GISA's secret base. Below the harsh surface and the depths of the hydrocarbon seas, the moon has a vast subterranean ocean filled with liquid water that can be accessed with a deep well.

I don't like the idea of sabotaging a vital life support system, but it *will* draw the attention of the base's defenders better than nearly anything else the mercs might contrive.

Our group slinks along our predetermined route, keeping to the shadows as we move toward the second camera's location. It's stationed above the door leading to the bunker's tertiary exit, but as we near, Streak signals a halt after peering around the building's corner. He turns to look over his shoulder, then beckons to me.

"I think we have company," I tell Sorin as I move past the others.

"Do not engage. Team two should be sounding a base-wide alarm any second."

Streak nods toward our destination, blocked by the polymer-coated steel wall on his left. "ZIEG," he hisses.

"Sorin says we should wait. They're—"

My whisper is cut off by the blare of the base's alarm system. A digitized voice issues from speakers throughout the dome, though I can't pinpoint their location. "Emergency response required. Water source compromised. Deep wells one and two are not responding. I repeat..."

I tune out the habitat's programmed recording and peer around the corner of the building. The cyborg is turned away from our group, speaking rapidly. I adjust my implants to pick up his voice, only to hear, "On my way." He breaks into a run and disappears behind the nearby buildings.

I look back at Streak. "We're clear."

"Good. Let's go."

Hammerfist takes aim at the camera and disintegrates it as efficiently as he did the first, then signals an all-clear to the rest of our team.

I wait while the others move ahead and resume my position next to Zinn. She signals team three behind us. We enter the bunker and find ourselves in a cramped room with an elevator console on the opposite side. I secure the door, and the blare of the alarms is mercifully muted.

"We're in," I tell Sorin.

"You can handle the console," he replies. "It should have the same set of defenses as the one outside the bubble."

"Copy that."

I engage the console and run through the same series of evasive maneuvers to bypass its security. It's easier the second time. I force it to accept my command to take us to the bottom level, where our prize should be. I don't withdraw my hand until the doors open at our destination.

"We're in the basement," I whisper.

"Your signal is still strong. Good. I was worried it would cut out once you were below the surface."

I grimace, glad no one can see my irritation through the reflective shield of my helmet. Sorin should have mentioned we might lose our damned comms before we reached this point in his operation.

Hammerfist leans out of the elevator to peer into the room beyond. From my position at the console, I can see several holoscreens on the opposite wall, and two people who appear to be technicians. I doubt that's all they are.

Hammerfist ducks back in the elevator and holds up four fingers. "Three GISA. One ZIEG."

I relay the intel to Sorin.

"Proceed. Team two is working their way through the ventilation system as planned. Team three is all clear."

I nod to the mercs at the door. "We're go."

"The big baddie is all yours," Zinn says as she lowers her face shield. "We can take the G-men."

Sorin's people draw their weapons and prepare to hole up in the elevator until the room is clear. The mercs burst into the room, weapons blazing, and I count to four while I alter my adrenaline and ACTH levels for optimal combat performance.

The mercs take cover behind one of the holoscreens as the GISA agents return fire. The cyborg begins to advance toward Streak, moving faster than a mere human is capable of. I'm at a greater distance from the screen than he is, and he'll reach Streak before I do.

I withdraw a nanosteel dagger from my belt and hurl it while I race across the room, a motion ingrained in me by Vee when I went through weapons training. Vee made damned sure I could hit a moving target with accuracy, even if I was running too, and we practiced every conceivable angle. I watch as the dagger spins through the air and embeds itself in the cyborg's right shoulder.

ZIEG armor is the best there is, but nothing can stop sharpened nanosteel.

The cyborg whirls in my direction with a howl of surprise, and I recognize the face behind the clear face shield of his helmet. It's Chadwick Cleary, one of the soldiers occasionally stationed outside the weapons lab.

Shit. I hadn't expected it to be someone I knew.

"Fuck," I say aloud.

"Slaughter, I need a status."

"Not now," I hiss as Chadwick withdraws the handcannon from his belt and takes aim.

I duck and roll, pushing myself faster than I ever have. His shot misses, and I hear the hiss of melting polymer behind me. I scramble to my feet as confusion flits across his features. I'm faster than he is.

Okay, I can do this. I *have* to do this.

I dart behind the nearest holoscreen, veer around its other side, and catch him aiming where I'd just been. I charge toward his injured right side. Blood and something else trickle down his arm, but he ignores it, amped up on adrenaline just as I am. He hears my approach at the last moment, but moves too late.

I slam a fist into his shoulder with as much force as I can muster. He staggers and drops the handcannon, but doesn't fall.

I can't afford to hesitate. I strike again, catching his chin with a savage uppercut. His reinforced teeth click together with the impact, and he crumples, unconscious. I retrieve the handcannon from the floor and wrench my dagger free of his arm. I like the dagger, and I've always wanted to fire a handcannon. I shove both into my belt and stand over Chadwick's form, indecisive as the mercs' battle with GISA comes to a finale on the other side of the holoscreen.

I don't want to kill him, but I can't risk word getting back to Zylar Inc. that an advanced cyborg was involved in this attack.

"ZIEG soldier down," I inform Sorin. "I can't… I don't want to kill him."

"He's unconscious?" Sorin asks.

"Yeah."

"You can interface with his data port through your armor. Wipe his most recent memories."

"Fuck. I don't want to tamper with his brain either."

Zinn arrives a moment later wearing a grin. "Tell Blue-eyes GISA's out of the picture." She points to another console, where Yao and Elise are at work. "We'll have his data soon. What's with the ZIEG dude?"

I relay her update to Sorin but ignore her final question. Wipe his memory, or kill him? There has to be another option.

"Team two has exited the ventilation ducts and has entered deep well three's facility. They're engaged with a GISA agent. Have you interfaced yet?"

"No. I—"

"You can't allow him to leave that bunker with his memory intact. Either wipe it or kill him, but whatever you do, act fast. Your time is almost up."

I nod and kneel beside Chadwick. I turn his body over, then establish a connection with his data port. "Fuck. I hate myself right now."

"You're engaged?" Sorin asks.

"Yeah. What do I do?"

I detach my thoughts and follow Sorin's quiet commands as I wipe Chadwick's most recent memories. He'll wake up without understanding why three GISA agents lay dead only a few feet away or how he was injured. My skin crawls as my conscience berates me, but this is the best outcome. Chadwick will walk away from this.

When I pull my hand away and turn to face the others, they're waiting at the elevator. I shove my self-loathing aside and sprint toward them. They're counting on me to get back to the surface, and I won't be the one who gets us trapped here when our time is up.

The return trip through Titan Base is a blur. I barely register when we rendezvous with team two at the same location we entered the bubble, and I update Sorin only sparingly. I remember little of our trek back to the shuttle, and don't fully comprehend we're there until I feel the craft shudder beneath me as it prepares to lift off.

My thoughts are stuck on Chadwick Cleary, the man who is now missing ten minutes of his memory.

Sorin sits down alongside me as the shuttle arcs through Titan's dense atmosphere. "You did the right thing."

"It doesn't feel that way." I shake my head, and realize belatedly that my helmet's still on. With a sigh, I pull it off.

"Kye, he deserves a chance to be freed from Zylar's restrictive coding. Your mercy has given him that chance."

"Only if you succeed," I reply. "If you don't, what then?"

"He has his life," Sorin says. "A different cyborg would have killed him. Hell, even Van was calling for it. It's better this way, and your secret remains safe. That's all that matters."

When I nod, he rises from his seat and walks back to the cockpit. Chadwick's alive, but that doesn't excuse the fact that I tampered with his brain. I'm no better than the company who produced us.

CHAPTER NINETEEN

THE PULSAR, THE MAINFRAME, AND THE PLAN

RESISTANCE COALITION HQ
COBALT ASTEROID, GAMMA CEPHEI SYSTEM

It takes six hours and forty-two minutes from the time we leave Titan until we reach our next destination. I'd assumed we'd return to Haven, but Sorin has other ideas.

We exit hyperspace in a system with a lemon-yellow star at its heart and five gas giants with a handful of habitable moons. The shuttle streaks past those and moves toward the star, entering a broad ring of asteroids and debris. I watch through the window as Sorin deftly maneuvers our craft through the field and we descend toward an enormous asteroid encapsulated in a habitat bubble. The bubble's surface reflects faintly blue in the distant star's light.

I query our location and learn we've arrived at Cobalt Asteroid in the Gamma Cephei system. It's a star system that supports few full-time residents. The habitable moons host mining colonies, but this system was bypassed by the colonizers generations ago. There are no terrestrial planets, the resources on the moons are finite, and there is nothing a tourist would find interesting about Gamma Cephei.

The asteroid we approach is marked as "slated for future habitation" on the 'net, but when I access the subset of files Sorin has given me clearance to browse, I learn the Resistance Coalition has been using Cobalt Asteroid as its primary base of operations for over four years. And now it supports a surface-wide city beneath the habitat bubble's reflective dome.

I haven't changed out of my armor. The mercs have taken over the cargo hold of the shuttle, and I have no desire to mingle, particularly when it comes to changing my gear. There's no privacy on a craft this small. So I stand at a window, helmet tucked under one arm, staring at Cobalt Asteroid as we approach.

The shuttle decelerates and comes to a stop outside an airlock designed for spacecraft. I hear Sorin in the cockpit, addressing someone on the other side of the dome. A few seconds later, Van emerges, wearing a smirk. His scarred face swivels toward mine. I look away, clenching my jaw against the rising tide of anger his presence elicits.

His heavy footfalls carry him to a position an arm's length from my right side. I refuse to acknowledge him.

"The call sign was a joke," he says.

I grind my teeth and swallow the tirade I want to spew. He's an asshole unworthy of my breath.

"Look, Johnston didn't tell me you were so fucking sensitive about the label," he continues. "My crew knows what you are, and you took down that ZIEG bastard in record time. It was just a fucking joke."

He doesn't move away. I ball my free hand into a fist and continue to stare out the window. If this is his version of an apology, it's terrible. And I'm in no mood to accept it.

He growls what I assume must be a sigh. "If we didn't need you so damned much, I'd have Johnston kick your ass to the curb."

"Fuck off."

"Are all you ZIEG pricks so full of yourselves?" he sneers. "Too much fucking trouble for what you're worth, and without a shred of humor either."

"Says the asshole who shut down my system. Do you even understand what that was like?" I turn my head to glare at him. "Until you do, leave me the hell alone."

"Watch your attitude, kid. Piss me off, and I'll do it again." Finally, he stomps away, but he's made his damned point.

I refocus on the view beyond the window. We're inside the airlock, waiting for the okay to proceed after atmospheric equilibration is achieved.

I need to talk to Sorin about the last set of override codes. There is no fucking way I'll let Van Duval use them on me after our latest conversation. I will not become that asshole's puppet.

I move toward the cockpit and tap on the doorframe. Sorin's in conversation with someone on the asteroid, but he waves me inside with a lopsided grin.

"…can't wait to see the full scope of your plans," the person says. It's a woman on the other end of the call.

"I've done nothing but put them together since we left Titan," Sorin replies. "The intel we received was good. The data was there, and the encryption was child's play to bypass. I'll call a briefing after my crew has time to rest."

"Good. We've been waiting for this opportunity for years." She pauses, then says, "Airlock's done pressurizing. You're clear to land."

"Thanks, Xia."

Sorin disconnects the call and glances at me as he eases the shuttle forward and out of the airlock. "We don't use AI systems here. It's too risky. They're all tied to Zylar Inc., and the former CEO didn't believe a colony could operate without one. His assumption is to our benefit."

I nod and look down at the helmet resting in my hands. I don't know where to begin, but he saves me the trouble.

"Is it Duval?"

"Yeah."

"Tell me."

So I do. Sorin's the only one who can fix this mess, and he promised he'd steal Van's copy of the codes.

"I *will* make this right," Sorin says, "but the codes are on Haven. He can't do anything to you right now. He was pissed, and when Duval is pissed, he makes threats he often doesn't follow through on."

I allow myself to relax. I'm safe for now.

Sorin guides our shuttle toward a dense cluster of low-profile buildings. Everything on Cobalt Asteroid is painted the same shade of dull gray, making it difficult to distinguish infrastructure from the natural landscape. I wonder why they've bothered to mask their buildings when the habitat bubble is clearly visible from space.

Sorin lands on a tarmac reserved for shuttlecraft, then rises from his seat to stretch. "I'm not used to sitting this long. I usually have someone else pilot, but with the mercs on board, I didn't think it was a good idea." He pauses to tap the console a few times, and the hum of the shuttle's gravity generator and life support systems shuts off.

My internal sensors warn me of the abrupt change in gravity, and I make the necessary adjustments. Cobalt Asteroid's gravity is less than half of Earth-standard.

"I'll show you around the Coalition base," Sorin says. "And I'll find you a bunk if you need to rest. The others are free to do as they please until I call them to the next briefing, and I'll avoid the mercs' usual hangouts. Come on."

I'm not tired after the tour of the base. When Sorin finally leaves me alone in a tiny room fit for one, the first thing I do is change out of my armor and into one of the Coalition's standard blue jumpsuits. Then I work the holoreceiver affixed to the wall and call Pablo.

He smiles brightly when he answers. "I almost forgot who Jerome Ells was," he says with a laugh. "Then I remembered it was you."

I chuckle. "Yeah. Sorin said he'll be changing my identity again soon."

Movement behind Pablo draws my eye, and I see Daaros walk behind him. The Botanaari is shirtless, his green skin smooth and unblemished, and his torso is utterly devoid of anything resembling muscles. It's a stark reminder that the Botanaari may resemble us, but they're definitely descended from *plants*.

Pablo glances over his shoulder, then turns around with a grin. "Daar's cooking tonight. Don't mind him."

"He cooks?"

Pablo tilts his head and frowns. "Yes. Sometimes he requires more than sunlamps, and Botanaari recipes are…interesting."

Daaros laughs in the background and says something our connection fails to capture.

"What did he say?"

Pablo shrugs. "That I'll get used to insects in my food one day if he has anything to say about it. They don't eat fruit or vegetables for obvious reasons, but meat and bugs are fair game. The bugs are hard to handle."

I pause to sit down on the end of the room's narrow bed and lean back. "But you're trying. That counts for something, right?"

Daaros appears over Pablo's shoulder and flashes a grin. "It counts for many things. Our Pablo is a sweet one." He plants a kiss on Pablo's temple and disappears from view.

Pablo blushes furiously. "He's usually not so…*open* about us with anyone."

"But you're happy. That's what matters."

His gaze strays off-screen and he smiles wistfully. "I am. So is he." He shakes his head after a moment and refocuses on me. "And how are *you*, Kye?"

"I survived the suicide mission, so I can't complain."

"Good. Did he find what he was looking for?"

"I think so." I pause to shrug. "I'll know more later."

He nods. "I'll tell Daar. He's been waiting for an update."

Our conversation morphs into a simple chat between two friends. It feels good to laugh, to *be myself* for a time, without the stigma of who and what I am to cloud the moment. We disconnect when Daaros reappears in the frame, this time wearing a loose white tee, and informs Pablo their dinner is ready.

"I'll call again when I can," I promise before signing off.

I lay back on the bed and stare at the ceiling. I want to call Kelsey, but Sorin told me calls to any location involving Zylar Inc., GISA, or the galactic military branches are blocked inside the base. Even if I tried to call her using my internal frequency, it wouldn't go through. Sorin coded every aspect of Cobalt Asteroid's functionality and created its singular system of firewalls, and I believe him when he says his security system's defenses are top-notch. I'm not willing to risk frying an implant just to hear my sister's voice.

I don't remember falling asleep, but I'm awakened later by someone rudely kicking the sole of my boot. I blink and peer up at Zinn.

"How the hell did you get in here?" I ask as I push myself to a sitting position.

"Good morning to you too," she says with a roguish grin. "I was sent to bring you to Ghosty's briefing. He said he tried to call you, but you didn't answer."

I frown and check my logs. Two missed calls from "Anonymous." I rise and follow Zinn to the door.

"That doesn't explain how you got inside my room."

She laughs. "If Sleeping Beauty wants privacy, he should lock his door."

I roll my eyes and stifle a groan. I should be more careful, and not only due to Zinn's propensity to invade my personal space. What if I wake up one day with her boss' override codes jammed in my neck, all because I failed to lock my damned door?

"You hungry?" she asks as we wind through the corridors of the base's apartment complex. "We have time to stop by the mess hall before the briefing."

I check my energy reserves and nutrition levels and decide breakfast is a good idea. "I could eat."

Zinn gives me a strange look. "You don't *feel* hunger anymore, do you?"

I shake my head. "If I go too long without food, I get warning messages, but I'm not to that point yet."

"That's…weird. Really fucking weird."

"They say it's more efficient," I reply with a shrug.

"It's also unnatural to have your organs ripped out and replaced with biomechanical equivalents," she replies. "Between you and me, you were pretty damned impressive against that ZIEG guy, but I would never trade *this* for what you have." She gestures to herself and struts seductively for a few seconds. "I'm proud to be one-hundred percent all-natural human, and I plan to stay that way."

When I don't respond, she says, "Look, I know why you did it. Earth's a shithole, and you were trapped. I'm not blaming you for making that decision, and I'm certainly not envious that you were forced to make it. And… I think I'm beginning to like you, Steel Guts."

I snort a laugh as we exit the apartments and move along the pedestrian path to the mess hall. "Steel Guts is a new one."

"The more I learn about you, the more fodder I have for nicknames." She winks and bounces ahead, clearly enjoying Cobalt Asteroid's low gravity.

The mess hall is busy when we enter, though the line moves swiftly. The menu is limited, but it still offers more variety than anywhere on Earth had boasted. Zinn orders an omelet stuffed with hot peppers and cheese. I've learned since my arrival on Megatropolis that I'm not fond of eggs, and too much of the other standard breakfast fare is packed with more sugar than I'm used to eating in a year. I stick to a protein shake, but branch out to a new flavor today. Cinnamon-vanilla.

Zinn wrinkles her nose as I place my order. "Is that all you eat?"

"They're better than protein cubes, and I don't see tacos on the menu."

"Okay, Shake Man, it is now my solemn duty to introduce you to the vast array of food the galaxy has to offer. You're seriously missing out."

"The shake has everything I need, and—"

"I will accept no excuses," she says, jabbing a finger at my face. "I'll break you of this ridiculous shake habit if it kills me—and I'm too stubborn to die."

Laughing, I collect my "ridiculous" breakfast and follow Zinn out of the mess hall to a nearby shuttle pad.

"Ghost Man scheduled his briefing on the other side of this rock," she says as we climb inside an automated transport. She scans the list of travel options and picks one from the menu. "All the tech is so damned manual here. I'm used to telling an AI where I want to go."

The transport lifts off and begins to glide noiselessly between the asteroid's low-profile buildings. There isn't much to look at on the ground, and the dome of the habitat bubble above is no better. From our angle, the dome is semi-transparent, but produces haze enough that the stars above aren't visible.

Zinn paces the length of the transport as she shovels bits of egg and pepper into her mouth. I'm not filled with the same level of nervous energy as she is, and after a few minutes spent staring out the window at…well, nothing, I sit down to finish my protein shake. I think I like the cinnamon in combination with vanilla—and the vanilla tastes far different than the expired protein cubes I'm used to eating had led me to believe.

I pause to glance at Zinn. "You know, I might take you up on your offer."

She lifts a pink eyebrow in question. "Which one, Mech-head?"

"The food. This is… It's better than I was expecting."

She rolls her eyes. "It's a damned protein shake. You've set a low bar for expectations." She chews a final forkful of egg thoughtfully, then says, "Next time we're on Megatropolis, I'm taking you on a food tour. We'll visit all the best places your fancy-ass Botanaari employer wouldn't dare set foot in. You'll get plenty of 'high-class cuisine' hanging out with him."

"He's trying to get Pablo to eat insects," I blurt.

She snickers. "Typical Botanaari. Do creepy-crawlies bother *you*, Metal Man?"

"Not unless they come in the form of six-foot-long cephalopods that want to eat me," I reply.

"That's a very specific description."

"Humboldt squid were a problem on Earth."

The transport glides to a stop and the door opens, sparing me from further discussion of the red devils and why I don't like them. I won't be surprised if Zinn decides to use my words to come up with yet another nickname, but my fear of the squid is warranted, even after my enhancement procedures. I don't think a mouthful of mechanical parts would deter those damned monsters, and cyborgs don't have the ability to breathe under water.

We exit the transport and Zinn motions for me to follow her toward the nearest building. The interior is a single long room filled with dozens of chairs and a raised dais at one end. A table has been set up near the door with a non-alcoholic drink dispenser. I pounce on the opportunity to disappear into the crowd and lose Zinn as she eyes the drink menu. Most of the people present wear Coalition blue jumpsuits, though there are a smattering of mercs in the crowd. I take an open seat in one corner next to Quiara.

Sorin appears on the dais a few minutes later and pulls up a display on the holoscreen behind him, showing a map of a subterranean structure. I scan the map and query the 'net for more information, then gape at what I find.

The structure is located in the heart of an artificial planet roughly the size of Mars. It's not located near any colonized star systems, but instead orbits a superdense pulsar. A dozen warnings accompany my search, indicating travel to the area is extremely dangerous. The pulsar emits bursts of gamma-ray radiation that commercial spacecraft can't fully shield its occupants against, not to mention the planet's designation as highly classified.

Sorin waits for the room to fall silent before he speaks. "The intel we retrieved from our mission to Titan Base contained precisely what we hoped it would. We now know the location of the AI government's mainframe." He points to the display. "This structure rests inside a Mars-sized planet constructed by Zylar Inc. more than a century ago. The planet was designed for one purpose: To house the AI mainframe."

"If we know the location, what's the next step?" someone asks from across the room.

"It's not going to be a simple mission," Sorin replies. "This world, designated as Z-1543, orbits a pulsar. Certain precautions must be taken for those assigned to the mission. Disabling the AI government is paramount, but I won't stand by and let my crew risk cancer or gamma ray poisoning in this endeavor. I have a team working on upgrades for our shuttles, and another on modifications to our standard hazard suits. That piece will take time."

He scans the audience, then his eyes fall on me. "Kye, you're the only one here who won't require additional protection. You already have it. You will accompany me as part of the strike team."

I nod, unsurprised by the order. "Understood."

"What sort of defenses will we be facing?"

I stiffen at the words and turn toward the speaker's location near the door. I should have expected Van would show up, but his presence sets me on edge.

"Some automated and some controlled directly by the AIs." Sorin crosses his arms and begins to pace. "The automated systems include electrical grids and laser cannons. They are designed to engage when intrusions are detected on the planet's surface. The AI-controlled defenses are more complex and include disruption of atmospheric conditions, gravity fields, and various projectile and plasma-firing weapons systems. I believe I can bypass some of the systems in place, but it's not a guarantee. The coding involved will be a challenge, even for me."

"What about ZIEG?" Zinn asks. She found a seat in the middle of the room.

"The records don't indicate a ZIEG presence on Z-1543, but that doesn't mean they won't show up. Zylar is aware of our incursion on

Titan, and my sources indicate they believe the Coalition is somehow involved. They know what we stole, and they're desperate to get it back."

"And what is your plan if we reach the mainframe?" a woman in Coalition blue asks.

"This strike will require three teams. One will provide a distraction, while the other two go deeper inside the structure. Duval's team will organize the distraction. I will lead one of the infiltration teams, and Brandy will lead the other." He motions to a tawny-haired woman in the front row. "Brandy's team will carry a virus designed specifically to cripple the AI systems. They'll head to the maintenance terminal here, where the upload can take place. My team will go to the mainframe and disable its firewalls. They will only be down for a short time, so Brandy's team needs to act swiftly once I give the signal to upload."

"If I'm reading the specs correctly," Brandy says slowly, "comms are going to be next to useless once the defense systems are aware of our presence."

"Which is why we have Kye," Sorin replies with a self-satisfied smile. "I will patch you into his frequency directly. The same goes for Duval. Kye will accompany me to the mainframe."

I bristle at the notion of having Van fucking Duval speaking directly into my head, but what choice do I have? If I resist, he still has those damned codes, and I won't be surprised if he makes a pit stop at Haven before we begin this mission to retrieve them. Despite Sorin's assurances, I can't bring myself to trust the scarred bastard.

"For now," Sorin says, "rest up. All of you. Once we have the necessary shields installed and the virus is finalized, we'll move. I estimate it will take three days at most, and our timing is crucial. If we wait too long, there will be ZIEG soldiers to deal with."

As if the AI's defensive systems and the pulsar aren't enough, we may be forced to fight ZIEG. And I won't have time to wipe the memories of every cyborg I'm faced with, assuming I'm capable of disabling them as I did Chadwick.

Fuck.

I hope for my sake, Sorin's people work fast, because I do not want to be labeled a murderer.

CHAPTER TWENTY

THE GALAXY'S WORST FIREWORKS DISPLAY

Z-1543, VELA PULSAR SYSTEM

"Nothing useful on the scanners yet," Quiara calls across our tiny shuttle.

This shuttle is designed to carry six comfortably, which is all Sorin has on his team. An identical shuttle ferries Brandy's team along a similar trajectory to ours, and a third, with the capacity for fifty, holds Van and his band of mercenaries. Zinn has been assigned to our team, and Felix is with Brandy. The remaining two slots on our team belong to Geo and Nate, veterans of the galactic military before joining forces with Sorin, and the only married couple to grace any of the strike teams.

I'm in my armor, including the helmet, while the rest wear hazard suits over their defensive gear. No one speaks, though Geo and Nate hold hands. The atmosphere inside our shuttle has been tense since the moment we dropped from hyperspace, and Sorin silenced the shuttle's desperate alarms regarding the nearby pulsar.

I can't see the stream of gamma rays pouring from the star as it rotates eleven times every second, but my sensors pick them up. Our shuttle and the people within are being bombarded with cosmic rays, and I'm the only one who doesn't risk cancer or radiation sickness if Sorin's engineered shields fail.

The pulsar itself is invisible to all of my optical channels, and I wasn't equipped with X-ray detection. But I know it's there, spinning impossibly fast at the heart of this system.

Quiara releases an aggravated groan. "There's too much interference from the pulsar. The planet should be within scanner range."

Sorin moves behind her and peers over her shoulder at the tablet in her hands. He mutters to himself, then says, "Kye, maybe you can assist."

I cross the space to their location, glad no one can see my confused expression behind the reflective face shield of my helmet.

"Our scanners require a link to the 'net, and the one we established when we came into this system has been washed out by the pulsar's ejecta," Sorin explains before I can ask what he needs. "I suspect yours is still working."

I nod in confirmation. "What do you need?"

Quiara's dark eyes widen behind her clear face plate. "Oh, he can act as a hot spot!"

Sorin chuckles. "That's the plan."

Zinn snickers behind me and mutters, "Hot spot." Great, I've just earned another nickname.

Grudgingly, I access the 'net and enable proximity access for select devices. I joined ZIEG to get the hell off Earth, not to become someone's temporary 'net provider. This is humiliating.

"Ah, I've got a *much* better connection," Quiara says with a grin. "Thanks, Kye."

I swallow my misgivings and inject false cheer into my tone. "No problem."

She taps her tablet a few times, then says, "There it is. Transmitting precise coordinates to teams Red and Silver."

"Give them Kye's frequency too," Sorin says. "We'll need to stay in constant communication from here on."

I grimace inside my helmet. "It will be easier for me to encode it directly into your tablet. There's an encryption and—"

Quiara laughs and waves a hand dismissively. "I know. Just connect here and upload."

In this moment, I feel exactly like the damned bot I've tried so hard to avoid being labeled as.

Then Sorin leans toward me and whispers, "After we finish this mission, I will update your identity again, and the encryption with it. He won't have access any longer."

I smile gratefully, though I know he can't see it. "Thanks."

With that assurance, I give up my personal frequency to Quiara's tablet and wait for the others to invade my aural implants. Sorin connects as well, and I'm grateful he'll be present to overhear and speak with the others, though it's jarring to hear him speak at the same time beside me.

"Beez online," Brandy's voice comes through first.

"Hey, Slaughter Bot," Van sneers a moment later.

I glare at the shuttle's ceiling and go rigid. He was supposed to have changed my fucking call sign.

"Ghost online," Sorin cuts in before Van can taunt me further. He places a hand on my elbow and lifts his eyebrows, a silent plea for me to remain calm.

The mercenary boss' dark laughter ceases. "Bull Shark here," he says.

Of course Van Duval would choose an apex predator as his call sign, although I'm pretty sure the bull sharks of Earth were wiped out when we polluted our seas. If they weren't, the overpopulation of ravenous devils probably ended them.

"Comms sound good all around," Sorin says with a nod of thanks to me.

"They may not stay that way," Brandy replies. "When your team descends into the deeper levels, there will be more interference, and not just from the pulsar."

"I don't think that will be a problem as long as our source remains online," Sorin counters.

"Sir?" Quiara interrupts. "I'm detecting readings from a shuttle on the planet's surface. It's broadcasting on a ZIEG frequency."

Sorin relays the news. "Watch for unwanted company as we proceed." He turns off his mic and studies me. "You'll need to enable your firewalls before we get any nearer. How is the strain on your system so far?"

"I can manage."

His eyes linger on my faceplate, but finally, he nods, seemingly satisfied. "Tell me at the first sign of fatigue. I have protein cubes in my tool case."

I'm still not used to the genuine concern Sorin seems to have for me after our shaky introduction on Haven. I nod uncertainly and mutter, "Thanks."

The now-familiar, angry buzz fills my head as I enable my firewalls. This was always part of our plan, even before we knew ZIEG was here, but I've been waiting until the last possible moment to do this. It's easier to think when it doesn't feel like a swarm of furious hornets has taken up residence inside my skull.

I check my system's status and note that between the firewall and maintaining comms with the others, I'm depleting my energy stores eight percent faster than my baseline average. Okay, maybe Sorin's protein cubes *will* come in handy later.

"We've reached the designated location," Quiara says.

"Copy that." Sorin folds his arms and clicks on his mic. "Bull Shark, you are clear to move. Beez, stand by for confirmation. My team is moving toward the secondary maintenance bay."

"Understood," Brandy replies.

"Alright, hell-raisers, let's do what we do best," Van growls. "We land in ten…nine…eight…"

"Planet-wide security systems coming online," Brandy says.

"…four…three…two," Van continues his count, unperturbed. "Let's fuck shit up! The Bull Shark has landed."

"Scanners haven't locked onto our ship yet," Quiara says to Sorin.

"Duval has been broadcasting Omega Prime's presence since we entered the system," Sorin replies.

"I know, but—"

"The AIs are still focused on him," Sorin cuts her off. "His people were hired to create distractions, and he's damned good at it. Look."

I follow Sorin's finger as he points through the cockpit window. The glow of plasma beams cuts through this otherwise dim section of space, briefly illuminating the planet's unnaturally smooth surface. I watch as several bulky silhouettes become visible, guns aimed at one of the planet's automated cannons.

Our shuttle banks toward a dark opening some distance ahead, and my view of the mercenary battle is obscured.

"And that's the maintenance bay. Keep your guard up. There's no telling what we'll encounter once inside." Sorin nods to Quiara. "Keep the engines primed after we land. We may need to evacuate swiftly."

"It's all part of the plan." She flashes a tight smile. "Good luck in there."

The shuttle is enveloped in shadow as we glide through the opening. Quiara flies using the navigational system alone; lights would only alert the planet's AI protectors to our presence sooner. I follow Sorin to the shuttle's exit as we touch down, but he gestures for me to go first.

"You're on point," he says, then taps his face plate. "Night vision."

I nod and switch optical modes as the door slides open. My world is abruptly painted in various shades of green.

"Six cannons disabled," Van says. "We'll keep attacking until the fuckers give up or there's nothing left to destroy. I don't think these assholes were prepared for my crew."

"Beez in position. We're moving on the target."

"Ghost has landed. Will update as needed."

I unstrap the plasma rifle from my back and flick off the safety as our group edges forward. The maintenance bay we landed in—if that's what the opening really is—feels cavernous. Even with my night vision engaged, I can't locate the ceiling, and the outer walls are distant. Everything is constructed of the same smooth metal, and there's enough gravity to keep us firmly on the ground. Our footsteps echo in the darkness; I hope the AIs remain too interested in Van's antics on the surface to notice our progression. I'm not sure I want to find out what other defenses they have in reserve.

I adjust my biochem levels to settle my nerves. I'm a fucking cyborg. I shouldn't be this anxious, but I am.

Someone from ZIEG is here, possibly more than one someone, and I'm expected to deal with them. Yeah, I've trained for it, but it doesn't change the fact that it might be someone else I *know*. What if it's Vee or Luna? What then?

I shake my head and shove the thoughts aside. I need to focus on *now*, not the random possibility that the ZIEG shuttle carried one of my friends. My helmet makes it impossible for anyone to recognize my face anyway, and my firewalls prevent any forced data breaches or scanner identifications. It doesn't matter if I know them. They won't know *me*. And I can deal with the guilt I'll inevitably experience.

I think.

Ahead, the space narrows into a corridor. Faint light pulses from somewhere further inside, the illumination making the arc of the corridor evident.

"There's a maintenance shaft at the end," Sorin says in a hushed tone. "It's accessible from an elevator or a stairwell. The stairs are longer, but it's the safer route. The AIs can stop the elevator at any time."

I nod, recalling the maps from his briefing. The mainframe is at the bottom of the shaft, but it's dozens of stories below our present location.

"Let me know if I need to slow down during the descent," I call over my shoulder. "I don't fatigue like the rest of you."

"Don't worry about us, Hot Spot," Zinn replies, a smirk in her tone. "We'll keep up."

"Indeed," Nate says firmly. "Focus on the way ahead."

I face forward as the corridor arcs toward the maintenance shaft and immediately signal a halt. There's an armored silhouette pacing along the shadows, the unmistakable shape of a rifle poking up above its shoulder. And when the silhouette turns, a green glow emanates from its eyes.

"ZIEG," I hiss to the others. "I'll handle this."

My voice sounds more confident than I feel, but none of the others can compete with a trained ZIEG soldier as I can. The cyborg's face shield reflects the dim glow from the elevator's console, obscuring the face within. Their frame is too large to be Luna or Vee; it's small consolation for what I must do next, but at least I won't be destroying one of my friends.

I dart forward, moving at an angle toward one wall, then veering sharply toward the other as the cyborg smoothly reaches for their rifle. I fire two warning shots, one aimed high, the other low. The second blasts into the elevator console with a hiss of melting polymer.

Maybe it's a good thing Sorin wanted to take the stairs. I've just rendered the elevator useless from this level.

The other cyborg fires a shot intended for my head, but I'm too fast. It misses as I zig-zag along the corridor. I'm within a dozen steps of my opponent when they suddenly vanish.

Shit. They have the CVRT-BT enhancements for stealth, but so does Vee. And they trained me for opponents like this.

I don't stop as many others would have when faced with a disappearing foe. I side-step and switch my optics to IR. The other cyborg's heat signature glares red-to-white as they slice the air with a dagger where I would have been if I'd stopped.

"What the fuck?" a male voice issues from within the cyborg's helmet.

I fire my rifle again and wince internally as plasma burns through his right arm, severing it just below the elbow. The hand holding the dagger drops to the metal floor with a clang. He howls in stunned surprise and rage, but I doubt he feels much pain. Plasma's good for cauterizing wounds instantly, and adrenaline masks the discomfort he experiences.

I dance around him as he pulls a pistol from his belt. "Who the hell are you?" he demands as he fires.

The shot strikes a point where my feet should have been if I were an average cyborg. But I'm not average, and according to Sorin, I'm one-of-a-kind.

I could answer his question, but I won't. He can't scan me, he can't see inside my helmet, but he *can* use voice recognition if I speak. And we're on borrowed time anyway; I need to finish this, as much as I don't want to. *Fuck.*

I raise my rifle, aim at his face, and pull the trigger.

Click. A warning message flashes across my vision, indicating a weapon malfunction.

My opponent laughs. "Your weapon's no good if its circuits are fried."

With a snarl, I hurl the rifle at his head. He ducks in time to miss most of the blow, but it grazes the side of his helmet as he lunges forward. I backpedal more swiftly than he anticipates. He keeps his footing, shaking his head in irritation.

I charge forward as he moves to regain his balance. As we collide, I wrench the pistol from his hand and send it flying down the corridor. Maybe one of the others can use it.

I pin him to the wall, utilizing every ounce of my superior strength to keep him there. He struggles, his severed right arm flailing uselessly at his side. I adjust my balance to account for his struggles and press my left forearm firmly against his throat.

I can't make out his face with my IR optics, but I can sense the vibrations that pulse through his body as he attempts to bury his fear under a flood of hormones. I'm glad I can't see his face. Recognition would only make what I have to do next that much harder.

"Who…the fuck…are you?" he wheezes.

I prime my strength, running as much power through my right arm as I can, and slam my fist through his helmet. My armored hand connects with flesh and bone, pulverizing his biological components and demolishing cybernetics as his skull caves beneath the blow. I swallow my disgust and strike again, even though he's already gone limp.

I can't risk leaving any witnesses, and I don't have time to erase his memory.

I hit him a third time, and his helmet cracks open like an egg, both halves falling to the floor. I release the cyborg's body and step back, shaking blood and brain matter from my gauntlet as I turn to face the corridor.

"We're clear," I relay to Sorin as I switch back to night vision mode.

The others appear moments later. Zinn twirls the cyborg's pistol in one hand and pauses to assess the scene as the others move toward the door to the stairwell. She studies me as she falls in line, then nods.

"I don't think the boss will give you a new call sign anytime soon," she says. "Slaughter Bot is too damned fitting."

I glare at her, though she can't see it, and step into the stairwell. I'm no fucking bot.

I'm Kye Verex, formerly of ZIEG, now an asset to the Resistance Coalition. And my mind will always be my own if I have anything to say about it.

The descent is uneventful on our end, but I hear chatter through the comms from Van's team about a few casualties as the planet's AIs adjust their defenses. Brandy's team arrives at their location ten minutes before we reach the mainframe with little to report. We race down *a lot* of stairs at Sorin's urging.

After my fight with the other cyborg, the rest of our group is motivated to move and get off this fabricated world as quickly as they can. I don't have to mention that ZIEG shuttles typically carry a four-person squad; they know it as well as I do.

When the stairs finally end, we're met with a reinforced nanosteel door with the most complicated security panel I've ever seen. Sorin wastes no time inspecting it. He whips out his tool kit, locates a device that looks similar to his damned suppressor, though with a blunt end, and jams it into the base of the panel. Sparks crackle across its surface in a spiderweb of electricity and the screen promptly goes dark.

"Was that supposed to—" Zinn asks, but stops abruptly when the door slides open.

The room on the other side is tiny compared to the cavern we entered above. It's shaped like a dome, with a single access terminal in the center. Sorin hesitates at the threshold, then motions to me.

"I need your scanner," he whispers.

The room is empty, but something about its atmosphere forces me to emulate his hushed tones. "What am I looking for?"

"Anything electronic embedded in the floor or walls. My glasses don't fit under this face shield, and it's too dark in here for me to see anything even if I could wear them. Look for circuitry, wires, anything that can be used as a conduit of information by the AIs."

I scan the room. "There are cables running from the terminal through the floor in all directions—"

"That's expected," Sorin replies. "Go on."

"Circuits are embedded in the floor too, but not everywhere. The first tile beyond the threshold, and then in a ring directly around the terminal." I shrug. "I can't tell you what any of it does. I'm not an engineer."

Sorin's expression is grim. "You don't have to. I suspect the first tile holds pressure sensors to alert the AI if someone enters this room.

The others… I'm not sure, but they're likely a trigger for the room's automated defenses."

"Can't we just blast the tiles and be done with it?" Zinn asks, tapping one foot impatiently. "No circuits mean no communication with the AI, yeah?"

Van's voice cuts through whatever Sorin says in response. "I hope you bastards are wrapping up, because we've found one of Slaughter Bot's buddies. Fucking cyborg has stealth enhancements."

"Do any of your people have IR upgrades in their helmets?" I ask while Sorin continues to discuss our options for the mainframe with the others.

"Yeah. That'll help?"

"It will. They can't mask their heat signature."

"Copy. Ah, now I see the fucker. Bull Shark out."

I refocus on the others in time to see Zinn aim the pistol she took from the cyborg I killed above and fire at the tiled floor just inside the door. Red lights begin to pulse inside as the door begins to slide closed. Something hisses from the ceiling of the room inside, but I ignore that problem for now.

I grip the door and strain against the force it begins to exert, but if I let it close, we'll be cut off from the mainframe and our mission will fail. I adjust my fingers for better purchase and pump more energy into my arms and hands.

"Can you pull the door out?" Sorin asks. "I don't care if we cause a little destruction."

With a renewed burst of strength, I tug on the door, hoping to wrench it free of its nanosteel frame. My fingers dig into the metal, leaving dents along its otherwise smooth surface, but the door continues to resist. I don't relent, and finally, I feel something above my head snap free.

A warning message flashes across my vision. "Energy reserves low. Refuel required."

Shit. I don't have time to pause and eat something right now.

I maximize the power in my arms and heave. With a metallic groan and a screech of torn metal, the door breaks free. I hold it awkwardly for a moment, then shove it along the wall and out of our way.

"Holy shit," Zinn breathes. "Remind me not to piss you off, Brutus Maximus."

I laugh. "That's a call sign I can get behind."

"I'll talk to the boss."

"The AI attempted to create a vacuum when the panel was triggered," Sorin says before our banter can continue. "I'm not sure it's safe for us to enter. It knows we're here now." He looks at me pensively, and I know what he's about to ask.

"You'll have to walk me through it, but first, I need some of those protein cubes."

"It can't wait?" Geo asks, his voice quavering. "We have food back on the shuttle—"

Sorin holds up one hand and rummages through his tool kit. "It can't wait. If he needs food, it's because his energy reserves are low. Maintaining comms puts a significant strain on his system."

He pulls out two packaged protein cubes and offers them to me. Both are marked as plain, but the expiration on the label hasn't passed yet. I think this is a first for me.

I run a brief scan of the atmosphere and note that while oxygen levels are low, I'll be in no danger if I lift my face shield for a few seconds. I take the offered cubes in one hand, flip open my shield with the other, and pop both into my mouth. The cubes are flavorless, but they don't have the same unpleasant aftertaste as those I grew up eating on Earth. I secure my face shield and give Sorin a thumbs-up as I swallow. The warning message disappears from my optical overlay, but the cubes have only restored me to seventy percent capacity. It will have to suffice.

"Avoid stepping on the tiles with circuits embedded if you can," Sorin advises as he hands me a slender rectangular device with an output jack on one end. "When you reach the mainframe, there should be a terminal on the other side with a port where you can plug this in."

I nod. "Cover me. If the AIs know we're here, so does ZIEG."

As I leap over the plasma-scorched tile Zinn shot, Sorin speaks into the comms. "The Ghost is on target. Slaughter is attempting the hack. Beez, standby for initiation."

Brandy's voice is filled with relief when she speaks. "Beez standing by. We're ready to get off this hellhole."

"I couldn't have said it better," Van snarls, his breathing heavy. "We just killed two of those ZIEG bastards, but my team's taking casualties."

"Pull back toward your shuttle," Sorin states. "This shouldn't take much longer."

"Hell yeah. Copy that, Ghost."

I pause as I near the ring of circuit-bearing panels around the mainframe. If Sorin's right, every automated defense packed into the dome will instantly target me if I misstep. There are two panels inside the ring, one on each side of the mainframe, that don't hold any electronics inside. I can make the jump, but it's the mainframe itself that worries me. The AIs *will* know when I plug in Sorin's device. I won't have much time to work before they react.

I skirt the circle of circuited tiles until I'm on the other side of the mainframe. Sorin stands in the doorway, his eyes locked on mine. He nods once in silent encouragement, and I take the leap.

"I see the port," I relay over the comms.

"Good. Don't plug the device in yet. I suspect the planet's overseers will react swiftly once it's in place."

"Yeah, I figured they would."

"Okay, this is what you need to do…"

I listen to Sorin's instructions carefully, memorizing each detail as he presents them. I can't fuck this up, or it's likely none of us will be leaving this fabricated world. I'm the only one who can move fast enough to escape this room if the AI triggers more of its defenses, and maybe not even then. But for the sake of my future and that of the other cyborgs conscripted by Zylar Inc., I have to try.

I draw a breath and steady myself. "Here goes nothing."

I plug in Sorin's device and proceed with his list of commands at lightning speed. I can hear the whine of something coming online above my head as I finish my task, and a new warning flashes across my visual overlay. I'm in the crosshairs of a plasma cannon.

Without waiting to see if my work is successful, I vault over the circuited tiles and charge toward the door. A blast of molten hell strikes the place where I'd been standing, but I'm already halfway back to the others. I hear the sizzle of the tiles and the mainframe itself as the blast vaporizes everything within a three-foot radius.

"Holy shit, that was close." I motion to the others to move as I jump over the last tile. "We need to get the fuck out of here."

"Beez, you're clear for upload," Sorin says as we begin to charge up the stairs.

"That was fast," she replies.

"Slaughter didn't waste any time." Sorin laughs, but there's a nervous edge to the sound. "I'm damned glad he didn't. We'll share the details later."

"Upload initiated." Brandy's tone remains calm, despite her next words. "We're moving out. The overseer has found us, and we have company."

"ZIEG?" The word spills from my lips unbidden.

Brandy doesn't answer. I hope it's because they're fighting off their visitor and she's too busy to respond, but fear worms its way through my gut. I increase my adrenaline levels to mask my unease. I have to focus on our group. Brandy's team is on their own.

"Status report," Sorin calls as we reach the midway point of the stairwell.

"Bull Shark at the launch pad. Shuttle's primed. Holding position until evac notice is a go."

"Beez here. We've taken some fire. Our visitor's not dead, but he'll be out of commission for a while. Black Wolf needs a medic."

"Copy. Ghost is ascending. ETA is ten minutes to shuttle if we don't encounter any more surprises."

Behind me, someone stumbles and pitches forward. I spin and catch Geo in my left arm. His face is pale beneath his face shield, and his breathing is labored. He doesn't look well.

"You okay?"

He shakes his head. "Wasn't planning…on running…*up* the damned…stairs."

"He has a heart condition," Nate says, concern in his tone.

I slide my rifle over my right shoulder and holster it. "We can't wait for you to catch your breath. Come on."

I haul him into my arms before he can protest and increase my speed to catch up to the others. Sorin nods in thanks and waves at the group to move faster.

"You don't have to do this," Geo whispers without meeting my eye. "But thank you."

"Despite Duval's name for me, I don't like seeing people hurt. Or dead," I add, certain he would be the latter if we left him behind. "And no one else can carry you out as easily as I can."

"The mercs are damned stupid if they don't think you have a heart," Nate says from beside us. "A bot wouldn't have bothered. A bot would have left him to die."

"I'm no fucking bot."

"And we're better for it." Nate smiles at Geo. "We're almost at the top. Hang in there."

Geo rolls his eyes and blushes faintly. He still doesn't look good, but he's doing better.

Ahead, Sorin stops outside the door that will lead us back to the cavernous space we entered from. The door is sealed, but he jams his gadget into its base as he did to the panel countless floors below. The door slides open and he waves us through as the panel smokes and crackles, protesting its demise.

We race past the corpse of the cyborg I killed, and I'm forced to switch back to night vision as the glow from the maintenance shaft behind us fades. I hear the hum of our shuttle's engines before it comes into view, and a wave of relief washes through me. Quiara's still here. She's safe and ready for us to board.

I set Geo down as we reach the shuttle doors. He blushes furiously and shakes his head, then mutters another thank you. I wait for the others to board, then step inside.

"Evac is a go," Sorin says as he climbs into the cockpit. "Comms terminating in ten seconds. Our conduit needs a break."

"Copy that," Brandy says. "We're in the air."

"Bull Shark's pulling out. Sawbones is going to be busy for a while."

Sorin nods to me as our shuttle lurches forward, and I disconnect all three frequencies from my own. I collapse into the copilot's seat a moment later. I need to sleep, and a snack might be in order too.

"Can I drop the firewalls yet?" I ask.

Sorin shakes his head. "Wait until we're beyond the AIs' sensors."

I stare out the windshield as he soars beyond the planet's pull. The shuttle dips and weaves as he evades cannon fire and a pair of lasers meant to slice our craft in two. Have I mentioned Sorin's a damned good pilot? Well, he is.

I settle back in my chair and take in the view of uninhabited space beyond the AIs' fabricated world. I itch to remove my helmet, but it's not safe yet. We're still well within the pulsar's range, and I'm no longer protected by the planet's insulating exterior.

"Where do we go from here?" I ask as I watch the view shift before us.

Sorin banks the shuttle around for a final view of Zylar Inc.'s secret facility. We're far enough away that I can no longer make out the planet's surface from the surrounding darkness until a plasma cannon erupts or a laser flares, revealing its malignant presence.

"Haven," he says. "We'll regroup there, and Van's people need their medic."

I allow my eyes to begin drifting closed. A brilliant burst of light above the planet snaps me back to wakefulness in an instant. I stare at the silent explosion, then turn to Sorin, certain I know what we just witnessed.

Sorin taps his console frantically. "Teams, report."

"Bull Shark here. We saw the fireworks too."

"Beez?" Sorin asks, desperation in his tone. "Beez, damn it. Answer me!"

Silence greets his order. He taps the console again, and I watch as his expression crumples beneath the glare reflecting from his face shield. He closes his eyes for several seconds, clenches his jaw, then shakes his head.

"Regroup at Haven. Ghost out."

I reach toward him, but withdraw my hand at the last second. I don't know what to say. He may not even want my sympathy.

"I'm sorry," I offer as I rise from my seat.

"Send Quiara in," he says after a long moment. "I need her to pilot. I can't…"

I nod and walk away, leaving Sorin alone to grieve in the wake of the galaxy's worst fireworks display.

CHAPTER TWENTY-ONE

INVISIBLE CHAINS

HAVEN
UNCHARTED SPACE

When we return to Haven, Sorin insists that I'm given a room adjacent to his. He fights through his grief and lashes out at the mercs when they question his orders regarding my placement. This new furious aspect of Sorin isn't something they're used to, and even the Coalition members are stunned by his abrupt change. They whisper amongst themselves, but no one summons the courage to question him.

I don't know the reason behind his demands, but I suspect it has something to do with my proximity to Duval and the lingering problem of the override codes. He clings to the fulfillment of his promise as though it's the only thing keeping him afloat. Maybe it is.

As soon as I'm shown to my room, I lock the door and begin the process of removing my armor. I hear Sorin's muffled shouts, then his door slams with enough force it rattles in its frame and vibrates through our adjoining wall. I'm half-dressed when the sound of heart-wrenching sobs shatters the silence next door.

I don't know the nature of his relationship with Brandy or her crew members, but at least one of them meant more to him than a mere acquaintance. He didn't shed a single tear during the flight here, but now that he's alone, his defenses have crumbled.

I pull on a white tee and perch at the end of my bed. Should I go over there? Should I call him? Would he even respond? Maybe he needs this time alone. I don't know him well enough to act the part of a comforting friend and I'm terrible at the role besides.

I pull up Pablo's frequency only to find my signal's blocked. Right. We're on Haven. No outgoing calls are allowed, unless they're through approved holoreceivers.

I groan and lay back on my bed. I slept during part of our flight here and won't need rest again for some time. The only thing I wanted to do, I can't, and I don't want to stay here where I'll overhear Sorin's anguish. Maybe I'm wrong, but I think he'd rather be left alone.

I push myself upright as a soft knock sounds on my door. I frown, confused that someone would be visiting *me*, and cross the room. I pull open the door to find Geo and Nate in the corridor. Geo looks better than he did in the shuttle, and both men offer me strained smiles.

"We thought you might like to visit the bar," Nate says. "We owe you a drink or two for your help, anyway."

"Sure." I leave my door ajar—I don't have anything the mercs can steal besides my armor, and it wouldn't work for them, anyway.

Geo glances warily at Sorin's door as we pass, and Nate shakes his head in warning. "We should leave him be," Nate says softly.

"Who was it?" I ask them. "Brandy?"

Nate nods, but it's Geo who answers. "They didn't have the smoothest relationship. In fact, they were on a break, but he never stopped loving her. He would have traded places with her if he'd known what would happen."

"She isn't the first he's lost to this fight either," Nate adds. "He takes every death personally, but Brandy was… She was special."

"And without you, he'd be mourning me right now too," Geo says. "I shouldn't have signed up for that mission. I knew what it would entail, but I wasn't going to sit by and let this guy take all the glory." He elbows Nate playfully in the ribs, eliciting a weary chuckle. "The heart problem's why I was discharged from the military, you know."

"Can it be fixed?" I ask, genuinely curious.

Geo shrugs. "Transplants are expensive, and I'd be the galaxy's biggest hypocrite if I signed up for ZIEG to have it corrected. Most of the time, I'm fine."

"We manage it," Nate adds pointedly. "I don't think we'll be doing any more marathon stair climbs, though."

The pair leads me to the mess hall, where most of the mercs have gathered around the bar. Duval stands atop a chair, a glass held aloft as he speaks. It takes me only seconds to realize why they've gathered; it's a toast in honor of their dead. Sorin wasn't the only one who lost people on Z-1543. Felix was on Brandy's shuttle, and Van had mentioned casualties before we even reached the mainframe.

"I didn't realize they were here," Geo whispers as Nate gestures toward the empty kitchen area on the opposite side of the room.

"Will Sorin do something similar?" I ask.

Nate shrugs and takes a seat along the kitchen's counter. "Probably, but it won't be today."

"He needs time to recover," Geo adds with a nod. He slides into the seat next to Nate and stares at the scuffed countertop in front of them. "We've lost people before, but never so many at once. Sorin plans everything so meticulously…"

"Casualties are rare," Nate continues as I move around the counter to stand facing them. "Our operations usually go smoothly, like the one on Titan. But we knew Zylar's false planet would be more difficult. Sorin dug up what intel he could, but it wasn't enough. We knew that going in."

Across the room, Van's voice carries over the crowd of mercs around him, and they fall uncharacteristically silent. He continues to hold his glass aloft, and the other mercs have followed his lead.

"I hope you bastards are ready to drink, because we have a list of names tonight. It's not just one or two. We lost eight yesterday." Van's eyes are distant, and I detect genuine sorrow in his tone, though his scarred countenance maintains a stoic façade. "You know the rules. One drink for each name, and two for someone in command."

"Shit," Nate says with a soft chuckle. "That's a lot of booze."

"It's more than my limit," Geo agrees. "It might be wise to leave before they get too drunk. Mercs tend to be rowdy."

Van waits several moments for his audience to quiet, then says, "Felix Shuraji was known to most of you as one of my captains. He was operating under the call sign Vortex when his shuttle was destroyed by Zylar's fucking AIs. Two drinks for Vortex, and his call sign will be retired."

Glasses are lifted to a chorus of shouts, then the mercs pause to down their drinks of choice. There's an unexpected camaraderie amongst Omega Prime, something I never imagined possible between a ragtag group of hired guns, but I find it strangely endearing. I'm beginning to understand why the mercs are so loyal to Van Duval despite his crass nature and terrifying reputation. He doesn't rule them solely by fear; they respect him, and he's earned it with moments like this.

I know what you're thinking. Am I *really* beginning to trust Van Duval?

Hell no. He still has the damned override codes somewhere on this space station. And in Sorin's present state, I don't have the heart to remind him of his promise to steal them. I trust Sorin, but he needs time to mourn.

"Oskar Jay was one of our rookies, but he was gutsier than some of you old-timers," Van continues after a time. He raises a newly filled glass. "Those guts bought us time, but ended his tenure too damned soon. Here's to the man you knew as The Kid."

As the mercs begin to down their next round of drinks, Geo points to the drink mixer on the countertop behind me. "We can make our own drinks, then find a quieter spot to talk. I don't want to stick around for the aftermath of this wake."

I nod in agreement and turn to face the machine. "What's your poison?"

Nate chuckles. "Get yours first. I'll put in our order when you're done."

Five minutes later, I'm following the pair toward the lounge, my drink in hand. Away from the mercs' impromptu wake, Haven's corridors are almost silent. The only person we pass is dressed in Coalition blue, and she's too preoccupied with her tablet to take note of us. The lounge is empty when we arrive. Nate and Geo move toward the plush chairs near the bookcase, and I begin scanning the various titles as I sit down. I don't recognize any of them, and I'm eager to peel back the covers to learn what stories await inside.

"Do you think the mercs would mind if I borrowed a couple books?" I ask.

Nate shakes his head. "I doubt it. I've only seen their boss read on occasion. The rest don't seem interested."

I lift my eyebrows, incredulous. "Duval reads?"

Both men laugh and Geo says, "He's remarkably well-educated for a hired thug."

"Then how did he end up with a rap sheet a parsec long?" I ask.

"That's a story I don't think even Sorin has heard," Nate replies. "Duval doesn't speak of his past prior to Omega Prime."

"And don't try to ask him," Geo adds pointedly. "He'll just get pissed off, and that never ends well for anyone."

I borrow three books from Duval's collection before I leave the lounge and return to my room. Sorin's door is still closed when I walk by, but I can no longer hear his sobs from within. I hope he's resting. If anyone needs a few hours of sleep, it's him.

I close and lock my door, then kick off my boots and settle down with a book titled *Summoned*. It wasn't the title that drew my attention, but the artwork on the creased cover; a fierce, dark-haired woman holds an antique-style pistol at the ready as she faces off against a hulking winged figure with crimson eyes. According to the summary on the back, she's a demon hunter protecting a city called Seattle, a city that was lost generations ago to the mountains of galactic trash that now smothers our home world in its fetid embrace.

If nothing else, the book should be entertaining. I need a diversion after the shitshow that was Z-1543.

I've been immersed in the grim story of the demon-hunting heroine as she stalks the rain-drenched streets of Seattle for several hours when I'm interrupted by a light knock on my door. I scowl and mark my place for later. It never fails; Pablo also had a habit of calling or showing up unexpectedly just as I was beginning to read a pivotal scene.

When I open the door, my irritation evaporates immediately. It's Sorin. His eyes are rimmed in red, his jumpsuit is rumpled, and his hair is mussed, but he looks like he's holding together.

"We need to talk," he says. "Can I come in?"

I step aside, then lock the door as he slumps in the room's only chair. I sit on the edge of my bed facing him but remain silent as I wait for an explanation as to why he's here. He stares at the scuffed floor, his expression shifting between determined and anguished, furious and fearful.

I don't need him to explain that he's received more bad news.

"Our strike on the mainframe was meant to silence the AI government," he says finally, raking a hand through his blond hair. "It's temporarily disabled, but it will be back online before long."

"What went wrong?"

He expels a sigh and shrinks into himself further. "More than I would have liked. Brandy's team started the viral upload, but fled before it was complete. Our team was focused on getting back to the shuttle, and I didn't monitor the virus' status while we ran. I don't have cybernetics to keep me in constant contact with everything like you do." He shakes his head as emotions threaten to overwhelm him. "I should have checked on the status when we reached a safe distance from the planet, but when Brandy's shuttle was destroyed…"

His voice cracks and he squeezes his eyes closed. Tears leak from his eyes, though he fights them with everything he has left.

I chew my lower lip, uncertain what to do or say. I settle on, "I know you loved her. You can't blame yourself for what happened."

A strangled laugh escapes his lips. "Who told you?"

"Geo and Nate."

"I'm not surprised." He groans and wipes at his eyes. "I'm sorry. I didn't mean to break down like this. I thought I had myself under control."

"Never apologize for grief," I reply, quoting something my sister told me after our mother passed. "It means you care."

A faint smile tugs at his mouth. "If anyone ever questions whether you're still human enough to feel emotion, that response is your answer. And after everything I've put you through…"

I shrug. "You're making it right. That's what matters."

"I'm not finished yet, but it won't be long." He crosses his arms as determination returns to his expression. "What I was trying to tell you before I fell apart again is that I need your help a second time. The virus didn't fully upload. The AIs noticed and took countermeasures, though their ability to strike back was severely limited at the time. When they tried to vaporize you and hit the mainframe instead, it compromised their systems significantly."

"I thought our exit went a little too smoothly," I admit. "I kept expecting another cannon to lock onto me at any second, or that we'd find the upper door sealed with no way to open it."

"With the mainframe destroyed, the AIs couldn't link to the planet's interior defense systems. It's a shame the automated systems on the surface remained operational." He hangs his head and takes several moments to collect himself again. "I received intel an hour ago that the AIs are being transported to Zylar HQ on Megatropolis. The only way to finish what we've started is to infect the primary servers there, and that will be no simple task."

"Which is why you need my help again."

"Yes, but not just yours. I need some of VaasTek's solar-powered devices to pull this off too. I need Daaros' backing."

"Will he help?"

Sorin shrugs helplessly. "I don't know. He gave me an ultimatum when we visited. I won't receive any additional funding until I fulfill my promise to you. I was hoping that if you spoke to him, he would change his stance."

"I don't know him that well, but I'll explain the situation."

A glimmer of hope sparks in his eyes. "That's all I ask. He's more willing to work with you than he is with me right now."

"I'm pretty sure that's Pablo's doing. I wanted to call him anyway, but I don't have access to the terminal."

"I'll make sure you get it. The Coalition needs this, Kye. Thank you."

I nod absently, my thoughts straying to the notion that *I need this too.*

I want to wreak havoc on Zylar Inc.'s long-standing system after all that I've learned from Sorin. My contract omitted the existence of override codes, and in my desperation to be cured, I gave up not only my life, but my very fucking soul. And they would have turned me into their puppet if I had refused to follow orders. As pissed as I was at Sorin when I first woke up on Haven, I'm now grateful that he acted as he did—and that he chose *me* as the cyborg he liberated from the invisible chains I didn't know existed.

"If you keep your promise, I'll do anything you want," I reply. "I want to bring them down as much as you do. Maybe more."

He rises from the chair and reaches forward to grip my shoulder. "I know. You're an ally and an asset to my cause, and I won't forget all that you've done. I will get those damned codes and destroy them. It's just a matter of time." When I nod, he releases his grip. "Get some rest. I'll call a briefing as soon as I can cobble together a new plan, and afterward, I'll make sure you're granted a call to Daaros."

"And Pablo," I add firmly.

He smiles. "And Pablo, if he isn't already present for Daaros' call."

"Thanks."

I watch him leave, content with the result of our conversation. I know he'll keep his promise, and he's given me a purpose. Before, I was merely a tool. Now, I'm an ally. An asset.

Zylar Inc. will rue the day they created those fucking codes. I will bring them crashing down, tear them apart, and hurl the pieces into the void of space where they'll never see daylight again. And then I'll grind the remains to dust under my heel.

Sorin will have the aid of the galaxy's only SLTR-BT series cyborg. And if the universe has any sense of justice, he'll break me free of the last of my invisible chains, the mercs be damned.

CHAPTER TWENTY-TWO

THE HEIR TO A DYNASTY

**HAVEN
UNCHARTED SPACE**

Sorin paces across the front of the room like a caged best, the embodiment of restless energy. Dark circles ring his blue eyes, but there is no trace of grief etched into his features. He's either worked through it in record time, or he's damned good at masking its effects. My bet's on the latter.

Behind him, the holoscreen shows a detailed map of Zylar Inc.'s headquarters on Megatropolis, a map I'm intimately familiar with. Half of the chairs in the conference room remain empty, while the other half are occupied by a mix of Coalition forces and hungover mercs. Sorin has summoned everyone on Haven as he prepares to unveil his plan.

Zinn collapses into the chair next to mine with a groan. I lift an eyebrow, amused. She reeks of alcohol, her mohawk is flattened in spots, and her eyes are bloodshot.

"Rough morning?" I tease.

"Shut up, Mech-Man. My guts don't have the processing powers yours do, and as our second-in-command, I couldn't exactly say no to the ritual." She presses her fingers into her forehead and begins to massage it. "I should have gone for the shitty beer Talon likes so much. Tequila was a mistake."

"You toasted all eight with tequila?" I can't stop the laughter that boils up and escapes my throat.

She glares in response. "Sometimes I can be pretty damned stupid. And if you don't reduce your volume, I might be forced to test just how spectacular a cyborg's healing capabilities really are." She pauses to groan and leans forward. "Fuck. No more tequila for Zinn."

"Need the trash bin?" I ask, more seriously this time.

She rams her elbow into my side. "No, Asshole, I do not need a fucking trash bin. I don't have anything left to puke up right now."

I snicker in response. "I'm just here to help, Pinkie."

"You did not just call me Pinkie." She side-eyes me with mock severity, and I laugh again.

"I could think of worse nicknames."

She lifts her eyebrows. "Doubtful."

"Hey, I learned from the best." I flash her my most charming grin.

She rolls her eyes. "I've created a monster, haven't I?"

Our laughter is cut short as Sorin signals for silence. The room has filled during our brief exchange, an even split between Coalition members and mercs. Van stands at one end of the holoscreen, arms crossed as he glowers at the crowd. His eyes are bloodshot, but he appears to be less affected by the evening's wake than most of his crew.

"Thank you all for coming, particularly so soon after the wake." Sorin clasps his hands behind him and stares up at the ceiling as he gathers his thoughts. "Most of you are aware by now that the operation on Z-1543 didn't go as smoothly as planned, and I'm not only referring to our collective casualties. The virus we hoped would cripple the AI government was detected before the upload was complete, and based on my most recent intel, the AIs have enacted a new set of countermeasures."

"Another firewall?" someone asks from the other end of the room.

"In part," Sorin replies. "I won't go into the finer details here, but I'll be putting together a team over the next several days whose sole responsibility will be to thwart the newest defenses and engineer another, more potent, virus."

He pauses to shift the holoscreen's view from the map of Zylar HQ to a GNN video he's queued. A middle-aged woman stands outside the columned entrance to an ivory-toned skyscraper that I recognize as one of the many government buildings on Megatropolis. As Sorin taps his tablet and the video begins to play, the shot pans skyward to reveal hundreds of emergency lights illuminating the night-darkened cityscape.

"I'm Margitte Lemieux, reporting this evening from Senate Tower on Megatropolis. As you can see, the emergency beacons on all government buildings have been lit as our AIs combat a grievous threat to our present way of life." The camera pans back to Margitte, who pauses to stare meaningfully at the camera before she continues. "Since the beacons lit up twenty-six standard hours ago, the AI government has remained silent, but the following statement has been issued by top Zylar Inc. executives."

The screen switches to text as Margitte reads the statement aloud. "A breach has been detected in the mainframe, and we are working diligently to both correct the issue and protect our AIs. The government-controlling entities have been relocated to our most secure facility, where we believe no future attacks can occur. No one has claimed responsibility for this act of galactic terrorism, but top GISA agents have been assigned to investigate."

The video flashes back to Margitte. "GNN will continue to cover this story and all new developments as they occur. Stay tuned for the latest updates. Margitte Lemieux out."

Sorin closes the video. "I plan to release a statement to Coalition channels claiming responsibility for the attack. Those who know where to look will find it, and I want Marim Zylar to understand the scope of what she faces in her new role as CEO."

Van cracks a feral grin. "It's about damned time. You've been working in the shadows for too long. Let the galaxy know who the hell the Resistance is." He lifts his hands and pops the knuckles loudly. "Omega Prime will also release a statement."

Sorin nods as the mercs erupt into a raucous cheer.

Zinn nudges me with an elbow. "They planned this, you know. The boss doesn't usually post anything publicly, so this should be entertaining."

"What will he say? Fuck Zylar? Omega Prime forever?"

She snorts a laugh. "No, he's more subtle than that, believe it or not. You're funny when you want to be, Earth Boy."

I smirk and lean back in my chair. At least she's not calling me Asshole anymore. Earth Boy is an upgrade.

"So what's the next step?" someone calls from the back.

The room quiets in the wake of the question, and Sorin waits until the chatter ceases completely before answering. "We know they've moved the AI mainframe to Zylar HQ on Megatropolis. Breaking in there won't be easy. I know we've done it successfully before, but this time, they'll be anticipating the strike. We'll have more than ZIEG to deal with."

"When do you plan to move?"

Sorin draws a breath and braces himself. "I don't know yet. We have to make sure this strike will be successful, and I want to make damned sure we're ready for *anything* those bastards might throw at us. I also need to design a better viral delivery system, and for that, I require certain difficult-to-obtain components. It will take time to gather the necessary resources, build the appropriate strike teams, and design a foolproof plan. I *will not* see us fail a second time."

Sorin fields several more questions, then asks me to remain behind as the rest of his people are dismissed. Van bellows for the mercs to regroup in the mess hall. A handful of Coalition members linger, seeking Sorin's ear away from the crowd.

I remain seated and begin to scroll through my newsfeed as I wait. Yes, I can still access basic 'net functions while in Haven, I just can't send any messages *out* unless I use an approved terminal. Only the outgoing frequencies are blocked.

GNN is filled with updates regarding the AI government, but there is nothing new since the clip Sorin shared. Whatever countermeasures Zylar Inc. is taking are being kept out of the public eye. I skip past the sports headlines; I've never been that interested in galactic athletics, although I'd probably do okay with them now. Cyborgs are banned from participating though, so it doesn't matter.

I'm skimming the celebrities and entertainment section when a dozen headlines draw my attention. "Botanaari Playboy Pops the Question" is followed by "Public Proposal is met with a Big YES."

I can't help but stare. I know I must look unhinged to the handful of people lingering in the room, but *holy shit*. I didn't expect to find out Pablo was getting married through galactic news channels.

I open the first link and am met with a celebrity reporter sporting neon blue hair gathered in an elaborate twist behind her head. She perches behind a white desk, an image of Daaros kneeling in front of Pablo frozen on the screen to her right. Daaros holds a flat, squarish box in his hands and looks expectantly up at my best friend, whose eyes are wide and shine with emotion.

"In the biggest news since the AI government was attacked, quadrillionaire playboy and CEO Daaros Syl'Vaasis took his human beau out for an elegant dinner at Sileca's last night. While their presence has become commonplace at the trendy restaurant, what happened next was a surprise to everyone but the Botanaari himself." She gestures to the image with a carefully crafted smile. "Inside the box was a pair of jeweled necklaces, designed and crafted on Botanaar by SunStone Gems, one of the galaxy's most elite jewelers."

The image changes to an overhead view of the necklaces. They're platinum bands a quarter-inch wide, meant to be worn in the manner of chokers. Both are adorned with a continuous string of polished opals. I'm no expert, but even I can see the craftsmanship inherent in the design, and I'm aware of the cost of platinum. Daaros spent a small fortune on the matching pieces.

"For those unfamiliar with Botanaari customs, these pieces are their equivalent to engagement rings. They will double as wedding bands once the two are married." The reporter flashes another of her brilliant smiles. "And for those simply *dying* to know the result of this proposal, his beau said yes. Daaros is no longer the galaxy's most eligible bachelor."

I shut down the newsfeed and stare at the floor, stunned. Pablo's getting married.

I access my personal messages, but there's nothing new. I sigh, momentarily disappointed until I realize I haven't received any new messages since I was taken from Zylar HQ by Duval's crew.

Right, I'm supposed to be dead. They cut off my inbox when the death certificate was issued, and it's probably too risky to have Sorin reinstate it.

Damn. I need to call Pablo.

"Kye, is everything alright?"

I startle and look up. Sorin stands in front of me, concern etched on his features.

A nervous laugh escapes my lips. "Yeah, it's fine. Daaros proposed to Pablo. I just… I haven't been in contact with them since before the operation, and I had no idea."

"I can set up a call from here," he offers. "What I wanted to talk with you about can wait."

I scramble to my feet. "Yeah. I need to talk to him. Pablo, I mean."

"I'll ping his frequency if you'll close the door?"

When I turn around after securing the door, I'm met with a blank screen, then an automated audio message. "I'm sorry, the person you are trying to reach is not accepting unsolicited calls right now. Please try again later."

"Shit," I hiss. "He's turned off his frequency because of the fucking paparazzi."

Sorin chuckles. "Don't worry. I'll call Daaros' apartment. Our call should go through there."

He disconnects and taps his tablet several times. Another blank screen pops up, but this time, I recognize the voice speaking when it answers. "Mr. Syl'Vaasis is not taking any calls at this time. If you're a reporter, please contact his PR team at—"

"Araan," I cut in. "It's Kye. Is Pablo there?"

The display flickers, and the face of Daaros' personal assistant appears. He grins and adjusts his white fedora. "Mr. Noriega is in final exams today and tomorrow," he says, "but our employer is available. I assume you saw the news?"

"Yeah. That's why I'm calling." I force a smile, but I can't hide my disappointment. I'd hoped Pablo would be there.

"I assume we can't reach you wherever you're presently located," Araan says with a pointed glance at Sorin. "If you schedule a timeslot this evening, I will ensure Mr. Noriega is present to receive your call. Would you like to speak with Daaros?"

"Sure. Why not? And we'll try to call after seven Galactic Standard Time."

Araan snickers. "Such enthusiasm. I won't mention it to Daaros. Just a moment while I patch you through to his personal line."

A few seconds later, Daaros appears on screen. He's wearing a black button-down shirt with the collar flipped up in the current fashion, but I can see the band he wears around his throat where the collar opens in the front. He grins, genuine excitement in his eyes.

"I knew you'd call," he says. "I wanted to tell you what I had planned, but given recent events, I never had the chance. And our mutual *friend* makes it extremely difficult to reach you," he adds with an imperious frown for Sorin.

"Yeah, well, congratulations. I was hoping Pablo would be there too. I—"

He waves dismissively. "I know. I was going to wait until after his final exams were finished, but when the *diivoraa* arrived, I couldn't." He tugs absently at his collar, revealing more of the opal-studded band beneath. "They are exquisite. My greatest fear was that he would say no. It is nothing to recoup the financial loss of acquiring these, but a rejection would have left me a broken man. He is my light."

"You didn't have anything to worry about," I assure him. "Pablo was smitten with you from your first meeting. And that party we went to sealed the deal."

"And you approve?" he asks, an uncharacteristic wariness in his eyes.

"Why wouldn't I? He's happier than I've ever seen him, and he fucking *adores* you. As long as you don't hurt him, I have no objections."

Daaros' smile is brilliant. "I wasn't sure how you would feel. I'm not human, and you are the closest thing he has to family."

"Honestly, I'm glad he met you. He needed someone in his life, and for many years, he wanted that someone to be *me*. I couldn't be that. He understood, but…" I shrug awkwardly. "He wasn't happy. And he deserves to be happy. With you, he is."

Daaros nods in understanding. "We have spoken of you at length. I feared I would never receive your approval. Telling my fathers of my intentions was easier than facing you, but I see now that I didn't need to worry."

"You didn't. How did your fathers take the news?"

Daaros rolls his eyes and expels a sigh. "Lord Syl'Vaasis was disappointed until he learned Pablo is in school to become an engineer, then he grudgingly accepted my decision. He values those with the ambition to make their own future, and solar engineers are valued in our society. It also helped when I reminded him I can still produce an heir to our dynasty with the help of a clinic. As the *paavylaar* of the pairing, any child I carry will bear the Syl'Vaasis name."

My mind is reeling with the onslaught of information. I understand the Botanaari term he used translates loosely into Standard as "seed father." I don't know the biological specifics, but I'll look them up later when I'm not in danger of blushing furiously in Daaros' presence. Instead, I latch onto the first detail he shared like it's a life raft.

"Your father's a lord?"

"Technically, he is the Vynaas, but 'lord' is the human equivalent, I believe."

"It's closer to 'king' or 'emperor,' if I'm not mistaken," Sorin cuts in. "Your father is akin to our monarchs of old."

I stare at Daaros. "If your father is the king, that means you're a blasted *prince*."

He rolls his eyes dramatically. "Yes, I am royalty according to your people's labels, and my *paavylaar's* heir. This is why I don't tell humans when I first meet them. You all treat me like I am the sun god of ancient times, and it's utterly *exhausting*."

This explains everything about Daaros. His mannerisms, his wealth, his position at VaasTek, his network of contacts... Everything.

"Why isn't it mentioned in your public record?" I ask.

Daaros lifts his eyebrows with a smirk. "It is. I believe it reads 'Heir to the Syl'Vaasis Dynasty.' For someone with unlimited 'net access in his head, your research skills are incredibly lacking."

I flush at his words. "I only looked up your record once, and I was still adjusting to…what I am."

"Then I shouldn't be surprised to learn that you don't know of my *siindolaar's* position in our society either." At my blank stare, he chuckles. "My *other* father. He is the Minister of Intelligence on Botanaar."

I glance between him and Sorin as more pieces fall into place. His fathers can't be publicly tied to the Resistance Coalition, so they funnel both money and information through their son. And Daaros' threats to pull funding weren't idle; he has the influence to do it if Sorin pisses him off. It also explains the paparazzi's fascination with the man I believed was just a wealthy CEO.

"Holy shit."

Daaros shrugs. "Now you know. And rest assured, I will do everything in my power to keep Pablo happy. He led a difficult life—as did you. I can give him anything he desires, and I will, if he asks for it."

"You love him, don't you?"

Daaros smiles wistfully. "I do. With every fiber of my being, I do."

"Can I ask you one thing?"

His smile falters, but he nods. "Of course."

"When you plan the wedding… Botanaari have weddings, don't they?" I feel heat rising in my face again. I really need to learn more about Daaros' people in my down time.

"We have *briia*, which is equivalent."

"Okay. When you plan the wedding, am I allowed to attend?"

He laughs, relieved and elated. "Yes. Pablo has already made me promise you will be his 'best man,' whatever that means for humans."

"I'm glad," I reply with a grin to match his. "Tell Pab I'll call tonight. I gave Araan a time."

"Yes, I see he's already placed it on our schedule." Daaros leans back and crosses his arms. "I'm glad we've had this discussion, Kye. It has alleviated most of my fears."

I nod and offer him a parting smile. "Congrats, Daaros. I'm happy for you. For both of you."

DAAROS SYL'VAASIS

CHAPTER TWENTY-THREE

WORST COOKS IN THE GALAXY

HAVEN
UNCHARTED SPACE

I shake my head in disbelief as Sorin disconnects the call. "I can't believe Daaros is royalty. How did I not know this?"

Sorin chuckles. "To most of the galaxy, he's a wealthy CEO who likes to host lavish parties from time to time. His link to the Botanaari Dynasty *is* in his public record—you can't hide something like that—but he doesn't like to flaunt his royal background. Unless I do something to piss him off, that is."

"It's why you did as he asked when you first brought me here."

"Yes. And you assumed it was only about money." He smiles ruefully. "That's enough about Daaros. I asked you to remain behind for another reason, though I'm glad the two of you talked."

"Yeah. Me too. So, what's up?"

"It's time we updated your identity credentials again."

"I guess I can't be a fake rum salesman forever." I force a laugh, but it sounds uneasy even to my ears. The process wasn't painful the first time, but it *was* awkward, and I'm not looking forward to round two.

Sorin motions me to follow him as he walks to the door. "We'll go through the update in my room. My tools are there, and we won't risk anyone walking in to interrupt the process."

He glances pointedly at the room's corners, and I wonder if the mercs have installed cameras. Sorin isn't wearing his glasses right now, but he has worn them here in the past. Maybe he doesn't trust his hired guns as much as I believed.

"Sorin?" I ask as we exit into the corridor.

"Don't," he says firmly. "We'll talk in my room."

I shrug and keep my mouth shut as I follow him through Haven's winding halls. We pass more mercs than Coalition members along our journey, but most don't pay us any mind. A few of Sorin's people nod in silent greeting as we pass, though none speak openly.

Something is going on, and I don't think I'm going to like it one damned bit.

As soon as we're inside Sorin's room and the door is closed, I blurt, "What the hell is going on?"

He holds up his hands, palm-out, in a gesture of surrender. "It's not what you think. Duval asked me to install security cameras throughout Haven. I had a team work on it overnight. He believes one of his people is feeding intel to GISA, and he's determined to catch them in the act. I also installed skimmers on the two holoreceivers capable of sending outgoing calls."

"So why the secrecy just now?" I cross my arms and lean against the wall, frustrated and confused, a state I don't enjoy.

"Two reasons. If Duval is right, whoever is feeding information to GISA may have access to the camera feeds. What I wanted to speak with you about can't reach an investigator's desk."

"Then why hold the briefing here? It makes no sense."

"The cameras are shielded from remote uplinks and only feed to a single tablet, which Duval locked in his control room. He ordered his entire crew to sit in on the briefing. The cameras can be viewed in real-time, but we've set them up so they can't record. Essentially, they don't leave an electronic record."

I stare at him blankly. I don't understand how this makes the situation any better.

He sighs and rakes a hand through his hair. "Let me try again. The cameras don't store what they're seeing. Only someone actively watching the tablet they're connected to can view what's on the screen at the moment it occurs. Since all of the mercs were in the briefing, there was no one inside the control room. The only way to send what we discussed to GISA is to record the video from a secondary device while watching the tablet."

"But can't the spy still *tell* GISA what was said?" I ask.

"Yes, but without concrete proof, GISA is at the mercy of a merc's word." He flashes a self-satisfied grin. "And I'm sure even you know how much weight that will carry."

"Not much. Okay, I get it." I pause to gather my thoughts and stumble across another question. "You said there were two reasons you wanted to meet here."

"Yes. I didn't think you'd like me plugging into your system where others might be watching."

I drop my arms to my sides with a nod, relieved by his answer. "You're right. I definitely don't want an audience while you're tinkering with my files. And if someone is watching, they'd know I'm here. There can't be that many missing cyborgs in the galaxy."

"Another reason why we need to update your identity."

"Who will I be this time? Not that the rum salesman was *bad*, but…" I shrug helplessly. How do I explain that I thought the notion of Jerome Ells from the Aloha Moon was ridiculous?

Sorin smiles knowingly. "It worked to get you through Ring Eight's checkpoint, and your next persona will need to as well. Which brings me to the other reason why I wanted to speak with you here."

"You need Daaros' tech."

"Yes, but I can't meet with him directly. Not on the Rings or anywhere in Zylar Inc.-controlled space, for that matter. And Daaros can't risk coming *here* or going to Cobalt Asteroid. He's being watched."

I frown. "Does he know?"

Sorin chuckles. "Of course, he knows. You know who his fathers are."

"Right." I tip my head back to rest it against the wall and stare at the rust-stained ceiling. "That's why you need me to go to him. I'll be…someone else, and we can talk safely in his apartment."

"Yes, but I can't send you alone. Duval doesn't know I destroyed the primary set of override codes, and he thinks you're cooperative because of them. Until I manage to extract the other set from his safe—which will be more difficult now with the camera system—you have to act your part. I'm sorry."

"Okay…" I expel a frustrated breath. "Who is my damned handler then?"

"Quiara will join you. Her record is clean, but I plan to update her credentials before you go just in case. Given Daaros' engagement, no one will be surprised when a pair of caterers arrive to meet with him."

"You do realize I've never cooked anything in my life?" I ask with a laugh. "I grew up on protein cubes and have only recently branched out to shakes and tacos. And from what Pablo has told me, Botanaari cuisine is...*different.*"

"If anyone questions you, Quiara is there to act as your assistant. Her background in solar tech is useful for the placement of sunlamps and the various wavelengths they should emit. You'll play the role of culinary expert. Do a bit of research on fine dining until you're confident you can answer any questions the AI kiosk may throw at you. It won't ask you to demonstrate your nonexistent cooking skills." Sorin lifts his eyebrows knowingly. "You'll be fine, Kye."

"Obviously, you've thought this through." I shake my head, amused. "Fine. I'll pretend to be a chef, but make sure everyone on this damned station knows I can't actually cook."

"I make no promises. And Zinn will act as your chauffeur," Sorin continues.

I stare at the ceiling again with an exaggerated groan. "She's going to love that."

"Duval won't let you operate without one of his people along for the ride, and she's taken a liking to you." Sorin shrugs. "It's better her than most of the others on his crew."

"I'm not looking forward to the nicknames I earn during this expedition."

"But it will give you a chance to see Pablo," he says. "And I think you want that."

"Yeah. Would it ruin our cover if I asked to stay there for a few days? I want to *talk* with him, Sorin. Not just discuss business with his...fiancé."

Damn, it's weird to say that, but I'm thrilled for Pablo. He's found his handsome prince despite everything life has thrown in our way.

"I'll create a fictional schedule for you," Sorin promises. "It's not unusual for someone of Daaros' bearing to require multiple days with prospective caterers, but I don't think I can promise you more than three days on Ring Eight."

I grin. Three days is more than I'd hoped for. "It's a deal. So, who am I this time, besides a phony chef?"

Sorin pulls out his tablet with a laugh and taps several times before turning the screen to face me. The fabricated profile on display shows my face next to a false name and a list of achievements I sincerely hope I'm never asked to provide evidence of. Orion Damascus is a graduate of the Galactic Culinary Institute and the owner of a private catering company that specializes in hosting parties for the wealthy elite. He's originally from New Paris, but relocated after completing school and now resides on Diamante, the entertainment capital of the galaxy. A client list three parsecs long follows his credentials.

I stare at the profile, then stare at Sorin. He's lost his damned mind if he thinks *this* identity is a good decision. The first security checkpoint I walk through is going to ping my credentials and broadcast it to everyone in the vicinity, even with my firewalls up. I don't want to be inundated with requests for my supposed services when I'm not even sure I know how to boil water.

"This is a joke, right?"

He presses his lips together as he tries and fails to suppress laughter. I begin to relax, then he says, "It's not a joke, Kye. The other caterers vying for Daaros' favor as he prepares for his *briia* will have similar public profiles. Your identity must be believable."

"But this *isn't*. No one has ever heard of—" I pause to check the name on the tablet, "—Orion Damascus, who has apparently cooked for the star of every holoflick that has ever been made."

"And Daaros is the heir to his people's monarchy. He isn't going to hire a random chef he met on the street. He'll hire the galaxy's *best*. It's your cover, and unless you can come up with something else that will get you onto Ring Eight without questions, we're sticking with it."

"I…" I slump against the wall with a groan. I hate that he's right, and I'm frustrated that I can't come up with a better solution.

"Orion Damascus has a nice ring to it," Sorin continues relentlessly.

"It sounds like one of those damned superhero characters from the holovids." I stare at the floor and refuse to look at Sorin. "If you were going for inconspicuous, that name fails."

"It's not that bad," he says, mildly hurt. "And I promise that no one will ask you to bake a souffle."

I don't even know what a souffle *is*, and I'm not in the mood to look it up. "If anyone asks me to do more than operate an automated drink mixer, I'm going to be pissed."

"They won't—"

"Even Zinn." I glare at him. "And she *will*."

"Zinn is an exception to every damned rule there is, and you know it."

He has a point, but I still don't have to like my supposed profession or the name he's chosen.

"Fine," I concede grudgingly. "I'll pretend to be Daaros' damned chef if it means I can see Pablo for a few days."

He grins and whips a cable from one of his pockets. "Shall we?" he asks as he plugs it into his tablet.

I slump further against the wall. "Yeah, let's get this over with."

"Your enthusiasm is contagious," he says dryly.

"It's fucking *weird* having someone rummaging around in my head," I snap. "I can feel you making the updates. I'm not sure I'll ever get used to it. It's one part of what I am that I wasn't expecting when I signed on with ZIEG."

He nods in understanding. "Typically, you wouldn't have needed updates like this, but anytime ZIEG required an adjustment to your 'net access or internal database, it would have been a similar process. I'm sorry I can't make this any easier for you."

His tone is so sincere, I immediately feel like an asshole for losing my temper.

"Sorry," I mumble. "It's not your fault. Let's do this."

Thirty minutes later, I am Orion Damascus to anyone scanning my biometrics, and we're waiting for Quiara and Zinn to arrive. Sorin wants to discuss the specifics of our next mission with them in person, and his room is the only space he believes is free of cameras or listening devices.

I sit on the floor while we wait. Sorin's room has a single chair and the cot I assume he slept on, and he's in the chair. It feels wrong to sit on his makeshift bed.

Sorin taps on his tablet for a few minutes, then says, "I've made a list of the items I'll need from the Botanaari in order to make our next strike work. I would send it to you, but your inbox is still sealed and I don't believe it's worth the risk to reactivate it yet."

I lift my eyebrows, certain he has something in mind as an alternative. "And?"

"I can upload the list directly into your databanks."

Great. That means he'll be tinkering inside my head again, but I understand enough about my system to realize his suggestion is valid. The list will be more secure inside me than it would be if he sent it over the 'net with the best encryptions available.

I nod absently. "Fine."

"No argument this time?" he asks as he crosses the tiny room.

"I'm not stupid, Sorin. I know why you asked." I lean forward, resting my forearms across my knees, then bend my head to expose the back of my neck. "Just make it quick. I don't want the others to see this."

"Okay."

He plugs the cable in, and I hear him tap on his tablet. The upload only takes seconds, but it's long enough for his door to swing open during the process. I glare at the door, then at Zinn as she strides into the room. When her eyes meet mine, the smirk dissolves from her face.

"Did no one teach you to knock first?" I snarl as Sorin pulls the cable free.

"Blue-eyes said it was urgent." She shrugs. "Everyone on Haven knows what you are. You don't need to hide it."

"Kye is still adjusting," Sorin replies softly. "Don't make it harder on him than it already is." He peers down at me, ignoring the brash merc as she perches on the empty chair. "You should have everything you need when you speak with Daaros."

I access the file and scan the list. Most of the items have technical names that I'm unfamiliar with, but as the CEO of VaasTek, I'm sure our Botanaari friend will understand. I'm not going to check out from the current conversation to look them up, not with Zinn staring at me in the strange manner she presently is.

I nod to Sorin, then shoot a frown at the pink-haired merc. "What?"

"Does it hurt when he…?" She gestures vaguely at the back of her neck.

"No."

"Good. Because I…" She shakes her head and averts her gaze. "Never mind."

I narrow my eyes, but she refuses to look at me again. What the hell was that all about?

A knock sounds on the door, sparing us from further awkwardness as Quiara arrives. I push myself up to standing and nod to her in greeting as Sorin closes the door.

"The boss must have told you about our little problem," Zinn says. "I don't know why else you'd insist on meeting here, Ghosty."

"He did," Sorin confirms. "I hope he takes care of it, because until then, your people are off my payroll, present company and Duval excluded."

"Yeah, he was pissed when he found out." Zinn leans back in the chair and stretches. "I've heard my share of rants when it comes to GISA, but he was in rare form last night. The wake didn't help matters either. Whoever is trying to fuck us over will be *lucky* if the boss tosses them out the airlock."

"And if they're unlucky?" I ask.

"He'll take his time with them. That shit isn't pretty, Earth Boy." She turns to Sorin. "Enough about our little problem. Why are *we* here?"

"I need to deliver a document to Daaros on Ring Eight. It's in Kye's database." Sorin nods to me. "Since your boss won't let him off Haven without merc supervision, he has allowed me to borrow you for this mission."

Zinn snorts a laugh. "When I signed on with Omega Prime, 'babysitter' wasn't part of the job description. It's a good thing I like our resident cyborg, or I'd be pissed with this assignment." She flashes a grin at me. "I'm not sure he likes me, but that's his loss."

"I'm not sure either," I reply with a smirk. "Tolerate, yes. Like is up for debate."

"But it isn't a *no*." She folds her arms and winks. "There are worse people to travel halfway across the galaxy with. At least I know you're good in a fight."

"I don't think you'll need to worry about fighting during this mission," Sorin cuts in. "You'll travel to Cobalt Asteroid with the rest of the Coalition when we leave. We have uniforms stashed on our base, and I believe you'll need them for this. You aren't going to loiter in the shuttle this time around, Pink."

"I assume you've tweaked my credentials, then?" she asks.

Sorin nods. "Yours and Quiara's. They're live now."

Quiara withdraws a tablet and begins to tap across the screen. Zinn makes no move to check what he's done to her identity.

"Just tell me, Baby Blues. I'm not married to my gadgets like your people are, and I don't have 'net access hardwired in my skull like our friend does."

"You're caterers," Sorin says. "Or rather, *they* are. *You* are their delivery driver."

"You don't think I can cut it in the kitchen?" Zinn asks, feigning hurt.

Sorin crosses his arms. "I remember the toaster incident all too well. No, you're better off driving."

"Toaster incident?" I ask.

Zinn shakes her head. "Not a chance, Killer. But I am curious to know what *you* will be cooking for the Plant Boy while we're visiting."

I roll my eyes and groan, then frown at Sorin. "I told you she'd ask."

He tips his head back and laughs. "That you did. I'm sure you can think of something before you reach Megatropolis."

"Not funny, Sorin." I turn to Zinn and shrug. "If he had assigned our roles based on culinary experience, I'd be the guy who washes your delivery van's windows, not the damned chef."

Zinn roars with laughter. "So you'll be making protein shakes for the Green Guy? *This* I need to see."

"No. Whatever you did to the toaster, I'm pretty sure I can do worse."

"You're on." She flashes a grin at Sorin. "Operation Worst Cooks in the Galaxy is a go. When do we leave?"

Sorin chuckles. "In two days. Then you'll stay on Cobalt Asteroid while I finalize a schedule for your visit to Ring Eight, among other things."

I'm back in the conference room with Sorin as he places another call to Daaros' apartment just after seven. Araan answers as he did before, and when he connects the video feed, he's grinning.

"I'll patch you through. Pablo has been pacing the apartment since he arrived home, and Daaros was beginning to fear he'd wear holes in the carpet." Araan laughs to himself and adjusts his hat. "I'll let them know your call is in the queue."

Seconds later, Pablo appears on the screen wearing the matching *diivoraa* to Daaros' opal-strewn band around his throat. He's alone, but I can hear something sizzling in the background.

"Kye!"

"Hey, Pab. I hear congratulations are in order."

He blushes, then nods. "Yeah. I wanted to call you as soon as it happened. I tried sending you a message, but your inbox is down. When Daar said you called earlier and would call again, I knew you must have heard."

"It was all over GNN's entertainment section," I tease, causing his blush to deepen. "I'm happy for you."

He beams. "I didn't think his fathers would approve. I mean, he's the Vynaas' *heir*. Part of me still doesn't believe this is happening."

"My fathers weren't the difficult part," Daaros calls from somewhere beyond the screen's field of view. "Your friend is the one who scared me."

I roll my eyes. "I already told him he had nothing to worry about."

"You have to be my best man," Pablo blurts, blushing anew. "Um, I meant for that to come out as a question."

I laugh. "You knew I'd say yes, so it's done. We can talk more about it later when I stop by for a visit."

"You're coming here?"

"I am. Only for a few days, but I'll take what I can get."

Pablo's grin nearly splits his face. "I can't wait to see you again." He turns to peer over his shoulder. "Daar, Kye's going to visit us!"

Daaros' reply is muffled and I can't make out his response.

Pablo swivels to face me, the grin still plastered on his face. "He says your room is as you left it. You never got the chance to fully move in before…everything happened."

"If I survive Sorin's bullshit, I fully intend to work through my contract with your boyfr—fiancé." I shake my head. "Still getting used to that."

"You'd better survive. We didn't scrape by all those years on Earth for you to die now." He crosses his arms and glares at Sorin, who stands silently in the corner of the room. "And you'd better keep your promise to him."

"I will," Sorin replies. "Don't worry."

"I assume your visit isn't just for fun," Pablo continues. "It's *his* business, isn't it?"

"It is, but Sorin's giving me a couple extra days with you. Like I said, we can catch up then." I offer him another smile. "It will be good to see you."

"Are you still going to show up as a… What was it? Rum salesman?"

I begin to laugh, recalling my earlier conversation with Zinn. "I've moved on. I'm now Orion Damascus, the worst chef in the galaxy."

"Oh, this sounds like a story I need to hear." Pablo snickers and flicks a glance at Sorin, who merely shakes his head, exasperated. "You'll have to tell me once you're here."

"Deal."

CHAPTER TWENTY-FOUR

A MARK OF FRIENDSHIP

RESISTANCE COALITION HQ
COBALT ASTEROID, GAMMA CEPHEI SYSTEM

The landing pad is a hive of frantic activity as we step off the shuttle on Cobalt Asteroid. A dozen other shuttles are prepared and waiting nearby, their crews scrambling to finalize preflight checklists before departure. About half wear the blue jumpsuits the Coalition seems to favor, while the rest are in body armor that looks suspiciously identical to the military variety I've seen Kelsey sport on occasion.

"What's going on?" I ask, hoping Sorin or Quiara will share a few details.

"Standard operations," Sorin replies with a shrug. "We always have a few running."

"Right." I scan the landing pad again and shake my head. This looks more involved than *standard operations*.

Quiara touches my arm lightly. "You'll learn soon enough. It's better if fewer people know the details. In case something goes wrong," she adds with a pointed look.

"Do *you* know the details?"

She laughs softly. "No, but even if I did, I wouldn't tell you."

"Think about it this way, Le Chef," Zinn cuts in. "What if Ghosty here wasn't as good with your ID as he thought he was? What if you're flagged at a checkpoint, and they make a connection between you and the Coalition? If you know the details of their operation, you're a security risk. Stop asking stupid-ass questions and focus on why we're here. We have our own mission to carry out."

"A mission that *they*," Sorin gestures at the Coalition forces around us, "know nothing of, for the same reasons."

"Fine. You've made your point," I growl.

I frown at Sorin's back as we walk toward the Coalition's main apartment complex. I understand his position and the reason for the secrecy, but I'd still like to understand more of what he has planned since I've been told I'm so crucial to his organization's success.

Or maybe *I'm* not crucial, but my cybernetics are. He still hasn't made an attempt to steal my codes back from Duval, and I'm beginning to wonder if he ever will. He's had ample opportunity, hasn't he? Why is he waiting? There has to be more involved than the mercs' fancy new surveillance system at play. Or was that just a convenient excuse meant to appease me for a while?

I bite back a frustrated snarl and follow behind the others. I hope I won't regret placing my damned trust in Sorin.

Zinn peers over her shoulder with an amused smirk. "Only *you* could manage to stomp around on an asteroid with half standard gravity, Metal Man."

"Jealous?" I ask dryly.

"Nah. I like lower gravity worlds. They put a spring in my step."

Sorin chuckles and Quiara rolls her eyes at the merc's attempt at humor.

I shake my head. "That was terrible."

"And you're too damned serious today. What's your problem? I thought you wanted to visit Ring Eight." She crosses her arms and scowls.

"I do."

I'm not going to voice my concerns to her. They might be unfounded anyway. Or they might be valid, in which case I'm better off not saying anything with Sorin five feet away.

"Then what the hell?" she demands, frustration seeping into her tone.

I glance at Sorin, but he's facing forward and doesn't see. "I don't want to talk about it."

Zinn's scowl morphs into a suspicious frown. "Fair enough. Maybe later."

"Don't count on it."

I haven't forgotten Zinn is Omega Prime's second-in-command, and I'm well aware she knows about the fucking codes. Until I see them destroyed, I can't trust her. I *want* to trust Sorin, but his delay has me on edge. What I need is a distraction, something to take my mind off this problem, if only for a short time. Dwelling on it isn't helping matters, and there's nothing I can do anyway.

I begin to browse the 'net's vast collection of culinary information as we walk. If I'm supposed to pass myself off as a chef, then I need to know the difference between a skillet and a saucier. And it can't hurt to learn how to properly make toast so I don't fall victim to Zinn's prior mistake, whatever it was.

No, she still hasn't told me. And yes, this is the first method of distraction that came to mind. Cobalt Asteroid isn't exactly bursting with entertainment venues, and I was forced to leave my borrowed paperbacks behind. Duval has a strict no-loans-on-interstellar-missions policy. Leave it to the scar-faced merc to become sentimental over *books*.

"Maybe I should ask Blue-eyes if he can update your attitude before we leave," Zinn replies. "I'm sure he has an anti-surliness program he can install."

I glare at her, only to receive her most mischievous grin in return. She's incorrigible.

"Zylar Inc. has a strict policy against tampering with personalities," Sorin says over his shoulder. "You'll have to find a way to make him more pleasant on your own, or learn to tolerate his moodiness."

I roll my eyes. I wouldn't be "moody" if Sorin just filched my override codes and destroyed them like he promised. Or if I didn't have to put up with Zinn's constant teasing, or the fact she calls me a bot every so often. Or if someone would finally just clue me in on the bigger picture and the specific role I'm supposed to play in it. To them, I'm just a tool, a curiosity, and a convenient receptacle for storing sensitive documents.

Yeah, I think I have every right to be "moody."

The sooner we reach Ring Eight, the better. Seeing Pablo will help, and hopefully I'll have time to talk with him alone. I doubt any of the present company fully understands what I've been through, and I don't know if they even care. Well, Sorin might. I shouldn't discount him.

"You'd be 'moody' too, if you were in my position," I growl. "I didn't sign up for this shit like you did."

Zinn's relentless grin falters, and I know I've struck a chord. Good.

She opens her mouth to respond, but Sorin holds up a hand in warning. We're almost to the entrance of the apartment complex, and I'm itching to lock myself in my room. I haven't had a moment alone in twenty-seven standard hours, and there's only so much of Zinn Jarek I can take. I surpassed my limit before we landed on this rock.

"Don't," Sorin says firmly. "Leave him be for now, Zinn."

"Fine. I'll let Bot Boy work through his PMS alone." She stomps past Sorin and through the door without another word.

Sorin releases a weary sigh and turns to face me. "You shouldn't provoke her."

"I wasn't—"

He lifts his hand again, and I snap my jaw closed. Why the hell am I in trouble with him too?

"Omega Prime has its uses," he says evenly. "The Coalition needs them, and we both need you. I know I haven't been entirely forthcoming—"

I snort derisively and cross my arms, but Sorin continues undeterred.

"—about your role, but it's better if you *don't* know every detail. Zinn had a valid point. If I missed a single line of code during the update of your profile, you *will* be flagged at the first security checkpoint you pass through. Your ID is a hell of a lot more difficult to update than hers or Quiara's. You don't understand the level of security Zylar Inc. put into your cybernetics, do you? And you certainly don't seem to grasp the level of risk I'm taking by sending you to Ring Eight right now."

I cross my arms and stare in challenge. "Maybe you should enlighten me."

Sorin clenches his jaw, then shoots a pointed glance at Quiara. "You should go. Your group needs disguises."

She nods and scurries through the door, eyes wide with concern. I'm pissed, but I'm not *violent*. Sorin is in no danger from me, but her reaction sends a lance of guilt straight through my gut. Maybe I'm overreacting.

"Look, I—"

Sorin shakes his head, cutting me off a second time. "I know you're frustrated. I would be too, but picking fights with your allies isn't productive."

I study him for several seconds. His heart rate is up, but that's due to his anger. I don't detect any deception in his expression and his tone is sincere, albeit furious. Okay, I'll admit I've fucked up.

"I want to believe you," I concede, "but how can I with those codes hanging over my head?"

"I *will* retrieve them," he says firmly. "Losing Brandy derailed my plans. I *meant* to take the codes while my team was installing the new camera system on Haven, but I was distracted. I couldn't focus. It slipped my mind, and I'm sorry, for your sake. But for mine? I haven't been given more than an hour alone to grieve. I know you've lost people, Kye. Try to understand."

I stare at him for several seconds, speechless. I've been a selfish bastard, haven't I?

"I'm sorry," I mumble. "I didn't think…"

"While you've had hours to yourself the last few days, I've had very few," he continues in a lower tone. "Keeping the Coalition's operations on track is never an easy task, but pushing through my personal anguish to make sure it's done? It has taken every damned ounce of energy I possess to do it. I'm running on fumes, but I have no time to rest. Not if I want my people to succeed."

I nod, chastised, but can't muster anything more to say.

"I *will* keep my promise," he says after a moment. "I just need more time."

He grips my shoulder, then motions to the door. "Zinn probably headed to the bar on the ground level if you want to avoid her. Or if you'd like to apologize. I'll leave that choice up to you."

I opt for an apology and locate Zinn right where Sorin said she'd be. The bar has a hatchet-throwing game, and she's predictably launching razor-sharp projectiles at holographic targets when I arrive. An untouched drink sits in a puddle of condensation on the empty table behind her.

The rage etching her face as she throws the nanosteel weapon forces me to momentarily reconsider. If I piss her off any more, she might hurl the next hatchet at my face. But I'm here, and I need to say *something*. My previous frustration wasn't her fault, but I chose to unleash it on her like the asshole I sometimes am.

I head to the bar and order a drink for myself, stubbornly hoping the alcohol will give me courage with its flavor alone. The trouble with my life as a cyborg is that I no longer feel the effects of my drinks; my ultra-efficient digestive system takes care of the liquor before it wends its way into my bloodstream. I can drink any merc under the table and never get a buzz.

It's not as fun as it sounds. Trust me.

I walk toward Zinn and wait as she throws another hatchet through the virtual target. The blade slices through a man-shaped silhouette and continues to spin in its deadly arc until it strikes the foam-coated wall beyond. The blade is buried several inches deep, a testament to the power behind her throw.

With her hands empty, I close the distance. "Zinn?"

She slides her eyes sideways to glare at me without turning her head. "What the hell do you want now?"

I swallow the upwelling of irritation that threatens to burst forth and close my eyes for a moment. "I talked with Sorin. I was being an ass."

Her head swivels toward me slowly, wary disbelief in her eyes. "I don't know what the hell Blue-eyes did to make you so pissy, but I'm glad you sorted it out. The last thing we need on Ring Eight is you losing your shit over nothing."

I grit my teeth. "It wasn't nothing, but I shouldn't have taken it out on you. I'm sorry."

There, I said it. She'll either accept the apology, or send me racing through the bar with a hatchet whirling toward my back. I *might* be able to avoid the weapon if I increase my speed to its max, but it's not something I want to test. Not when the alternative is death or maiming.

"Look, maybe I don't seem like the caring type, but you know what? You've grown on me. When we were sent to Zylar HQ to off Big Bad Reg and pick you up, I didn't think anything of it. It was just another damned job, and you were just another weapon to add to our arsenal. I didn't realize cyborgs retained so much of their humanity." She sighs and picks up her drink, then downs it in a single gulp. "What they did to you was fucked up. I don't really blame you for acting out. Hell, I would have trashed Haven and put so much plasma through Ghosty and the boss that they'd be nothing more than bloody slag heaps if I'd been in your position. You have more restraint than I do."

"It's not restraint." I finish my drink and set the empty glass on the table next to hers. "Do you know what the override codes do, beyond knock me unconscious? Do you know why they wanted them so badly?"

She shakes her head. "The boss didn't mention anything, and like I said, it was just another job. I didn't ask questions. The merc's code and all that."

Can I trust her with the truth? I don't know, but I feel like I owe her *something.*

"Let's just say I'm more afraid of what those codes can do to me than I am of dying in Sorin's bullshit schemes." I gesture at the bartender for a refill. "It's why I've 'agreed' to help him. If I don't, I'll be worse off than I was back on Earth."

"The fucking Ghost is blackmailing you?" Zinn's eyebrows rise in genuine surprise. "I didn't think he had it in him."

I shrug. "So is your boss."

"Now *that* I can believe." She signals to the bartender, then hops onto her chair. "Sit down, Earth Boy. I want to hear your story. Maybe I can help."

"I doubt it." I slump into the seat across from her and stare at the tabletop. "You know I joined ZIEG to get off Earth. Things were…bad there. Not just on the planet, but for me. The average life expectancy for someone living there is thirty-five. Not the galactic standard of a century and a half. *Thirty-five.*"

I look up as the bartender arrives with our refills and nod in silent thanks. Zinn's eyes never leave my face during the exchange.

"When I was offered the post with ZIEG, I took it. They promised the gene therapy I needed to become eligible for space travel, but when I met with their doctor at the spaceport, they found tumors too. A lot of them." I pause to take a drink and brace myself for the rest. "Without Zylar's help, I'd be dead right now. Another fucking corpse left to rot among the garbage heaps. Or maybe my neighbors would have tossed me in the water for the damned squid to feast on."

"They offered to patch you up if you agreed to sell yourself to the corporate empire," Zinn says with a nod. "I've heard they target the galaxy's most desperate. Who else would agree to their terms? Shit, Kye. I feel worse about the abduction now than I did before."

A smile crosses my face. "You used my name."

She leans back in her chair, the hint of a smirk twisting her lips. "So I did. Don't get used to it." She sips her drink, then says, "Consider it a mark of friendship. Now, I want to hear the rest of it. Spill."

With a nod, I decide I'll tell her everything. Maybe if Sorin can't steal my codes, she can. And if she doesn't… I can't land myself in a worse situation than the present, can I?

In a rare display of restraint, Zinn doesn't ask any more questions until I'm finished. The first words out of her mouth are, "Well, that explains a lot. I can't help you with the safe or those damned codes, but I can put in a good word for you now and then with the boss. The more he thinks you're worth keeping as-is, the less likely he'll be to plug you in."

I shift uncomfortably in my seat. "Thanks?"

I don't know what I was hoping for. She is Omega Prime's second; it was stupid to hope she'd promise to help Sorin steal the codes. Mercs aren't loyal to many things, but they are to crew and credits. I'm not one of them, and her response makes that abundantly clear.

"Hey, I can't piss off my boss. I like this gig. But like I said, I'll tell him you're better off unplugged." She shrugs. "He'd probably make me run your systems anyway, and as much as I like you, that would make things pretty fucking awkward, wouldn't it?"

"Yeah." I slump in my chair and look away. "He can't know I told you."

"Who? My boss, or yours?"

I force a laugh and internally cringe at the hollowness I hear in my tone. "Both. Sorin doesn't want his fancy trade secrets spread across the galaxy—and I don't really want anyone else to know either. And your boss would probably plug me in if he found out, just because he can."

She nods knowingly and signals the bartender for another round of drinks. "Look, despite my better judgment, I like you, Pretty Boy. Your secret's safe with me. Besides, the codes are on Haven. If I piss you off too much, I'll wind up like that bot you slaughtered on Z-1543."

I grimace and risk a glance in her direction. She leans back in her chair, arms folded, that ever-present smirk plastered across her face. She's teasing me.

"I'm not proud of how that fight ended," I reply uneasily. "My fists were faster than aiming a gun, and I had to make sure he wouldn't follow us. And he wasn't a damned bot."

She tips her head back and laughs. "I'm not accusing you of ruthlessness, Bud. I'm just pointing out that you can be scary as hell when you choose to be. And I can't match your speed, so it'd be stupid to provoke you. That's all." She pauses to accept her refill from the bartender, then says, "As for the 'bot' part, how do you know he wasn't plugged in? How do you know he was in control?"

A chill ricochets along my spine. "I… I don't."

"My point. You're the only cyborg in the galaxy who can't be manipulated by Zylar's execs. Your codes are beyond their reach, so you're safe. And I'll do my damnedest to make sure the boss doesn't follow their lead. We're supposed to be taking them down, yeah? What good is overthrowing the Man if we act the same way? The galaxy needs change, and that's why Omega Prime stepped in to help Ghosty's Coalition."

It's not a promise of *help*, exactly, but it's something. It's the best I can hope for, given the circumstances and who I'm talking to.

"Thanks." I reach across the table and offer my hand.

She grins, studies it for a moment, then shakes. "I wasn't sure you'd understand, but I'm glad you do."

"Politics and shit. I get it."

She laughs. "Yep, I think I like you. *Kye.*"

CHAPTER TWENTY-FIVE

MISPLACED JEALOUSY

MEGATROPOLIS, TRAPPIST-1 SYSTEM

"Do not say a word. Not a fucking word."

Zinn jabs a finger at my nose as I hold back a laugh. The Coalition has outfitted us in white caterer's uniforms, but part of her disguise is a change to her hair. Gone is the copious amount of gel that usually holds her mohawk in place. The thin strip of hair is parted and combed back to cover most of her bare scalp, then secured at the back in a short ponytail. She's even dyed it a murky shade of brown. I almost don't recognize her.

"You look almost professional," Quiara replies with a shy grin as she peers at us from the shuttle's cockpit.

"What did I just say?" Zinn asks, swiveling to face her, hands on hips.

Quiara shrugs and returns her attention to driving. We're nearing Megatropolis' atmosphere, and shuttle traffic is picking up. "You told *him* to shut up, not me."

"Fair point." Zinn crosses her arms and shakes her head. "And I'm supposed to be driving now, yeah? That's my job."

"You'll drive after we land and switch vehicles," Quiara replies. "I'm too busy at the moment to switch with you. Atmospheric Traffic Control keeps pinging us."

I freeze and stare through the windshield as our shuttle maneuvers through the lane of inbound shuttles. "Why?"

"They've tightened security since the 'incident' with the mainframe." She shrugs and taps at the console. "It's all routine. Nothing to worry about yet."

I nod absently and begin to pace. The news has made me restless and edgy. Sure, I could flood my system with dopamine and serotonin to calm my nerves, but I'm better off reserving my energy for a fight if my new ID fails to pass the checkpoint's scanners. A boost of adrenaline is more fun anyway, and I might need it later.

Minutes pass as we hover almost motionless over the hazy blue expanse of Megatropolis' atmosphere, the dark bands of its artificial rings arcing across our view. The line creeps forward toward the checkpoint ahead. Red and white lights illuminate the AI kiosk that we'll be forced to interact with soon, and I note the telltale green-blue flares of superheated exhaust from small craft as they patrol around the planet's circumference. They're likely military, but I'd be stunned if a few ZIEG soldiers weren't tasked with maintaining Megatropolis' defenses.

"Is there anyone at the kiosk with the AI?" I ask Quiara.

"Based on my interactions so far, a GISA agent may be up there. We're too far away for me to verify, and it may only be someone on the surface tasked to monitor this checkpoint." She pauses to peer over her shoulder. "Don't you have special optics? Maybe you can tell."

"IR isn't going to do us any good," I reply as I stalk toward the cockpit. "If an agent is there, they'll be in a full environmental suit. I won't see anything that way, but…"

I switch to night vision after I stop behind Quiara's seat, then focus on the illuminated kiosk ahead. My eyesight is damned good now, but we're too far away for me to make out many details. I can see the AI console and a cylindrical shape adjacent to it that should be a maintenance cubicle. Smaller objects are lost to the shadows.

"I can't see anything yet."

A message flashes across the console, warning Quiara that the shuttle will be scanned when we reach the checkpoint. "You may want to raise your firewalls if you haven't already."

"Right."

I'd been putting it off, but I can't wait any longer. Sorin's hacking skills may be unparalleled, but I'm not stupid enough to take the risk. The firewalls prevent the reinforcing matrix in my bones, the filaments in my muscles, and my biomechanical organs from showing up on scans, as well as protecting me from electronic invasion by a malicious

AI. And after our attack on their mainframe, the AIs may be prone to lashing out if they suspect our involvement.

I can tolerate the buzz if it means we coast through undetected.

We creep forward, and I continue to pace. Zinn shoots me periodic glares, annoyed I can't stand still. But if even one line of Sorin's code is faulty, we're screwed. How can I pretend calm knowing that?

We reach the kiosk fifteen minutes later, and I brace myself for the incoming scan as the shuttle's console chimes, "Verifying passenger identifications."

The scan takes seconds, but in the maelstrom of my whirling thoughts, it's an eternity. I prime myself for a boost of adrenaline should we be forced to fight or flee.

The console chimes again. "Identifications verified. Customs scanning initiated."

I release an explosive sigh and collapse into one of the seats next to the window. Sorin's damned hacking skills worked. We're clear. And we have nothing that will trigger a customs search, unless Zinn has smuggled something on board. I doubt it, though; she's not stupid.

Zinn rolls her eyes at my reaction. "How many times did I tell you to relax? Everything went fine."

"I know, but—"

"For someone with the ability to eliminate his anxiety, you're a damned worrier," she interrupts. "Relax and enjoy the ride down to the planet."

"Customs scanning complete," the console chimes. "Welcome to Megatropolis, and enjoy your stay in our galaxy's beautiful capital world."

Zinn snorts as the AI disconnects from our shuttle and Quiara accelerates forward. "Beautiful world, huh? That bot has never been to the Aloha Moon or Eden Prime."

"You have?" I ask, skeptical.

She grins. "Sometimes jobs take me to paradise. It's a perk of being a merc."

"Hmm."

"Have you considered what you'll do when we're done with the Coalition's bullshit?" Zinn asks pointedly. "The boss could use someone like you on his crew."

I cross my arms. "I won't work for him. You know why."

"Yeah, well, let Ghosty figure out what he'll do, then maybe you'll consider it."

I shake my head. "No. Besides, I already told Daaros I'd uphold my contract with him. I'm not interested in Omega Prime."

She snickers. "If it was anyone else, I'd say he couldn't match what the boss would pay you, but since it's *him*, I doubt the boss could match his offer even if he drained our accounts. Chances are the Prince of Plants will take you somewhere tropical while you play bodyguard."

Quiara laughs from the cockpit. "I dare you to call Daaros that to his face."

"Challenge accepted, Little Hack," Zinn replies with a wicked grin.

The rest of our flight to the surface passes without incident, and Quiara lands the shuttle on top of the same skyscraper Sorin did when I was last on Megatropolis. Zinn is familiar with the building's layout, and leads us to the elevator, then through the vacant lobby on the ground floor. Our footsteps echo in the space, and I wonder how the mercs afford the rent on a building they rarely use.

As we step outside into a pale and overcast Megatropolis morning, Zinn points away from the building. "Wait over there. I'll meet you with our *catering van* in a few minutes."

I resist the urge to roll my eyes. "I know about the garage."

She frowns and jabs her finger at the desired meeting place again. "I don't care. The boss doesn't want the two of you knowing how to get inside. He's still pissed about Ghosty's joyride from the last time you were here."

I snicker and follow Quiara away from the building. "I know where the control panel is. Sorin showed me," I tell her once we're some distance from Zinn. "She doesn't know it, but they train ZIEG soldiers in basic hacking. I could break into that garage if I wanted to. Or if we need to later on."

A small smile forms on her lips. "It's always good to have an escape plan."

"Yeah, I thought so too." I shrug and lean against the polished nanosteel plate on the building's side. "I can't share specifics, but I don't trust the mercs. Zinn might be an exception, but I haven't made up my mind yet."

"Don't worry," Quiara replies softly, "Sorin doesn't trust them either. They're useful tools, but Van has his own agenda. It's good that you're cautious."

A few minutes later, a small white shuttle arrives and stops in front of us. Zinn flashes a grin through the window and beckons impatiently. I allow Quiara to take the front passenger seat while I climb into the back. I know I'm not going to like Zinn's method of driving, and in the windowless rear of the tiny shuttle, I'm less likely to witness her aerial antics.

Seconds later, we're lurching skyward, the shuttle's engine groaning in protest. Zinn spews a litany of curses at the console.

"It's not rated for this speed," Quiara informs her calmly. "You need to accelerate more slowly and at a lesser angle."

"Whose job is it to drive?" Zinn counters with her characteristic wry smirk. "Not yours, Assistant to Le Chef."

I release a groan and force myself to look forward. "Just listen to her. I'll be pissed if you crash the shuttle before we reach the Rings. And of the three of us, I'm the only one rated to survive that type of impact."

I cross my arms and sit back as the shuttle's nose dips and our angle drops significantly. If Sorin had thought through our roles for any length of time, he would have set *me* up as the driver. I have the specs for this shuttle's model stored in my databanks and flying it would have been easy. It would have been better than watching Zinn push the little craft dangerously toward its stalling point.

She begins to understand the shuttle's limitations after a few minutes in the air, then we begin to ascend again. This time, the ride is smoother as we follow a gentle arc toward Megatropolis' exosphere and the Rings some distance beyond.

I settle back into my seat and do my best not to think about the next security checkpoint outside Ring Eight and Daaros' private hangar. We made it past one; the second shouldn't be an issue. Yet I worry. Security was tighter around Ring Eight than it was around the planet's perimeter when I visited with Sorin. This time won't be any different. It'd be bad press for Megatropolis' security forces if something were to happen to their wealthiest residents, so they'll spare no expense.

I hope Sorin's forgery skills are as good as he claims and my firewalls are as strong as I've been led to believe. If either one fails, I'm screwed.

I'm not very good at *not* thinking, am I? Don't answer that.

Zinn slows the shuttle as we approach the security checkpoint outside Ring Eight. There aren't any craft ahead of us in the queue, and the kiosk is dark until we cross an invisible line marking our proximity to it. Lights blaze across the kiosk's screen, and moments later, the AI's voice issues from the shuttle's speakers.

"Scanning passengers," it says in a bored tone.

I glance at Quiara in question. She shrugs. Maybe AIs are just as susceptible to boredom as we are. Until now, I've never considered it.

The scan draws on longer than I'm accustomed to. My tension grows with every moment it continues, and I'm certain the AI will find something amiss with our credentials. Then we'll...

I'm not sure what we'll do. Zinn's in the pilot's seat; I'm pretty sure she'd turn around and race away at speeds this model isn't designed for. And then we'll either break apart as she attempts reentry into Megatropolis' atmosphere, or we'll crash into something along the way. Both scenarios end in a fiery and swift death for all of us. Cyborgs aren't designed to withstand starship explosions, even small ones like our current shuttle would create.

"Why is it taking so long?" I hiss through my teeth, unable to contain my anxiety any longer.

"I told you they've increased security," Quiara replies calmly. "Your culinary displays will last a few extra minutes, Chef."

Right. I'm supposed to be playing my part too.

"Well tell that damned bot to hurry up," I snarl, injecting false condescension into my tone. "My sculpted sugar will shatter if this shuttle vibrates any more, and if that happens, I will see to it that Megatropolis' security pays for my services threefold."

Yes, I did some research. I wouldn't trust myself to melt or color sugar, let alone sculpt it into the fragile works of art the *real* chefs of the galaxy can create, but I can pretend for the AI's sake.

"You heard the boss," Zinn drawls. "Hurry up with the scans. Our client will be pis—*furious* if you're responsible for damages."

She flashes a grin over her shoulder. She's enjoying this.

"Additional requirements have been added to the scanning process," the AI snaps, clearly irritated with our impatience. "It is beyond my ability to speed them up any further. Conversation will prolong the experience."

"And I thought your kind was developed for multi-tasking," Zinn replies with a laugh. "You can't speak and scan at the same time?"

A blast of static erupts from the speakers as the AI's temper flares. "Surely even chefs are aware of the recent attacks on the government mainframe? Every AI in the galaxy is running at limited capacity until it can be restored to working order. My bandwidth has been severely reduced, yet they insist I do more work than ever."

Zinn laughs. "I doubt you have much work to do out here. How many people come and go from Ring Eight on any given day?"

Another blast of static, more furious than the last, assaults our ears. "You insist on talking, now you also ask me to run calculations while I finish the scans? Humans are cruel beasts." There's a pause, then, "On average, four hundred twenty-seven people approach Ring Eight each day."

"That wasn't so hard, was it?"

I grimace as more static pulses through the speakers. "That's enough. Let the poor bot do its job."

She peers over her shoulder with a knowing smirk and I hope with every fiber of my being she keeps her damned mouth shut for once in her life. The AI can't know I'm a cyborg, no matter how much she yearns to toss a jibe in my direction.

"I know many humans do not understand the distinction between a robot and an artificial intelligence, but I can assure you I am no *bot*, Mr. Damascus." The AI's tone has shifted from irritated to resigned. "The scans are complete. You may proceed."

Zinn shakes with laughter as she guides the shuttle toward Daaros' hangar, but she mercifully keeps her comments to herself until after we've landed.

"Your ID must have checked out just fine," she says as we climb out of the shuttle. "The fucking AI reprimanded you. *You!*"

"At least you didn't blow our cover," I growl as I stomp toward the door leading into Daaros' apartment. "I thought you were going to."

"A joke at your expense would have been a stupid move on my part," she concedes. "If you're flagged as problematic, we'll be too. And I'm too pretty to be thrown in prison, Le Chef." She feigns brushing hair from her eyes, and I can't help but laugh.

"So, keeping your thoughts to yourself is only a matter of self-preservation?" I ask.

"I'm a merc, Metal Man. If I don't look out for me, no one else will."

The door to the apartment slides open and Pablo appears, a grin plastered across his features. He's dressed in designer jeans and a crisp, button-down shirt embellished with swirls of metallic thread at the collar and cuffs. Behind his collar, I spy the platinum *diivoraa*. He's a healthy weight for the first time in his life, a far cry from the half-starved version of my best friend who fled Earth at my side. And the smile he dazzles us with can only be the result of his relationship with Daaros. I've never seen Pablo this happy.

He rushes forward and pulls me into a fierce hug. "I'm glad you're here. I'm glad you're safe."

I chuckle as he pulls away. "We're okay, Pab. The scans took longer than usual, but nothing came of them."

"Zylar Inc. has been claiming their scans are foolproof, that they'd catch anyone trying to come into Megatropolis space under a false identity." He chews on his lower lip for a moment, then motions for us to follow him to the door. "Daar said you'd be okay, that Sorin's forgeries are infallible, but I still—"

"Hey, we're here now, and that's what matters."

"You're right. You made it here, and I know you need to talk to Daar. He's at his office right now." Pablo shrugs uneasily and flicks a glance at the others as we stop just inside the threshold. "Introduce me, Kye?"

"Of course."

Once introductions are out of the way, Pablo shows Quiara and Zinn to the guest suite. It has four separate bedrooms around a central seating area. Zinn immediately claims the room with a window facing out toward dark space, then sidles up to me as we wait for Quiara to deposit her belongings in the room she's chosen. Pablo leaves with the promise he'll be in the main living room when they're finished.

"Your friend's cute," she says. "I can see why the Plant Man fell for him."

"He's not interested in you," I reply with a smirk. "There's a zero percent chance you'll manage to tempt him away."

"Ah, but *you* can," she counters with a knowing look.

"No, I can't. And I won't."

She folds her arms. "Touchy, aren't we, Earth Boy?"

"Just drop it," Quiara says from behind her as she emerges from her room. "Kye's preferences are irrelevant to our mission here, as is the availability of Pablo."

"And if you try to sabotage his relationship with Daaros, I will personally toss you out the airlock," I add. "He has a good thing here. Don't fucking ruin it."

"I won't," she promises, unfazed by my display of temper. "As you said, he's not interested."

"Zinn," Quiara cuts in, warning in her tone. "Stop."

Zinn shrugs and pushes past me toward the suite's exit. "Fine, I'll play nice. For now."

I clench my jaw and storm after her. There is no way in hell that I'll subject Pablo to her alone. I'm not sure how he'll take her incessant teasing. Someone needs to be present to act as a buffer, and that someone has to be me.

Quiara grips my elbow as we enter the corridor. "She'll calm down. I don't think she expected your friend to greet you quite as he did."

I frown in confusion but wrench away from her grip. "We grew up together. Pablo is my best friend. I don't see how his greeting matters, least of all to *her*."

Quiara releases an exasperated sigh. "You don't see it, do you? She's taken you under her wing, not because her boss asked her to, but because she *likes* you. And I don't mean as a friend, Kye. She's had her eye on you since the day they brought you to Haven."

I scowl at Zinn's retreating form. Why does this always seem to happen to me? I'm not interested. In *anyone*. Why can't the rest of the galaxy just leave me the hell alone?

"She's wasting her time. And her jealousy is misplaced."

"Do you want me to speak with her?" Quiara offers, her tone compassionate. "I think I understand."

I almost refuse. Zinn doesn't need more fodder for her jibes, and this is a point of frustration for me. But she won't let up unless someone explains it to her.

I rake a hand through my hair and groan. "I should say something, but... She'll be more willing to listen to you. If you don't mind?"

She smiles. "Not at all. I think she'll settle down after we talk. Try to enjoy your time with Pablo while you have it. We won't be here long, and I'm not sure when you'll see him again."

Relieved, I match her smile. "Thanks. I'll owe you one."

"You'll owe me nothing." She strides ahead, then pauses to glance over her shoulder. "You should be safe here. You can drop your firewalls."

I force an uneasy laugh. She knows maintaining my defenses causes my temper to fray. I won't deny she's right in thinking the buzz in my skull is at least partially responsible for my previous outburst; it is, and maybe I owe Zinn an apology. But only if she offers one first.

CHAPTER TWENTY-SIX

GOODBYE

I avoid Zinn like the flamboyant plague she is and focus entirely on Pablo until his fiancé arrives several hours later. We chat about everything—the end of his first term at MSTI, how I'm coping with recent events, my spat with Zinn, and what we like best about our lives away from Earth—but the conversation inevitably spins back to his engagement to Daaros. He's not just enamored with the Botanaari; *he's in love.* And the brief interactions that I've witnessed between them from the far side of a holoscreen tell me that Daaros feels the same.

I'm glad that Pablo's happy. He deserves it.

When Daaros arrives that evening, he's preceded by Araan, who nods in welcome to me as he hangs his white fedora on a peg next to the door. Daaros enters in his wake, as poised and self-assured as ever. His expression is calculating as he studies Quiara and Zinn, but I'm offered a grin.

"Hello, Kye. I think our business should be concluded swiftly. Come." He spins away, headed toward his private office, then calls over his shoulder, "Araan will order food for everyone while we're busy."

I offer Pablo an apologetic smile as he shoos me after Daaros. "Go. We'll talk more over supper."

"Fine. Order me something. I don't care what."

He laughs as I turn away. "Be careful what you wish for. You might end up with a Botanaari entrée."

"It has to be better than expired protein cubes."

When I enter his office, Daaros motions to the door. "Please close that. I trust Quiara, but I do not trust the merc who came with you."

He sits down behind a sleek black desk ringed by holoscreens. The desk's surface is pristine, each item placed carefully. There is no clutter. It's so blatantly *Daaros*.

I take one of the chairs opposite him and lean forward, eager to have this task over with.

"Are you aware of what I have?" I ask, speaking in vague terms in case he fears a security breach somewhere.

"Yes, I'm aware, and I'm prepared to extract it. Sorin took a risk sending it with you, but I suppose it was less than the risk he would have taken if he'd sent it through the 'net." Daaros looks away, his expression troubled. "You should not be entangled in his games. Not after everything you've gone through."

"I can't exactly escape," I reply, thinking of the codes stashed in Omega Prime's vault.

"I know. I attempted to buy the codes from Van Duval directly. He refused." Daaros crosses his arms and shrinks into himself. "No amount of money will change his mind. It seems the possibility of his very own cyborg, one he can command and control on a whim, is more tantalizing than endless wealth. I have tried, Kye. I have *tried*."

I pause to stare at him, stunned. "I wasn't blaming you. Hell, I didn't even *know*."

"Nor did Sorin," he admits with a tired shrug. "But you deserved to hear it from me."

"Sorin has a plan," I offer, hoping to buoy his spirits. "I think he'll follow through. You said I should trust him."

Daaros nods as a faint smile graces his lips. "Good. I hope he'll meet with more success than I did. You are in more danger from Omega Prime than you are from GISA or Zylar Inc."

"I don't know. GISA and Zylar Inc. can toss me in a prison where I'd never see the light of day again."

Daaros crosses his arms. "Omega Prime can make you a puppet. I can't think of a worse fate, and I will see you freed of this threat if I can." He closes his eyes for a moment, then shakes his head. "If I know Sorin, some of what he included on his list will assist him in his plans for *you*. I will ensure he has all that he needs."

I nod and chew my lower lip. "How do you want to do this?"

"In truth, I don't want to do it at all. It must be humiliating for you."

I shrug helplessly. "I think I'm starting to get used to it."

He scowls at the desk between us. "Sit on the edge of the desk with your back to me. I'll try to make this quick."

I snicker, but move as he asks. "You make it sound like a medical procedure. It isn't. And it doesn't hurt, Daaros. I'll be okay."

"Pablo will never forgive me if you aren't." There's a sharp edge to his tone, one that forces the smile from my face and kills the laughter in my throat.

"I'll be fine," I assure him. "I've been plugged into tablets more times than I care to count. It doesn't hurt me, and there isn't any other way to extract your list. I'll tell you if anything feels wrong."

He doesn't respond for several seconds, and I turn to look over my shoulder. He's staring at the desktop, a helpless expression on his features and a cable dangling from his hand. He wasn't lying when he said he didn't want to do this.

"Hey, I'll be okay. You want the list, right?"

He shakes his head. "Not like this. But I have an idea."

"And that is…?"

"Can you read the file from within your system?"

"Yeah. But how does that help you?"

He begins to laugh. "Go back to the chair, Kye. There is another way. A better way. It will take longer, but it's safer for both of us. No cables, no electronic signatures on my end, no traces leading back to Sorin."

He rummages beneath the desk as I return to the chair, producing a flat sheet of something vaguely gray in color and what appears to be a stylus. The end is pointed and too sharp to be used on a tablet's glassy surface.

I cross-reference what I'm seeing on the 'net, and I'm surprised to learn the stylus is exactly what I thought it was, but it's not meant for use with electronics. It's for paper, or the grayish Botanaari equivalent produced from compressed insect wings. The Botanaari don't condone the destruction of plants, for obvious reasons.

"You're going to write it all down?" I ask.

He nods. "Did you have other plans I'm not aware of before supper arrives?"

"I… No."

"Then we'll do it this way." He flashes a grin. "It's better, isn't it?"

"Yeah," I agree, unexpectedly relieved he's chosen to treat me as a person rather than a convenient data repository. I don't think anyone else would have hesitated to plug into my system if given the opportunity. "Thanks."

"Of course. Pablo thinks of you as family. It's only right that I do the same."

There are sixty-four items on Sorin's list. Some are familiar, but most are described only as a series of numbers. I hope Daaros understands what each one is as I rattle off line after line, while he dutifully transcribes them to his version of paper. I can't read his words; I think he's using Botanaari, or maybe some form of code. The symbols are unfamiliar, and despite all of my internal tech, I can't place them. None of my programming included Botanaari text, though if I spent some time studying their language, I could probably learn to decipher it. But I'm not interested in doing it right now.

"That's everything." I sit back in the chair while Daaros finishes writing. "Thanks again. I didn't realize how much it would mean when you…when you chose not to plug in."

"Your people… Your *government* made it impossible for you to leave your home world, despite the deplorable conditions there. That they forced you to become something inhuman in exchange for survival is fundamentally wrong. You deserve better than this, but as I understand it, what they've done cannot be *undone*." His voice is tight with a righteous fury I never expected to hear. "I will squeeze Sorin if I must, Kye. He *will* see you freed, or he will have the might of the Botanaari people to contend with."

I blanch at the notion. "You can't start an interstellar war over *me*, Daaros. I'll adapt. It's what I'm best at."

He sets his stylus aside and peers at me, his dark eyes unreadable. "The galaxy requires change. It's why my fathers agreed to help the Coalition. I was merely their messenger until I met Pablo. Now, I am fully invested. For our future, and yours."

I stare at him as my thoughts spin. He's serious. He really *would* send his people to war to help me.

"Why?" The word spills from my mouth of its own accord.

A slow smile spreads across his face. "It's the right thing to do. I failed to comprehend the scope of your AI government's influence, or its corruption at the hands of Zylar Inc. until recently. When I learned of the override codes, I was furious."

I look down with an uneasy laugh. "I remember."

"You only witnessed the aftermath." His smile widens to a grin. "Afterwards, I demanded Sorin tell me the truth about the ZIEG program. He spared no details, and I realized for the first time precisely what is at stake. It isn't merely your people's way of life that is threatened, but their very freedom, particularly for people like you."

"But isn't getting involved in Sorin's plans dangerous for you? You're the *heir*, Daaros."

"I have my fathers' backing," he replies with a shrug. "And with that, our people's. Do not worry about me."

"Just promise me one thing."

He tilts his head as he studies me, then nods.

"Keep Pablo out of this. Keep him safe."

"Believe me when I say that Pablo's welfare is my top priority."

I believe him; there is no deception in his dark eyes, only a fierce determination borne of his desire to protect the one he loves. Pablo is in good hands.

"Hey."

I look up from the novel I'm reading to find a chagrined Zinn standing in front of me. I don't have to ask why she's sought my company, and I'm not looking forward to this conversation. I was in a really good part of the book I borrowed from Daaros' library. I push my fleeting irritation at being interrupted aside, mark my place, and set the book on the end table beside my chair.

"Hey," I reply. "I know—"

She holds up a hand, and I fall silent. She closes her eyes briefly, her expression torn between frustration and genuine guilt.

"Look, I'm shit when it comes to apologies, but I owe you one. Or maybe a dozen."

"You didn't know."

"Yeah, and now that I *do*, I feel like a complete and utter asshole. All that time I spent goading you, calling you 'Pretty Boy' and the like… It never fazed you for a second, did it?"

"Zinn, I—"

"And then *I* got worked up when I saw you with Pablo. But there isn't anything romantic between you. He's just your blasted friend." She groans and stares up at the ceiling. "I should have known when you didn't even *attempt* to flirt. I should have fucking *known*. And now I've made an ass of myself." She strides to the nearest cushioned chair and collapses into it. "I made a scene, caused chaos… It's what I always do. And I'm sorry."

"You didn't know." I lean forward to rest my elbows on my knees. "And before you ask, it's not a cyborg thing. It's a *me* thing. It always has been."

She shakes her head, stubbornly refusing to meet my gaze. "It doesn't make everything I've said to you any better. The teasing. The failed flirting. I really thought I was losing my touch. And it was shitty of me to bring Pablo into it. He's a sweetheart, now that I know him better."

"He is. He's my best friend, and the only reason I survived on Earth as long as I did. He doesn't have any family left, but he has me. I've always thought of him as a brother."

She risks a glance in my direction, questions in her eyes, but remains silent.

"I think I know what you want to ask," I continue. "It's simple. The idea of intimacy is…repulsive. I'm good with friendship, but I can't offer anything more. And if it makes you feel any better, I didn't realize you were flirting. I'm shit when it comes to recognizing someone's advances."

"More like you're blind as a damned bat." She laughs, and the familiar mischievous grin breaks across her face. "I think we have another nickname: Bat Boy."

My laughter joins hers. "If you're giving me new nicknames, does that mean we're okay?"

"Yeah. Feel free to call me Captain Asshole if you want. I deserve it."

"I think I'll leave the nicknames to you," I reply with a grin.

I hold out my hand. She eyes it for a moment, then grasps it firmly.

"To friendship," she says, a serious glint in her eyes.

"To friendship," I agree.

The rest of our stay on Ring Eight passes entirely too fast. I'd rather stay and begin my role as Daaros' bodyguard than return to Haven and the prospect of fighting Sorin's battles, but I know I can't. If I don't return, Omega Prime will eventually come for me. As much as I like Zinn, I don't think she can stop her boss' plans. Only Sorin can, which furthers my obligations to him.

I try not to dwell on the mess my life has become, instead focusing on Pablo. He's collected a plethora of links to wedding sites—everything from attire to catering to décor. I sit with him for hours as he debates his preferences and whether Daaros will agree. I don't tell him this, but I'm confident Daaros will accept any decision Pablo makes, so long as their union moves forward. Daaros doesn't seem concerned with *how* the ceremony plays out, only that it will.

Daaros still has a company to run, and he's absent from the apartment for several hours each day. He returns with Araan each evening, usually with a stack of take-out boxes in his arms. Daaros spares no expense on the cuisine.

Zinn and Quiara keep to themselves more often than not, which is fine by me. Quiara works on projects for Sorin, and Zinn manages to convince Daaros to allow her to use his simulator. She spends more time slaughtering digital monsters than socializing, but at least the tension between us is gone.

Zinn and Quiara head to the shuttle once our time is up, but I linger just inside the apartment, reluctant to leave. I don't know all the details of Sorin's next scheme, but I know enough to suspect this might be the last time I'll see Pablo. I try to mask my fears behind a smile, but he's aware of my unease. I've never been able to hide a damned thing from him.

"It will be okay," he says, drawing me into a final, fierce embrace. "Believe in yourself, Kye. You're a survivor. You'll get through this too."

I force a nod, but my throat is too constricted to speak. I don't want this to be our last goodbye, but I can't shake the feeling that it is. Maybe this is why Sorin allowed me to visit Ring Eight. Our visit wasn't meant as a diversion for me, though it served that purpose well enough. Our visit was planned as my final farewell.

And I'm rendered speechless from emotion.

Pablo steps back, but continues to hold me at arm's length. "We'll see each other again. Don't worry."

His words are meant to cheer me up, but the pain in his expression ruins their effect. Damn it, he's going to make me cry.

"Pab, I…"

I stop to clear my throat, hoping it will dislodge the lump forming there. It doesn't, but I continue anyway. He needs to hear this.

"If I can't make your wedding, I want you to know I'm happy for you. Daaros is a better match for you than I would have been. You're good together."

Tears spill from his dark eyes and he jerks away, then swings wildly. I let his punch connect solidly with my ribcage, though I could have easily evaded it. He's never been good with grief, and I can take a little punishment.

"Don't you *dare* talk like that," he hisses. "You'll be there. You're my best man."

I shake my head. "I *want* to be there, but I can't guarantee it. You've seen what they've done with security around here, and I… I won't make a promise I can't keep."

His wounded expression does nothing for the turmoil raging in my heart. I wish I could offer him something more. I wish I didn't have to go back to Haven. I wish life had been different in so many ways, but this is my reality.

"I'm sorry," I offer. "If I make it through this, you'll be the first one to know."

He wipes at his eyes and looks away. "You'd better. Don't forget your firewalls."

I stand rooted in place as he turns away and disappears down the corridor. I knew leaving would be difficult, but I never imagined I'd botch our goodbye so thoroughly. *Damn it.*

Daaros appears several moments later, his mouth twisted in a worried frown. "Pablo's upset. I knew he would be, but—"

I shake my head. "He'll give you the details when he's ready. I can't… I can't right now."

He nods in understanding. "Trust Sorin. He will see you through this to the best of his ability, but don't trust anyone else."

"I'll call you when I can. Take care of him for me, Daaros. He'll need you now more than ever."

I turn away and trudge through the door to the hangar. It will be a miracle if I see Ring Eight again.

CHAPTER TWENTY-SEVEN

OVERDUE DESTRUCTION

**HAVEN
UNCHARTED SPACE**

"I know what will cheer you up, Metal Man. Come on."

I look up from the tabletop in Haven's mess hall and my untouched breakfast, but can't muster a smile for Zinn, even with the reappearance of her trademark pink mohawk. Since our return from Ring Eight, I've been fighting a bout of depression so dark I need my night vision to navigate Haven's rusted halls. I've spoken with Quiara, but her boss isn't ready to share his plans yet. Waiting only makes it worse.

"I doubt it." I pick up the fork and poke at the pale yellow mass that is supposed to be scrambled eggs. They don't look any more appetizing than they did ten minutes ago.

She releases an aggravated snarl. "Damn it, Kye, I know you didn't want to leave Ring Eight, but we need you for Ghosty's next operation." She takes the unoccupied chair across from me and leans forward. When she speaks next, her tone is a bare whisper. "Look, you need to snap out of it. The boss is going to notice, and you don't want that."

I shoot her a sullen glare. She doesn't have to say it, but I know what she's thinking. If Duval doesn't trust me to play my part, he'll use the damned codes and force me to. No, I definitely *don't* want that, and Sorin isn't currently here to stop him.

"Fine."

I force myself to swallow a mouthful of eggs. They're tasteless and just as awful as I suspected they'd be; my second attempt with eggs isn't going any better than my first did. But I need to eat. My energy levels are lower than they should be, and I think I'll need them boosted to adjust my serotonin output. I doubt there's anything else I can do to elevate my mood at this point, and I doubt whatever scheme Zinn has planned will help. I also haven't eaten since we left Ring Eight thirty-six hours ago.

"Do you always wait to eat your eggs until they're cold?" she asks.

I shrug. "I haven't tried them scrambled before. They're…not good."

"They're better warm."

I'm skeptical that heat will improve the flavor and continue eating. It's better than expired protein cubes.

"You'll eat anything, won't you?" she asks, her lip curled in disgust.

"If you'd grown up on Earth, you wouldn't be picky either."

"I need to take you out, like I promised before." She sits back with a shake of her head. "Too bad there were so many damned security checkpoints when we were on Megatropolis. I could have introduced you to *real* food. Not the pretentious crap Plant Man ordered in or the shit you choose for yourself."

"Hmm."

"Talkative, I see." She crosses her arms and flashes a grin. "That's fine. With what I have planned, you don't need to talk. Just…hit."

I lift my eyebrows, my interest piqued. "The exoskeleton?"

"Hell yeah, the exoskeleton. I thought you could use the exercise, and the boss agreed to let me, ah, assist."

I smile in spite of myself. Venting my frustrations on an armored merc will certainly take my mind off my parting words to Pablo. And I might even feel better afterward.

"Okay. I'm in."

"I knew you couldn't resist. I think there's a part of you deep inside that *wants* to live up to your call sign."

I shoot her a warning look. "Fuck the call sign."

"Ah, but you don't deny it, do you?" she teases.

I push my empty plate away and stand. "Now I *need* to hit something. Better the exoskeleton than the annoying merc sitting in front of me."

"Ooh, you need to work on your terms of endearment, Earth Boy." She rises from her seat with a laugh and swaggers toward the exit.

I swallow a groan and follow her. We've gone back to our previous version of banter, and I can't see any difference in her behavior now that she understands I'm only looking for a friend. Was she really flirting before? I'm so damned confused.

Away from the mess hall, Haven is quieter. There aren't as many mercs currently stationed here as there were before I went to Ring Eight, and only Quiara and I represent the Coalition. I haven't seen her since we arrived, but I haven't been looking for her either.

Zinn leads me to the cargo bay where the exoskeleton is parked, a hulking monstrosity of nanosteel looming in the darkness while she fumbles for the lights.

"I should get my armor," I mutter as the overhead lights blaze into life.

"Nah," Zinn replies with a grin. "I'll go easy on you today. Besides, I'd like to see how you fight without it. Does the armor give you strength and speed, or is it your…ah…?" She grimaces and looks at me hopefully.

"My cybernetics?" I ask with a laugh. "It's a little of both, but mostly my cybernetics. The armor just gives them a boost."

"What about your defenses? I mean, the physical ones, not the shit that goes on inside that metal skull of yours."

"For the record, my bones aren't metal. They're reinforced with a matrix of carbon nanotubes that makes them almost unbreakable. But to answer your question, my defenses are better than those of a normal human. I'm less likely to sustain organ damage, but it's still a possibility. And if enough force is applied, I can still be hurt… Or killed."

"Right. You punched that guy's skull in on Z-1543." Zinn chews her lower lip thoughtfully. "You know, Ghosty mentioned they haven't made any more of your…series. You're still the only Slaughter Bot in the galaxy."

"Except they think I'm dead," I remind her, bristling at her use of the call sign.

"It's better for us that way." She shrugs, then turns to face the exoskeleton. "I'll go easy on you today. Blue-eyes will be pissed if I break you while he's gone."

I force a smile as she moves toward the contraption. I haven't forgotten my conversation with Vee, even though it seems like a lifetime ago. Jen lost an arm to a pirate raid, and as far as I know, Mat is the only person in the galaxy capable of making repairs of that nature. Sorin might know how to do it, but he hasn't mentioned that he has a lab where he can grow stem cells. I need to remember I'm not invincible, that I *am* more vulnerable without my armor.

Zinn hauls herself into the driver's seat and secures the harness as I study her through the shatter-proof, clear protective panes.

"What do you have in mind for easy?" I ask.

She grins. "Just a little dancing, Pretty Boy. I won't hit you if you're fast enough."

The first hour goes well enough. I dodge the exoskeleton's swings, duck beneath its punches, and taunt Zinn periodically to keep her motivated. I needed a diversion more than I realized, and she's having a blast operating her boss' fancy machine.

After another twenty minutes, my system starts to warn me I'm low on energy again. I shouldn't be surprised after not eating for a day and a half, but I am. I'm supposed to have a highly efficient digestive tract, and I haven't burned through the eggs already, have I? I ignore the warnings until a blaring red message cascades across my vision. I'm no longer low, I'm borderline *empty*.

I stagger backward, narrowly dodging a swing from the exoskeleton, and hold up my hands. "I'm done."

My limbs feel impossibly heavy and my ears begin to ring. I sit down in the center of the cargo hold and focus on my breathing as I stare at the dingy floor between my legs. I hear Zinn power down the exoskeleton, then clamber from the driver's seat. The sound of her boots on the floor echoes loudly as my system continues to blare internal warnings.

Fuck. I should have stopped when the low energy alert was triggered. I shouldn't have fallen into my old habit of refusing food because I was upset. I'm a damned idiot.

"Hey, are you okay?"

I shake my head. "No. I'm too stupid to be okay."

An uncertain laugh escapes her throat. "Normally, I wouldn't argue, but this isn't like you."

Heat creeps up my neck and into my face. Apparently, my energy levels aren't low enough to prevent me from blushing from embarrassment. Or maybe that wasn't factored into my enhancements.

"I need to eat something. Soon."

"Can you walk?"

I shrug but make no effort to rise.

"Look, I can't help you if you don't talk to me."

I grimace at the floor and brace myself for the inevitable jibes, then tell her exactly what went wrong.

"You *are* stupid, but it's nothing that can't be fixed. At least now I understand why Blue-eyes carried extra protein cubes for you on Z-1543." She winks mischievously, then says, "Stay here. I'll grab you something from the mess hall. You're probably too heavy for me to drag along, anyway."

"Water too." I pause, then add a pathetic, "Please."

Zinn returns six minutes later with an armload of snacks, two enormous bottles of water, and a fancy cocktail in a martini glass that glows the same vibrant shade as her hair. She sets the water down at my side and dumps the snacks on the floor beside them.

"What's that?" I nod at the drink in her hand.

"Payment for my trouble." She flashes a grin, then sits across from me. "I brought you a sample of everything the boss' new vending machine had inside. Protein cubes of four different flavors, chocolate bars, powdered doughnuts, the works."

I reach for the chocolate first. It has become my weakness since I discovered it in protein shake form, and a solid bar is heaven. I'm halfway through the chocolate bar when I notice Zinn is shaking with silent laughter.

"What?"

"I think I've learned that the way to a cyborg's mechanical heart is with dark chocolate."

"It goes a long way to further our friendship," I admit between bites. "And it's better than protein cubes."

"And the doughnuts?"

"Never tried them."

"Damn, you *were* deprived as an Earthling." She reaches for a package and tears it open, then thrusts it toward me. "You have to try one. You won't be disappointed."

I finish my chocolate bar while eyeing the unwrapped doughnut skeptically. It's fried dough encased in what I think is cinnamon-sugar, and a brief scan tells me it's made entirely of carbohydrates and fat. It's not a great snack for most people, but my system can handle questionable food choices without causing me harm. It's one perk of my new physiology that I'm learning to appreciate.

I turn the doughnut over in my hands. I like cinnamon with vanilla, but I'm not sure about the dough or sugar parts. This is why I didn't want to be a fake chef even for a few days. My experience is too damned limited, and research only goes so far.

Zinn sips her drink, then kicks the sole of my boot. "Try it. The anticipation is killing me!"

I take a tentative bite. The dough is dense but surprisingly soft. And the combination of cinnamon and sugar isn't bad. I might even like it. I take a second bite to be sure.

"I think Cyber-boy approves." Zinn smiles triumphantly. "I thought he might."

I down half a bottle of water, then nod. "Thanks."

"For?"

I gesture at the pile of snacks, the water, and the discarded wrappers. "For dealing with a stupid cyborg who ignores his warning messages. I needed this."

"Maybe you shouldn't go on a hunger strike the next time you're upset," she replies, compassion in her gaze. "Your cutie-pie friend would be pissed. And if he's pissed, that means his boyfriend is too. I won't risk Plant Man's wrath. A merc can't survive on the wrong side of someone *that* powerful."

With a chuckle, I shake my head. "You'll make me eat as a form of self-preservation?"

"For both of us. *You* might be stupid, but I'm sure as hell not."

I try to ignore the insistent tapping on my door. I'm in a good part of this book, and there's no reason for anyone to interrupt me. Not at this hour, anyway. It's three in the morning, Galactic Standard Time.

The tapping continues while I attempt to finish one last paragraph, then escalates to a loud knock. I release an irritated snarl, mark my place, and stomp to the door. I wrench it open to find Sorin in the corridor. I stare at him for several seconds, trying to piece together when he arrived and why no one seemed to know he was coming. Or maybe the mercs knew and chose not to tell me. It wouldn't surprise me.

"We don't have long before the security cameras come back online," he says. "Grab your things and meet me in cargo bay four in ten minutes. Don't forget your armor."

"You want me to put it on?" I ask, concerned by the urgency in his tone.

"No, there's not enough time. Just bring it with you. We need to get the hell out of here before Duval wakes up."

I nod uncertainly. "I'll be there in five."

What the hell is going on? I haven't heard a word from Sorin since leaving for Ring Eight, and that was almost two weeks ago. Now he shows up, demanding I leave with him in the middle of the fucking night, and the mercs are obviously unaware of whatever he has planned. I sense that I'm being extracted, that he's trying to protect me, but why now?

I shove my scant personal items into a pack and sling it over my shoulder. The armor is bulky and won't fit, so I'll have to carry it and hope I don't encounter anyone in the hall as I run toward the cargo bay. I don't have adequate answers to the inevitable questions that will arise.

Daaros has told me numerous times that I should trust Sorin. I'll have to put my faith in the Botanaari's judgment and hope I don't regret it later. And I'm tired of skulking about Haven, avoiding its scar-faced boss at every turn. Zinn has been great, but she's the only merc who bothers to interact with me. The rest keep their distance, and Van leers each time I fail to evade his presence, a silent reminder of the power he wields over my life.

Maybe that's what Sorin's unexpected arrival heralds.

A spark of hope ignites in my core before I rapidly extinguish it. I don't need false hope. I need action, answers… But distance between myself and Haven is a decent alternative too. I'll take what I can get.

Quiara stands near the airlock as I arrive in the cargo bay. She nods to me, then beckons me to hurry. I don't hesitate. As I approach, I note a ship's umbilical is attached to the airlock. It isn't a standard shuttle, but a freighter. There's no way Omega Prime didn't see this thing coming a parsec off.

"Get inside," Quiara hisses as I frown at her in question. "We'll explain once you're on board."

"Why the—?"

"Get *in*." She shoves me toward the umbilical and the temporary corridor that will lead me inside the freighter.

"But Sorin—"

"He's inside. Go." She glares at me, fiercely determined to ensure I stop stalling and comply.

I frown and trudge past her. I'll get answers from Sorin this time. I'm beyond tired of waiting for them.

The umbilical is a narrow space, and I have to duck slightly to avoid hitting my head. As I pass beyond Haven's gravity field, my mechanical stomach plummets for a moment before I adjust to near-weightlessness. I clutch my armor tighter, fearful it will attempt to float away if I lose my grip. After a few awkward steps, I'm within the freighter's gravity field and my body is forced to adapt again. Another few feet brings me through the umbilical's far end and into another cargo hold.

Sorin stands near a stack of crates, arms crossed and blue glasses in place. He motions for me to follow, and soon we're headed toward the ship's massive bridge.

"What's going on?" I blurt as soon as we're out of the hold.

"We're leaving Haven."

I roll my eyes. "I can see that. Why?"

"Daaros followed through on the list you delivered, and I would like your help with a project or two while we prepare to strike the AI mainframe." He pauses to consider his next words. "I don't want to repeat myself, so I'll wait until Quiara and our *associate* have returned. They shouldn't be much longer."

"Okay. I'll wait, but I want answers."

He nods once. "You'll have them."

When we reach the bridge, I'm stunned by the number of people at work inside. The freighter is huge, so a crew of more than three isn't unexpected, but there are *dozens* here. All of them wear the blue jumpsuits of the Resistance Coalition. I scan the holoscreens filled with schematics and ship specifications as we walk toward the command deck and frown.

"This isn't a freighter, is it?" I ask.

Sorin chuckles. "I suspected you'd pick up on that. No, it's not a freighter. It's a warship we've disguised as one. It can hold a crew of three hundred, but we only number eighty-two at present. That's counting you, Quiara, and our friend, of course."

He stops before the vast window that spans the width of the command deck and clasps his hands behind his back. I can see Haven's flank on the left side, scarred and battered by decades spent enduring interstellar abuse. On the right is the inky expanse of space, dotted with myriad stars.

"Who's the mysterious friend?" I demand as I set my armor on the floor near my feet.

"You'll see. They wanted it to be a surprise."

I cross my arms and scowl out the window. There are only a handful of people that might fit his description. His use of "they" could mean anyone, but it makes me think of Vee. Would they have willingly left ZIEG if they learned of the override codes? I think so. Would they agree to assist the Coalition? Maybe.

Zinn's a possibility too. She's been a near-constant in my life since I was dragged away from Zylar HQ, and despite her connection to Omega Prime, I've begun to trust her. But would she leave with Sorin, risking her boss' fury in order to help me escape? I don't know.

And then there's the remote possibility that my best friend did something incredibly stupid and got himself tangled up in this madness. He'd think himself endearing, a dashing hero come to save the cyborg who can't seem to save himself. But if Pablo walks onto the bridge, I will be seriously pissed. He has no business here.

There's an even smaller possibility that Kelsey might stride through the door, but I doubt she'd risk her career or clearances to openly help

Sorin. She's worked too damned hard to throw it all away just because I've become mired in this mess.

Sorin turns away from the window as footsteps approach. "Disconnect from Haven," he commands his crew. "Then get us the hell out of here before the mercs realize we've paid them a visit."

I tear my gaze from the outside view and pivot to face the newcomers to the command deck. It's Quiara and Zinn. I stare at the pink-haired merc, uncomprehending.

"Hey, Metal Man." She flashes a self-satisfied grin.

"Okay, what the fuck is going on?" I demand, my patience gone in a heartbeat.

Zinn gestures to Sorin, who withdraws a familiar device from his pocket. A chill pulses through my veins as I recognize the override codes.

"You… You came through." I can't hide my disbelief or mask my joy. "You actually fucking did it!"

I cross the space between us and wrap Sorin in an unexpected hug. He grunts at the impact, then wheezes, "Kye, you're going to break my ribs."

I release him and step back with a grin. "How did you do it?"

"With some inside help," Sorin says, gesturing at Zinn.

She shrugs. "Hey, I promised I wouldn't let Scar do to you what Zylar Inc. threatened. After I talked to you on Cobalt Asteroid, I went to Blue-eyes here. I told him I'd help."

I shake my head. "But why? If your boss finds out—"

She laughs darkly. "I've set him on a false trail. I left a note in the vault that indicated we ran off together. I suppose we *have*, in a way." She pauses to gaze wistfully through the window as Haven's battered hulk rapidly fades behind us. "Consider this my official resignation from Omega Prime. The Scarred Bastard isn't my boss anymore."

"And I was always supposed to leave covertly overnight," Quiara explains. "Van knew, of course. My disappearance won't arouse suspicion."

"As for *how*," Sorin cuts in, "Zinn agreed to spike the drinks last night."

"I can be *very* persuasive when it comes to alcohol," she cuts in with a laugh.

I snicker. She's not wrong.

"The mercs should still be asleep for a few more hours," Sorin continues. "After we docked, I hacked into Haven's security system and set the camera feeds to loop for thirty minutes. It was enough time to extract the codes—and you."

"You'll destroy them like you did the other set?" I ask the question because I have to be sure.

Sorin nods. "I'm set up to do it in the lab. We can go there now."

"Let's do it."

I'm a jangle of nerves and humming with anticipation as I follow Sorin through a warren of corridors to the space he calls the lab. Zinn trails behind me, uncharacteristically silent, but I think I understand. She's processing everything she's just done and contemplating her future. I don't know how long she was with Omega Prime, but I suspect it was years. And now she's free. Adrift. Solo.

The lab consists of a square room in the heart of the freighter. Three rows of black workbenches break up the space. Two are filled with a variety of complex apparatuses, some of which I recognize immediately, and some that I'm forced to look up. A brief scan shows me everything here is designed for work on electronic components, and some are made specifically to repair and create cybernetics. None of it is powered by AI, and the 'net claims it's outdated.

I don't care. I feel safer knowing there won't be a link back to Zylar Inc. should Sorin need to repair me for any reason. Any AI is a potential threat, a near-certain enemy.

Sorin leads us to the rear bench, the only one uncluttered by equipment and components. At its center is a deep basin. I think I know what he plans to do, and this time, he doesn't risk setting Daaros' apartment ablaze in the process.

He places the override codes in the bottom of the basin, then withdraws the suppressor from within one of his pockets. Sorin's expression is pensive as he looks at me.

"Are you ready?"

I nod once. I've never been so damned ready for anything in my life. I want those codes destroyed, obliterated beyond repair. I want them *gone*.

Zinn reaches toward me and grasps my hand. I glance at her, surprised, but she merely smiles and squeezes my fingers between her own.

"This is for you, Metal Man," she whispers.

Sorin turns to face the basin and plunges the suppressor into the center of the blasted device that has haunted my subconscious for weeks. Sparks erupt as he withdraws his hand, sizzling against the basin's dark sides. A wispy stream of bluish smoke begins to waft from the device, signaling the overdue destruction of my override codes.

I squeeze Zinn's hand and untangle my fingers a moment later, a grin stretching across my face. It's done.

I'm finally free.

ZINN JAREK

CHAPTER TWENTY-EIGHT

SORIN'S ENDGAME

"I thought Haven was a derelict shit heap, but look at that." Zinn plants her hands on her hips with a shake of her head, her gaze fixed on the metal monstrosity looming before us through the command deck's window.

My scans indicate that it's a conglomeration of at least fourteen different vessels, welded and mashed together in a seemingly random pattern. From the outside, it looks like an angry giant crumpled the steel together to form a tangled ball of dented and scarred metal, then cast it aside in a fit of galactic rage. As I study it, tiny yellow lights blink to life along the exterior at intervals, illuminating the craggy surface of the space station in stark relief before fading into the lightless void beyond.

Sorin calls it Station Six-Theta. It's a Coalition stronghold in the depths of uncharted space, floating through the Oort cloud of its distant star and safely on the opposite end of the galaxy from Omega Prime's Haven. The area is desolate, cold, and dark, the system's star so far away that it's little more than a large pinprick against the backdrop of space.

"We designed it to appear like nothing more than an asteroid to search drones," Sorin calls from a console not far away. "Typically, the exterior lights are off, but I turned them on for our final approach."

"Don't search drones scan for electronics?" I ask. "I just—"

Sorin laughs, cutting me off. "Zylar Inc. doesn't waste its resources checking for electronics this far away from civilized space. They don't know this base exists."

I would love to search through my former employer's classified database to verify his claim, but Station Six-Theta is light-years away from the nearest 'net relay. I'm cut off from the instant information I've grown accustomed to. I can rely on my personal databanks for weapon and vehicle specs, but not random data regarding a star system that won't be colonized for another century.

I turn back to the window to watch the freighter approach. The station is massive; there's a shadowy recess directly ahead that could engulf the disguised warship with room to spare, and it looks tiny compared to the expanse of twisted metal surrounding it. We're headed for the recess, and I suspect it's a docking bay. A few more seconds tick by, then lights blaze inside.

Yep, it's a docking bay.

"How long did it take to build this thing?" I ask without tearing my gaze away from the space station.

"Not as long as you might think," Sorin replies. "It was just a matter of collecting the galaxy's abandoned spacecraft and gathering them here, then making the interior suitable for habitation. You'd be surprised by the number of ships left rusting for one reason or another."

I snort, my thoughts flitting back to my salvaging days on Earth. "I'm well aware of the numbers. I also understand that less than a quarter of them wind up back home, but it's still enough to poison the planet and everyone stuck living there."

My words are laced with a bitterness that surprises even me, and Sorin falls silent. If by some miracle I survive his lunacy, I hope to return to Earth. Not to stay, but to do what I can to help those who remain. There are few others in this damned galaxy who understand the scope of suffering the natives of Earth are forced to endure every fucking day, and I want to make a difference.

Yes, I promised Daaros I'd fulfill my contract with him, but I don't think he'd be opposed to assisting me with some charity work. All celebrities do what they can to polish their PR image. He's no different.

And *yes,* I'm free now and could leave if I wanted to. Since Sorin fulfilled his promise, I feel obligated to help him with this final piece of his mission, and oddly enough, I *want* to. Bringing down the AI mainframe and Zylar Inc. with it gives me another opportunity to help.

We could destroy the override codes for the rest of ZIEG. We could free them too.

Maybe my time with Sorin has turned me into something of an optimist. He has that effect on people.

"Docking sequence initiated," someone behind me calls as the ship slips inside the gaping recess hollowed out of the faux-asteroid's side.

I stoop to gather the pieces of my armor where they're piled on the floor. I glimpse Sorin's expression in my periphery; he's contemplative, but there's sorrow etched into his features too. My sharp words must have struck a chord.

Good. The galaxy needs to know what humanity has done to Earth, what we've done to the souls left stranded there. The galaxy needs to make things *right*.

Sorin's Coalition is trying, but maybe it's time I ask him for more than his immediate plans. Overthrowing Zylar Inc.'s programmed government is a start, but will it be enough? Does he plan to do *more*, once he achieves his goals? Or is wresting control from the megacorp the extent of his scheme?

I turn to face him as he scans the crowded bridge from our position on the command deck. "I have questions, Sorin."

He nods. "Is this about the Coalition?"

"Yeah."

"I'm not surprised. Follow me after we've docked. We'll talk in private."

Sorin lingers on the command deck as his crew disembarks for the space station. Zinn paces nearby, reluctant to leave my side even for a moment.

I still don't fully understand why she threw away her career with Omega Prime for *me*. Don't misunderstand; I'm grateful she did, but I'd like to know why. She seemed happy with the mercs. Now, her future is as uncertain as mine.

As the last of the crew departs, Sorin motions for us to follow him. He says nothing while we walk, lost in his own thoughts.

Zinn falls into step at my side, a pensive expression on her face, but she also remains silent.

"Why did you do it?" I ask as we move through the cargo hold, unable to keep the question to myself any longer.

She laughs softly. "After you spilled your story at the Coalition's base, I finally understood why you were so edgy, why you hated Van Duval so fucking much. He had you pinned under his damned thumb, and you couldn't do anything to free yourself. With all your tech and fancy upgrades, ZIEG didn't exactly make you stealthy."

I snort a laugh. "They had enough of that series already by the time I was brought in."

"My point is, I was compelled to help," she replies with a shrug. "Part of my job as Scar-face's second was to keep him in check. I spoke to him about the codes, you know. He refused to give them up. He said he wasn't willing to 'lose the greatest fucking tool' he had in his arsenal over a point of 'irrelevant morality.' I told him to piss off. Then I called Sorin."

"When he finds out I'm gone, he'll know—" I begin, but she cuts me off with a wicked laugh.

"I'm counting on it, Metal Man. And it doesn't matter now, does it? He can't do a fucking thing to you. The codes are a slag heap in Ghosty's lab."

"So, you did all this because it was the right thing to do?" I ask, still skeptical. This aspect of Zinn Jarek doesn't mesh with the irreverent merc I've come to know—and call a friend.

"Tell yourself that if it helps you sleep at night, Pretty Boy," she replies with a mischievous wink. "Or maybe I did it because I *like* you."

I groan and look away as heat crawls across my face. Pablo once warned me about this when we were back on Earth, and I discounted his opinion as that of my best friend doing his best to cheer me up. But he was right. Too many people find me attractive, and I'd rather not draw their attention at all.

Zinn nudges my arm with her elbow. "I'm kidding, Mr. Serious. The truth is the boss had been pissing me off for a while. When he assigned me to shadow you, I thought it was a form of punishment. Babysitting a cranky cyborg was never in my job description, but he claimed he didn't trust anyone else to make sure Blue-eyes here didn't

run off with his 'asset.' I resented him—and you—for that. But then…
Against my better judgment, I started to like you. You're funny when
you aren't brooding, and you gave me an excuse to drive the
exoskeleton a few times. And on Z-1543, I learned just how fucking
scary you can be. I won't lie to you. It was a turn on."

I don't think my face can flush any hotter. Thankfully, we're at the
entrance to the umbilical and the passage is so narrow we're forced to
move single-file. I step ahead of her and hope my skin cools down
before we emerge on the other side.

I clear my throat. "Is that when…?"

Her laugh echoes behind me. "I think so. But don't worry. I know
now that I was wasting my time, and I won't force the issue. My point
is I started to *care* about you. Not as one of the boss' toys, but as a
person. And when you finally told me everything, I couldn't let him
hold you prisoner. It wasn't right, and he would have *never* willingly
released you. You're too valuable."

"And her call provided me with the opportunity I'd been waiting
for," Sorin says over his shoulder. "I take my promises seriously, and
I meant to fulfill the one I made to you, but I lacked a way in."

"That's me. The inside woman," Zinn replies with another laugh.
"But I had to get some assurances from Ghosty first. The boss will
hunt me to the ends of the galaxy when he finds out."

"You're part of the Coalition now," Sorin says, then pauses as he
steps from the umbilical into the pressurized hangar beyond. He
doesn't speak again until we've both emerged. "I look out for my
people, as much as anyone can. I promised I'd set you up with a new
identity, and it'll be a permanent one this time. We can discuss the
questions you both have while I work."

He leads us through a staging area where a number of his people
are already at work, sorting supplies and equipment. Tiny yellow-
orange lights illuminate our path toward an exit, while brilliant white
lights shine from the ceiling above. Crates and boxes are arranged in
rows through the space, and more are added every minute as three
cranes work in synchrony to move more supplies from the belly of the
freighter into the hold.

There's enough here to last all of Sorin's crew months, but I hope
we're not planning to stay that long.

"And how do you plan to update my ID when we're sitting at the ass-end of the galaxy?" Zinn asks, hands on hips. "I know enough about the process to understand it requires 'net access to update. You can't plug into me like you can him."

"I can still craft the ID," Sorin replies with a dismissive wave. "It won't update until we're within range of a 'net relay, but the bulk of the work can be done here. And I appreciate the reminder. We should update your ID too, Kye."

I grimace and force a nod. It's necessary, but I don't have to like the process.

We follow Sorin out of the staging area and into a warren of metal-plated corridors. Overhead lights flick on at our approach to illuminate the way ahead. We pass countless closed doors, each marked with a placard indicating what lies on the other side. An infirmary, a bio lab, an electronics lab, a weapons lab…

Our path turns and carries us through a residential section, but it has the feel of a place that hasn't been used in years. The air smells faintly metallic, an odor I've come to associate with space.

"Was the atmosphere turned off before we arrived?" I ask.

Sorin nods. "I turned it on at the same time I turned on the exterior lights. There's no point in generating breathable air or gravity if no one is here to use it. It's a waste of resources."

"I assume you had a backup plan if your systems didn't come online?" Zinn muses.

"I didn't get this far without contingencies in place," Sorin replies with a wry grin. "It's the only way the Coalition has survived so long, the only way it'll *keep* surviving. I have to stay one step ahead of Zylar Inc., GISA, and the galactic military, and adapt to whatever they decide to throw at us next. And they *will* throw something soon."

"Yeah." Zinn's tone is uncharacteristically somber. "They're still pissed about the mainframe. Someone has to pay for that shitshow."

"Which is why we need to strike before they do." Sorin pauses in front of a door and slides his glasses in place. "This is the room I took for myself. I'll answer your questions inside."

I watch as he moves his hands to a hidden panel in the middle of the door. My scanners detect the wiring inside, the biometric lock that can only be opened by him. He places his palm against the panel, and the door slides open with a soft whir. As we follow him inside, I note the door is four inches thick. He could use this room as a vault. Or a bunker.

Lights flick on overhead to reveal the sparse interior. A cot is crammed into one corner, and a handful of battered chairs are scattered in a haphazard ring in the center. The metal walls are bare, there are no windows, and the only thing I spy that might be considered a form of decoration is the bright red emergency kit leaning against one wall. It's obvious Sorin hasn't spent much time here.

I remain standing as Zinn risks perching on one of the chairs. It wobbles, one leg slightly shorter than the others, but she manages to balance well enough. Sorin sits down in another across from her as I begin to pace. I'm too restless to sit. I have too many unanswered questions spiraling through my mind, questions I'm sure only Sorin can answer.

Sorin leans forward to rest his elbows on his knees, his eyes keen behind the blue lenses of his glasses. He studies me as I pace, and I'm certain he can see every damned circuit and cable woven through my body as I move. Part of me wishes he'd set his glasses atop his head as he so often does, but another part doesn't give a damn anymore. Let him study the cyborg tromping across his room. He already knows what I'm capable of, even if I'm still discovering it for myself.

"You want answers. Ask away."

Zinn peers over her shoulder at me, then shakes her head with an amused smirk. "I think I should start. Metal Man needs time to settle down." When I nod, she says, "Your endgame. What is it?"

That was one of my questions, and I'm relieved she asked it first.

"I don't believe in 'endgames,'" Sorin replies with a shrug. "The path I'm on doesn't allow for it. Dismantling Zylar's stranglehold on the galaxy is only the first step. No single entity should be allowed so much power, and I don't plan to replace the megacorp's reign with an equally vile substitute. It will take time, but I hope to reinstate the Galactic Senate of two centuries ago, staffed by *biological* entities elected to their posts by popular vote. The AIs served their purpose at first, but their motives have become twisted, and as you're both aware, I no longer trust them."

"And what about people like me?" I demand, shooting him a frustrated glance. "I'm not fully *biological* anymore. Where do you see cyborgs in your grand future?"

"You were fully human once," he replies, his tone soft, contemplative. "That makes you biological, Kye."

"We have different needs than normal humans," I continue, unrelenting. "Will you give us representation too? Will you destroy the cache of override codes hidden in Zylar's vaults? Will you see the rest of them freed?"

He nods patiently. "We have already planned for all of those things. After my conversation with you the night we visited Ring Eight, I realized my mistake. Destroying your codes was only a portion of what I put in motion when we returned to the Coalition's HQ. I have amended our new Galactic Charter to include at least one cyborg representative in the future senate, and yes, I *will* see the rest of ZIEG freed. The proposed creation of the override codes was why I left Zylar Inc. to begin with. To knowingly subvert a person's free will… It's an atrocity that should have never been allowed." He pauses, then says, "We have a constitution too. That document outlines the new government's authority, its limitations, and the freedoms every citizen will be granted. The charter is the framework. It details how we'll enact the constitution."

I remember the constitution, but the charter is new.

"Can I see the charter?" I ask, unable to shake my uncertainty and skepticism. I need to see for myself what he plans for the galaxy. For *me*.

"Of course. I'll upload the latest version to your databanks when I create your new identity." He smiles ruefully. "I don't share draft copies with others, but in your case, I'll make an exception. You have defenses in place we mere humans lack. It will be safer in your head than it is on my tablet, and having a backup stored somewhere can't hurt."

"As long as you don't make a habit of using me as a data repository, we're good," I reply with a frown. "This will be twice now."

"This time, I am entrusting you with the beating heart of the Coalition," Sorin replies, his tone serious. "As I said, I don't share copies of the charter with others. I've let them view it under supervision, but you will be the only person in the galaxy to possess a copy. I am trusting *you* as much as you are trusting *me*."

I concede he has a point, and he *has* upheld his promises so far. "I'll read it tonight. Is it drastically different than the one I read before?"

"It is. We can talk again tomorrow if you have further questions," he says with a faint smile. "As I'm sure you will."

"Now that Metal Man is satisfied, I want to know exactly what you plan for me," Zinn cuts in, crossing her arms. "A new ID is a start, but anyone working with Omega Prime will recognize me, even if I dye my hair and change its style. Which I don't want to do," she adds firmly. "I need assurances, Blue-eyes. I've helped your cause when the boss wouldn't. You owe me."

"Wait," I cut in. "I wasn't—"

Zinn shoots a pointed look in my direction that causes the rest of my words to die on my lips. I cross my arms and glower at her, but I'll wait for Sorin to answer her before I ask anything else. I can be patient. Sometimes.

Sorin appears amused by our exchange. He leans forward, focused on Zinn. "I'm prepared to offer you a position in the Coalition's strike teams. You've proven yourself—both at Titan Base and on Z-1543. I'll ensure no one asks questions about your past. Most won't on principle—we're all here for our own reasons, and some of those reasons might appear…questionable. I doubt I can match Omega Prime's pay, but you will be compensated for your work."

Zinn tilts her head. "Is there hazard pay?"

Sorin laughs and leans back. "Of course. I'd be a terrible leader if I didn't offer it. Our missions are almost always dangerous, as you know."

She frowns at the floor, then nods. "I shouldn't expect anything else. Nothing's certain until we bring down the bots. Fine. I'm in."

Sorin shifts his gaze to meet mine. "You wanted to say something else before you left?"

"Yeah." I hesitate, unsure if he'll answer or if he expects me to read the Coalition's proposed charter first. "If you succeed, what do you plan to do *after?*"

"Ah. The *big* question." He studies me for a moment, then says, "Much of our plans for the future are outlined in the charter I gave you. I hope to reinstate a fair government, one where *every* planet has a say in its fate, including Earth. I haven't seen the devastation for myself, but your stories paint a grim picture. Something must be done to help those we've left behind, to prevent more situations like yours."

"Yeah, and I'm glad to hear it."

"But?" He prompts.

"I want to know what *you* plan. For yourself."

Zinn nods her agreement. "I'm with him on this piece, boss. We don't need to trade one dictator for another."

Sorin manages a weary smile. "No, we certainly don't. I plan to disappear from the public eye if we succeed. I'll help establish the new senate, of course, but I want no part in the political games that will inevitably ensue. I'd rather retire to some backwater planet where I can tinker in a private lab, light-years away from the spotlight and the stress of running an underground organization. It might surprise you, but I'm getting too old for this shit."

Zinn tips her head back and laughs, while I scan Sorin in silence. There is nothing to indicate he's lying; his heart rate is steady, he doesn't sweat, he maintains eye contact, and appears at ease.

I decide to believe him. If I don't, what hope do I have in surviving what comes next?

CHAPTER TWENTY-NINE

A WRAITH

Sorin was right. I have even more questions after reading his draft of the new Galactic Charter, but they're minor when compared with those I asked him previously. I'd like to know how he plans to implement elections in a galaxy that hasn't seen them since the AIs replaced human senators, and I need clarification on some of the nuances involved in his proposed judicial system.

But my big questions have been answered, and I'm ready to set aside my misgivings to assist him.

I don't want to join the Coalition as Zinn did. I'm unwilling to sign up for another organization after ZIEG, and I'm determined to fulfill my contract with Daaros once Sorin's schemes are finished. I think I'm better off working for the Botanaari heir than I am for any human.

Sorin's great most of the time, but I don't know if I'll ever fully forgive him for using the override codes when he did. To know I could have been *his* puppet rather than Zylar's is not a comforting thought. He may have corrected his mistake, but my trust will always remain fragile.

And I still have to survive his final scheme first. Despite his assurances, I'm not sure I will. What he plans to do isn't just risky, it's suicidal. It makes what we did on Titan seem like a stroll through the park. It will be a damned miracle if we aren't caught and executed.

I doubt Marim Zylar will be lenient with us after the death of her father and our first attack on the AI mainframe. The AIs sure as hell won't be. They aren't programmed to understand mercy.

An elbow nudges me out of my clouded thoughts. I glance to my right as Quiara slides into the chair next to mine.

"I understand your digestive system is efficient, but I don't think glaring will help you process your lunch." She offers a small, mischievous smile.

"Right." I came to the make-shift mess hall to eat, not to brood over possibilities that may or may not happen.

"You're still thinking about the briefing, aren't you?" She picks up a pale protein cube from her tray and scrunches her nose in distaste. It smells slightly rancid, but so do mine.

"Yeah. And that cube won't hurt you. I've had worse."

She shoots me a skeptical look. "I know you have, but what if that was part of the problem? Pablo said—"

"I had tumors. Yeah." I shrug uncomfortably and stuff a protein cube in my mouth. I don't want to talk about the planet that nearly killed me; it will only lead me back to thoughts of ZIEG, and I'm better off without those careening through my skull.

Quiara doesn't reply, nor does she attempt to take a bite. Damn it, now I have to say something.

I swallow and point at the protein cube between her fingers. "I don't believe for a second that our expired protein cubes were to blame for our medical problems. The tumors came from our salvage work. I was exposed to unshielded starship engine cores on a weekly basis, and barrels of toxic waste were more common than the devils were. Hell, even the atmosphere was contaminated. The tumors weren't caused by our food."

She nods and risks a small nibble, then grimaces. "It tastes off. And what devils?"

"It was what we called the Humboldt squid." I sigh, then pick up another protein cube as an idea strikes me. "Would you feel better if I scanned yours?"

She brightens. "Yes! I didn't think of that."

The scan takes only seconds, and as I suspected, nothing harmful is found. The strange taste Quiara complained of is the result of a synthetic protein breaking down somewhere within the cube, but the byproduct isn't dangerous. When I share my findings, she visibly relaxes.

"Thanks, Kye."

"Any time."

My attention is drawn across the table a moment later as the chair across from me is pulled out. I look up to find Zinn… With different hair. She still sports the mohawk—I doubt she'll ever willingly part with her preferred style—but it's now a brilliant shade of cerulean.

She crosses her arms and smirks, but doesn't immediately sit down as she pauses to gauge my reaction.

"I thought you didn't want to change your hair."

She flashes a grin. "I didn't at first, but it turns out blue goes better with these Coalition jumpsuits."

"Since when did you care about matching?" I ask, genuinely surprised.

She taps one finger against her lower lip, feigning thoughtfulness. "Since yesterday, when I was officially sworn in. You know, I've never been a part of anything like this before. And Blondie has a way of inspiring people that my former boss lacks."

I lift my eyebrows. "He's Blondie now?"

"Blondie, Ghosty, Blue-eyes, whatever." She laughs, then points at the last protein cube remaining on my tray. "Lunch looks appetizing. Do they have a drink mixer in here? I'm going to need something to wash the aftertaste out of my mouth."

"Over there." Quiara gestures vaguely toward one corner of the room, where a short queue has formed.

"I think some of Sorin's crew had the same idea," I add with a snicker.

Zinn tosses her head. "Ugh. Lines! I think I'll wait." She sits down and watches as I finish my last protein cube. "The boss said you've decided not to join, that you only plan to help, then go on your merry cyborg way."

I nod once, suspicious. "Yeah. Why does it matter?"

"It doesn't. I'm just nosy." She winks mischievously and looks like she'll say more, but falls silent as someone claps their hands for attention behind me.

Twisting in my seat, I find Sorin standing in the doorway, flanked by two Coalition members I recognize only vaguely. Without access to the 'net, scanning their identities is impossible. I'll have to wait for introductions like everyone else.

Sorin waits for the room to quiet before he speaks. "We've decided on an official plan, and I think most of you will be happy to learn we'll be leaving this station in five days."

A chorus of cheers and a smattering of applause follows his words. He smiles, but his eyes betray his exhaustion. I wonder if he's slept at all since our arrival.

Sorin gestures to the woman on his left. She's easily the shortest person in the room, but the auburn hair piled atop her head in an elaborate, twisted bun makes her appear several inches taller. She wears a Coalition jumpsuit, but I note her black boots sport a considerable heel. Her expression is stern, and despite her stature, I have the distinct impression she's not someone to be taken lightly.

"Trin will hold an official briefing in two days," Sorin continues as the woman nods. "Strike team assignments will be covered in Trin's briefing, and those assigned will meet with their designated leaders separately. Some of you will be assisting me directly."

Sorin's eyes meet mine, and I know where my name has fallen on his lists. I'll be with him.

The man on Sorin's left steps forward with a nod. There's more gray in his hair than brown, and his close-cropped beard is mostly white, but he sports the lean physique of an athlete. When he speaks, his voice is hoarse, and it's only then that I notice the scarring on his neck, half-hidden by his collar.

"Those assigned to other duties will report to me," he rasps. "You'll know where you've been placed after the briefing. In the meantime, I suggest you all prepare yourselves for our planned departure."

The trio disperses as the room erupts into excited chatter.

I turn to face Quiara. "Who was that?"

"Maximillian Burkhardt-Davies," she replies with a faint smile. "Former colonel in the galactic military and Sorin's go-to for secondary operations."

Zinn's eyes follow the lithe soldier as he crosses the room, her expression unreadable. "I've heard of him. I may have sabotaged a few of his ops in my early days with Omega Prime."

"Are you worried he'll recognize you?" Quiara asks.

Zinn tips her head back and laughs. "It would be surprising if he did. Fourteen years changes a person in more ways than one, and unless one of you assholes decides to tell him, he'll never know I was involved. Omega Prime protects its own, and we were never caught on those missions."

I lift an eyebrow. "But you have been caught before. I've seen your rap sheet."

She grins. "I'd be a shitty merc if I didn't have one, and you'd be a shitty cyborg if you hadn't looked it up."

I chuckle and shake my head, amused. "Your secret's safe with me."

She shrugs. "I wasn't worried about you. It's the quiet one that I can't read."

Quiara flushes slightly. "I won't say anything, but there's a good chance he already knows. Sorin shares almost everything related to personnel with Max."

"Hmm. I suppose I'll have to trust Ghosty's judgment. He's done okay by us so far, hasn't he, Metal Man?"

I nod in agreement. "Yeah. He has."

Trin is significantly older than I'd assumed, based on my brief assessment in the mess hall. She hides the signs of aging behind a thick application of makeup; it's artfully done and wouldn't be noticed by anyone lacking a scanner or infrared optics in their head. I have both, but I keep quiet about my observations as we await her briefing. Trin doesn't seem the type to appreciate that brand of attention.

She paces across the empty room she's chosen for her meeting, heels clicking briskly in time with her footsteps. There are no chairs, but someone has set up an array of empty shipping crates that we use as seating. Most of the warship's crew is present as I sink onto a crate beside Zinn.

Sorin leans against the wall behind her, his eyes closed. He doesn't sleep, though I think he needs to. The dark circles that ring his eyes have only expanded since his brief announcement two days ago.

Max stands a few paces from Sorin, his arms crossed as he surveys the room. His military background is apparent in his every movement, his stoic façade, the pristine condition of his jumpsuit, and the shine on his boots.

A pang of longing rips through my core as I make the connection. Damn it, I miss Kelsey. I haven't spoken to her in weeks.

Not that I've been given an opportunity. Haven was almost as isolated as Station Six-Theta is, and I wasn't going to ask Van Duval for time with the holoreceiver.

Trin stops pacing after a time while she scans the room. She nods, seemingly satisfied, then turns to face us directly. "As you're all aware, we have established the parameters for our next mission. It will not be simple, and even with careful planning, we expect there will be casualties."

A few whispers rustle through our ranks, but I remain silent. If Sorin's next step is what I suspect it is, we'll be lucky if anyone survives. I glance in his direction, but he's staring at the floor, his mouth twisted by a troubled frown. He doesn't like the odds, but he's pushing forward anyway. Great.

"Strike team assignments have been meted out to each team's captain," Trin continues. "Four teams will enter Megatropolis space covertly, and each will await the final signal before beginning their designated tasks. The signal will come from Sorin directly. If you receive communications from anyone else, assume it is an attempt by GISA to infiltrate our ranks and disrupt our operations. You are not to engage. Instead, immediately forward any suspicious communications to me, then await further instructions. Are we clear so far?"

Nods and murmurs of assent echo through the room.

"Good. The captains designated for each team are as follows. Quiara Jaide, security systems and oversight; Nate Braxxus, infiltration team one; Yao Ilu, infiltration team two; and Perrie Alarus, infiltration team three. You've been given a list of your team's members and their specialties. Meet with them before we depart to ensure everyone understands their role and our expectations."

Trin pauses to gesture toward Sorin. "There is one final team that has been chosen to assist the Blue Ghost directly. He will lead that team personally. It is imperative that the rest of you are prepared not only to complete your assigned duties, but to adapt and assist his team as circumstance requires. His team *cannot* fail."

Sorin pushes away from the wall, draws a breath, and scans the crowd for several moments. Finally, he says, "Xia Kavan, Zinn Jarek, Kye Verex, and Max will accompany me to the AI mainframe at the designated time. I'd like to meet with the four of you privately after we're finished here."

Zinn leans toward me and nudges my side with her elbow. "I figured he'd take us both," she whispers with a grin. "He needs the firepower."

"Hmm."

I can't muster the same level of enthusiasm. That nagging sense in the back of my mind that first reared its ugly head when I left Ring Eight hasn't disappeared. I don't know if I'll see Pablo again, or Daaros, or even my sister. I've agreed to help Sorin—maybe that wasn't the brightest idea I've had in my twenty-six years of existence—but I won't back out now. He helped me. Now it's time I reciprocate, no matter the end result.

I hope I'm wrong. I hope we succeed and that I'll find myself working as Daaros' bodyguard in a few weeks' time, but I can't shake the foreboding that grips me in its savage claws. It's persistent, relentless, and refuses to be dislodged.

I only half-listen to the designated captains as they rattle off the names of their assigned teams. I don't recognize many, and it wouldn't matter if I did anyway. I'm assigned to Sorin's crew, and I doubt it's for my combat abilities alone.

I cross my arms and scowl at the floor while the other teams file out of the room. Trin hesitates briefly once the room is empty of everyone except Sorin's group, but Sorin inclines his head toward the door, and she leaves without another word. I wonder what her role in all of this is, beyond facilitating the strike teams and their placement.

Sorin begins to pace as the door to the room whirs shut. "Nothing we say from this point forward leaves this room. The other teams cannot know what I have planned, for our safety and theirs."

"You know I'd never speak a word of your plans to anyone," Max replies, a worried frown creasing his face.

"It's imperative that *no one* learns," Sorin reiterates, blue eyes flashing fiercely. "I've chosen this team because I believe each of you *can* be trusted." He gestures at Max. "You've been here since the Coalition's inception. You've sacrificed more than anyone I know to help bring us to this point. Your loyalty isn't in question."

"I still don't like that we'll both be on Megatropolis for this mission." Max sighs with a frustrated shake of his head. "If our team is compromised or overrun, who will carry the mantle of the resistance? Trin's efficient, but she's not personable."

Sorin shrugs indifferently. "I need you there as backup. No one else knows the sequence to disable the mainframe, and I'm not going to risk installing those instructions in our cyborg friend's head. He'll be in danger as it is."

"No shit. Half of ZIEG will recognize my armor on sight, and if I don't wear it, they'll know my face. How exactly do you plan to avoid that?" I demand.

Sorin chuckles. "We'll be making a stop on Botanaar before we head to Megatropolis. The list you gave Daaros consisted of items required for this mission. Some we'll deploy while inside Zylar Inc. HQ, but some of those components were earmarked for a different purpose." He grins. "The Botanaari agreed to manufacture you a new set of armor. It will link with your cybernetics just as the other set does. And I plan to add a firewall to your armor itself, which should free up some of your system's resources for other tasks. To any of Zylar's scans, you'll be a nameless soldier wearing gear they've never encountered before. In effect, you'll be untraceable. A wraith."

I gape at him. "You can do that?"

"With the help of Botanaar's brightest minds, yes." He crosses his arms, clearly pleased with himself. "Don't worry. Your inclusion within our ranks won't be a problem, and Daaros oversaw the allocation of resources for this project himself. If I've learned anything about the Vynaas or his heir, it's that they will do *anything* to protect their allies. And their people will follow their commands without question."

"I didn't realize Daaros was involved with this," I mutter, stunned.

"He wouldn't have bothered if it were anyone else," Sorin replies. "But it isn't anyone else. It's *you.* You have Pablo to thank for his interest."

"I know."

I can't help but feel guilty about how I left Ring Eight. Pablo wanted assurances I couldn't give him. But now? If this new armor is everything Sorin claims, I might walk away from Megatropolis unscathed after all. I might see my best friend again.

I look up to meet Sorin's gaze. "When do we leave?"

CHAPTER THIRTY

BACK IN BUSINESS

BOTANAAR, VYNAAS HOME/KEPLER-47 SYSTEM

I've never seen a binary star system, and even with the green expanse of planet looming in the shuttle's windscreen ahead, I can't stop staring at the twin suns crouching in the system's heart. We're far enough away that both stars appear no larger than Earth's sun did from my home world's surface, but there's something captivating and *alien* about a binary system. One star glows yellow-white, the other a glaring red.

"That's Botanaar?" Xia asks from beside me. Her voice sounds as awestruck as I feel.

"Yes," Sorin replies from his post in the co-pilot's seat. "We've been granted special access to visit by Vynaas Caaram Syl'Vaasis himself."

"They're requesting our clearance," Max cuts in as he taps the console in front of him.

Sorin swivels in his seat to face forward once more and begins to input a complicated sequence. I ignore the two men piloting our shuttle and return my gaze to the view of space beyond the shuttle's windscreen.

We're on the dark side of the planet, but its verdant nature is still evident. Deep green swaths are intersected by lighter bands of jade and lime, then punctuated by small clusters of glowing white. A brief query of the 'net informs me that each white cluster marks a Botanaari city. The planet is roughly four and half times the diameter of Earth, and nearly every inch of it is covered in plant life. The Botanaari have cultivated their world and it thrives, even as they've begun to take to the stars.

I thought Megatropolis was stunning with its recreational gardens and vine-covered skyscrapers, but its flora is minimal when compared with the lush expanse of greenery that marks Botanaar. And we're still looking at the world from space. What must it be like on the surface?

"Are there palm trees?" I muse aloud, thinking of a long-ago conversation I had with Pablo. Earth used to have palm trees. I've always wanted to see one.

Zinn snorts behind me. "You're one of only a handful of humans who has ever been granted access to Botanaar, and you're asking about palm trees? Damn, Metal Man. You need to get out more."

I ignore her and research the topic on my own. The Botanaari don't allow non-native species of plants on their home world, so the palm trees I recall from watching holovids won't be present. It's disappointing, but I note there are several similar trees that grow in the equatorial zone. The leaves are slightly broader, the trunks smoother, but in basic shape, they're a close approximation. Maybe I'll see some form of palm tree after all.

A trio of Botanaari Sun Cruisers materialize out of the darkness ahead, yellow lights blinking unspoken commands.

"Our escort's here," Max says uneasily.

I tense involuntarily and enable my firewalls, knowing they'll scan the shuttle and the identities of those aboard. Sorin has updated our IDs, and I'm now masquerading as Jason Mironov, starship mechanic. Zinn hasn't told me what her new name and history are, and I'm not sure she will.

The shuttle's console chimes, indicating the initiation of the Botanaari scans. I force my heart rate to remain steady, but my sensors scream that the others' are accelerating. Even Sorin's beats faster.

Shit. It's a bad sign when *he's* nervous.

A burst of static pulses through our shuttle's speakers seconds later, then a smooth voice states, "We've been expecting you. We're here to guide you to the Vynaas' complex in Sylvii City."

It doesn't immediately register that he speaks Botanaari until Sorin lurches toward the console to enable the ship's translator. I think I'm too relieved to process it, until I pause to think it over. I relay the Botanaari's words as Sorin taps frantically on the display.

Sorin peers at me over his shoulder. "I didn't realize they'd added aural translation implants into the ZIEG cybernetics."

I shrug uncomfortably. It's probably buried in my system spec documentation somewhere, and I've never bothered to read it. As we both know, I have a history of that.

"I didn't know."

"It will be faster to have you speak with them," he replies, then motions toward the console. "Tell them we're prepared to follow their lead."

I move forward, then hesitate. I can understand Botanaari, but I don't know if I can speak it. "Um…"

Sorin looks up at me, a quizzical expression on his face. "The translator implant was supposed to work both ways. Did they only perform a partial implementation?"

"I don't know."

He chuckles and holds up a hand, then starts tapping on the console once more. "Don't worry about it. We can figure out the nuances of your implant later. We don't have time to go over it now." He sits back after several seconds with a nod. "They'll understand the text-based message well enough."

"Would the information be somewhere in my specs?" I ask.

He nods. "Probably. Search for aural communications translator."

I query my databanks, and… Nothing. "Huh."

Sorin lifts an eyebrow. "No luck?"

I shake my head. "No. This is the first time I haven't found a spec for something they…added."

He frowns. "I can take a look at it later. The failure to upload the spec to your system is unusual, and now I'm intrigued."

Max laughs dryly. "Of course you are. Any mysterious tech will pique your interest."

"Prepare for atmospheric entry," the same smooth Botanaari voice says through the speakers.

I relay the message, and Max sits up straighter, immediately alert. Sorin gestures toward the shuttle cabin.

"We'll need to focus for a few minutes as we navigate Botanaar's skies," he says. "We'll talk more once we're on the ground."

"You know I can interface directly with the shuttle and make piloting easier for you all, right?" I ask as I turn away. Irritation seeps into my tone; I'm more capable than Max is, and I can react faster. I don't understand why I'm always relegated to the role of passenger.

Sorin chuckles. "We know, Kye. But I'd rather not overtax your systems needlessly in the face of our upcoming missions."

And there it is. I'm too valuable to play pilot. I'm only good for two things in Sorin's eyes: defending him and his data, and slaughtering enemy cyborgs. *Fuck.*

I cross my arms as I move toward one of the cabin's side windows to glare outside. One of the Sun Cruisers banks on our shuttle's right, visible through the window, yellow jets of superheated plasma discharging from its exhaust as it angles toward the blue-green haze of Botanaar's upper atmosphere. Our shuttle banks a half second later, matching the Sun Cruiser's trajectory. The Botanaari craft are sleek and appear more aerodynamic than our standard shuttle, a testament to the craftsmanship and elegance their people value so deeply.

The Sun Cruiser's mechanical beauty reminds me of Daaros and the collection of finery housed in his apartment. It isn't the result of his upbringing as the Vynaas' heir, but his heritage as a Botanaari that makes him crave and covet the galaxy's most exquisite items.

The shuttle vibrates and shudders as its nose penetrates the atmosphere. We descend rapidly, the Sun Cruisers flanking us on either side, with the third some distance ahead. We lance through Botanaar's midnight sky, then begin to arc in an easterly direction. Within minutes, light blazes across my view as we near the planet's daylight side.

The world below is dense with forest. Trees tower to unimaginable heights, some taller than even Megatropolis' skyscrapers, their trunks as wide as the freighter-turned-warship we left behind during our brief stop on Cobalt Asteroid. Soft lights illuminate some of the boughs we pass, and I realize the Botanaari have built their homes, their cities, their businesses *within* the trees. The lights shine from inside rooms, through windows set into the sides and ceilings. I'd never imagined such architecture was possible.

Humanity has tried to incorporate nature into its building designs on occasion. The vines and gardens on Megatropolis are proof of that, but we've never managed to do it so seamlessly. We're better at obliterating the natural beauty of our surroundings, poisoning them with our toxic shit and apathy.

Yeah, I'm still bitter about what we've done to Earth. I always will be, unless we fix it.

The forest below slowly thins, then gives way to a vast grassland. Lakes and streams glimmer at intervals, many surrounded with more impossibly tall trees. The shuttle slows as we approach a new expanse of forest. A suspended landing pad comes into view, held up between the gnarled branches of a dozen trees. Lights sparkle from beneath the forest's canopy, indicating more Botanaari buildings are nearby.

Max lands in the center of the pad, and only after our engines are turned off, the Sun Cruisers land too.

I stare at the massive branches around us as we exit the shuttle. From a distance, I couldn't make out the details, but now, I see they're twined with innumerable vines and draped with flowers and leaves from dozens of other plant species growing directly on the bark. A breeze rustles the flora, but the soft susurration is nearly drowned by a persistent, droning hum. I automatically adjust my aural implants to reduce the volume of that particular noise.

"What the hell is that?" Zinn asks, clapping her hands over her ears.

A familiar laugh sounds to my left. "It's sun hopper mating season. They sing."

I swivel to find Daaros standing between two of the Sun Cruiser escorts, a knowing smirk on his lips. The pilots of the Sun Cruisers exit their craft moments later and offer him salutes, which he acknowledges with a brief nod. They begin to relay our journey in Botanaari, while we stand in a tight cluster, awaiting the heir's next command.

Daaros holds himself in a self-assured manner, his face an expressionless mask as they speak. The hair-like fringe on his head is combed and styled carefully in his usual manner, but his clothing is of a higher quality than anything I've seen him wear before. The collar of his shirt is open just enough to display the opal-studded *diivoraa*, and he sports cufflinks to match. He *looks* the part of royalty here.

I frown. Daaros' presence raises a dozen questions in my mind. And if he's here, where the hell is Pablo? I hope he wasn't stupid enough to leave my best friend alone on Ring Eight, knowing what

Sorin has planned for Megatropolis. Pablo has no damned business getting tangled up in that shit.

Daaros motions the pilots away, then beckons to us. "Come. My fathers are expecting you."

He leads us past the spacecraft to a suspended bridge that disappears amidst the dense foliage ahead. I'm bursting to ask him questions, but Sorin's sharp glance silences the urge.

I search the 'net for information on Botanaari customs, but find very little. The Botanaari don't share the intimate details of their society with the wider galaxy, and I learn we're only the third group of humans to set foot on Botanaar in the past century. Most of what I've learned about their people has come from my interactions with Daaros on Ring Eight, where he was a famed curiosity and wealthy businessman. Here, he is more.

And I don't know what constitutes proper interactions with Botanaari royalty.

The bridge winds through the trees for a short distance before opening onto a broad plaza, also suspended between the trees. The plaza rests at the foot of the largest tree we've encountered so far, and is ringed with a series of carefully-tended gardens packed with an array of white flowers. Their scent carries on the wind, floral with a hint of something spicy. Cinnamon, perhaps.

The tree we face is ringed in glass from the level of the plaza all the way to the highest branches far above. I crane my neck to take in the sight and only manage to make myself momentarily dizzy. It seems impossible that trees should grow this large, yet here they are.

We're led through a glass door and enter the dappled, sunlit realm of the Vynaas' complex. Comfortable benches ring the interior wall of the first tier, their backs brushing against the massive tree's bark. Daaros strides through the room toward an elevator some distance from the entrance. A pair of armored Botanaari stand sentinel outside the elevator, and they salute Daaros as we approach.

"My father's guests have arrived," he says in Botanaari. "Your scanners will likely pick up falsities in their identifications, but given who they are, it's to be expected."

I lift my eyebrows and glance at Sorin, startled and concerned. He forces a tight smile and shakes his head.

"Their tech is superior to ours. Don't worry," he whispers.

One by one, the others are allowed to enter the elevator, but I'm left outside until the end. Something *is* wrong, even if Sorin won't admit it.

Daaros crosses his arms as the sentries scan me for the second time. "Drop your firewalls, Kye."

I nod uneasily and comply. One of the sentries gapes at his scanner, as though he can't believe what the display is showing him. The other points at the screen and mutters excitedly.

"A real cyborg! I thought they were a myth."

"The last time I checked, I was very real," I reply with a scowl.

The sentries glance at Daaros; they don't speak Standard, but they're aware my comment was directed at them. Daaros rolls his eyes at me, then translates my words.

"Let him through," he finishes. "*He's* the reason why the others are here. And I'm sure Pablo would love to see him."

"Pablo's here?" I ask, my irritation immediately forgotten.

"Of course," Daaros replies in Standard. "Do you think I'd risk leaving him behind while the Coalition storms Megatropolis? I would never forgive myself if something happened to him. Besides, wasn't it you who threatened my life if I ever did anything to hurt him?"

I flush and flick a glance at the sentries. Their eyes dart between us, but they remain silent.

"They don't speak your language," he assures me. "It's fortunate. If they knew of your past threat, you'd be made to stand trial for the affront and likely found guilty. Sorin needs you, and Pablo would be distraught if my father tossed you in prison." He smiles knowingly. "Come. They've delayed us long enough."

The sentries part at Daaros' command, and we're finally allowed into the elevator. Sorin arches an eyebrow in question, and I shrug in response. I'll let Daaros explain what happened and why.

"I wasn't sure they'd let you through, Metal Man." Zinn leans against the elevator wall across from me, her arms folded across the denim jacket she wears.

Daaros taps a button on the console, and we begin to rise. He turns to offer Zinn an appraising stare. "Kye's firewalls disrupt our scanners' ability to read him, and my father's guards were under the impression cyborgs aren't real."

"Is this going to be a problem?" I growl at Sorin. "I can't parade around the galaxy without my damned firewalls enabled. Botanaar may be safe, but nowhere else is."

"Your system's defenses were designed to subvert standard galactic technology," Sorin replies smoothly. "The Botanaari Sun Cruisers who met us above employ standard tech. The Vynaas utilizes a superior system in his complex, one that isn't available outside Botanaar."

"Okay, I get it. Royalty has its perks." I release a sigh and slump against the glass wall behind me. "I just hope this is all worth it."

Daaros chuckles. "It will be. Some of my best scientists created your new armor based on the schematics Sorin shared. I suspect they were stolen from ZIEG directly, but I don't want to know their origin. It's better if I don't." He pauses to stare outside as we ascend past tier after tier of glass-enclosed and lavishly decorated spaces. "The armor will interface with your body just as your other set did, but with significant improvements to its functionality. I think you'll be happy with the end result."

The elevator chimes and the doors slide open. Daaros steps outside and motions for the rest of us to follow.

"But first, you must meet with my fathers."

More sentries greet us as we approach a room whose outer walls are opaque, a first in the towering complex. We're scanned again, then Daaros leads the procession through the wide double doors and into the room beyond. A dais sits at the opposite end, where two Botanaari stand awaiting us. On the steps below them are another set of guards, two more Botanaari dressed as immaculately as Daaros, and one dark-haired human with the warmest smile in the galaxy.

I grin at Pablo but resist the urge to run forward to greet him. I don't know the protocol here. We're in the presence of the Vynaas and his partner, the Minister of Intelligence. I'm pretty sure every word we say and every move we make will be scrutinized and dissected by the two men standing atop the dais.

Daaros stops at the base of the steps and nods to his fathers, who continue to study our group with impassive gazes. I don't know which

Botanaari is the Vynaas and which is the Minister, and Daaros' features are a perfect blend of the two. They don't look any older than he is, but I've read that Botanaari don't show age as humans do. It has something to do with osmotic pressure and cell walls, though I don't recall the exact science behind it.

One of the men steps forward. His hair-like fringe is loose and falls nearly to his shoulders. He has the same nose shape as Daaros and the same trim build beneath an embroidered vest and matching pants. His arms are bare to the shoulder, and I'm once again unsettled by the lack of muscle tone that my once-human eyes expect to see. I have to remind myself they're *plants*.

"I am Uros Taal'Sym, Minister of Intelligence on Botanaar, and life partner to our venerated Vynaas," he says in flawless Standard. "Our son and heir has arranged this meeting at our behest. It is past time we met with the Resistance Coalition and its leadership face-to-face."

Daaros nods again. "Fathers, this is Sorin Johnston, the Coalition's founder and leader, and Maximillian Burkhardt-Davies, his second-in-command." Daaros gestures to them each in turn. "With them are their special escort, Xia Kavan, Zinn Jarek, and Kye Verex."

The minister's eyes focus on mine at the mention of my name. My heart rate begins to accelerate under his scrutiny, but I don't adjust my biochems to slow it. The Botanaari need to see I'm still partially human, and unchecked nerves are the best way to show them. I don't want them to think I'm nothing more than a convenient piece of tech. I'm more than that.

"You're the cyborg our son believed he saved," the Vynaas says, breaking the silence.

I flick my gaze in his direction, and note he sports more jewelry than the *diivoraa* and cufflinks the others wear. Rings sparkle along his green fingers, and a belt of platinum links is threaded through the loops of his black pants. He wears an ivory button-down shirt that looks to be made of real silk that shimmers softly in the sunlight spilling in through the ceiling. His eyes rake across my form, calculating and emotionless.

"Yes, sir," I manage, unsure if I should say anything more.

His lips twitch into a smile. "Good. It pleases us to know the Coalition upholds its promises. Daaros will take you and the others to the compound's private laboratory while we speak with Sorin and Maximillian privately."

Twenty minutes later, we've relocated to the laboratory, where a set of cybernetic armor sits proudly on display across a workbench. Pablo has joined us, as have the two Botanaari we encountered in the Vynaas' chamber. Kaalor and Iinas are Daaros' brothers, though both bear the Taal'Sym name. I learn Daaros is the only Syl'Vaasis their fathers have produced.

"We were summoned here ten days ago," Pablo whispers to me as we walk across the lab. "When Sorin sent word he was preparing to strike, the Vynaas felt it was too dangerous for us to stay on Ring Eight."

"Isn't your second term at MSTI supposed to start soon?" I ask.

He nods. "I've been transferred to Sylvii University here on Botanaar. The Vynaas insisted." He blushes and looks away. "I don't know what Daaros has told him, but he's accepted me and expects that I receive nothing but the best education. I... I'll hold the title of Elnaas when Daaros replaces his father."

A brief query tells me Elnaas is reserved for the life partners of the Vynaas alone. I lift my eyebrows in surprise. "Seriously? You'll be...a prince. Or close to it."

"I know." He shifts uneasily as we stop near the workbench holding my new armor. "I never expected any of this to happen."

"That makes two of us."

I grin and begin to inspect the armor, while Daaros waits in silence on the other side of the bench. His brothers stand a short distance away, speaking animatedly with Zinn and Xia. I ignore their conversation and conduct a brief scan.

The armor is tailored to my genetic signature. How Daaros managed that, I don't know, but I suspect Sorin had a hand in it. This suit shares the precise dimensions of my other set, but the exterior isn't as garishly obvious. It's a deep green, almost black, with lighter green highlights around the seams. The helmet's visor is tinted and reflective to hide my face, and there's a tiny interface socket in the back that will align with the data port on my neck.

I look at Daaros and shrug. "It will fit, but there's only one way to know if the interface works as intended."

He nods, a mischievous smirk sliding across his lips. "Then I suppose you'd best try it on."

I recall my first time interfacing with my other armor and the disorientation that ensued. It didn't last more than a few seconds and I wasn't prepared for it, but this time, I am. I haul the armor off the workbench and set it upright, then strip off my clothes and step inside. The suit responds immediately, enveloping me like a second skin.

Several seconds pass before the sensory onslaught abates, but this armor has integrated more seamlessly with my systems than my other set ever did. And Sorin wasn't lying about the firewall; it's part of the armor and was activated the moment I put it on. That will definitely free up my resources for the upcoming mission.

Pablo hands me the helmet. "I helped design the visual interface," he says shyly.

I flash him a grin before I set it in place. "Thanks, Pab."

The interface displays atmospheric conditions that I'd typically need to query separately, and when I look at a person, their vitals are visible on the right-side overlay. Both will be useful when we storm Zylar HQ.

"Look at that," Zinn calls, her tone amused. "Slaughter is back in business, and he looks even deadlier than before."

CHAPTER THIRTY-ONE

CYBERNETIC MONSTERS

MEGATROPOLIS, TRAPPIST-1 SYSTEM

We've made it through every security checkpoint between Ring Eight and Megatropolis' nanosteel and concrete laden surface, and are hidden in a warehouse somewhere beneath the financial district. We've been here for three days while Sorin ensures the strike teams are in place and finalizes his plans. I'm tired of waiting.

The warehouse is empty except for our gear, and only Xia and Zinn have been allowed to leave on occasion. Xia usually returns with bottles of water and news. Zinn always comes back laden with bags and boxes of food. I've learned I like tamales, pineapple, and barbecued meat of any form. I don't care for onions, and I discover cilantro has the flavor of rancid soap. Not all food tastes better than expired protein cubes.

Beyond the excitement of trying new foods, I'm restless. I read novels from the 'net, but miss the tactile feel of a paperback in my hands. And Zinn finds it "fucking creepy" when I stare into space for long periods of time. Apparently, that's what it looks like when I'm reading through my 'net interface.

Max and Sorin discuss strategy for hours each day, pausing only to eat or share updates they find important. I don't know what more they have left to plan; everything seemed set when we left Station Six-Theta.

Which leaves me.

I'm anxious. I crave action, but dread it in equal measure. Sorin's next call to arms is going to change the damned galaxy one way or another, and I'm not sure I'm prepared for my part in it. Yeah, I'm just acting as his bodyguard for this mission, and he *might* need my interface, but I'm also aware of the potential consequences if we're caught. My new armor skews the odds slightly in our favor, but not enough to let me relax.

I'm still pretty sure this is going to be a suicide mission for some of us. Will I be one of the casualties? I don't know. There's only one way to find out… And I'm not ready. Not yet. But I *am* bored.

Zinn returns during the afternoon of the third day, two bags laden with old-Earth Thai-style cuisine in hand. The food smells delicious, and everyone takes a carton but Sorin. He leaves Max to eat and begins to pace the length of the room. I frown as I eat my chosen noodle dish; it's spicy and savory, filled with julienned vegetables and strips of real pork, then topped with chopped peanuts. It's fantastic, but my enjoyment of our meal is dulled by Sorin's edginess.

My sensors indicate his pulse thunders, his breathing is shallow, and he's covered in a cold sweat. Either something is wrong, or he's about to deliver the news I've been waiting—and dreading—to hear. My bet's on the latter.

Sorin says nothing until we've finished eating and are collecting the cartons for disposal. He continues to pace, but his face has become an expressionless mask, the visage of a man prepared to do what is necessary to fulfill his goals, no matter the cost. His vitals have calmed but remain slightly elevated. He exchanges a glance with Max, who nods subtly in return.

I know what's coming. I've been watching, waiting, *fearing* this moment for the past half-hour. Fucking hell, I wish he'd issue the orders and be done with it.

Waiting is the worst.

Sorin stops and swivels to face the rest of the group, his spine rigid. "Gear up. It's time."

Zinn is the only one brash enough to speak up. "I knew something was on your damned mind, boss. Next time, just say it."

Sorin replies, but I'm not listening anymore. I walk to the cubicle in the corner of the room where my armor is stashed while mentally preparing for what's to come. I know we'll face ZIEG soldiers. Maybe not our team specifically, but they'll be in Zylar Inc. HQ. I hope Luna's squad has been dispatched elsewhere. I don't want to face her or Vee, and I *really* don't want to be forced to make a life-or-death call when fighting one of them.

They'll see me as a fucking traitor. Maybe I am, but if they only knew about the override codes, they'd understand.

I grimace and swallow a groan, pushing those thoughts away. I can't dwell on what-ifs. I have to focus on what *is*.

I trade my borrowed Coalition jumpsuit for the sleek, dark green armor Daaros commissioned, then take a final inventory of my other supplies. The pouch on my utility belt holds six protein cubes and two hydration packets. It's enough to see me through this operation and another full day, if needed. A pair of nanosteel daggers clip to my belt, and a ZIEG-style handcannon holsters at my hip. Extra ammunition clips line my belt opposite the pouch; projectile rounds, plasma rounds, and several varieties meant to incapacitate, but not kill.

The last item I set in place is my helmet. Sorin has already linked his comms to it, and is in the process of patching in the other strike team leaders when the audio connects to my implants. It's another improvement to my old armor; the helmet acts as the relay instead of my head. I should be able to maintain focus and react more swiftly without that constant drain on my resources.

I exit the cubicle and walk toward Sorin's location near the warehouse's exit. He's changed into a white uniform and a blue lab coat with the Zylar Inc. logo above the breast pocket. It's the same lab coat he wore the day I first met him, before I knew who he was. The day he stole my fucking override codes and set me on this damned path. The iridescent blue glasses are perched atop his blond hair, but he slides them over his eyes as I near.

He studies me for a time, then nods. "Your connections are flawless. Daaros' people did a better job than I believed possible."

"You thought they'd do a subpar job?" I ask, incredulous. I'm not sure it's in a Botanaari's nature to do anything half-assed. I certainly can't picture it.

He chuckles and shakes his head. "The Botanaari aren't familiar with cyborgs, and you're one-of-a-kind. I knew they were capable of following the specs I sent, but I didn't know they'd create this masterpiece. How does it feel? I never asked you on Botanaar."

I flex my fingers in response. "Great. It responds a few nanoseconds faster than the other set, but it's the extra features I like best."

"The firewall?" he asks.

"And the relay. I can focus better without maintaining external data streams."

"Good. I think you'll need that focus tonight."

An hour later, we're crammed into a shuttle meant for three, parked on the ground level near a maintenance entrance to the Zylar Inc. company headquarters. I'm sprawled in the storage compartment behind the rear seat, the only space available to my armor-bulked frame. The others wear stolen corporate garb, and Zinn dons a beret with the ZIEG logo to hide her mohawk. I'm the only one who doesn't sport a company logo somewhere.

"INF-team two in position," Yao's voice states in my helmet. "We're through lobby security."

"Good. Standby," Sorin replies from the front of our shuttle.

Seconds later, Nate speaks. "INF-team one has landed. Rooftop's clear. Standing by."

I count the seconds as we await team three's confirmation. They're supposed to follow team one through the lobby after two hundred seconds have passed. My chronometer ticks past two-twenty, then two-thirty. I peer over Xia's head toward Sorin, but he's facing forward, his expression drawn.

"INF-team three in position," Perrie's voice cuts through the tension. "En route to the forty-seventh floor."

I exhale silently, relieved.

"Stand by for security override," Quiara says, a smile in her tone. "Building security breach in five…four…three…two…one…"

"Power next," Sorin says.

"Yep, working on it." Quiara is business-like, unfazed by the enormity of what we're attempting to do. "And…done."

With her words, the entire sector goes dark. Illuminated signs and building lights wink out on all sides. As I clamber out of the shuttle, I look up at Megatropolis' night sky; the stars are visible without the light pollution to wash them out. It's a rare sight on this world. I switch to night vision.

Xia moves to the door we've been monitoring, the others following closely behind. I take up the rear, my palm on the butt of my handcannon as I peer along the shadowed alley. I hear traffic overhead, but no emergency sirens wail through the night. Not yet.

A click behind me is followed by a hiss. "Got it," Xia mutters.

I glance over my shoulder, watching as first Zinn, then Max dart through the open door. I continue to scan our surroundings until everyone else has entered the building, then I follow them inside, pulling the door shut behind me.

"Takedown team in position," Sorin says over the comms.

"Power coming back online in three…two…one," Quiara replies.

Harsh overhead lights glare into life, and I grimace involuntarily. I switch back to standard vision, then take in our surroundings.

We're in a small nanosteel-lined chamber with an elevator on the opposite side. Next to the elevator is a door leading into a stairwell. Our plan was to take the stairs into the depths beneath Zylar Inc. HQ, where the AI mainframe was relocated. The elevator is too risky, and Sorin's intel indicated the security system along the stairs is easier to compromise.

We'll know how good his intel is in a few seconds.

"Camera system override in three…two…one…"

"You all know what to do," Sorin says. "Good luck. We'll see you back at Cobalt when this is done. Infiltration teams maintain radio silence until this operation is complete."

Zinn yanks open the door to the stairwell and steps inside, leading with the barrel of her plasma pistol. She looks up, then down, then gives us the all-clear signal.

I scan the levels above as I step into the stairwell, but detect no vital signs beyond those of our group. It doesn't mean we're safe or alone—the CVRT-BT series cyborgs have the ability to mask their vitals from scans, a handy addition to their stealth capabilities. I have neither, but I *do* have infrared vision. They can't hide from that. I switch modes and glance upward, but there's nothing to see.

I nod to Sorin, and we begin a rapid descent. We don't speak, though our footfalls are indication enough of our passage. I continue to scan the levels above and hope our route remains undiscovered.

We're four levels below the ground floor when Quiara provides an update. "Zylar Inc. has detected our initial breach. They haven't managed to break through our overrides, but someone was dispatched to ZIEG HQ for backup. We should have seven minutes before ZIEG arrives, given traffic patterns and the maximum speed of the shuttle they've deployed."

"ZIEG shuttles are faster," I warn.

"I've factored that in."

Seven minutes. We have another six floors to descend, a security console to hack, and a mainframe to eradicate in that time. Sorin believes the mainframe won't be left undefended, which means there will likely be a skirmish of sorts before he can begin the viral upload. And then there's the matter of our escape.

Seven minutes isn't enough damned time, but we all knew that going in.

"The infiltration teams are there to provide a distraction," Sorin reminds us as we race down the stairs. "Our task is what must be accomplished, no matter the cost. And we'll do it."

Max nods in silent agreement as Xia says, "We know the stakes."

"And we're still here," Zinn adds with a grin. "Don't sweat it, boss."

We reach the bottom of the stairs with five minutes to go. I position myself on the bottom step and scan the floors above, while Sorin begins the process of disabling the security console attached to the wall next to a steel-plated door. The others fan out between us, with Zinn and Xia focused on the door, weapons drawn in preparation for whatever we encounter on the other side.

Reluctantly, I pull the handcannon from its holster and flick off the safety. It's loaded with plasma rounds; they're safer than projectiles in our steel-coated surroundings. Plasma doesn't ricochet.

I hear the whir of the door's locking mechanism disengage behind me, but I don't turn around. We have four and a half minutes at best before ZIEG arrives, and I doubt they'll show up in small numbers. I will not leave our rear undefended until we're through that damned door.

"Be ready," Max warns.

Seconds later, someone pulls the door open, and they begin to file inside. A single shot is fired from close range—Zinn or Xia, maybe Max—and then Sorin tugs at my elbow.

"Three ZIEG soldiers at the mainframe," he hisses.

I spin around and charge inside, making sure he's behind me. I can take more punishment than Sorin, and he's the only one who can hack the mainframe without causing us further delays. But three soldiers are more than we've counted on.

One is crumpled in front of the holoscreen used to access the mainframe. A single bullet hole leaks blood and brain matter from the center of his forehead. The shot came from Xia then; she's the only one with projectile rounds loaded in her weapon.

Relief washes through me as I fail to recognize the first casualty. It wasn't Luna or Vee. It wasn't Chadwick or Captain Wax or any of the cyborgs I knew in passing.

One of the others is engaged with Zinn, while the third crouches behind the console, her vital signs masked. She's focused on Zinn, but draws a plasma rifle carefully from her back and aims.

It's only then that I realize she's in stealth and I'm the only one who can see her. Her hair is loose and obscures the side of her face. I don't know if we've met, but I sure as hell won't let her kill Zinn.

I level the handcannon and fire before I can overthink my actions. Plasma blazes through the room, searing a white trail of molten fire across my infrared vision before it pierces her shoulder.

Shit, my aim was low.

She inhales sharply at the impact and loses her grip on the rifle with her left hand. The acrid odor of burned polymer mixes with the stench of charred flesh. A gaping hole in her armor reveals the blackened and cauterized wound beneath. Her armor has melted in a crater formation around the site of the impact.

She swivels her head to face me and rises to her feet, murder flashing behind the crimson glow in her eyes. She repositions the rifle in a smooth motion while I dart forward, utilizing my ungodly speed. If she didn't know what I was before, she does now.

I wrench the rifle from her with my free hand and toss it behind me. It clatters to the floor, beyond her reach and hopefully out of commission for the rest of the fight. I glance briefly toward the other

ZIEG soldier and note both Xia and Max have joined Zinn. Their cyborg was the only one smart enough to wear a helmet.

I focus on the woman again as my sensors indicate the other cyborg is a DFNR-BT series. Now I understand why they engaged Zinn first. They can withstand an onslaught and survive, while their stealthy companion was supposed to make a fatal shot. They weren't expecting another cyborg to crash their party.

But here I am.

The woman glares at me as she whips a nanosteel dagger from her belt. I sidestep her blow, moving faster than she can track. I bring the heavy butt of the handcannon down on her skull, but she twists at the last moment. It's a glancing blow, but leaves her stunned and reeling for a second.

I need to end this dance, even if the guilt consumes me. *Fuck.*

I aim the barrel at her temple and fire. Her expression doesn't change, even as the light fades from her cybernetic eyes. They're blue, I realize, as she collapses to the floor, steaming holes in her skull where the plasma entered and exited.

The other cyborg roars within his helmet. The sound is the embodiment of unbridled rage and incomprehensible pain, a dangerous combination in anyone, let alone a ZIEG cyborg. He twists away from the others to face me, and I know I'm in for one hell of a fight.

I never sparred against a DFNR-BT series while I was with ZIEG, and I'm pretty sure Chadwick Cleary was my first encounter with one. There aren't many of them, and there wasn't one in Luna's squad, but I have learned a few things since then—like the importance of reading specs on the other series so I know what to expect in a fight.

DFNR-BTs aren't invincible, but they're harder to take down than their counterparts. Even my defenses can't compare, but I have the advantage of strength and speed. He'll be a true test of my abilities, with or without the handcannon to assist me.

And we have three minutes left until reinforcements arrive.

I can see his eyes through the clear visor of his helmet, chocolate brown and seething. Dark eyebrows wrinkle above them as he begins to charge forward with all the momentum of a pissed off rhinoceros.

I hold my ground, calculate his speed, and push a jolt of adrenaline through my system. Time seems to slow. At the last second, I pivot. He charges past me and skids to a halt.

I don't wait for him to charge again. I rush forward, fueling my movements with a strength no human was ever born to possess. He turns, too slow to evade. My right shoulder slams into his rib cage with enough force that his armor cracks. He wheezes as the air flees his lungs. My momentum carries us into the wall, where I slam my left fist into his faceplate. The clear polymer doesn't break, but it crumples.

He sucks in a breath and shoves me away. I keep my footing and smirk behind my helmet. He isn't used to fighting someone stronger than he is.

His eyes bore into mine, but now there's a wariness present that was missing before.

"Slaughter, we need the console." Sorin's voice cuts through my battle-induced haze like a scythe.

I draw a breath and aim the handcannon at the other cyborg's face as he charges toward me again. He has incredible defenses, but no one is immune to a plasma round. And I'm faster than he is.

I squeeze the trigger when he's four steps away. The bolt lances through his damaged faceplate, but his body continues to rush forward another two paces before it registers he's dead. His body falls to the ground at my feet, and I stare at it for several seconds, relieved and repulsed by my actions.

I killed two ZIEG soldiers in the span of three minutes. *Fuck.*

Sorin pushes past me and descends on the mainframe, his toolkit in hand. I note the woman's plasma rifle is now strapped to his back. Good.

"Reinforcements are arriving," Quiara states over the comms, her voice dragging my thoughts away from the dead cyborgs that litter the room.

"Shit, they're early," Zinn hisses.

Max shrugs and motions for both Zinn and Xia to join him at the exit door. I walk past Sorin and the mainframe toward the rear of the room, where a second door is closed tightly against incursion. If Zylar Inc. suspects why we're here, I doubt they'll send ZIEG along the same path we used. They'll come from the other direction, the classified route, the one they don't realize we're aware of.

I glance at Max and nod once. I'll hold off anyone who tries to bust through this door.

He swallows and returns the nod. He knows the plan. His only role from here on is to get the others out of the building. For Sorin's plan to work, the Coalition must be kept whole after the mainframe is permanently disabled.

"Twenty seconds until completion," Sorin says, his voice tight. "Fifteen…Ten…"

The rear door crashes open as I knew it would. Two ZIEG soldiers enter, then three more. I can handle two, but not this many. Not alone.

"Five seconds," Sorin whispers as an array of weapons take aim.

I have to make a choice. The Coalition will fail without its founder and his technical abilities. I don't want to see it fail.

But I also don't want to die.

Safeties click off as I pivot toward Sorin and charge. Three seconds until the virus is uploaded and the mainframe is dead.

I shove him away from the console, lift him off the ground, and toss him toward the exit. Zinn and Xia are running outside, but Max lingers. Sorin hurtles into him with a wordless exclamation, then Max drags him through. Two seconds until upload.

I duck beneath the rim of the console as two plasma rounds blast through the air inches from my helmet. My internal sensors shriek a momentary temperature warning, which I ignore. If I'm going to die today, it won't be as a failure. One second remains for the upload.

Boots stomp toward my location. I know I'm surrounded.

I lift my hands in a gesture of surrender, releasing the handcannon from my grip.

"He's a fucking cyborg," someone growls behind me. "My scans don't—"

Their words are cut off as an alarm pierces the air. The console and the holoscreen above it flash red, then white, then red again. Static pours from a speaker nearby.

"What the hell did you do?" A fist connects with the back of my helmet and I stumble forward—not from the impact, but from recognition. It's Luna Zeta.

"I can explain," I reply, hoping she'll recognize my voice too.

If she does, I may just live to see tomorrow. If she doesn't, I'm screwed.

Silence follows my words, but no one fires the dozen or more weapons currently aimed at my person.

"Take his other weapons," she commands. "Vee, take Jace up the stairwell. Maybe you can flush out the rest of the vermin."

The pair jog away, Vee with a disappointed shake of their head. A burly cyborg steps forward to pull the daggers from my belt, but pauses at Luna's next words.

"Be careful with this one. He was designed as a weapon without the need for blades or barrels."

I lift my hands higher and stare at the ceiling while the man disarms me. "I didn't want any of this shit to happen."

Luna steps around me and assesses me with a scowl. "We thought you were dead."

"I was *taken*," I snarl. "If you want the truth, ask your fucking CEO about your override codes. *All* ZIEG soldiers have them, you know. *They* had *mine*."

"They being who? The assholes who killed old Reg, Jen, and a dozen others that night?" She rests her hands on her hips. "I'll know if you're lying, Kye."

So will everyone else currently in the room. We're all cybernetic monsters.

"Omega Prime," I reply. I'll keep Sorin's people out of this as long as possible, but I have no love for Van Duval.

Luna folds her arms. "Truth. Fine, you were taken by Omega Prime. Explain the codes you mentioned, and just maybe I can convince Marim and GISA to let you live. But first, take off that damned helmet so we can see your face."

I disconnect from the Coalition's channels, then pull off my helmet. Luna's scowl deepens as her suspicions are confirmed.

"Spill, or I shoot you where you stand." She aims a pistol at my throat to emphasize her words.

So I tell her everything I know about the override codes and what they did to me. I omit the fact that they've been destroyed and manage to avoid sharing Sorin's involvement. Until I find a way out of this, those are secrets I'll hold dear.

The exit door opens as I finish, but I don't take my gaze from Luna. My sensors indicate Vee and Jace have returned alone.

"This is above my pay grade," Luna growls. "You aren't lying, but I wish to hell you were." She motions to the others around us. "We'll take him upstairs. Agent Malachi will be *very* interested in his story."

Someone steps behind me and wrenches my hands behind my back, while Luna takes my helmet and begins to examine it carefully.

"This isn't the armor you were given before your abduction."

I shake my head. "It's new."

"We've known for some time that Omega Prime was acquiring lab space," someone offers, sparing me the trouble of fabricating a defense they'll see right through.

Luna appears unconvinced, but nods. "It's not for me to decide your fate, but you will speak with GISA, Kye."

CHAPTER THIRTY-TWO

SENTENCING

MEGATROPOLIS, TRAPPIST-1 SYSTEM

A dozen ZIEG soldiers are tasked to escort me from Zylar Inc. HQ to the judicial district, where I'll be held in the planet's only solitary confinement cell until my meeting with GISA. I go willingly and don't speak a word beyond what I've already shared with Luna.

My armor is taken for further examination by Zylar Inc. scientists, but Mat isn't with them. I'm forced to change into a plain gray prison jumpsuit. The fabric is stiff and scratchy, irritating my skin on contact.

Before I can alleviate the itching, I'm fitted with shackles identical to the ones Omega Prime used when they abducted me. They leave the shackles in place when they close the door of my cell, and I'm left alone to stare at the tiny six-foot square space. It's furnished with a ragged cot too short for my frame and a toilet affixed to the opposite wall.

The cell block employs 'net scramblers much like the ones on Haven. I'm cut off from any means of communication. I hope Sorin and the others escaped unscathed, that my decision to face ZIEG alone spared them from a similar fate. My escorts were silent, and I wasn't stupid enough to ask.

Anything I say or do can be used against me. Some things haven't changed in centuries.

I perch uneasily on the cot and wait, while my shoulders begin to protest that my arms are still pinned behind me. I shift slightly, but my attempt to ease my discomfort is met with failure. I prompt my system to release endorphins, and the pain disappears for a time. It's a temporary fix, but it's better than nothing.

My internal chronometer tells me I've been abandoned in this cell for almost four hours before a faint click issues from within the door.

I stare at it sullenly as it swings open to reveal a contingent of armored ZIEG soldiers surrounding a man in civilian clothes. The cyborgs are all helmeted, but I can see their eyes through the clear face shields. Some hold questions, some animosity, others wary recognition. None of them speak.

The man steps into the doorway, taking in my cell with a calculating look. He's tall and lean, with short-cropped dark hair and piercing blue eyes. He wears a charcoal gray suit with a pale blue shirt underneath. The brass shield-and-sickle badge of GISA is displayed prominently above his jacket's left breast pocket.

His eyes meet mine briefly and tighten imperceptibly in anger. "We'll take him to interrogation room five."

Two cyborgs enter the room as he turns away, and I rise from my seat. Hands grip my elbows on either side as I'm herded through the door and into the corridor beyond. Our speed is hindered by the shackles around my ankles; I can't move forward at more than a shuffle, but the soldiers flanking me don't seem to care. They drag me forward when I stumble, wrenching my shoulders painfully.

I shouldn't be surprised by the treatment. I've killed several cyborgs now, and in their eyes, I'm nothing but a murderer. They won't see it as self-defense, even though Sorin and Van have both lost numerous people throughout the years. The government doesn't acknowledge the casualties of so-called terrorist organizations and certainly won't listen to the reasoning behind their supposed crimes.

I'm complicit. I know that. I knew it the moment I willingly decided to help Sorin, and again when I made the decision to save him at the cost of myself. I don't regret my actions.

The interrogation room is two levels above the cellblock where I was held. It's windowless, furnished only with a narrow table and two chairs that look as comfortable as the rickety crate I used as a stool back on Earth. Cameras glare from every corner of the room as I'm led inside and made to sit down. They're recording the interrogation, as I knew they would. I'll need to consider every word I utter carefully.

I have no intention of giving them anything they deem useful. Zylar Inc. and GISA can collectively fuck off.

The GISA agent slides into the chair across from me and motions for the cyborgs to leave. He says nothing for some time, even after the door is closed and we're seemingly alone. I know we're being monitored by someone in an adjacent room as they diligently scrutinize the camera feeds. I've read enough crime thrillers in my time to know how this typically works.

Finally, the agent leans forward, steepling his fingers in front of him. "I'm agent Jeron Malachi, lead investigator into the recent attacks on Zylar Inc. and the AI government's mainframe."

I stare at him impassively. What does he expect me to say? I'm not here to congratulate him on his post.

"State your name and affiliations for the record, please."

I consider silence, but he already knows who I am. "Kye Verex."

"And your affiliations?"

I stare at him, daring him to contradict me as I say, "None."

He meets my gaze unflinchingly. "I see. Well, Mr. Verex, we're here to discuss the charges laid against you. Consider your options carefully as we proceed."

"I'm listening."

"You are accused of the murders of three ZIEG soldiers, destruction of corporate property, sabotage, conspiracy, and the virtual homicides of forty thousand one hundred twenty-six artificial intelligences."

I force my expression to remain neutral. I'm terrified of what this means for my future, but relieved Sorin's virus worked. The AI government is gone, and with it, Zylar Inc.'s stranglehold on the galaxy. No more preying on the desperate and destitute, forcing them to work for a company that sees them as little more than puppets on a string. No more favoritism based on corporate greed. No more gatekeeping… As long as Sorin keeps his promises.

"You didn't enter Zylar Inc. headquarters alone," Jeron continues. "The squad that apprehended you stated there were others when they arrived. Who were they?"

"Did the squad also tell you of Omega Prime?" I counter. "Did they tell you about the override codes?"

A flicker of irritation passes through those blue eyes. "Yes, I took their statements personally. I'm aware of your claims, that you acted under duress." He pauses to emphasize his next words. "However, none of it can be verified."

"You mean Zylar Inc. doesn't want its dirty secrets exposed." I lean back in my chair and glare at him. "I may have grown up on a world this fucking galaxy has forsaken, but I'm not stupid. You're still in their pocket. You'll keep this quiet, because you'll benefit from the arrangement."

He smiles, seemingly amused, but the reaction never touches those glacial eyes. "We're not here to discuss conspiracy theories, Mr. Verex. I'd like to hear your story for myself."

"And if I refuse?"

He shrugs and leans back slightly, feigning indifference. "Based on the charges against you, you'll face execution. If you share your story with me, it's likely the sentence will be reduced to life in prison."

I resist the urge to roll my eyes. I know where they send people with life sentences. Those they've deemed too important to kill, but who present significant dangers to Zylar Inc.'s carefully controlled systems. Primordia-1 is a hellhole that makes Earth look like paradise.

But maybe, if I play my cards right, it won't be permanent. Sorin spent time there, and he got out. And if Sorin succeeds in the rest of his plans...

It's a calculated risk, but I decide to take it.

"Mat can verify the existence of the override codes," I reply. "He designed them and installed them in every member of ZIEG. I don't know how Omega Prime stole mine, but I'm acutely aware of how they work. I was given the option to obey willingly, or be turned into Van Duval's damned puppet. Can you imagine what it's like having someone plugged into your head, controlling your every fucking movement while you're trapped inside, conscious of everything but unable to so much as twitch without permission? Do you even fucking care?"

Jeron leans back in his seat, his expression unreadable. "Mat Shukan was killed in the raid last night."

I freeze, my one ticket to potential freedom vaporized by his statement. How the hell am I supposed to get out of this now? Mat was the only one who had clearance to develop and install the override codes, and he answered to no one. Except...

"Then ask Marim Zylar."

I know it's a long shot. I don't believe he'll actually contact her or ask her to verify my claims. But it's my *only* shot.

"Perhaps I understand the source of your anger, but that doesn't explain why you struck at the AI mainframe. The AI government and the entities responsible for maintaining our day-to-day lives were not involved in the production of your alleged override codes." Jeron steeples his fingers again and pierces me with his gaze. "According to the reports of Captain Zeta's squad, you rescued one of your accomplices before they took you down. It was an act of free will, not compulsion. Why?"

I clench my jaw. I will not bring this down on Sorin or his Coalition, but there is one thing I can safely say.

"That man destroyed my override codes without Van Duval's knowledge. I owed him for my freedom."

Jeron frowns in momentary confusion. "Why would one of Duval's people betray his boss? By all accounts, Van Duval is not a forgiving sort."

I shrug awkwardly in my shackles. "He's not. He's a prick and a bloodthirsty asshole who wanted control over a ZIEG-trained soldier. I don't really care what happens to me, as long as Van Duval pays for what he did."

"You hate him." Jeron's tone betrays mild surprise.

"Yeah. Wouldn't you?"

Jeron studies the tabletop between us, contemplating his next words. "Maybe we can come to an agreement. We know Omega Prime has a base outside of colonized space. Are you willing to give us the location in exchange for a life sentence?"

My next words will make me Omega Prime's greatest enemy, and if I ever manage to regain my freedom, I'll be hunted throughout the galaxy. But it will spare Sorin from further investigation, it will keep both Pablo and Daaros safe, and I'll have some measure of vengeance against the scar-faced merc who refused to do the right thing when given the chance.

"Yeah, I am. I'll tell you everything I can about Haven."

I'm returned to solitary confinement after Jeron determines our interview is over. He doesn't accompany the ZIEG squad tasked with my imprisonment, but their mood is markedly different now than it was earlier. Their sharp hostility is gone, replaced with unspoken questions and uneasy glances.

Someone overheard our conversation about the override codes. Good.

One of the cyborgs pauses in the door after I'm led inside. He studies me, curiosity warring with fear as he contemplates his question. I know it's a question based on the way he chews on his lower lip. I meet his gaze, waiting for him to break the silence.

"Is it true?" he asks finally.

"Yeah. Luna can confirm I wasn't lying about the codes."

A troubled frown etches his craggy features. "This is…shitty." He heaves a sigh and shakes his head. "We'll make sure you're treated okay until they move you. It's the least we can do."

He closes the door and the electronic locks click into place. I'm alone again, but someone stops by every six hours with a handful of protein cubes and a hydration packet. They're always ZIEG, always silent, always efficient with the task.

I lay on the cot with my feet hanging off the end and stare at the stark white ceiling for the better part of five days. I can't access the 'net, and my request for paperbacks is denied. I'm bored out of my damned skull.

But my trials have only started, and boredom is the least of my damned worries.

On the morning of the fifth day, Jeron returns with a full squad of ZIEG soldiers to escort me to the courthouse. Additional shackles are added to those on my wrists and ankles, making it almost impossible to walk. Someone must believe I'll try to run or fight back. Or maybe the additional restraints are just an overt display of Zylar Inc.'s residual power.

I'm led outside the holding center and into a mob of reporters. GNN cameras hover and flash, capturing my image for the universe's entertainment. Questions are hurled in my direction and demands are made of Jeron, but neither he nor I speak as the ZIEG squad encircles us and pushes through the throng.

The courthouse sits across a grassy plaza, designed in a style meant to mimic the columned structures of Ancient Rome, an architectural choice that has been repeated throughout human history so often it was considered cliché four centuries ago. But humans are creatures of habit and resist change, so it's not terribly surprising the style has made its way to Megatropolis, forty-one light-years away from our ancestral home.

The reporters flock around us like starving vultures, keeping pace as we move across the plaza. They stop only when we reach the courthouse steps and the security line surrounding it, but continue to shout questions even after I'm inside and the doors are locked behind me.

In that moment, I do not envy Daaros one damned bit. He's forced to deal with them no matter where he goes or what time it might be. Ten minutes and twenty-six seconds was more than enough media scrutiny to last me a lifetime.

My escort doesn't pause once we're inside, and I'm led down a hall and through a security checkpoint staffed by four armed guards. They're not ZIEG, and I note with a small measure of satisfaction that the AI kiosk is offline. It must have been one of the forty-thousand one-hundred twenty-six I'm charged with destroying.

The guards wave the other cyborgs through, then manually verify my shackles are secure before I'm told to follow them. We move down a wide hall and stop at a motion from Jeron outside an ornate arched door. A digital display next to the door claims it's Courtroom Six, and my case is the only one on the docket this morning. *Kye Verex vs. The Galactic Government.*

We all know who will come out victorious here. This isn't a trial; it's a formality. I'll be found guilty and sentenced to life on Primordia-1, where Zylar Inc. can prod me for questions and hope one day I'll break, revealing the full scope of what transpired.

I don't plan to indulge their fantasies.

We linger outside the courtroom for another two minutes. The door slides open, and I'm led inside. Hundreds of seats line the aisle on either side, but the majority are empty. Our footsteps echo in the vast space as I'm led before a panel of three human judges robed in traditional black. One of the judges is Marim Zylar.

I know damned well she has no legal background and that she's present only to prove a point. I glare up at her as I'm moved into position, unrepentant and defiant. I can prove a point too.

One of the other judges speaks first, a woman with graying hair and stern eyes. "We have reviewed your case, Mr. Verex. You have been found guilty of all charges laid against you, namely three counts of first-degree murder, three counts of conspiracy to commit murder, one count of conspiracy to destroy a government entity, seventeen counts of sabotage, forty-thousand one-hundred twenty-six counts of virtual homicide against an artificial intelligence, and sixteen counts of aggravated destruction of corporate property." She pauses to draw a breath. "Do you deny any of these charges?"

I resist the urge to smirk. I have no use for denial; they've already decided my fate. "No."

The man next to her clears his throat and fixes me with a grim stare. "In light of your testimony and your cooperation with GISA in the matter of Omega Prime, we have determined a death sentence is no longer warranted."

Good. Jeron kept his promise on that front. I wasn't entirely sure he would. Some gambles pay off, after all.

"You are hereby sentenced to life imprisonment as an enemy of the Galactic State, to be carried out with conditions on Primordia-1." The man glances down at a tablet and begins to read the official sentence of the court. "For your role in recent events, you will be tasked with hard labor, to be carried out in solitary confinement for the foreseeable future. As a former ZIEG soldier with unique cybernetics, you will be responsible for powering a cell block of your overseer's choosing, to be determined on your arrival."

Marim leans forward in her seat, cold fury in her dark eyes. "You will regret your decision to expose corporate secrets to those without clearance. Physical isn't the only form of hard labor a cyborg like yourself can be subjected to. You are, after all, one of the most efficient batteries we've ever designed if managed and inserted into a power grid properly."

Some of my ZIEG escorts freeze at her words, and others curse audibly inside their helmets. I can do nothing but gape as real terror coils around my heart in a vice-like grip.

Oh, shit. What form of hell have I landed myself in now?

CHAPTER THIRTY-THREE

WELCOME TO HELL

ULTRA-MAX CONFINEMENT CENTER
PRIMORDIA-1, VAN MAANEN'S SYSTEM

I stare through the window of the processing center, unable to tear my eyes from the hellscape featured beyond. Primordia-1 is a world blasted by intense solar radiation from its proximity to the system's glaring and bloated white star. It's a rocky world filled with wind-carved spires and jagged canyons, only visible on rare occasions when the dust storms have abated.

It's calm beyond the window today, which is why I'm here now, rather than a week ago when we arrived in the system. The dust storms make navigation impossible, even with the best instrumentation available. Primordia-1's dust is coarse and irregular, with edges sharp enough to pierce the hulls of standard shuttles, and when kicked up by a windstorm, it produces enough static to disrupt both navigational aids and communication.

A dark smudge looms on the northern horizon, heralding the approach of the next set of storms. My escorts stare through the window too, edgy and impatient as we wait in the queue. They want out of this hellscape before the storms arrive.

The sandstorms and wind are the least of my problems here. There is no possibility of escape from a facility on Primordia-1. The atmosphere is comprised mostly of methane, with hints of nitrogen and hydrogen sulfide gas. I may be a cyborg but I still breathe like I've always done, which requires oxygen.

And if that weren't enough, there are the temperature extremes. During the day, temperatures can skyrocket to over one hundred degrees Celsius, but at night, they plummet to a frigid negative eighty.

I've been enhanced to withstand a wider set of extremes than a normal human, but nothing on this level. I don't even think my armor could have held up against that. I'm better off staying inside the facility if I want to live.

"Since that asshole killed the AIs, processing has taken forever," someone ahead of us grumbles.

I wince and look away from the window. I'm that asshole, as far as the galaxy is concerned.

To my relief, the speaker isn't one of the burly men behind the processing desk, but one of the handlers of the prisoner in front of me. He'll be gone soon. That's one less punishment I have to look forward to.

A pair of armored guards enter the processing area from behind the desk and take up positions flanking the man ahead of me. He's led through the door they exited from, while his handler is told to speak with the people at the front desk for his payment. The handler whirls around, eager to collect his credits, but slows as his eyes land on our group.

Both of my handlers are in ZIEG-issued armor and have more weapons on them than any civilian has a legal right to possess. He peers at my face as he strides past, and I'm acutely aware that he recognizes me. I'm not surprised; my face has been plastered across every GNN station in the galaxy for the past week.

"You're that—" he begins, only to be rendered silent by the soldier on my right as he draws the plasma rifle from his back and aims.

The man lifts his hands in surrender and scurries away. The soldier on my left jerks on my elbow and drags me forward to the desk. The man directly across the desk lifts an eyebrow, unimpressed and unamused.

"Name and number," he drawls.

I clamp my mouth shut. I've been warned that my handlers will do the talking, and if I so much as utter a sigh, I'll regret it. I don't doubt it's a valid threat; Marim was thoroughly pissed off that day in the courtroom.

"The prisoner is Kye Bradley Verex, galactic prisoner number two-five-alpha-nine-four-two-six-two-eight-delta-five-eight," my escort on the left growls.

Both men behind the desk look up to peer at me, wary surprise written on their features. "This is the big bad cyborg, eh?" the one in front of us asks. "The overseer's been expecting you."

I grind my teeth to keep silent. Anything I say is only going to make my situation worse, and I'm pretty sure my time here isn't going to be even close to pleasant. Marim Zylar will have seen to that.

"I'll call him," the other man offers, then leaves his post for the holoreceiver on the wall behind the desk.

"I have a few more questions about the prisoner before his escort arrives," the first man says, tapping at his tablet. "Yes or no answers only, Verex." When I nod, he continues. "Your planet of origin is Earth?"

"Yes."

"Your age at the date of this booking is twenty-six?"

"Yes."

"You are..." He pauses to lift his eyebrows and whistle. "...an SLTR-BT series cyborg?"

I scowl. "Yes."

He laughs darkly. "Now I understand the necessity of all those fucking restraints. Don't worry, Ajax has the *perfect* setup for you."

I glare at him as he continues to laugh at his own joke. I have some idea of what I'm in for, but I'd rather not dwell on it yet. I'll have *years* to think about that shit if my luck continues to follow its typical course.

Two minutes later, a hulking man who makes the two guards at the desk look tiny enters from the rear door, surrounded by a contingent of armored security guards. The giant is armored as well, but unlike the others, his bald head isn't encased in a helmet. I'm not entirely sure they manufacture helmets that size. A scar runs along the left side of his face, from temple to chin, carving a gnarled cavern in his pockmarked flesh. He sports a tattoo in the same location on the right side of his face; a wide black band with a series of faded reddish numbers running through its core.

He stomps toward us, looks me over, then jerks his chin toward the exit. "I'll take him from here. Paxton at the front will arrange your pay."

The giant leers as my ZIEG escorts disappear, revealing a set of yellowed and crooked teeth. "I'm Ajax, the overseer of this level of hell. Let's get you settled into your new home, shall we? We've set it up especially for you."

His minions swarm me as the big man lumbers through the rear door. I have no choice but to stumble after him as one of the guards jabs the barrel of a weapon into my back. They aren't supposed to use deadly force here, but I'm convinced it must happen on occasion. This is the *Ultra*-max ward, after all.

I'm led down a maze of corridors with cells on both sides. Each cell is comprised of solid polymer-coated nanosteel with a single door. The doors sport both physical locks and an electronic security system, as well as a tiny window. Some of the inmates peer out at me from within, their eyes and brows visible from the other side. Others don't bother to watch our procession. Only a handful of cells are dark.

Ajax strides past them all and doesn't stop until we've reached an area of the ward that looks like it's meant for maintenance rather than prisoner housing. He gestures to a solid door with a placard above it that reads, "Server Room."

Time seems to slow as I stare at the door. Marim Zylar didn't *really* mean what she said in the courtroom, did she? Weren't her words all for show?

The guards nudge me roughly forward as Ajax taps the security console next to it, and the door slides open. The interior lights blaze into life, and my eyes move past the banks of data centers, the network of cables and wires intertwined like vines, and the electrical panels that adorn the walls to the metal contraption bolted to the floor in the center of the room. It's roughly the shape and size of a chair, but lacks a back. Instead of armrests, a series of shackles much like the ones I currently wear gape open, awaiting someone to devour. More shackles are affixed to the contraption's seat and legs. A bundle of cables as thick as my wrists hang above it, gathered and spliced together at a single junction, fitted with an input jack.

One look tells me that jack will slide seamlessly into the data port at the base of my neck.

Panic envelops me in its rotten embrace and I freeze, even as another of the guards jams a weapon into my side. I can't go in there. I can't do this.

Oh, fuck, fuck, *fuck*. This can't be happening. I'm going to wake up in ten seconds and realize this was just another nightmare, and I'll still be in orbit above Primordia-1.

I don't wake up.

The nightmare is real.

Ajax's crew shoves me inside the server room and into the maw of the metal beast that will become my world. My torso and legs are secured before they begin removing my temporary shackles. My arms are pinned down one by one.

I writhe in the restraints, terrified and desperate to escape, but it's too late. That ship has blasted off and is on the other side of the galaxy by now.

"Settle the fuck down," Ajax growls as he drags yet another contraption from the room's corner and sets it up at my side. "This will go easier for you and me both if you aren't thrashing like an unwilling whore."

The second contraption is comprised of a holoscreen, two reservoirs, and a tube connected to what looks like an ancient gas mask. One of the reservoirs is filled with a clear liquid, the other with a brown sludge. A brief scan tells me it's water and a protein slurry. They plan to force-feed me to keep me alive once I'm wired into their system.

I shake my head, the only part of my body I can still move somewhat freely. Ajax sighs, disappointed and exasperated, then motions to one of the guards.

"I'll hold him down while you strap the mask on. This little shit isn't going to keep still otherwise."

Ajax moves to stand behind me, and I stare at him, pleading with my eyes for him to release me, to laugh and tell me this is just some sort of cruel joke, a hazing ritual, *something*. His eyes narrow and he shakes his head. Enormous hands envelop my skull and press down.

"We all know what you did to piss off the galaxy's super powers," he says as the guard draws the mask toward my face. "You've had this coming."

It's strapped to my head and secured, covering everything from my cheekbones to my chin. Ajax moves to the holoscreen and activates it. As it lights up to display my vitals, something snakes through the mask and up my nose, and moments later, I feel it enter my throat. I gag involuntarily, but I can't dislodge whatever the hell just violated my nasal cavity.

Ajax nods once, then motions to his crew. They file out of the server room and close the door. I'm alone with my oversized tormentor.

"Zylar Inc. deemed you too important to kill, but too dangerous to be held in the usual manner," he says. "This device here will ensure you have all the nutrition and oxygen you need, with the added bonus of keeping you silent."

I follow him with my eyes as he begins to pace, warming to his tale. "You see, you aren't the first damned cyborg to find his way to Primodia-1. We know how to deal with your kind."

He pauses to reach for the cables hanging above my head and holds the input jack in front of my eyes. "With your cybernetics, we can increase the speed of our communications systems tenfold. All I need to do is plug you in."

I shake my head again, silently begging him to rethink my punishment. This is almost worse than the override codes.

"You should have considered your life choices before you decided to kill every AI in the fucking galaxy," Ajax snarls.

He moves behind me, the jack still clamped in his meaty fist, then holds my head firmly in place with his free hand. "Welcome to hell, asshole. Here, *I'm* the master of your fate."

The jack slides into place, and I'm immediately inundated with more streams of data than I can count or analyze. It overwhelms my human senses and sends electrical impulses like fire through my cybernetic enhancements.

I scream, but the mask dampens the sound. I squeeze my eyes shut, but bursts of virtual light explode across my overlay. My heart rate accelerates beyond its biomechanical safe zone and the holoscreen blasts a warning through the room. I'm only dimly aware of Ajax as he moves to the screen and taps in a sequence of commands.

My heartbeat slows, but the fire in my implants remains.

"It always takes a few weeks for you bastards to adjust," he whispers next to my ear. I can barely hear him over the cacophony of communication channels rattling through my aural implants. "But you *will* adjust. And we'll keep you healthy to keep our comms online."

He clamps a hand around my shoulder. "Someone will pay you a visit every six hours. Your fuel tanks will need to be refilled. In the meantime, enjoy your stay."

My chronometer keeps me apprised of the time I spend trapped in Ajax's variety of hell. Two days pass before I muster the energy required to filter out most of the comms traffic that ricochets through my brain. I mute everything at first, then realize absolute silence is almost as bad. I select one comm channel at random to leave open in an attempt to keep hold of my sanity.

It turns out to be the outgoing line from the super-max ward. The inmates housed there are allowed one hour per week to place a call outside. I overhear some very interesting conversations, but nothing that will help me find a way out of this situation.

I'm well and truly fucked.

Was saving Sorin in those last moments on Megatropolis worth this unending nightmare? Was refusing to tell GISA about the Coalition's involvement?

I hope Sorin makes the most of the chance I've given him. I doubt I'll ever see sunlight of any form again.

The server room is dark until someone opens the door to refill my tanks, but the holoscreen display of my vitals is always visible. At some point during my first week as the comm center's new relay, I switch my vision to night mode and keep it there. It allows me to see everything in the room at any time, but makes me wince when the door is unexpectedly opened, which happens sometimes.

I embrace that momentary discomfort. It's a reminder I'm still alive, trapped in this waking nightmare. As long as I'm alive, there's a slim chance I'll see the outside again.

Every six hours, someone arrives with more protein sludge and water, but once a week, a pair of maintenance techs enter to perform routine upkeep. They always keep their distance, even though I'm clearly incapable of freeing myself, and it's never the same people twice. Each time, I'm met with wary glances and fearful stares. I'm sure the damned mask strapped to my face doesn't improve my image.

Even with constant refills, my energy levels remain at a steady fifteen percent every hour of every day. Ajax gives me just enough nutrition to stay out of danger, but not enough to regain my strength. And it's sapped incessantly with the demands of the comms system.

After my first month in the server room, I finally resign myself to my fate. I chose to save Sorin at the cost of myself. I chose to protect Pablo and Daaros, knowing I'd take the fall for everything the Coalition has done. I chose to give up Van Duval and Haven in exchange for my life—but now I wonder if that wasn't the greatest mistake I've made in all my twenty-six years.

Execution would have been swift and painless, but I feared I'd never see Pablo or Kelsey again. Now that I'm here, I know I won't see them anyway.

I should have kept my damned mouth shut and left my hatred for Van Duval behind.

I will die here. I understand that now. But it will be at a date of Zylar Inc.'s choosing, not mine—and I'm pretty damned sure they'll keep me here to power the comms for as long as my body holds out.

As a cyborg, that might be a *very* long time.

CHAPTER THIRTY-FOUR

BLINDNESS BORNE OF LOVE

ULTRA-MAX CONFINEMENT CENTER
PRIMORDIA-1, VAN MAANEN'S SYSTEM

At some point, I stop opening my eyes when someone pays me a visit. The maintenance techs don't speak while they work, and Ajax's goons don't bother with niceties as they refill the water and protein tanks. Ajax is the only one who says anything, but his visits are rare, and I've started to ignore him. It's better for my sanity that way.

My chronometer indicates that it has been one hundred eighty-three days since I entered the ultra-max facility on Primordia-1. That's just over six standard months for those who are bothering to count.

I bother. I don't have anything better to do between the super-max holocalls I listen in on.

I have gleaned a few tidbits of news from my eavesdropping. Zylar Inc. still hasn't reinstated the AIs; I'm not sure they know *how*, so many centuries after they were first developed. There were riots on Megatropolis not long after I was inserted into my present version of hell, and the military was called in to enforce martial rule. I bet Kelsey *loved* that assignment.

News regarding the Resistance Coalition has been absent, but I expected the silence. Sorin's operation works better when they aren't in the spotlight or the focus of GISA investigations.

And speaking of GISA, Agent Malachi was promoted after his dealings with me. It seems his promotion also included access to Marim Zylar's bedroom on more than one occasion, which the GNN gossipmongers—and some of the female inmates—love to discuss.

I hear almost nothing regarding Daaros, only that the "pretty Botanaari" hasn't left his home world in months. It's a relief to know he and Pablo are out of the spotlight, safely away from the shitstorm I had hoped to protect them from.

I'm listening in on a call between an inmate and his adult daughter when the data stream inexplicably cuts off. It isn't a common occurrence, but it happens sometimes, usually during the worst of the sandstorms. Trapped in the bowels of the ultra-max ward, I have no way of knowing what the weather outside is like, and I don't care. The stream will come back online once the outside receivers are no longer inundated with the planet's savage variety of dust.

I disconnect from the super-max call line and pull up the prison guards' private channel. Most of the time I don't bother listening in on their conversations. They never say anything interesting, but it's the fastest way to learn what caused the disruption in the other data stream.

I'm greeted with static. Their line is down too.

I snap my eyes open seconds before the door to the server room slides open. Ajax looms in the doorway, his hulking figure seething as he steps into the room. He ignores me for once, concerned only with the display on the holoscreen. My vitals are normal, my tanks won't need refilling for another two hours, and there are no error messages present.

His face contorts into a snarl as he whirls in place, seeking a problem somewhere in the room.

"What the fuck is going on?" he bellows, then storms out the door without giving me a second glance.

The lights click off. I close my eyes once more and begin to scroll through the rest of the prison's comm channels. All of them are offline.

This isn't the work of a sandstorm, and I know only one person capable of pulling this off. Hope rears its nearly unrecognizable head somewhere deep in my chest, a feeling that has become so foreign, I almost can't name it.

When the door opens again, I don't immediately open my eyes, thinking it's Ajax again, or one of his techs. The sharp inhalation of breath, muffled only slightly by an armored helmet, forces me to reassess the situation. Footsteps race toward me as I open my eyes.

The helmet's face plate is tinted black and I can't make out the features of the person inside, but I recognize the matte black armor as military-issue. The armor is dark where the wearer's name and rank should have been displayed.

"Oh, shit," a familiar voice issues from within. "Ghost, I've found him."

I can't speak her name through the mask, but I'm as stunned as I am relieved to know it's Kelsey. She hasn't given up on me. She's *here*. And working with Sorin, if he's the Ghost she's speaking to.

"I don't know how to safely disconnect him," she says after a moment's pause. "He's wired into the server room on block D-14."

It's so damned good to hear my sister's voice, but her presence here raises more questions than it answers. My questions will have to wait. We don't have time, and I couldn't ask them right now anyway.

She tilts her head to listen, then nods firmly. "Copy that. I'll stand by."

She unholsters the plasma rifle from her back and leans toward me. "I don't know if you can hear me, but we're going to bust you out of here, little brother. Just hold on a few minutes longer."

I nod feebly as tears moisten my eyes. She spins away, her rifle aimed at the server room's door.

I'm not going to die here, after all. Or if I do, it will be as a free man, going down in a blaze of cybernetic glory. I won't fucking die in this chair.

When the door opens next, a pair of Ajax's techs stumble inside, their faces drawn and pale, then ashen as they're faced with Kelsey's rifle. She doesn't hesitate. Two pulses fire from her weapon, both hitting their marks. The techs are dead before they comprehend what happened.

She moves to drag them away from the door, then glances over her shoulder. "We knew there would be casualties. I'm not going to be one of them."

I nod imperceptibly. I understand her reasoning better than she knows.

Another minute crawls by, then Kelsey steps forward to open the door. Sorin jogs inside, followed by another helmeted person with a tinted face plate. Sorin wears armor, but his helmet has a clear shield across his eyes. His glasses are in place beneath, and I relax slightly. He'll know how to extract me from this hell.

"Cover me," he says to Kelsey and the other person, who moves to a position sideways from the door.

Sorin studies the cable running between the mask and the holoscreen contraption, then moves to the bundle of wires hanging from the ceiling and plugged into my neck. He grips the bundle, then hesitates.

"This might hurt."

I nod once. It can't hurt any more than the first days after Ajax plugged it in. The input jack slides free, but instead of pain, I feel… Nothing. Okay, maybe not *nothing*, but the absence of pain is so profound after six months that my body almost feels numb.

The door slides open again, and both our protectors immediately fire. Ajax stumbles backward, a plasma bolt searing through his right shoulder, while a projectile tears through his left forearm. The report of the projectile gun is deafening in the enclosed space, and my ears ring momentarily.

Ajax roars, the sound muffled while my ears and aural implants struggle to recover. Kelsey fires again. The blast hits him directly in the face, melting his scar and vaporizing half his bald skull in an instant. He crumples in the doorway, but Kelsey doesn't attempt to drag him out of the way. I'm not sure she has the strength to move his oversized frame.

Sorin ignores the commotion and focuses on the holoscreen. He taps a few buttons, and the tube lodged in my nasal cavity withdraws. Another overdue relief, and one I didn't know I needed until now.

"Give me a hand with the restraints," Sorin calls over his shoulder as he unstraps the mask from my face. "We need to get the hell out of here."

Kelsey remains at the door, but the other person darts away from their position to do as he asks. I breathe in deeply, taking in real air for the first time in months.

"Oh, Slaughter. You look like shit."

I force a laugh that turns into a rasping cough. My vocal cords haven't been used in a while, and my resources have been taxed to their limit since Ajax put me here. I didn't bother to divert my energy to healing the damage the damned tube he lodged in my throat had caused.

"Yeah." My voice cracks and wheezes, but it feels good to speak, despite the raw state of my vocal cords. "I'm glad…you're here, Zinn."

She shakes her head as the dozens of restraints holding me in place are disengaged one at a time. "Stop talking, Metal Man. My throat hurts just listening to you."

I stand once I'm free, but immediately stumble. I'm weaker than I anticipated.

"Easy," Sorin says, sliding an arm under my shoulders. "I know exactly what they've done, and it's not something you'll heal from in a couple minutes." He pauses, then adds, "Switch to standard vision. That green glow will give us away."

I do as he asks. After months spent looking at my prison through the night vision's filter, color is almost overwhelming. I shake my head and do my best to focus.

Kelsey beckons for us to hurry, and I let Sorin support some of my weight. Maneuvering past Ajax's body is tricky, but after a few seconds, we're in the corridor outside.

"This way," Zinn says.

She takes the lead and moves along a hall I wasn't taken down on my previous trip through the ultra-max ward, gun held at the ready. Kelsey follows behind, determined to watch our rear as Sorin and I half-jog, half-shuffle as fast as my exhausted muscles can manage. We meet four more armored Coalition members at the end of a corridor, where they're grouped around what appears to be the entrance to a maintenance shaft.

"It's just a short climb up, then a straight shot to the warship's umbilical," Sorin assures me as the others duck inside.

Zinn and Kelsey wait for us to enter before joining us, then they secure the grate. I watch as the other group climbs the rungs of a ladder to a tier ten feet from the floor. It's not a long climb, but I'm not sure I have the strength to make it that far.

I hope Sorin has a whole crate of protein cubes reserved for me on his ship. I'm going to need that and more to recover.

My internal sensors scream warnings as I divert my dwindling energy reserves into muscles that haven't seen action in six months. I have to climb this damned ladder and get out of here. It's more than my life at stake if I fail.

"Team two is back onboard," Sorin says as I begin to climb. "Team three is waiting for our exit."

I want to ask him how many of his people he's risking in this operation, but I'll save my energy for questions later. Hands reach for me and haul me up the last few rungs, then guide me toward the wall. I lean against it as I wait for Sorin, panting for air. I don't think I've ever been this weak, even back on Earth.

"Come on," Sorin says as his arm slides around my shoulders once more. "We're almost there."

I manage a nod and force my feet forward. I can see the umbilical's attachment point ahead, the way to my freedom clear…

Until shots ring out behind us. I glance over my shoulder as Sorin urges me on. Zinn's at the top of the ladder, gun aimed at something below. I don't see Kelsey.

"My sister," I rasp.

"It's a single guard. Your sister can handle them."

He's right. I know he is, but part of me still wants to turn back to ensure Kelsey is okay. She's career military, she took down Ajax, and did who-the-hell knows what else to help me escape. And in my present condition, I'd only be a liability.

"Yeah. Fine."

Sorin pulls me along toward the umbilical and pushes me inside ahead of him. The space isn't large enough to walk side-by-side, and he obviously thinks I'm of greater concern than he is. It's bullshit; the Coalition wouldn't last a week without him at the helm, but I'll humor him. I'm too damned tired to argue anyway.

I stumble into the ship's vast cargo bay after two minutes spent dragging myself through the umbilical. Sorin darts into the space behind me and steadies me before I fall. I nod my thanks, take another ten steps, then collapse into a sitting position behind the nearest crate. He pulls his helmet off and shakes his head, worry creasing his brow.

"The rest of my crew is on the way. Your sister is with them," he adds pointedly. "They'll be here any time."

"Why is she…here?"

Sorin chuckles uneasily and sits down facing me. "When news of your arrest broke, she called Daaros and demanded access to my direct line—after giving him an earful, I'm told. He didn't give her my frequency, but he arranged a call. Kelsey was livid and demanded an explanation. I told her everything, including what you did." He pauses to study me. "I still don't understand why you did it. Why you risked your life to save mine."

I shrug and lean my head back against the crate. "I needed you to succeed."

"And I would have without your intervention," he replies evenly.

"You don't get it." I clear my throat, but it only makes the soreness worse. "I've watched you with…the rest of your people. Max is great, but…he's not you. Your Coalition needs *you*."

His frown deepens. "You're too damned stubborn for your own good."

Laughter erupts behind him. "I've been telling him that for years," Kelsey says. "He never listens."

She's pulled off her helmet, and her dark hair is plastered to her brow, slick with sweat. She stares at me intently, frowns, then points somewhere behind me.

"I'm going to the mess hall. Tell me what you need, and I'll get it, Kye. Once you've eaten, I want some damned answers."

"I'll eat just about anything right now," I reply.

"Something with high protein and high carbs would be best," Sorin cuts in. "And bring him some water."

As she strides away, the ship lurches upward.

Sorin gazes at the ceiling, his expression pensive. "We'll know in thirty seconds if we've escaped cleanly, or if we've landed ourselves with a tail."

"You said this was a warship."

He nods. "It is. And I have every gun on this thing armed and operational. If there's a tail, we'll be rid of it quickly." He focuses on me once more. "Did you know they wouldn't execute you?"

I shake my head. "I gave them Haven for my life. Van's probably pissed."

"He is, and he'll place a bounty on you the moment he learns of our jailbreak." Sorin laughs softly. "I don't like him, particularly not after the override codes incident. But for now, Omega Prime is on the run. They can't return to Haven, and until he establishes a new lair, I doubt he'll make any serious attempts at retaliation." His gaze flicks to someone behind me, and he nods. "No tail. That's good."

A moment later, another familiar face strides across my field of view to sit cross-legged next to Sorin. I stare at them, recalling the last time we met. I was a disappointment, a failure, a *traitor*.

"Vee?" I croak.

They smile knowingly. "Luna uncovered evidence of the override codes three months ago. Many of us have been quietly 'disappearing' since. We come here. Or rather, to Cobalt Asteroid, once our histories have been verified. What you did was brash and stupid, but it was right. For *us*. But brash and stupid has always been your forte."

"Is Luna here too?"

Vee shakes their head. "She has chosen to stay behind in Megatropolis."

"She's one of our inside sources," Sorin adds.

"Then taking out the mainframe… It wasn't enough." I close my eyes as another wave of fatigue washes over me, this one borne of disappointment rather than my physical condition.

The silence is broken a few moments later when Kelsey returns. "I sure as hell hope you haven't killed my brother due to boredom after everything he's been through."

I open my eyes and manage a weary grin. "I'm okay, Kels."

She sits down at my side and shoves a bottle of water into my hand. "Drink first, then I'll give you one of Zinn's prized burritos. Or a doughnut. Your choice."

The water is cold as it slides down my throat, almost burning in its intensity. Or maybe it's the raw state my throat is in that makes it feel that way. I don't care; this pain is *good*.

I empty the bottle and set it aside. "Burrito. I can smell the sausage."

"You always were a carnivore," Kelsey teases, holding the plate out of my reach.

"I haven't tasted anything in six months. I want the damned sausage."

She laughs and sets the plate carefully in my lap. "I'm glad we found you in time, little brother. I'm glad you're going to be okay."

There's a hitch in her voice I don't think I've ever heard in it before. I glance up, my mouth full of sausage and cheese and warm tortilla, to find my sister crying. I force myself to swallow and set the burrito down.

"Kels—"

"If it wasn't for me, you wouldn't be in this mess."

"That's not true. I was stupid—"

She shakes her head firmly. "You were, but I was *blind*. Which is worse, Kye? Stupidity driven by a desire to do what's right, or blindness borne of love? I wanted to get you off Earth so damned badly, I didn't consider what they'd do to you at ZIEG. That single-minded desire almost killed you at least three times that I know of. If anyone is to blame for this, it's me."

She rises to her feet and strides away. I stare after her, at a loss for words.

"I'll talk to her," Sorin promises as he stands. "Eat, Kye. We can discuss everything that has happened later." He glances at Vee as he begins to walk away. "Keep an eye on him. He isn't known for resting when he should."

"Of course," Vee agrees. "It'll be just like old times."

KELSEY VEREX

CHAPTER THIRTY-FIVE

HUMANS ARE ALL ASSHOLES

"I'm *fine*, Sorin."

I've been fine for three days. I can walk again, spar with Vee and Zinn without tiring, and my throat doesn't feel like it was recently sandblasted. My reflexes are a little slow, but I think it's just part of the natural healing process. My recovery has been two weeks in the making, yet the past three days have been the best I've had in months.

The hard part has been convincing Sorin. And my sister.

"I won't risk your health yet. Not on a minor excursion." He crosses his arms and fixes me with a pointed stare. "I pushed you into situations you had no business engaging in before. I won't do it again."

I roll my eyes. "You're just afraid of Kelsey."

He doesn't deny it. "Your sister is a force of nature when she's angry."

"Look, I'm no good to anyone cooped up here," I say, trying a different tactic. "If you're that concerned about the state of my cybernetics, run a diagnostic scan. I'm giving you permission."

I'm aware that he's wanted to run a scan since we returned from Primordia-1, and I'm also aware that he's been too afraid to ask after my treatment in the prison. I'm not looking forward to having *anything* plugged into my data port, but if it eases his mind, it's for the best. I can handle a few minutes of discomfort.

He rakes a hand through his hair, dislodging the blue glasses perched atop his head. He curses as they clatter to the laboratory floor. He snatches them up with a scowl, then returns his attention to me.

"A scan is definitive, but I think it's too soon."

I slam my fist into the benchtop I'm leaning against and feel it crack from the impact. "Why? I told you I'm fine."

He pinches the bridge of his nose and exhales slowly. "Physically, yes. Psychologically… Vee has a number of concerns."

I grimace and look away. My room is adjacent to Vee's on this station, and I've awakened them numerous times as I battle nightmares. Ajax is featured in many of them. I haven't been able to sleep beneath a blanket; it's too constricting and reminds me of the shackles that once pinned me in place. Dozing in a chair is no better. The position triggers something primal in my brain, and I wake up trying to claw myself free of imaginary restraints.

And then there was the sparring session yesterday. Vee managed to surprise me with a feint and struck an area too near the data port. I froze, and it took the combined efforts of Zinn and Vee to snap me out of a flashback I didn't know was coming.

Okay, maybe I'm not *fine*.

I push away from the workbench and stalk toward the door. "You're right. I need to work through this. Somehow."

"Talk to Max," Sorin advises. "He knows something about PTSD. I think that's what you're suffering from."

Post-traumatic stress disorder. Yeah, that would fit, wouldn't it? I've certainly experienced my share of fucking trauma.

"I will," I promise, but don't add that it won't be today. I need to come to terms with it first.

I wend my way through the halls of Station Six-Theta, seeking the virtual targeting range where I'm sure to find my sister. She has always been the person I talk to when Pablo isn't available. We haven't spoken much since she tried to blame herself for everything that happened, but I need her now. She'll understand; she always does.

She's where I expected to find her, but she's in the company of someone I didn't anticipate. I loiter in her periphery as Kelsey fires a series of rounds at moving targets, hitting each with a precision few but career military or cyborgs could achieve. Her lanky companion stands with his dark arms crossed over his chest, a smirk on his lips as he observes.

"Fifteen targets. Fifteen bullseyes." Tariq Osirius shakes his head in disbelief. "I can't beat that."

Kelsey holsters her pistol and pivots to face him with a triumphant grin. "I know. Which means you lose."

Tariq flicks an uneasy glance in my direction before addressing her once more. "It was never easy with you. Everything was always a damned competition. It's tiresome."

"And you enjoyed every minute," Kelsey counters. "But that's the past, and I have no desire to rehash our relationship in front of my brother. Accept your defeat. I expect to see cupcakes enough for the whole crew sometime tomorrow."

I snort a laugh, unable to stop myself. "This was about cupcakes?"

"A little-known secret about Tariq: He's a fantastic baker." Kelsey grins and motions to the door. "Go on. I don't think Kye wants an audience for whatever he needs to discuss."

Tariq rolls his eyes and strolls toward the exit. "I've missed this, Kels," he calls over his shoulder before disappearing into the corridor.

Kelsey releases a groan once he's gone. "I never expected him to show up here, but he was one of the first to defect."

"He knew you'd be here."

She swats at my shoulder. "Sorin said the same thing after he learned about our past. I don't know how I feel about him walking back into my life. Did you ever work with him before you were taken?"

I shake my head. "I met him a few times over holocalls with you. That's it."

She grimaces. "He was intense, even when he wasn't on missions for ZIEG. I thought I was in love with him. His passion, his fire. And then I realized we'd never last. He's right, you know. I *do* make everything into a competition." She pauses to shake her head, her eyes on the ceiling above. "You didn't come here to listen to me complain about my ex. What's on your mind, little brother?"

"I…" My voice falters and I scramble for an alternative topic, inexplicably panicked. "I never thanked you for the rescue. But I've been wondering—what happens to you now?"

Her dark eyes study me; she knows it wasn't what I planned to ask. "I resigned from my post at OMMA two days after your hearing. Even if I had wanted to stay, there was too much heat from upper command. They were calling for it." She shrugs. "I spent my last two days looking up every schematic and map of Primordia-1 I had clearance to view. I was going to get you out of there one way or another."

"Sorin told me you called Daaros."

"I did. I gave him an earful, and Sorin one too, once he called me." She gestures toward the door. "Let's walk. This conversation is making me restless."

She sets a brisk pace once we're in the corridor, and I allow her to take the lead out of habit. It was always the same back on Earth, before she left me with Pablo and his father to enlist. Some things don't change, no matter the time or distance that separates us.

"And you joined the Coalition just like that?" I ask after a time.

She laughs. "You know me better than that. No, they had to convince me. An encrypted holocall with Sorin and a lengthy explanation on his part allowed me to understand what happened on Megatropolis. You were a fucking idiot, Kye." Her tone is a mixture of exasperation and fondness, the same tone I've heard her use numerous times over the years when I do something incredibly stupid.

"I had to make a choice," I reply, defensive. "I could have run and left him there, but it felt wrong. He saved me, Kels. I thought I owed it to him."

"At the expense of your damned life? Were you out of your mind?" Emotion shines in her eyes. "Damn it, Kye, you were only the third cyborg in the history of…cyborgs to be imprisoned on Primordia-1. They did the same to the others that they were doing to you. It was going to fucking kill you, and I was helpless to do anything about it!"

A tear traces an erratic path down her cheek, and I hang my head. I remember her words in the cargo bay after my extraction. *I'm glad we found you in time, little brother.* I didn't consider the implications then; my sole focus was on a damned burrito.

"You weren't helpless," I murmur after a time. "You joined Sorin, and you came."

"Has Sorin run a diagnostic scan yet?" she asks pointedly.

I hesitate, then shake my head. "He thinks it's too soon."

She rolls her eyes. "Then you don't know the true extent of the damage to your system. Sorin gave me the files on your…predecessors. Neither lasted more than a year. The constant drain on your system was slowly frying your cybernetics, and it could have left you with permanent brain damage. He needs to do the damned scan so he can repair what you can't on your own."

"He won't," I admit. "Not until I talk to Max."

"Burkhardt-Davies?" she asks, puzzled. "Why him?"

I shrug uncomfortably. "I've been having nightmares. Flashbacks. Sorin thinks—"

"He's probably right." She expels a sigh. "He's afraid to run the scan because he has to plug you in. Shit. I should have realized." She grasps my forearm and drags me into the next corridor. "We'll visit Max now. You need treatment before Sorin can patch you up, and knowing you, you'll procrastinate until you're an old man unless someone pushes you."

"I'm not *that* bad," I reply defensively. "I'm capable of making decisions when needed."

"Only those that involve the worst possible outcomes. Anything labeled *good* for you was never something you'd willingly arrange."

I want to argue, but she has a valid point. How many times during my teenage years did she set up doctor visits for me, knowing I'd never do it myself? This is no different.

"I'll even have Tariq save *two* cupcakes for you," she says with a grin.

I release a dramatic groan. "Fine, but you didn't have to bribe me with food."

"I think I did. You make better decisions when your stomach is involved."

She laughs as I scowl at her, as though she knew exactly which expression her words would elicit from my face.

I'm so damned glad she's here.

"I don't know if I agree with Sorin's stance," Max says thoughtfully after I tell him why we're here. He sits in a scuffed and battered chair, his right ankle propped across his left knee.

I sit in an equally questionable chair facing him, though my eyes refuse to move beyond the bare patch of floor between us. Kelsey paces behind me, restless as a caged predator. Her footsteps are swift and steady, keeping time with my pulse.

No, I haven't bothered to alter my biochems. It doesn't seem worth the trouble, and knowing my luck, I'll only make matters worse.

"Is there anything we can do?" Kelsey asks.

"There are a few things we can try," Max replies. "The simplest, in my experience, is exposure therapy. Basically, we'd help your brother face his fears by triggering them."

I continue to stare at the floor. "You want to plug me in."

"That's the most direct method."

A prickle of unease traces its way along the length of my spine to lodge at the base of my skull. A flash of unwanted memory invades my thoughts, unbidden. I'm strapped in the server room, surrounded by the hum and pulse of the prison's communications system, calls from the supermax ward blaring through my aural implants. Ajax leers at me from above, his bald head shiny even in darkness, but I can see it, see *him* with a clarity only grayscale night vision can produce.

I'm on my feet and halfway to the exit before I realize I've moved. My sensors indicate Max and Kelsey's heart rates are elevated, that I've done something to produce a fear response. I'm still, my fists are clenched, and I'm shaking. From anger or pain or fear of my own, I don't know.

"Kye?" Kelsey asks after several seconds.

I squeeze my eyes shut and remain still. I'm afraid to know what I've just done. "Yeah?"

"I think we'll try another method," Max says softly. "Do you want to talk about this?"

Hell no. I don't want to relive the months I spent acting as a communications array under the watchful eyes of a sadistic asshole with too much power. And yet… I need to know what just happened. What I've done.

I turn around to face them, taking note of the wreckage of the chair I had occupied only moments before. Shards of plastic litter the floor, jagged edges glittering in the glare of the overhead lights.

"Shit. I didn't mean to…"

My world crumbles, and I'm suddenly more helpless than I've ever been. I sink to my knees and hold my head in my hands, ashamed, horrified, overwhelmed. I don't remember striking the chair; I only recall the memory and Ajax's leer.

Kelsey's arm wraps around my shoulders. "We'll get through this, little brother," she promises. "You and me. Okay?"

I nod as hot tears streak down my face. They don't sting like they used to; my eyes are cybernetic and can't feel them, but my tear ducts still work.

I haven't cried like this in years, but I don't know what else to do. What if I had struck Kelsey or Max instead of the damned chair? One of them would be injured… Or worse. My inhuman strength is a liability now, a danger to everyone around me until I can get these fucking flashbacks under control.

If I can get them under control.

"Talking through your memories might help," Kelsey says softly.

I don't look up at her. I can't. "It's not safe. For you."

She withdraws her arm and moves to face me directly. "Will you talk with someone present who *can* restrain you if it becomes necessary? I'll be there too. You don't have to face this alone."

Reluctantly, I nod. "Get Vee. And maybe another."

"Done."

She summons Vee and Tariq through the station's internal coms, while Max locates another chair. Both cyborgs arrive in full armor, and Tariq sports a stunner on his hip. I hope he doesn't have to use it, but I don't fault him for taking the precaution. I slump in my new seat while Kelsey explains the situation to them. Vee's gaze meets mine a few times, compassionate and understanding. Until this moment, I didn't realize how much I'd missed them.

Sorin arrives behind them and speaks in hushed tones with Max. Part of me is irritated that he's here, but another part is relieved. He understands how my cybernetics work better than anyone else, and if Vee or Tariq can't maintain order, I trust Sorin has some trick of technology hidden in one of his jumpsuit pockets that can.

Finished with her explanation, Kelsey crosses the room to stand at my side. Sorin and the two former ZIEG soldiers remain somewhere behind me; I'm aware of their presence, but they keep out of my periphery. I'm grateful for that small kindness as Max resumes his seat and leans forward intently.

"Typically, I would prefer to conduct a session like this in private," he says apologetically. "I don't think it's wise to attempt it after your episode earlier, and since you've agreed…" He trails off and heaves a sigh.

"I need them here," I reply without looking at him.

"I understand the necessity, but this might become awkward."

"I know, but I'm used to awkward. My life has been nothing but awkward since I left Earth, and I didn't exactly fit in there, either." I cross my arms and scowl at the floor between us. "I've always had some damned condition that marked me as different. Why change now?"

Kelsey grips my shoulder reassuringly. "Remember what I said," she whispers, though I know both Vee and Tariq can hear her words. "We'll get through this."

"Let's start from the beginning," Max says evenly. "Describe what happened at Zylar HQ after you tossed Sorin out of the room."

I hear a rustle behind me, and Max looks up sharply with a shake of his head, silencing whatever comment Sorin planned to say before he uttered it.

I draw a breath and begin. I tell him of my conversation with Luna as I was arrested, my brief stay in Zylar HQ's main conference room as GISA was summoned, and the holding cell I was taken to while I awaited my hearing. He asks questions when I pause, but only to coax the story from me and keep it moving forward. I sense no judgment from him, and the words come easier after a while.

I tell him of Jeron Malachi's interrogation, his unspoken refusal to involve Marim Zylar after I insisted she could verify my words, and the media frenzy that accompanied my escort to the courthouse days later.

He stops me at that point with an upraised hand. "You're doing well so far, but I know what comes next won't be easy to share. Would you like a break?"

I shake my head, determined to see this through before I lose my nerve. I'm terrified of how I'll react, but I'm among friends who can prevent me from hurting anyone. My heart rate spikes as I shove the memory of Ajax's face firmly out of my mind. I have to speak of Primordia-1 next.

It's time to get this over with.

"I could use some water," Kelsey says, shattering my momentary resolve.

"And it's almost noon. We should eat," Vee adds in a pointed tone.

"Yeah," Tariq agrees. "We *all* should."

I suppress a groan. I'm outvoted, and knowing Vee, they'll insist I eat no matter how much I protest. Kelsey will side with them, and Tariq with her...

"Fine," I concede, "but I expect another cupcake as compensation."

Tariq's resonant laughter erupts behind me. "There will be plenty, as long as your sister gives me the time to actually bake them."

I follow the others from the room as they make their way to the mess hall. Tariq is flirting with Kelsey, who appears unimpressed by his efforts, and Sorin is once again in conversation with Max. Vee walks alone, but pauses to allow me to catch up, a knowing look in their eyes.

"The break is necessary. Your pulse was accelerating," they inform me, blond eyebrows lifted in a no-nonsense expression.

"I know."

"We all have limits, even those who choose to ignore them," they reply with a smirk. "Your sister asked that we stand by to look out for your welfare. She was more concerned that you'd hurt yourself than someone else."

I glower ahead at Kelsey's back. "I broke a fucking chair. Not an old wooden one or the cheap plastic type, but a solid-cast polymer chair. The kind that are supposed to be almost indestructible. You know what the worst part is? I don't remember doing it."

The memories threaten to encroach again, but I hurl them violently away. Damn it all, I want to cry *again*. Or scream. Or punch something.

Okay, the last option is out. I've already destroyed enough for one day.

"I know," Vee replies in a soothing tone. "Tariq and I will make sure you don't hurt anyone, but that includes *you*, Kye. Refusing to acknowledge your system's warnings is never a good idea. We had to step in."

"Fine." I don't tell them I wasn't receiving warnings yet. It's not worth an argument.

The mess hall is serving protein cubes as usual, but they're not expired today. As we step inside, Kelsey waves us to a table she and Tariq have reserved. Our group isn't alone, and I can feel the stares, the unspoken questions from the others as I cross the room. Maybe it's only my imagination, but I can't escape the notion that I'm being scrutinized like a bug under a damned microscope. I've kept to myself since my rescue, avoiding common areas like this as much as possible.

They all know something of what I endured. They crave details I'm unwilling to share, not now when I'm so fucking vulnerable.

My face burns as I slide into the unoccupied chair beside Kelsey. I refuse to look up, to scan the faces of the curious for even a second. I don't want to be here, but I don't want to be alone.

Vee pats my shoulder but doesn't sit. "I'll bring you a plate."

"Thanks."

Kelsey nudges my arm with her elbow. "You're doing good so far, little brother. We'll get through this."

I shrug but make no effort to respond. I can sense the hush in conversation that surrounds our table as those nearest strain to overhear our words. I won't give them the satisfaction. They're like the mob of reporters that swarmed us as I was marched from the holding cells to the courthouse on Megatropolis, their only difference being they choose silence over eager shouts in their quest to gain my attention.

"Kye?" Kelsey asks, concerned.

"I'm fine." It's a lie, and she knows it.

"We should go back," Sorin's voice cuts in.

Startled, I look up to find him standing next to Tariq's chair, Max a step behind him. Heads turn to stare at us, visible in my periphery. I clench my jaw in frustration, but nod before averting my gaze. They're all fucking vultures, ready to pounce on my misery and discomfort the moment I enter the room. Why can't they mind their own damned business?

Kelsey pushes back from the table and begins to guide me toward the door as soon as I'm on my feet. Tariq carries her portion of protein cubes without comment, as though he's done this for her countless times. Maybe he has. She never shared the minute details of their relationship with me during our holocalls.

No one speaks until we're back inside the room Max has been using as his office. Sorin studies me in silence as I accept my plate from Vee, but I know he has questions. Hell, they all do, but they wait for Max to take the lead. This is his project, after all.

"Tell me what was going through your mind in there." His tone is calm, even, non-judgmental.

I chew my lower lip and stare at my plate of untouched protein cubes. I grapple with the urge to lash out at something, and somehow manage to resist. Finally, I tell him. I omit nothing of my thoughts and end with a wry attempt a humor. "Humans are all assholes, aren't we? Some are just better at hiding it."

Max chuckles, Tariq laughs, and Vee nods in agreement. Sorin's concerned frown morphs into an amused smirk momentarily, while Kelsey lifts her eyebrows.

"I think that's enough for one day," Max says after a time. "We'll regroup tomorrow to continue your story. You should rest. Sleep, if you can."

CHAPTER THIRTY-SIX

SHATTERED

I sleep late the next morning. It's unusual for a cyborg, but I think I'm still catching up on what I lost during my captivity on Primordia-1. I didn't dream for the first time since my rescue.

I'm stunned at the reading on my internal clock. It's after nine, and if I don't get my ass moving soon, I'll miss my chance at breakfast. There is no way in hell I'm going through a second session with Max on an empty stomach. And the added delay will give me a little more time to prepare.

I know what's coming next, and I do my best not to think about it as I pull on a pair of black cargo pants and a plain white tee. When I emerge from my room a few minutes later, I'm not surprised to find Vee leaning against the wall across the corridor, arms crossed as they wait for me. They brush strands of blond hair from their eyes and gesture for me to follow.

"Sorin sent me to check on you," they admit after a few seconds. "I sensed you were in a sleeping rhythm until a few minutes ago. I thought it was best to let you rest until you woke naturally."

"Thanks." I chew my lower lip, self-conscious. "How long were you waiting?"

A faint smile forms on Vee's lips. "It doesn't matter. You needed to sleep, and now you need to eat."

"I didn't realize you were monitoring my metabolism too," I tease.

"I'm familiar with your habits, and Pablo isn't here to watch over you," they reply with a shrug. "In spite of everything you've been through, your lack of self-regard hasn't changed."

"My system isn't in warning," I reply defensively. "I'm fine."

"From what I understand, you told Sorin the same thing yesterday *before* you demolished that chair." Vee stops walking and pivots abruptly to block my path, arms crossed. "You are not fine, Kye. You need this treatment, and you need to take care of yourself. As one friend to another, I'm not going to stand by and let you self-destruct. Maybe you don't see it, but everyone around you does."

I stare at them, gnawing at my lip some more. I don't know what to say. I didn't realize my struggle was so apparent, so *obvious* to everyone.

"Zinn mentioned you did the same thing after the mission to Z-1543," Vee continues. "She said you refused to eat for several days, then had a minor physical breakdown. You aren't on Earth anymore. There is no point in starving yourself—there are rations enough to feed the entire galactic army for a month on board this station."

I bristle at the accusation, despite its damned accuracy. "For the record, I was planning to eat before facing Max again. Maybe not because I *want* to, but because I'm not ready to rehash the absolute hell I experienced on Primordia-1. No one understands what I went through. You can imagine, but you don't fucking *know*."

I'm shaking, on the brink of losing control. I want to smash my fist into the nearest wall. I'm pissed, but I'm also terrified—and that realization scares me even more.

I stare at the floor, unable to meet Vee's blue-eyed gaze or accept the unspoken compassion they express. Something inside me was broken on Primordia-1, and it may be beyond repair. I'm almost as terrified by that prospect as I am of how I'll react when Max begins to coax the rest of my story from my unwilling lips.

Strong hands touch the sides of my face, and I peer up at the only cyborg I've ever considered a real friend. Tears shine in the corners of their cybernetic eyes.

"We don't know, but we want to help. Don't shut us out, Kye. You are not on this path alone."

I nod, but make no reply. My throat's too tight to form words.

Vee studies me for a moment, then steps away. "Breakfast first, then we'll meet up with the others. Between me and Tariq, we won't let you hurt anyone. You're *safe*, even if you don't know it."

I manage another nod and follow them along the corridor. I'm safe, but no one else is. Does Vee understand what I'm fully capable of? Are they prepared to shoot me, or use Sorin's fucking suppressor if I become a real threat?

I hope so. I'd rather be dead than unknowingly hurt or kill someone I care for. I hope Vee will do whatever is necessary as the situation evolves. I'm not sure anyone else possesses the resolve.

The atmosphere in the mess hall is tense as we enter, as though a storm is visible on the horizon and they're merely waiting for the first flash of lightning before taking shelter. Despite the late morning hour, almost twenty people are gathered. They're armed and armored. Some carry helmets tucked beneath their arms, others hold ration sacks. Something *big* is about to go down.

I glance at Vee in question. I don't think they're preparing for the same mission I asked Sorin to join the day before when he refused to run a diagnostic scan. That had been a supply run, a routine mission to Cobalt Asteroid to restock food stores involving little risk. With the firepower this group is currently packing, they're involved in something else. Something *more*.

Vee shakes their head. "I don't know the details any more than you do. If Sorin thinks it's relevant, he'll tell us, but you need to focus on yourself right now. Ignore them."

I glower at them, but I know an argument won't do any good. My path is set until I get through Max's damned therapy sessions and Sorin's satisfied it's safe to run a diagnostics scan. I won't be going on any missions for a while, no matter how much I protest, pout, or plead.

We eat our share of protein cubes in relative silence. Vee scrutinizes my every movement, while I stare at my plate and flick covert glances toward the armored group as a few more of them trickle into the room. Zinn appears amongst them, her hair redyed to its familiar flamingo pink hue. She notes my gaze after a time and pauses to wink mischievously before turning her attention to the others.

They leave as a unit a minute later, and I'm granted a final smirk accompanied by a wave as she exits the mess hall. The room falls silent in their wake; Vee and I are its only remaining occupants.

"I want to know what's going on," I grumble as I rise to my feet, intent on putting my empty plate in the dishwashing bot's queue.

"So do I. This isn't a minor foray into occupied space." Vee follows me across the room, and we move toward the exit together. "Nik Davenport and Wen Valor were with them."

The names mean nothing to me. "Former ZIEG?"

Vee nods. "I suspect Sorin would have asked me and Tariq along, if not for you."

"I'm sorry."

Vee chuckles. "Don't be. I wouldn't change this for all the credits in Zylar Inc.'s encrypted vault. We've always had an understanding, Kye, even from the beginning. I want to be here, to help you through this. I want to see you recover and thrive." They pause, a distant look in their eyes. "In the last days we worked together as ZIEG soldiers, you were beginning to. And then everything went to shit."

"Yeah." I heave a sigh and look down. "I thought I was happy. I had a future, a life to look forward to. I didn't have that before. And now I don't know if I'll ever have it again." I grimace at the admission and rake a hand through my hair. "*Fuck!*"

This time, I don't resist the urge to demolish something. I pivot and smash my fist into the nanosteel-plated wall. Pain erupts across my knuckles, but I welcome the distraction it brings. When I pull my hand away, the impression of my fist is imprinted on the wall's surface.

Vee lifts their eyebrows. "Feeling better?"

I massage my right hand with my left and laugh. "Actually, yeah. Maybe I should have hit something sooner."

"Maybe. I'll ask Sorin if he has any more chairs he's not partial to."

I frown in confusion before realizing Vee is teasing me. "You're hilarious."

Max and Kelsey are in the conference room when we arrive. The chairs we used the previous day have been removed, as well as the table that had been pushed against one wall, leaving the room empty. I think I understand.

"You slept late," Kelsey says as I approach.

When I shrug, Vee says, "He needed the additional rest."

"I'll call Sorin," Max mutters as he turns toward the exit. "He needs to be here before we begin."

Kelsey snorts at his departing back. "Sorin might be a while."

I cross my arms and frown. "Yeah. What's going on, Kels? We saw—"

She shakes her head. "That mission is classified to those not involved."

"And you're involved?" I press.

"Indirectly."

"Tariq?" I won't relent until I get an answer.

"He's not. He went to the storage bay to look for sugar." She laughs at my confusion, then says, "Cupcakes, remember?"

"Oh. Yeah."

It's another ten minutes before Tariq arrives, and almost an hour before Sorin appears. Sorin's face is drawn and lined with worry, and he says nothing beyond a perfunctory greeting. Max indicates we'll stand at the center of the room, several feet apart, while the others arrange themselves behind me, out of my direct sight.

"I thought it best to work through the next piece of your story while standing," Max explains. "I'll guide you as I did yesterday, and we'll stop if things get too…intense."

I take a deep breath and nod.

I can do this. I *need* to do this.

"Let's start with your transport to Primordia-1," Max says. "Did you know what they planned before you arrived?"

I shake my head. "Marim alluded to it, but in vague terms. My ZIEG escort at the courthouse was just as shocked as I was at the sentencing. I… Part of me hoped she was only posturing, you know? I didn't think they'd actually…"

My voice cracks and catches. Fucking hell, I didn't think it would be this hard to talk. I'm not even to the worst part of my story yet, and already the walls are drawing in, moving closer, threating to realign themselves into the dark confines of the server room.

My breathing becomes a pant, my heart stutters rapidly, my mind races. Shadows obscure the edges of my vision, and I see that damned chair, the holoscreen, the fuel tanks…

Hands grip my shoulders, and I blink, stunned to see Vee inches from me. The darkness recedes as rapidly as it appeared.

I stare at Vee, eyes wide, as I work to slow my breathing.

"You're free," they whisper. "You're *here*. Never forget that."

"If I do anything…" I chew my lower lip and look away. "If I do anything, you'll stop me, right?"

"It's why I'm here. You're strong enough to fight this, Kye. And we'll help you through it."

I nod and begin again as Vee steps away. Max guides me through the journey from Megatropolis to the orbit around Primordia-1, and the week we spent waiting for the sandstorms to clear. I was shackled then too, but was allowed to move about my six-by-six-foot cell. I was given protein cubes and water daily, and I'd begun to think my time on Primordia-1 wouldn't be that bad. It would just be an extension of my confinement on Megatropolis, nothing more.

As we all know, I was very fucking wrong.

Max halts my story as I reach the part where I meet Ajax for the first time. "You're doing great, but I need to know how you're feeling. The next part will be the hardest."

"I'm…" I frown up at the ceiling as I search for the words needed to convey my thoughts. "I'm holding together so far, but I feel…fragile. Like I'll crack at the least amount of pressure. I don't know what will happen if I do."

Max nods and flicks a glance at someone behind me. I peer over my shoulder, following his gaze to Sorin. His blue glasses are in place as he studies me in silence.

"I believe it's safe to continue," he says after a moment. "I don't detect any warning signs yet."

"His vitals are stable," Tariq adds. "Slightly elevated, but I think that's normal in this situation?"

"It is," Max replies. "We'll continue."

I remind myself that I am on Station Six-Theta, in uncharted space, amidst friends and family. I am not on Primordia-1 and Ajax is dead. I will get through this. I *will*.

Max stops me often, forcing my mind to focus on his questions rather than allowing the hell to envelop me anew. It takes hours, but finally, my story is told in full, and I haven't fallen victim to another flashback. I haven't harmed anyone.

But I'm left shaken after the telling. I feel cold and sick.

Vee steps into my field of view again, Kelsey not far behind. My sister draws me into a fierce hug and doesn't let go. She buries her face in my shoulder as hot tears seep through my t-shirt, and my resistance crumbles.

I begin to sob, to grieve for myself in a way I've never done before or since. Kelsey doesn't waver, doesn't push away, doesn't comment. She holds me as she used to when I was a kid and upset by something that would seem trivial now. I haven't needed this from her in at least two decades, but she understands. She's here, and in this moment, it's the only thing that matters.

I've shattered, but now I can finally start to rebuild.

Sorin runs a diagnostic scan the following day. Vee and Tariq stand by in case the process triggers another flashback, but I focus on Sorin, on his intent to *heal*, and the darkness is kept at bay.

He taps on his tablet a few times after I'm plugged in, then shakes his head. "The damage is more extensive than I realized. I have the materials and tools to repair it, but it will be a slow process."

"What do you see?" Tariq asks uncertainly.

"His aural implants require almost complete reconstruction. The cybernetics responsible for fast reflexes were likewise damaged, and some were completely destroyed. He's—"

"I thought so," Vee says softly. "Kye has been slower when we spar."

"Why didn't you say something?" I ask, bewildered.

"I didn't want to make the damage worse," they reply with a shrug. "You were too fragile, even if you didn't see it yourself."

I look down at my hands, helpless and frustrated. "What else?" I ask Sorin.

"Most of your biomechanical organs will need repairs too," he says gently. "And your 'net implants will need to be replaced. I'm..." His voice cracks, and I look up to find him struggling to maintain a stoic façade. "I'm sorry we didn't come for you sooner."

"But you said you can repair the damage."

He nods. "I can, and I will—if you'll allow it."

I don't hesitate. "I will."

Tariq grins from his post behind Sorin. "I think this is a better reason for cupcakes than losing a bet with your sister. I'll start on them once we're done here."

"I'm finished," Sorin says, then gestures to the cable connecting his tablet to my data port. "You can disconnect, Kye."

I smile faintly as I reach behind to pull the cable loose. Sorin refused to plug it in, insisting that I should be in control of who and what is in contact with my cybernetic system. I respect him for giving me the chance to mend my psychological wounds during this process too. Without Sorin and Max, I would have been an unstable threat to myself and anyone around me for years to come.

I hand the cable to him with a nod. "Thanks."

His smile is strained. "Don't thank me yet. The repairs won't be easy. I'm sure you remember some of what Mat did when you were originally brought to ZIEG headquarters."

I nod. "I know. I've started to read my system specs, believe it or not. I can handle this, Sorin. I've been through worse."

"You've been through *hell*," Vee interjects. "Now, we'll help you rebuild."

Sorin nods appreciatively in their direction. "We will. I could use some assistance when we begin, if you're free?"

"Of course. I will do anything to help Kye."

CHAPTER THIRTY-SEVEN

A FUTURE, DESPITE EVERYTHING

BOTANAAR, VYNAAS HOME/KEPLER-47 SYSTEM

It takes Sorin almost two weeks to finish reconstructing my cybernetics and repairing the damage to my biomechanical organs. There is pain, but nothing I can't endure. As I've said, I've been through worse, and he explains every step of the process.

Unlike Mat, Sorin works without the aid of an AI. He's methodical, double-checking every adjustment and reconfiguration against the specs stored in his tablet or in my databanks. I'm awake the entire time, and watch with a mixture of fascination and horror as he operates on various parts of my body.

When he's finished, I feel better. Stronger. I'm back to the same level I was before my imprisonment.

"I'd like you to take a break," he says as I disconnect from his tablet for the final time. "And I don't mean one or two days, Kye. You need a real break. A *vacation.*"

"Where would I go?" I ask. "It's not safe to show my face anywhere but here. The news of my escape was probably all over fucking GNN."

He chuckles dryly. "News of *an* escape was, yes. Zylar Inc. has repressed the name of the prisoner who continues to elude them and has only said that GISA is 'working on it.' But don't worry. I have a destination in mind."

Two days later, I'm aboard a compact shuttle on my way to Botanaar. Vee accompanies me after Sorin updates their identity. We're both posing as starship merchants interested in solar tech, scheduled for a week-long visit with the Vynaas' heir.

I don't care what guise we're operating under. My thoughts are on Daaros and Pablo, and I'm so damned eager to see them I can't sit still. Vee is amused by my restlessness but doesn't comment on it as they navigate through the Kepler-47 System toward Botanaar.

We're met by an escort, much like my first visit to this system. I pace through the tiny cabin as we wait for their scans to complete, but we're allowed through and given coordinates to VaasTek's headquarters on Botanaar.

I don't know if Daaros is aware that we're coming. Station Six-Theta is cut off from the 'net, and I wasn't paying attention to the comings and goings of Sorin's crew as he repaired my system. There is always *someone* flying to the remote space station, but whether or not Sorin sent someone out with a message for Daaros is a mystery. I'll find out soon enough.

"I've never been here," Vee says as we begin our descent through the atmosphere.

I grin, recalling the time Vee took me to the gardens on Megatropolis. "I think you'll like it. It's a quiet world and *very* green."

Vee laughs and taps at the console. "I can see that from here."

We fly along a different trajectory than my first visit, veering north and west across the forested world below. The scale of the trees remains breathtaking, even though I was prepared for the sight this time. Vee openly gapes as they guide the shuttle toward our final destination.

"There are rumors about the trees here, but I never imagined…" They trail off, awe-struck.

"Have you met Daaros?" I ask as we close in on a cluster of glass-encased trunks much like those I remember from the Vynaas' compound.

"No. I know *of* him, but we haven't met." Vee pauses to maneuver the shuttle onto a landing pad. "It was big news when his father recalled him to Botanaar. The tabloids had a field day with their speculation."

I laugh. "I can imagine. I'm glad he was here before I… Before my trial. Pablo's association with me would have brought a shitstorm down on him. I would have hated myself even more for that."

Vee rises from the pilot's chair and fixes me with a stern gaze. "We are not here for you to wallow in self-pity or recriminations. We are here for your recovery. No more."

"But, I—"

"I said, no more." Vee crosses their arms. "Positive talk only, or your sister will hear of it."

I groan and follow them to the door. "Fine. Kelsey's scarier than you realize."

Vee laughs as we step into the midafternoon sunlight. "Kelsey loves you more than you realize. You're damned lucky to have a sister like her."

Before I can reply, we're approached by a familiar face wearing an immaculate white suit and matching fedora. I turn away from Vee and grin, thrilled to see Araan again.

"When we were notified of your visit, Daaros was confused," he says with a smirk. "We should have known Sorin would send you back here eventually. We have your armor."

"What?"

Araan chuckles. "He didn't tell you? It was acquired from Zylar Inc. about five months ago. They didn't understand the new tech and tossed it in storage for analysis later. Daaros bought it from them at an auction. He knew you'd want it back one day."

I glance at Vee. "Did you know?"

Their self-satisfied grin is all the confirmation I need. They've always had a knack for surprising me in the best possible way.

"Sorin wanted to tell you, but I thought this was better." Vee offers their hand to Araan, and they shake in greeting. "I'm Vee Domineaux, former ZIEG, former trainer to this clueless ass, and current overseer of his recovery."

"Araan Bin'Doriist, executive assistant to Mr. Syl'Vaasis and Mr. Noriega." Araan grins. "Welcome to VaasTek. I'll show you to Daaros' office, then I'm sure he'll ask me to give you the grand tour."

"You're assisting Pablo now too?" I ask as he leads us across the landing pad.

"I am. It's customary when the Heir chooses a partner that the staff also serve him." He shrugs, then points to an array of sleek, silvery craft parked along one side of the pad. "Those are some of our latest designs. We'll market them as the Solar Flare, the fastest solar-powered personal shuttles in the galaxy."

"How is Pablo?" I ask. "Is he okay?"

Araan lifts his eyebrows knowingly. "Yes. He was…inconsolable when news of your arrest broke, and even more so after the sentencing. They broadcast the hearing on GNN after you were escorted off Megatropolis. We—Daaros and I both—tried to persuade him not to watch it, but he refused to listen. Ms. Zylar's words to you nearly broke him."

I grimace as my biomechanical heart squeezes painfully in my chest. I should have known what the news would do to Pablo. I hope he'll forgive me, that he'll be pleased with my unexpected visit.

"When we received word from the Coalition about your rescue, he asked for permission to visit you," Araan continues as he leads us through a wide glass door and into a sunlit corridor decorated in VaasTek's signature white and lime green hues. "He was informed you required time to recover and would visit once you were well enough."

I'm relieved by his news. Pablo will be happy to see me, and he knows I'll show up eventually—just not today.

We enter an elevator, and Araan taps the icon for the highest level. "Daaros will be glad to see you, but I'm afraid your reunion must be brief. He is booked for a meeting in twenty minutes."

"It's okay," I reply with a grin. "I'm just glad to be here. Sorin gave us a week."

Araan nods thoughtfully. "And he aligned it with Pablo's midterm break. Of course."

I glance at Vee again, who does a poor job of hiding their smirk. "You knew about this too?"

Vee shrugs. "Surprises are good for the soul."

Daaros is elated that I'm here, and pulls me into an unexpected and firm embrace the moment I step into his spacious office. I've never been this close to him, and I'm struck by the lightly floral scent of his green skin. He steps back with a roguish grin, but continues to hold me at arm's length.

"You look well," he says. "Pablo will be thrilled to see you."

My face grows hot under his scrutiny, but I manage a nod. "I hear he's on break."

"He is." The holoscreen behind him chimes, and his smile falters. "I'm afraid I can't extricate myself from this meeting, but once I'm finished, I'll find you. Araan, will you show them the facility? Then prep one of the Solar Flares. I'll be leaving the office early today."

Daaros releases me, and I follow Araan into the corridor. Sunlight streams through the clear panes overhead and glimmers on the polished tile floor.

"What would you like to see first?" Araan asks. "We can tour the laboratories, the production floor, the engineering wing, or the relaxation gardens. It's up to you."

When I don't reply, Vee says, "The gardens. We don't often see plant life thriving like this. It's…beautiful."

Araan beams. "This is nothing. The gardens here are cultivated to bring a sense of serenity to VaasTek's employees when they need a break from their duties. But if you want a truly magnificent display, ask Daaros to take you to his father's private garden while you're here. The Vynaas' garden is unparalleled on Botanaar."

We take a different elevator to a middle tier of the building. It opens into a circular corridor with a clear glass ceiling, but the exterior wall is opaque and ink-black. Araan leads us to a door, then pauses with one hand over the exit controls.

"Most humans never get to see the gardens here," he says. "It's rare that you're allowed in our system, and the few visitors we do receive rarely ask to see the gardens."

"Why not?" I ask, mystified.

He smiles sadly. "Often, they are too rushed to bother with 'trivialities.' Your people are always on a schedule. You never truly relax. I see it often enough with Mr. Noriega, though he's beginning to adapt."

"That's the trouble with corporate types," Vee replies. "But *we* are here on vacation, and the gardens will do this guy more good—" Vee jerks a thumb in my direction, "—than a tour through the labs will."

I chuckle and run a hand through my hair. "I've spent enough time in Sorin's damned lab the past two weeks to last a lifetime. Let's see the garden."

Vee doesn't have to say it, but they know lab spaces still make me edgy. Yeah, I've overcome my fear of *Sorin* plugging me in, but I'm not ready to let anyone else near me with a cable.

My psyche is still fragile, though I've been trying to downplay that fact, and since I discovered nature in the form of Megatropolis' hidden garden, I've learned it brings me a sense of peace. And peace is something I need right now.

Araan opens the door, and I stare in wonder as we step outside. The garden is perched on a broad ledge encircling the glassed-in building and the massive tree at its heart. Smaller trees and shrubs are planted artfully in carefully tended plots, then surrounded by multitudes of flowers. Each plot features flowers of a single color, though the shapes and forms are nearly endless. The plot directly in front of the exit is an array of yellows and golds, while the one to its right features shades of purple and violet. Between the garden plots is a fountain in the shape of a fanciful woodland creature with antlers and six legs. Water spills from the antlers and across the creature's stone flank to pool beneath it.

Vee moves ahead and kneels at the edge of the nearest flowerbed. They close their eyes and tilt their head back to allow the sunlight to spill across their features. I walk slowly toward the fountain, drawn by the statue of a creature I can't name.

"It's a *kiiru*," Araan says a few moments later. His tone is hushed, as though he fears to disturb the serenity of this space. "They are grazers that inhabit this world's forests. I think they may be similar to your Earth's extinct reindeer."

I query the 'net for reindeer, then *kiiru*. They're similar, but Earth's version only had four legs and much less impressive antlers.

"Will we see any?"

Araan laughs softly. "Yes. The Vynaas has adopted a herd, and it lives in his personal garden. Some have been tamed for riding."

The idea lodges in my brain and won't let go. I've never experienced something like it before, but I imagine it's both incredible and terrifying. Would the Vynaas allow me to ride one of his *kiiru*? Would it be considered an insult if I asked?

I grimace as I realize I don't know, and I'm scared shitless at the prospect of offending Daaros' father. Or rather, *fathers*. They're both powerful men capable of crushing me with their political might the instant I become a nuisance.

Araan smiles knowingly as he watches my face. "Daaros can arrange it, if you'd like. His fathers won't deny him."

I chew my lower lip momentarily, then nod. "Yeah, I would like that. But I've never…ah…"

Araan laughs and motions for me to follow him deeper into the gardens. "Don't worry. The *kiiru* keeper is my father. I'm well versed in riding, and I'm more than happy to teach you."

I lift my eyebrows. I can't imagine Araan, with his crisp suits and immaculate appearance, sitting astride a massive *kiiru*.

"You are surprised," he says.

"Yeah. What else don't I know about you?"

"I was appointed Daaros' assistant at age five," he replies. "It's customary for the Vynaas' heir to be paired with an assistant at birth, and since my father works for *his* father, it was arranged."

"I didn't realize you were older than him." I laugh softly as we near a garden plot filled with flowers in shades of pink, magenta, and salmon.

"You didn't check my profile?" he asks, genuinely curious.

"I don't like to pry unless I have to."

He nods. "I understand. Yes, I am five years older than he is. It was often assumed by outsiders that we would pair—it has happened often enough throughout history—but Daaros always sought a different path. It led him to Pablo, and by proxy, to you." His tone is thoughtful, calm.

"Do you wish it were otherwise?" I ask.

He shakes his head. "I've known since childhood it would never happen. I accepted it and moved on. My partner is a solar engineer, though he is currently on leave from his duties. He is in gestation."

I blink, then offer him a grin. "Congratulations. I didn't know."

He laughs again. "It's not surprising. It happened after your capture, and you've had more important things to focus on than your friend's assistant becoming a father."

I look away, taking in the fragrant array of flowers in front of us. "Yeah. I was a mess when Sorin pulled me out of there. Sometimes, I still am."

"He was right to send you here," Araan replies. "Botanaar has always been a place of rejuvenation and healing. I will ensure your stay is restful."

We wander the gardens in silence for a while, eventually completing the vast loop around the central tree. Vee is where we left them, but is no longer alone. They speak with Daaros in quiet tones that even my aural implants have difficulty picking up until we're within a few feet of their location.

Daaros flashes a grin at Araan. "I've taken the liberty of having a shuttle prepped while you were showing Kye around."

Araan nods stiffly. "I should have called it in sooner."

Daaros laughs. "How long have we worked together, Araan? There is no reason to apologize, and I'm glad you've indulged him with this." His smile falters as his gaze slides over to meet mine. "Sorin sent me information regarding your…condition a few minutes ago. I will do everything in my power to assist in your recovery."

I flush and look down. I didn't expect Sorin to share the details of my therapy sessions with Daaros, and I'm not sure how I feel about it.

"I don't want to be a bother," I reply. "Max thinks I'm well enough…"

Daaros shakes his head. "Our contract states I will provide you with the best medical care the galaxy has to offer. Unless you have changed your mind since we last spoke, I intend to uphold my portion of our agreement. And I was hoping you'd still be interested in the job."

I pause, startled by the reminder. I haven't given our contract any thought since my capture on Megatropolis, and he's never brought it up like this before. "You'd still let me work for you? After all the shit that's happened?"

He tilts his head, then reaches toward me, resting his hand on my shoulder. A worried frown creases his expression, but the compassion in his eyes is clear. "Kye, it will be an *honor* to have you on my staff. That hasn't changed, and it never will."

I don't know what to say. I stare at the man who has given me opportunities no one else ever has, the man who has won over my best friend's heart, the man who would take me in and treat me as family when I've done nothing to deserve his generosity. Daaros confounds me, but I know in my heart he genuinely cares.

"Why?"

The word hangs between us for several moments. He studies me, amused, then squeezes my shoulder.

"You know the reasons, Kye. And after hearing of your recent exploits, I've begun to understand the sort of man you are. Loyal, brave—"

"You mean stupid," I interrupt with a smirk.

He shakes his head. "What I'm trying to say is your character speaks for itself. Any future Vynaas should be fortunate to have *you* acting as their head of security."

"Wait." I hold up my hands. "I thought this was just a bodyguard gig."

Daaros folds his arms and nods once. "It is. But when I replace my father one day, I'll require more protection. More than a single man— enhanced as he might be—can provide. You will lead the team. If you still want the job, that is."

He's offering me a future, despite everything. I'll be the galaxy's greatest dumbass if I turn him down.

"Yeah. *Hell*, yeah."

"Good." He turns to Araan. "We should go. The shuttle should be ready by now."

Vee falls in step beside me as we exit the gardens and follow the two Botanaari to a different shuttle pad than the one we landed on.

"I hope the future head of the Vynaas' security force remembers his friends from before," Vee teases. "Maybe he could use the assistance of a fellow cyborg."

I laugh, carefree in a way I've seldom been. "I hope you'll be expecting the call when that day comes. I don't really know what the hell I'm getting myself into."

Vee snorts. "You never do."

CHAPTER THIRTY-EIGHT

BOTANAARI CUISINE

BOTANAAR, VYNAAS HOME/KEPLER-47 SYSTEM

I lay on my back, staring up at a patch of twilight sky through the interwoven branches of the canopy overhead. Stars twinkle in the darkness, a sight I'm still unused to seeing, despite my time away from Earth's perpetual haze. It's no wonder the ancients loved stargazing. The night sky is breathtaking and heartbreakingly beautiful.

The soft grass beside me rustles as Pablo turns over to rest on his side. I peer at him, his contented smile half obscured by shadow as he leans on his elbow, watching me.

"What's up, Pab?"

"We haven't had time alone like this since we left Earth," he replies. "Sometimes, I miss our place. I miss you."

I lift my eyebrows in surprise. "You have Daaros. I didn't think you—"

He cuts me off with a laugh. "I love him, Kye, but he's not you. He's not my best friend. He's not the person who has always been there, through everything…"

"But he will be." I shift my gaze back to the sky. "I wasn't sure about him at first. I didn't trust him. Rich guys tend to hurt those around them without thinking, and he's fucking *loaded*."

"And now?" Pablo's voice trembles with unspoken anxiety.

"I know better. He's not like the rich human bastards that litter the galaxy. He's genuine, and he's smitten with you." I crack a smile. "Leaving Earth was the best thing you could have done. You just didn't know it."

"The Vynaas is pushing for us to set a date for our *briia*," Pablo says after a time. "I don't want to make anything official until I know you'll be there. Daar understands, but his father… The Vynaas can be very demanding."

I grimace and sit up, brushing stray blades of grass from my hair. Daaros won't officially employ me until Sorin's schemes are finished; he believes if the Coalition succeeds in undermining Zylar Inc.'s hold on the galactic government, my name will eventually be cleared. Until then, I'm on loan to Sorin—once I'm well enough.

"Has he told you I'm still working for the Coalition?"

Pablo nods. "I wish you weren't, but I understand the politics involved. Once it's over, you'll come back here, and we can spend more evenings like this."

"You mean sneaking into the Vynaas' garden after visiting hours without his permission?"

"If we're caught, Daar will vouch for us." He grins. "I doubt his father will care that we're here, as long as we don't touch the *kiiru* or trample any of the rare flowers."

"Araan said he'd teach me to ride."

Pablo beams. "You'll love it. And with your reflexes, you'll have no trouble. It took me weeks to learn how to guide them along the path *I* chose, and I still have trouble with them sometimes. You won't."

"How do you know?' I ask, incredulous. "I'm not fully human anymore, remember? I've heard animals pick up on things like that."

He shakes his head. "I just know, Kye. There are some things you've always been better at than I am, and I'm pretty damned sure this will be one of them."

Abruptly, he rises to his feet and extends his hand. "We should go back inside. We've been out here for hours, and if I don't show up soon, Daar will send the guards to look for me."

I accept his hand and allow him to pull me to my feet. "He's protective of you, isn't he?"

"No more than you ever were." He flashes a grin, then frowns. "I didn't realize it was so dark. Can you, ah…?"

I chuckle and take the lead, switching to night vision. "Don't worry, Pab. I won't let you trample any of your future father-in-law's favorite plants."

"Thanks. He'd forgive me eventually, but I'd rather not piss him off this close to our *briia*. Daar says his fathers like me, but I don't know how to read the Vynaas yet." He clasps my hand tighter, and I feel him shudder through our grip. "I know I shouldn't be afraid of him, but I can't help it. He's the Vynaas! And I'm just some poor kid from Earth with nothing and no one to his name."

"I'm someone," I reply, more defensively than I'd intended.

He's silent for a few seconds, then says, "You're right, and I'm sorry. You've been away for so long, and I... I didn't think I'd see you again. Not after your arrest." He sniffles and pulls his hand away.

I turn around to face him. "Hey, I'm here. I'm okay."

He shakes his head miserably. "You're here, but you aren't okay. I read Sorin's report."

I squeeze my eyes shut and swallow my disappointment in silence. *Of course*, Daaros would share that report with Pablo. I'm not sure either of them is capable of keeping secrets from the other. *Fuck.*

"Then you know why Sorin wanted me to visit."

"Yeah." Pablo's voice is strained, laced with a pain borne of empathy. "I want to help, but I don't know how. I'm an engineer, not a psychiatrist. I feel so damned useless!"

Tears threaten to spill from his dark eyes as I open mine to look at him again. "I just need a friend, Pab. That's why I came."

He nods and wipes at his eyes, then inexplicably begins to laugh. I stare in confusion. I have no idea what I've done to cause his mood to veer from frustration to mirth in the span of a heartbeat.

"Your eyes glow," he says, still laughing. "You look ridiculous."

"It's a side-effect of night vision. I thought you didn't want to ruin the Vynaas' flowers." But I'm laughing now too, and it feels damned good. I've missed this. I've missed him.

"I don't, but if his guards pass by, they'll see you." He laughs again and grabs my hand. "I thought cyborgs were supposed to be stealthy."

"Some are. I'm not."

"Even ZIEG knew you're shit at blending in." He snickers and motions vaguely toward the glass door that will lead us back inside the Vynaas' complex. "Lead the way. I can't see the path very well."

I smile and move forward, recalling our last years on Earth when my distance vision was going to hell, and Pablo was often the one taking the lead. Our roles are reversed tonight, and though it feels damned weird, I'm content. He doesn't realize it, but his presence has healed a portion of my ruptured soul.

Maybe, if I'm lucky, I won't dream tonight. Maybe my best friend's proximity is enough to keep the nightmares at bay for a while.

I'm never as lucky as I hope to be.

Ajax stalks my dreams, his towering form looming above me as I writhe in bonds I can't see. His leering face is clear, while the rest of my surroundings are dim, shadowed approximations of the objects I became familiar with inside the server room.

I must have screamed aloud at some point. When I wake up, Vee stands at the edge of my bed wearing a pair of baggy plaid pajamas, their blue eyes filled with concern. I push myself upright and disentangle from the sheets, which I note were torn nearly in half during my struggles.

My heart pounds and my breathing is ragged, but I adjust my biochems to steady them. It was only a nightmare, and I haven't hurt anyone. The sheets can be replaced.

Vee sits alongside me and tilts their head. "Do you want to talk about it?"

I grimace. My natural instinct is to say no, but Max insists it helps. I haven't had any flashbacks in over a week, only nightmares, so maybe he's right. And I trust Vee.

So, I tell them of my nighttime hellscape while I stare resolutely at the floor, my face burning with unspoken shame. I want to move on with my life. I have a future here on Botanaar, but my past hangs over me like Earth's noxious haze. I need to get past this. Somehow.

"Your sister made sure that bastard was dead," Vee replies once I'm finished. "He can't hurt you anymore. You're *safe*."

Vee uses Max's words to reinforce their point. I'm safe. Ajax is dead. I know this, but my fucking subconscious refuses to relinquish its fears in the depths of the night. Instead, it throws them viciously in my face when I'm helpless to prevent its attacks.

My subconscious is a terrified asshole.

"Thanks," I mutter. "I'm sorry I woke you."

Vee shakes their head. "Never apologize for this. And I was awake, reading one of those awful books you like so much."

"Awful?" I ask with a laugh. "They're entertaining."

"And gory as hell. It's no wonder you have nightmares when you spend half your afternoon reading about cannibalistic serial killers who feed people their own fucking brains!" Vee rolls their eyes in mock-exasperation, but their amusement is clear.

"But I did spend the evening with Pablo," I remind them. "I wasn't reading right before I fell asleep."

Vee sighs dramatically, then rises. "I'll leave you to get dressed. The first sun will rise soon, and you promised Pablo you'd meet him for breakfast. We're on Botanaari time now, and breakfast means first dawn."

When I nod, they disappear through my door. We've been given a suite on one of the middle levels of the Vynaas' compound. Our bedrooms connect to a central seating area, which someone—Pablo, I suspect—had stocked with books not long after we arrived. I'm not sure how the Botanaari feel about the human penchant for paper products, given their biology and the reverence they have for their world's magnificent trees.

I pause to stare through the clear glass ceiling above, noting the wash of color beginning to paint the wispy clouds overhead. Vee's right; I need to make myself presentable soon, because Pablo will be waiting. Probably Daaros too.

I pull on a plain gray t-shirt and black cargo pants, run a comb through my hair, then slip on my latest pair of work boots. I didn't pack anything nicer—I don't *own* anything nicer—and I hope the Vynaas isn't offended by my lack of fashionable attire. I doubt he'll join us for breakfast, but there's a good chance I'm wrong. We're in his home, visiting his son and Pablo, staying in rooms he's loaned us, after all.

When I emerge from my room, Vee is already at the exit door, dressed in similar fashion, the book they teased me about minutes ago in hand. They flush slightly and set the book aside, while I smirk knowingly.

"Awful, huh?" I tease.

"No comment."

I laugh as I follow them from our shared suite into the glass corridor beyond. The light outside is steadily growing brighter, and the clouds overhead blush more orange as I watch. We make our way to the elevator and step inside. I tap the console for the ground level, where we promised to meet Pablo the day before. The compound's kitchen is somewhere above the guest suites, so I assume he plans to go elsewhere for breakfast.

When the elevator opens into the expansive lobby, my eyes are drawn to the cluster of Botanaari gathered around a wall-mounted holoscreen a short distance away. Pablo stands at the rear of the group, his expression troubled. I spy the GNN icon in the upper right-hand corner of the display.

I glance at Vee as we walk toward them. "This can't be good, can it?"

They shrug. "There's only one way to find out. Listen."

I filter out the whispered conversations of the Botanaari as we stop alongside Pablo, and focus my aural implants on the voice issuing from the holoscreen. The volume is low, but since Sorin patched me up, I can once again tune my hearing to specific frequencies or voices.

A trim, dark-haired reporter in a light gray suit speaks from the screen, an image of Zylar Inc. headquarters behind him. His brown eyes focus on his viewing audience as he relates the details of the galaxy's latest breaking news.

"…still unsure of casualties, but we have confirmed the CEO of Zylar Inc. has been abducted. A ransom note was found in her apartments only moments ago. GISA has refused to comment so far, but state they are actively investigating this new breach in the interim government's security."

I turn to face Vee, eyes wide. "Was this…?"

Vee shakes their head. "I don't know, but we shouldn't speculate. Not here," they add in a whisper.

The holoscreen switches to an image of suited GISA agents combing through an apartment more luxurious than Daaros' had been on Ring Eight before returning to the reporter. "Marim Zylar, as acting galactic president, is missing. We will continue to update the citizens as more information becomes available."

"Holy shit," I hiss as Pablo grabs my elbow and steers me toward the exit door. Vee increases their stride to keep up.

"Daar is outside," Pablo says after a few seconds. "I think he'll know more, but if he doesn't, his fathers will. They've made reservations at one of this sector's premier restaurants."

I wince and hope he doesn't notice my reaction. As I said earlier, I'm never as lucky as I hope to be, and Pablo has always been observant.

He shakes his head as we walk outside. "Did you seriously expect to avoid the Vynaas and the Minister of Intelligence for the entire week?" He snickers and points to a private shuttle waiting nearby. It's one of Daaros' new Solar Flares, painted a lustrous shade of ruby red. "Some things never change. I'm glad you're still mostly *you.*"

"I—"

"He's a little battered, but we're working on it," Vee interrupts before I can spill the story of my latest nightmare.

I shoot them a frown over my shoulder, and am met with an unimpressed expression in return. Sometimes, Vee is as protective of me as Kelsey is. I'm not sure how I feel about that.

My irritation vanishes the moment we step inside the Solar Flare. Windows line two sides of the cabin, tinted so only those inside can see through the seamless panes. Several plush sofas are arranged along its sides, and there's a bartender bot and a fully stocked bar in the rear. A sliding panel shields the cockpit from the remainder of the craft, but it's open and Araan's trademark white fedora is visible above his seat's headrest. Daaros lounges on one of the sofas, his arm thrown over the back as he stares outside. He's dressed to impress, as usual.

He turns to flash a grin our way as we enter. Pablo wastes no time settling in next to him, and Vee takes a seat across the cabin. I continue to stand just inside the door, taking in every detail of the luxury craft. The furnishings alone probably cost more than a full year of Pablo's tuition.

"Are all of your Solar Flares set up like this?" I ask.

Daaros chuckles and shakes his head. "No. This one is mine, designed for my tastes." He leans forward to peer into the cockpit. "We're ready, Araan."

The door behind me slides shut, and seconds later, the craft silently lifts off. As we begin streaking through the dawn-lit sky, Pablo tilts his face toward Daaros, questions in his dark eyes.

"Do you know anything about Marim Zylar's abduction?" he asks.

Daaros shifts slightly in his seat and stares through the window behind Vee for several seconds. "No, but I have a theory."

"And?" I press, determined to know more.

Daaros lifts his eyebrows and fixes me with an unreadable gaze. "It is part of Sorin's endgame. I believe my *siindolaar* can tell you more, though I can't promise he'll be forthcoming."

Pablo laughs softly. "He's never forthcoming about his work, Daar."

"And he can't be," Daaros counters with a fond smile. "He deals in secrets to better protect the citizens of Botanaar, which you will soon be."

I swallow a sigh. "You didn't tell me you were granted citizenship, Pab."

"It's not official yet," he replies. "Since I'm human, I can't apply for it. It only comes through *briia*. I'll have it once we're recognized as partners in the ceremony."

Now I feel like an ass. He hasn't scheduled the ceremony yet because of *me*. He's putting his life on hold again because of *me*. I'm not sure I'm deserving of a friend like him. I haven't done anything in my life but struggle to survive, then I fuck things up when they're finally going right.

"I'm sorry," I mumble. "I didn't know. You shouldn't wait for me. You should—"

"Enough," Daaros cuts in, his tone unyielding. "*We* have made the decision to wait for your availability, however long it may take."

My mouth takes this opportunity to blurt the question I've been dreading to ask, the one I've managed to keep to myself so far. "And what if Sorin's plans end with me dead?"

Pablo's expression is stricken as he looks away.

Daaros frowns and says, "Then Sorin will have bigger problems than what to do with Marim Zylar. If any further harm comes to you during his final missions, then by the suns, I will personally see to it that he regrets every breath he takes for the rest of his miserable life. And it *will* be miserable."

For the first time since I've known him, I'm afraid of Daaros Syl'Vaasis. He's a powerful man with more money than most colonized planets possess, and I have no doubt he'll make good on his threats. And with the backing of his fathers…

I shake my head. "Why do you care so much about what happens to me, Daaros? Pablo I understand. We've known each other forever. But you… It *still* doesn't make sense."

Daaros' expression softens, a faint smile quirking his lips. "We've been over this before, Kye. Pablo cares for you as he would a brother. I protect those I love, and by extension, their families. That includes you."

"We're here," Araan calls from the cockpit.

Daaros nods and rises from his seat, offering Pablo his arm. "Let's forget this talk for a time and enjoy our breakfast. Maybe my fathers will tell you what they know of Sorin's latest exploits. Maybe they won't. Regardless, the food here is exquisite—if you can stomach Botanaari cuisine."

It turns out Botanaari cuisine is some of the best food I've had in the galaxy. I'm aware it's entirely protein, most of it from insect and arachnid sources, but they know how to create flavors and textures with their food that I've never experienced. And it's damned good.

Okay, I also acknowledge that I'm no culinary expert, despite my history as a fake chef, and that I spent most of my life surviving on expired protein cubes. Maybe my opinion is worthless, but I enjoyed our breakfast.

The conversation afterwards… Not so much.

"So," the Vynaas says slowly as our plates are cleared away, "I want to learn more about the once-human my son and heir has employed as his future head of security."

I splutter through the sip of water I was attempting to drink and almost cough. I know damned well Vee can sense the rapid increase in my pulse, but they remain silent across the table from me. I flick a glance at Daaros, who only shrugs.

Shit. I wasn't prepared for this.

"Uh… What would you like to know?" I manage.

The Vynaas steeples his green fingers and leans forward, the beginnings of a smirk identical to his son's appearing on his lips. "I have read your public file, obviously. I have also read your classified file." He gestures to his Minister of Intelligence, who nods once, his face an expressionless mask. "But your files tell me nothing about your personality, about *why* my son believes you are the best candidate for the job."

I fumble for answers that my mind refuses to conjure. It's blank, and the deafening buzz of silence blankets my ears. They're all waiting for my answer. I don't know what to say. Not to the Vynaas and his partner. *Fuck.*

Vee kicks my foot, and I glance at them, hoping they'll help. They look pointedly at Pablo.

Of course. I latch onto the idea like it's a life raft and my only means of salvation from the red devils that have overtaken Earth's forsaken seas.

"Pablo is my best friend," I begin, forcing my words to conform to a measured pace. "He has always been there for me. He made sure I had enough clean water and food for months when he was accepted into MSTI… Before I was offered the contract with ZIEG. I've never had the opportunity to repay him for everything he's done. I will do *anything* for Pablo."

I draw a breath and some of my nervous energy dissipates. "Pablo fell in love with Daaros, and Daaros with him. I want them to be happy. If anyone deserves joy in their life, it's my best friend."

I pause to study the faces around me as I consider my next words. The Vynaas' expression has softened, and he appears genuinely interested in what I'll say next. His partner appears thoughtful, but I still can't read any emotion in his green countenance. Vee offers a nod of encouragement, Pablo smiles, and Daaros grins. I'll take the last as a sign that I'm doing something right.

"I'm still not sure how Pablo convinced him to do it, but Daaros bought my contract from ZIEG," I continue. "For that alone, I owe him my loyalty. No one else would have shown such compassion to a poor scavenger from Earth who would have died without signing on with ZIEG. But there's more. He's proven to me that he cares for Pablo just as much as I do. Daaros will give Pablo the best life he can possibly ask for. I want to help him provide that for my friend."

I realize as I stop speaking that this is what I've been feeling all along. I haven't been able to articulate it, but it has been there since the moment I learned Daaros had proposed to Pablo. I don't have to reiterate what a headache it is to deal with the GNN paparazzi; they know the details all too well. I don't have to explain why I agreed to help Sorin; override codes aside, Daaros asked me to, because *he* believed it was better for our collective future, and in turn, Pablo's.

I've always felt helpless to reciprocate all that Pablo has done for me over the years, but now, I have that chance. Now, I can protect him as he's always tried to protect me. And with my cybernetics, he'll never have a better bodyguard.

But the Vynaas isn't finished with me. "And what will you do about the bounties Zylar Inc. has placed on your head?"

I gape at him. "What?"

Beside him, the minister chuckles. "You didn't believe you escaped Primordia-1 without someone taking notice, did you?"

"I… I didn't…" I shake my head as my face flushes in frustration. "No one told me—"

"Father," Daaros hisses, clearly incensed by the question.

"Sorin didn't tell him," Vee cuts in. "He and Max felt it was better if he didn't know, given his recent diagnosis."

"We have an excellent treatment for that," the Vynaas replies with a wave of his hand. "I have arranged it for tomorrow, and afterward, his armor may be returned to him, if he wants it. Kye will be cured in a far more efficient fashion than anything the humans have concocted so far." He turns to me. "Think on it, Kye. What will you do about the bounties? That little problem must be resolved before I allow you to work for my son."

I manage a terse nod. My stomach would have roiled if it wasn't a biomechanical wonder, and I'm forced to adjust my biochems to slow my heart rate.

Maybe I don't like Botanaari cuisine after all.

CHAPTER THIRTY-NINE

CURED

BOTANAAR, VYNAAS HOME/KEPLER-47 SYSTEM

"So, how the hell does this work?" I ask nervously.

I'm perched on the edge of an uncomfortable nanosteel table at the epicenter of four sun lamps, each one focused on me. A trio of Botanaari doctors monitor holoscreens, while a fourth attaches electrodes to various points on my torso, neck, and skull. I hope the Vynaas' people know what they're doing, because if not, my cybernetics will be fried. *Again.*

Sorin will love that.

I'm just lucky the Vynaas' miniature interrogation the day before didn't fry them first. Daaros' fathers terrify me even more now that I understand how fiercely they guard their son. And Pablo's damned boyfriend didn't have the decency to warn me first.

I should be angry with him, but I'm not. How can I, after everything he's done for me and Pablo? And now I'll be indebted to his royal damned father for my current treatment too. *Fuck.*

The doctor attaching electrodes pauses in his work to study me. "As with all things on Botanaar, we utilize the power of our suns. In this case, to heal the rift in your brain. Our scans indicate a portion of your amygdala was damaged due to prolonged exposure to a difficult event. We will repair it."

"And it won't damage my cybernetics?"

He shakes his head, smiling. "No. The Vynaas contacted your primary engineer, and he has approved of our proposed methods."

I frown. "You mean Sorin."

"Yes."

I suppress a sigh. I should have known Sorin was involved in this, that my visit to Botanaar was more than a brief vacation to see my best friend. What else does he have planned for me that I'm unaware of? I'm convinced there's something—he wouldn't be so concerned about treating my PTSD otherwise.

"Are you comfortable?" the doctor asks.

"Yeah."

I don't tell him I'm resisting the urge to squirm in my seat, that the electrodes are almost too similar to the restraints that once held me in place, that I'm doing everything in my power to focus on *him* rather than the remnants of memory that threaten to overwhelm me. I'm determined to get through this without another episode.

"Relax," he says. "Lie down. We'll begin momentarily."

"You didn't fully explain how this works," I reply, desperate to think of anything other than the server room, that damned chair, the fuel tanks…

His voice cuts through the shadowy haze that tries to descend. "The electrodes are powered by the sun lamps. I've placed them at precise locations, where they'll focus their energy toward healing the damage I mentioned. You'll feel heat at each point an electrode contacts your skin, but they have been adjusted to your unique physiology. It should not burn. If it does, you must tell me immediately. Do you understand?"

I nod and reluctantly lie down. "Why are there electrodes on my chest if the damage is in my brain?"

"All of your nerves have a pathway to your brain," he replies, "and a subset of your cybernetics follow the same paths. We will use your cybernetics to channel the energy and focus it where it's needed most. Are you ready?"

I shake my head. "One more question. How do you know so much about neuroscience? The Botanaari are—"

"We evolved from plants, yes, but we have also developed something remarkably similar to your human nervous system. That aspect of our anatomy isn't so different." He steps away from the table and nods to the others. "Let's begin."

I clench my jaw and ball my hands into fists, prepared to experience some form of discomfort as the sun lamps are turned on one by one. I squeeze my eyes shut as the first blinding beam of solar energy focuses on my prone form. The second turns on, then the third…

I open my eyes and immediately regret it. The light is so brilliant, it hurts my cybernetic eyes. I snap them closed, then begin to relax. There is no pain from the electrodes, only a gentle warmth, like true sunlight on my skin on a clear day. It's unexpectedly soothing.

"How do you feel?" the doctor asks after several minutes pass.

I'm growing drowsy, but I feel fine. "Good," I reply. "This is…nice. Weird, but nice."

"We'll begin channeling the energy along your cybernetics in a few seconds. You'll notice a change."

I do, but it's pleasant too. Warmth trickles along my cybernetics and gathers near the center of my skull. My internal sensors detect the energy transfer, but nothing goes into an alarm state. Heat builds inside my head, and I struggle to remain awake. I want to sleep, though I don't need to, according to my system analysis. I fight the urge for a few seconds, then willingly give in.

I don't need to be awake for this, do I?

When I wake up, I'm in a comfortable bed. Soft pillows cradle my head, and a puffy blanket envelops me. I'm still shirtless and barefoot as I was in the clinic, but when I open my eyes, I'm in my room in the Vynaas' compound.

I blink experimentally, but I don't feel any different than before.

I run an internal scan. Nothing is out of the ordinary; everything is within prime operational parameters. But my system also claimed that in the days after I was rescued from Primordia-1, and only Sorin's full diagnostic scan revealed the true extent of the damage I'd sustained. My internal scans are only designed to monitor my vitals, not the state of my cybernetics.

It's a design flaw I'd love to see fixed.

My room is dim, the sky growing dark through the skylights overhead. I can see the first stars twinkling in the clear sky, the silhouettes of enormous tree branches arcing across my field of view, and a pale bluish glimmer partially obscured by the compound's central tree that could only be Botanaar's smallest moon, Kaas. I must have been asleep for hours.

I push myself into a sitting position and untangle myself from the blanket. I switch to night vision to assess my exterior, but the electrodes the Botanaari doctor attached to me earlier in the day have left no marks on my skin. I don't know if their treatment was successful. As I said, nothing feels different.

I locate a clean shirt and pull it on, then switch back to standard vision before opening the door to the common area between my bedroom and Vee's. Soft light illuminates the room, and I spy Vee lounging on one of the plush sofas in the center. Across from them are Pablo and Daaros. All three turn toward my door as it slides open.

Pablo springs to his feet and crosses the room in an instant, pulling me into another one of his fierce hugs. Tears seep through the fabric of my shirt as he releases a shuddering sob.

"Pab?" I ask, confused by his reaction. "What's going on?"

Daaros rises from his seat and moves toward us, his expression lined with concern. "After the procedure was complete, they failed to wake you. We weren't sure what happened, and without Sorin here…" He shrugs helplessly and looks away.

I glance at Vee, who stands a few steps behind Daaros. "They aren't used to treating cyborgs. They don't have the right tools or equipment to run a systems diagnostic on us, but I told them I thought you'd wake up given time. Your vitals were steady."

"How long was I out?" I look down at Pablo as he wipes his eyes and pushes away.

"About thirty hours," Vee replies.

"My fathers have stopped by every few hours to check on your status," Daaros adds. "My *paavylaar*—the Vynaas—feels responsible for what happened. I have rarely seen him so concerned."

Thirty hours. That means I met with the doctors yesterday morning. What the hell happened? And did their treatment ultimately work, or am I still the broken mess I was two days ago?

Vee crosses their arms. "Sorin is on his way here with Max and a few others. It's good you're awake. You can tell him what happened."

There's a soft tap on the exit door, and Daaros moves toward it. "That will be one or both of my fathers."

"My sensors indicate everything is okay," I explain as Pablo guides me toward the sofas. "But I know they aren't a reliable indicator for some forms of damage."

Vee sits across from me, but Pablo remains glued to my side. He's finished crying, but he's still rattled by what happened. Whatever the hell it was.

Daaros returns from the door with the Vynaas, and they seat themselves alongside Vee. The Vynaas' expression is weary and lined with concern as his deep green eyes scrutinize every detail of my appearance.

"I'm glad you're awake. I feared we had miscalculated your treatment to catastrophic effect." The Vynaas leans forward, elbows on his knees, to peer into my face. "How do you feel?"

"Normal, I guess. Nothing seems wrong." I shrug. "When they started to run the solar energy through my cybernetics, it made me sleepy. I couldn't fight it, but I didn't want to. It was…nice. I was comfortable."

He turns to Vee. "Is this reaction typical?"

Vee shrugs. "I don't know. I'm not sure any cyborg has gone through even half of what Kye has. Sorin will know for sure."

Pablo clasps my hand in what would have been a painful grip before my muscles and bones were augmented. "But you're okay. Aren't you?" he whispers.

"Yeah, I think so."

"I can't lose you, Kye." He pulls away, his eyes fixed on the floor.

I'm desperate to change the subject, if only for a few seconds. "When will Sorin be here?" I ask the Vynaas.

"He's scheduled to arrive in our system in approximately one hour. I've directed my people to escort him here." He rises to his feet, though his eyes are locked on mine. "If you require anything, send for it. Araan and some of my staff are in the hall for this purpose. I will return with Sorin. In the meantime, I implore you to rest. I will not see my future son-in-law heartbroken if I can help it."

He smiles fondly at Pablo before turning to leave. Daaros watches him go, unspoken questions in his eyes, while Vee leans forward to peer at me.

"Do you need to eat?" Vee asks pointedly. "And don't say no out of habit, Kye. I'm in no mood to tolerate your brand of dumbassery. Tell me honestly what your vitals say."

I don't feel like eating, but I know Vee is right. "I'm at forty-six percent."

Pablo is on his feet in an instant, moving toward the door in the Vynaas' wake. He speaks rapidly, asking for a meal to be brought to our suite, and Araan's self-assured tone responds seconds later.

I cross my arms and scowl at him, irritated that he'd immediately take action without consulting me first. It may be for my own damned good, but I don't have to like it. I'm not helpless, and I'm not a child.

He notes my expression when he turns to face us once more. "Don't," he snaps. "If you won't take care of yourself, *we* will. And if you argue, I'll make sure Kelsey hears about it."

I groan and swallow my momentary anger. He's acting out because he cares. I still don't fucking like it.

"You'd tell my damned sister?"

"It wouldn't be the first time," Pablo replies with a smirk. "I learned a long time ago that if you wouldn't listen to me, you *would* listen to her. And she doesn't put up with your bullshit, even when she's half a galaxy away."

I frown and turn to Daaros. "Has anyone told her what happened?"

He nods. "She's on the ship with Sorin."

"So is Tariq," Vee adds with a chuckle.

"They're going to wind up together again," I blurt without thinking.

Pablo resumes his seat next to me and rolls his eyes. "Didn't I tell you that after she said they broke up? From what you've told me, Tariq would do anything for her, and she's almost as oblivious as you are. *Almost.*"

"Hey, that's not—"

"He's not wrong," Daaros chimes in with a grin. "You turn heads wherever you go, and Botanaar is no exception. Do you know how many of my people have enquired about you? I'm not the only one who finds humans strangely alluring."

Heat creeps into my face and I look to Vee in desperation. They'll know how to put an end to this conversation. They'll come to my rescue. I hope.

Vee shakes their head, amused. "Don't look at me."

I feign outrage. "I thought we were friends."

"We are. But this is one discussion I won't participate in."

Running a hand through my hair, I lean into the cushioned back of the sofa. "I'm—"

A smart rap on the exterior door cuts me off. Vee rises and strides to the door, where I'm sure Araan is waiting with a tray or three of food.

Pablo tilts his head thoughtfully and smiles. "I think you *are* okay. You've been more yourself since you woke up than…before."

"I guess we'll know for sure once Sorin is here," I reply with a shrug.

I know he'll ask to plug into my data port to run the scan, but the notion doesn't send tendrils of fear creeping along my spine. I stare at my hands for a moment, contemplating this realization. It gives me hope.

Maybe the Botanaari treatment worked. Maybe Pablo's right.

Maybe I *am* okay.

Every time I try to stand up, Pablo or Vee intervenes, and I'm forced to remain sitting. Vee monitors my every movement, ensuring I not only rest as the Vynaas ordered, but that I eat everything Araan brought for me too.

There's a tray filled with a Botanaari facsimile of tacos; the soft wraps are made of water and finely ground insects, but the texture is almost identical to the tortillas I discovered on Megatropolis in my ZIEG days. The filling is meat—*real* meat—that Daaros claims is venison. I'm not sure I've had venison previously, but it's good, if a bit gamey.

And despite my inclination to stubbornness, my appetite gains the upper hand. I eat every damned morsel on the tray.

"Do you want more?" Daaros asks as I finish, his tone amused.

"No, I'm good." I lean back into the sofa and offer a wry grin. "Thanks. I needed this."

Vee rolls their eyes dramatically, then looks to Pablo. "Is he always this difficult?"

Pablo laughs and nods. "Yeah. It's one thing about Kye that will never change."

"You should have warned me sooner." Daaros grins mischievously. "I'm not sure I'm prepared to act the part of caretaker to my future bodyguard."

"Hey," I protest. "It's not *always* like this—"

"Don't listen to him, Daar," Pablo interrupts with a playful grin. "It *is* always like this."

"Then, by the suns, I hope you can manage him," Daaros replies with an air of mock-exasperation.

"Don't worry," Pablo promises. "I've had a lifetime of practice managing this stubborn asshole. He'll behave. I'll make sure of it."

Our conversation is cut short by another knock from outside. Vee waves at me to remain in my seat and moves to the door. They pull it open and step aside as the Vynaas, his partner, Sorin, Max, Kelsey, and Tariq enter the room. Even with the two enormous plush sofas that dominate its heart, I don't think there are enough seats for everyone. I begin to stand, only to have Pablo throw an arm across my chest.

"You're supposed to rest," he whispers. "Sit still. Araan will bring more chairs if they're needed."

I glower at him, then look up to see Kelsey push past the others and race to my other side. Between Pablo and my sister, I won't have a say in anything that happens to me for the next few hours. They're both worriers—especially when it comes to me. And I'm *fine*.

"How are you, little brother?" Kelsey asks, unable to mask the concern in her dark eyes.

"I think I'm okay. I'm—"

"He woke up an hour ago," Pablo informs her as he shoots me a pointed glare. "He was unconscious for thirty hours. He's *not* okay."

Kelsey nods at Pablo, then refocuses on me. "Do they know what happened?" Her question isn't directed at me, though her eyes never leave my face.

"Fucking hell, I'm right here! Stop talking around me like I don't exist." I cross my arms, seething, as I pause to look at each of my unwanted visitors in the eye. I've had enough of this shit.

"Kye…" Kelsey's tone is laden with exasperation, a tone only an older sister can muster and utilize to effect on her younger sibling.

I frown petulantly. "Fine. Just talk to *me*. I'm right *here*. In this fucking room."

"We don't know if the treatment was successful," the Vynaas cuts in smoothly. "If it failed, we feared how you'd react to a…scan."

I roll my eyes and stare at a point on the wall, one of the few places I can't see any of their faces in my periphery. I'm beyond pissed; I'm *livid*. Why won't anyone fucking listen to me?

"Just have Sorin do his magic. He's done it before. I'll be fine," I mutter through clenched teeth.

"You're sure?" Kelsey asks.

"Yes! I'm tired of being handled like I'm made of glass. I'm a damned cyborg! I don't break that easily. And I'm pretty fucking sure my brain is fine." I cross my arms and stare a challenge at my sister. "You weren't around for most of my life, Kels, and I know you still feel guilty about that, but *stop*. I'm a grown man. I'm not the little kid you left behind in Baja Colony."

She winces. I know I've gone too far, but I don't stop. My tongue seems to have gained a mind of its own. I turn to Pablo.

"And you. You're my best friend. I know you got used to making sure I stayed hydrated and had enough to eat back on Earth, but those days are behind us, Pab. I survived my cybernetics. I survived Ajax's hell. I'm still alive, and I plan on staying that way for a long time."

The room falls silent after my outburst. The others exchange glances or watch me warily, as though I'm no longer the thing they must protect, but something they just might fear.

Finally, Sorin withdraws a tablet from one of his jumpsuit pockets and moves toward me. "You said his name, and you didn't react adversely. It was conversational." He stops in front of me and kneels to look me in the eye. "A scan will confirm…"

He pulls a cable from another pocket without taking his eyes from mine and holds it up for my inspection. There is no fear, no threatening darkness, no unwanted blast of memory to cloud my vision and steal my breath.

"Do it. I'm fine."

"Would you like some privacy?" Daaros asks uncertainly.

I shrug. "I don't care if you're here or not."

"As a precaution, I'd like Vee and Tariq to sit beside you," Sorin says. "I don't think they'll need to restrain you, but if I'm wrong, I don't want to see anyone hurt."

"Okay," I agree. "I don't want to hurt anyone, either, but I don't think it'll come to that."

Sorin smiles faintly and plugs one end of the cable into his tablet. He offers me the other, but I shake my head.

"I want to prove to you that I'm fine." I point at the data port on the base of my neck. "You do it."

Sorin frowns and waits for Pablo and Kelsey to switch places with Vee and Tariq. He slides his blue glasses in place and studies me through the lenses, perplexed.

I sigh in frustration. "Let's just get this over with."

Sorin slides the cable in place, and a heartbeat later, I sense his diagnostic scan begin to assess the parts of my system I can't verify myself. He glances at me, his expression unreadable as he taps on his tablet.

"I'm okay, Sorin. There's nothing… No memories. No…fear." I shift my focus to the Vynaas, who stands with his arms crossed next to Daaros. "I think your treatment worked."

He stares at me impassively. "I will not deem it a success until Sorin is finished with your scan."

"I'm done," Sorin replies absently. "There is no sign of damage to your cybernetics. I can only assume you blacked out due to the reconstruction work the doctors performed on your amygdala. I read the files from the clinic on my way here," he adds for my benefit. "I wasn't expecting to find you completely unharmed."

I shoot Pablo and Kelsey a pointed look. "I told you I was fine."

"And we didn't know for sure," Kelsey snaps. "Damn it, Kye, we were worried about you. Don't be like this."

I return her glare for a few seconds, then relent. She's always been better at maintaining her anger than I am. "I just wish you would listen to me sometimes."

"You can disconnect now," Sorin says quietly.

I remove the cable from my neck and flash him a grin. "Thanks for confirming what I've been trying to tell them since I woke up."

Sorin nods. "I'm glad I could. No one was sure what happened, and I wish I had a better answer. But for now, it seems you're cured, which is fortunate."

I lift my eyebrows. "You have something planned?"

He laughs. "I always have plans. This time, it's not a mission. It's a party." He pauses to glance at the others. "Everyone is invited to Cobalt Asteroid. We're celebrating the Coalition's imminent ascension and Zylar Inc.'s permanent downfall."

CHAPTER FORTY

UPGRADES

BOTANAAR, VYNAAS HOME/KEPLER-47 SYSTEM

"I'm afraid I must decline, as must my heir," the Vynaas replies.

Sorin's smile falters. "I understand."

"I recalled him to Botanaar under the pretense that galactic security has been subpar since the attack on Z-1543," the Vynaas continues. "We must maintain appearances for our sake, as well as yours. Mr. Noriega will remain here too. I will not allow my son's partner to risk himself unnecessarily."

Pablo is crestfallen, but he manages a nod. Daaros moves to his side and wraps an arm around his waist, pulling him close as he whispers something most of the room can't hear. "I promise we'll throw a better party for our *briia*, one without such restrictions. Cheer up, love."

Sometimes I wish my aural implants weren't so damned sensitive. I don't mean to eavesdrop on my best friend's private moments, but when they appear without warning, I can't help it. I flush and stare at the floor, waiting for someone to pick up the conversation.

"Then you *did* have something to do with Marim's abduction," Vee says to Sorin. "We suspected, but no one here would confirm."

"No one here *knew*," Sorin replies. "Apart from Max, that is. Marim's alive and well, and when I left Cobalt Asteroid, my interrogation team was confident they'd have the final piece of information I require to undo all the damage Zylar Inc. has caused before our return."

The Vynaas crosses his arms and peers at Sorin, his expression unreadable. "The control codes."

"Exactly. Without those, we can't wrest control of the non-AI systems from Zylar Inc." Sorin begins to pace, more animated in his speech than I've seen from him in some time. "And we need to remove their chokehold on those systems. My plans for a galactic senate will never come to fruition otherwise."

"You will continue to have Botanaar's support, as long as you ensure my people will have a voice in your new government," the Vynaas says evenly. "I trust you to follow through on your promises."

"I will," Sorin assures him. "You should know that by now."

"I believed I did, until I learned the details of Kye's story." He narrows his eyes and frowns at Sorin. "You used him, threatened him with a life of unwilling servitude, all to further your agenda. I believed Zylar Inc. capable of such crimes, but not the Coalition."

"I've done everything in my power to rectify that mistake," Sorin replies, wounded.

"Nevertheless—"

"Hey, I've forgiven him," I cut in before the Vynaas can continue his tirade. "*And* he freed me from Van Duval. I… It's why I felt obligated to save him on Megatropolis and took the fall for the mainframe. I owed him that much."

Behind Sorin, Kelsey rolls her eyes dramatically. She mutters under her breath, but I catch the phrase "fucking stupid" before Tariq snickers beside her, drowning out the rest of her words.

"While your actions were noble, they were reckless," the Vynaas chastises me. "You may have saved the Coalition from a significant setback, but your loyalty to its leader does not excuse his previous actions."

"I plan to destroy every set of cyborg override codes stashed in Zylar Inc.'s vault once I seize control," Sorin says heatedly. "I've offered the Botanaari seats in the galactic senate once it's established. I plan to include at least one cyborg representative too. I can't undo the past, Caaram, but I'll make damned sure the future is better for all of us."

"You should trust him," Daaros says softly, breaking the uneasy silence following Sorin's outburst. "I do."

The Vynaas narrows his eyes at Sorin. "I will heed my heir on this matter—for now. Do not, as your people like to say, fuck it up." He turns on his heel and strides toward the door. "You do not want to make an enemy of Botanaar."

"I won't," Sorin promises, though I doubt the Vynaas hears him. He's already gone from the room.

"My father is protective of those he cares for," Daaros explains, "and by extension their families. He considers Kye to be Pablo's family, just as I do."

Sorin releases a heavy sigh. "I'm aware of how your father operates. He'll relax once I fulfill my end of the bargain."

"You might want to make sure Kye doesn't stay long on your base," Pablo adds. "And make sure no one plans to crash your party."

"Trin and Quiara have been monitoring the necessary chatter while I've been away," Sorin replies dismissively. "No one will show up without an invitation."

"So, what?" I ask. "You take us back to your base, you get Marim's codes, then leave for Megatropolis while the rest of us celebrate?"

"Yep. That's my plan." Sorin shrugs. "We're down to the endgame, and most of the work is finished."

"I hope you aren't planning to go back to Zylar HQ alone," I reply, unable to shake my skepticism. "It can't be that easy. Nothing ever is."

"A select team will accompany him," Max says. "I've insisted on it."

"And ZIEG won't stop him," Tariq adds. "Luna's made sure of it. Zylar won't know what hit them."

"Just enjoy the party, little brother," Kelsey says with a smile. "You won't be put in the crosshairs again. You've done enough."

I shake my head. Something still bothers me about the situation, but I assume it's just my lack of details regarding Sorin's plan. And I know he won't share them with anyone not part of his select team.

"Fine, but I want my armor before we leave. Just in case."

"That can be arranged." Daaros flashes a knowing grin. "And we've added a few upgrades I think you'll like."

I match his grin with one of my own. "Okay, now I'm intrigued. Show me."

Daaros asks Araan to prep a shuttle, and thirty minutes later, we're flying to VaasTek's corporate office in Daaros' crimson Solar Flare. Pablo, Vee, and Sorin accompany us, but the others stay behind. I suspect Tariq wanted time alone with Kelsey, and Max hoped to speak with the Vynaas again. I don't know Daaros' more powerful father well, but I doubt he'll be in any mood to speak with a Coalition representative today. Max might have better luck with the Minister of Intelligence.

"What improvements have you made to the armor?" Sorin asks eagerly. "I've always wanted to tinker with a set, but I left Zylar Inc. before they gave me clearance to access the armory. And I designed the first prototype! I should have been allowed to work on its predecessors."

"You gave us the specs before we built this set," Daaros replies with a shrug. "You should know some of its capabilities."

"I do, but I want to know what *you* have done to improve it." Sorin's blue eyes are alight with excitement. Sometimes I forget he's an engineer at heart, and not just the Coalition's overworked leader.

Daaros smiles fondly at Pablo. "One of the improvements was a design project Pablo implemented as part of his curriculum. It's his place to tell you."

I turn to face Pablo in time to see a blush creep up his cheeks. "It was meant as a surprise for Kye if…*when* he came back."

A grin begins to stretch across my face. "Solar tech?"

"Yeah." He looks away and chews on his lower lip. "Daar let me look at your system specs as well as the armor's. The way it connects to your cybernetics is fascinating. I realized your energy stores are used for more than how much power you can put toward fighting or running, but they also help maintain your 'net access and any other external communications. And your firewall, although we solved that problem previously."

"I think I know where you're headed with this," Sorin replies thoughtfully.

Pablo nods. "I adapted the solar tech typically used to power indoor lighting and atmospheric controls to fit inside your suit, then connected it to the cybernetics responsible for your digestive system. If I set up the interface correctly, you should be able to choose between storing power for later, or replenishing your energy on the go—as long as light hits the exterior of your armor somewhere."

"The armor acts as a capacitor, but the energy can be accessed any time he requires it," Sorin says with a nod. "That's brilliant."

Pablo's blush deepens and Daaros beams proudly. I grin at the pair; together, they make an unusual but near-perfect match. And I couldn't be happier with my best friend's fortune. I've always believed Pablo deserved better than what Earth had to offer, than what *I* had to offer.

"How can I get a set?" Vee asks.

"Kye's is a prototype, but if it functions as intended, we'll put it into production later. Provided Sorin accomplishes what he hopes to," Daaros adds pointedly. "I will not sell VaasTek's design assets to Zylar Inc. or one of its subsidiaries."

Vee pivots to face Sorin. "You'd better not fail, or you'll have every former ZIEG soldier on your ass about a missed opportunity. And I'll be nicer than most."

Vee's grin is feral, and I laugh at Sorin's stunned look of surprise. He hasn't grasped the nuances of Vee's brand of humor yet.

Sorin chuckles, recovering some of his usual poise. "I don't plan to fail. Not this time."

They continue to chat, but I tune them out and turn to face the window. Outside, trees blur by against the backdrop of Botanaar's clear night sky. Both of its moons are visible this evening, the smaller bluish one, Kaas, outshining the irregularly-shaped gray one. I could look up the name of Botanaar's larger satellite, but I don't. I'm not interested in accessing the 'net right now.

Pablo sidles up to me a few minutes later. "I hope my update to your armor works as it theoretically should. What Sorin said… That's the highest praise anyone could have given me."

"Are you worried it won't work?" I ask.

He shrugs. "I don't know. I understand the solar tech involved, but your cybernetics are…" He sighs and shakes his head. "Without you here to test the design properly, I didn't know if it would interface with your…system. I had to rely on the schematics Sorin gave Daar, and I've learned that sometimes, design specs aren't one hundred percent accurate."

"Then think of this as your test run," I reply with a smile. "If it doesn't work, you can tweak the design as needed once I come back from Sorin's base."

Pablo gnaws his lower lip and nods. "I wish I could go with you. I love parties."

"I know, but I think the Vynaas is right. You're safer here."

I don't tell him about my current unease with Sorin's plan. I don't have all the details, and it's possible I'm only being paranoid given everything I've gone through while working with the Coalition.

But Pablo is perceptive. "You think something will go wrong."

I glance at Sorin. He's still talking with Vee and Daaros on the other side of the cabin, unaware of our conversation.

"Yeah, I do. I don't know why I feel this way, and maybe it's just me, but… I think I'm going to ask Sorin to be part of the base's security detail during the party."

"It will give you a reason to show up wearing your armor," Pablo says thoughtfully. "Do it. You were never one for parties, anyway. You'd rather stay at home with a book."

"Books are usually more interesting than most people," I reply with a grin. "You've always been the exception."

He groans, exasperated. "Don't try to flatter me, Kye. If you're right, you need to be careful. If GISA shows up…"

I nod and look through the window. He doesn't have to say what will happen if GISA crashes Sorin's party and finds me there. It will get bloody. I have no intention of having my ass shipped back to Primordia-1. Six months there was more than enough for one lifetime.

"I'll do what I have to, Pab. I won't be captured again."

Golden lights draw my attention through the glass. We're approaching the executive landing pad at VaasTek. The shuttle begins to slow, and I turn away from the window to face Pablo. He's chewing his lip again, unspoken concern in his dark eyes.

"I *will* come back," I promise. "Araan doesn't like to relinquish his duties as pilot, but I'm capable of flying any craft in the damned galaxy." I tap a finger against my temple. "All the specs for Zylar Inc. craft are stored in here, and I can interface with anything that has a data port. Don't worry. No matter what happens, I'll come back this time."

He stares at me in challenge. "You'd better. I can't go through it again, Kye. I watched the… the trial. And Daar told me how they found you. What they did."

"I won't be captured again," I repeat more fiercely. "I won't hold back this time, and I'll never surrender."

"Good. Daar will protect you while you're here."

"So will my fathers," Daaros adds from directly behind us. "And GISA isn't the only credible threat to your person. Do not forget Omega Prime."

Right. I have a fucking bounty on my head, one that I have to clear before the Vynaas will approve of my prospective role as Daaros' bodyguard.

"If Van Duval shows his ugly mug at the party, I'll deal with him then." I cross my arms. "He's smart, but he's a cocky bastard. I'll use that to my advantage."

"There has been no intel regarding Omega Prime *or* GISA surrounding the party," Sorin says, his tone weary. "Nothing is going to happen."

"And I want to be prepared, just in case," I snap, my tone harsher than I intended. "Let me work security for your party. If you're right, nothing will happen. But if you aren't…"

He frowns, then says, "It can't hurt, but I hoped you'd take the night to relax. If anyone deserves a little downtime, it's you."

I'm spared from further discussion as the shuttle lands and the door slides open.

I'm not going to argue with Sorin. I will be part of the security detail whether he wants it or not. And I doubt he realizes that I'm not terribly excited about parties, no matter what we're celebrating. Pablo is right. I'd rather stay home with a book and endure Vee's teasing about my genre choices later.

Daaros leads us across the landing pad and into his corporate headquarters. We take an elevator down several levels to the laboratories, a site I skipped on my previous visit in favor of the gardens.

"What more did you add to his armor?" Sorin asks as we descend. He bounces on the balls of his feet, unable to contain his excitement.

"We upgraded the firewall," Daaros replies with a shrug. "Now, even Botanaari scans will be unable to pierce them. Such precautions may become necessary in the future. My *siindolaar* suggested it, and I trust his judgment on matters of the Vynaas' security. We won't include that feature in production models, for obvious reasons."

"So once again, Kye's the exception to the rule," Vee teases. "Typical."

"Maybe your best friend should hook up with a rich Botanaari," I reply with a laugh. "It worked for me."

Vee rolls their eyes. "My best friend isn't interested in 'hooking up' with anyone."

I stare at them as a knowing smile crosses their lips. I wasn't expecting that admission from Vee. I knew they kept to themselves, even amongst Luna's former crew, and I didn't know they considered *me* their best friend—but I'm honored.

"Come on," Pablo says as the elevator door slides open. "I need to know if my solar tech interface works as intended. My grade for this term kind of depends on it."

"You designed this upgrade before you knew I'd be able to test it?" I ask with a laugh. "What if I hadn't come back, Pab? The armor is keyed to my genetic and cybernetic signature."

"It was a risk I was willing to take," he replies stubbornly. "But you're back now. It's the only thing that matters."

I look to Daaros for a better explanation, but he merely shrugs. "There was no dissuading him from this project."

We follow the pair along a glass corridor to a room with opaque walls and a door with a security kiosk outside. Daaros places his hand against the sensor, and a second later, the door opens with a soft chime.

This lab space is larger than any I've been inside previously. A few Botanaari in white VaasTek uniforms are at work amidst the array of shining instrumentation and black countertops, but most ignore our entrance. Only the nearest two look our way. Both nod deferentially to Daaros, then scan the rest of our group with unconcealed curiosity. Their eyes follow us as Daaros leads us to a small alcove along one wall, where my armor rests on a stand.

"There is a privacy door you may activate inside," Daaros explains. "Once you've suited up, Pablo can run his version of diagnostics on your system."

"I'll need to make a copy of the data too," Pablo adds uneasily. "I… I hope you don't mind. I need it for this term's final report."

"I don't mind," I assure him. "If it works as you hope it does, letting you make a copy of the scan data is the least I can do. This is going to be *epic*."

He laughs nervously. "If you say so."

"I do." I flash him a grin, then step inside the alcove. "See you in a few."

The privacy door is activated by the push of a button, and I'm left alone with the familiar green-on-green armor Daaros' scientists designed for me months ago. I believe Pablo's upgrade will work; he's meticulous when it comes to his engineering projects, and he had access to all of my specs. There is no reason why it *won't* work according to his designs.

I strip off my clothes and boots, then remove the armor from the stand, allowing it to bond to my body piece by piece. The sensation still feels strange, but it's not the shock it once was. I pick up the helmet last, and carry it in the crook of my left arm. I shouldn't need to put it on for Pablo to run his scans.

My internal display alerts me to the armor's newest upgrade. I can toggle between energy storage or consumption as it's gathered from the light of my surroundings. I opt for storage; I didn't eat that long ago, and I'm currently at ninety-nine percent.

I turn toward the button that opens the door, then pause. Is this what it feels like to be a Botanaari, taking sustenance from nothing but the light around me? It's weird, but I think I'll get used to it. And I won't have to carry protein cubes to replenish my power reserves anymore.

Excellent.

I open the door and step into the lab. Pablo holds a tablet and a cable, chewing his lip as he looks up at me. Sorin, Daaros, and Vee stand a respectful distance away, chatting amongst themselves, though Sorin peers at us surreptitiously a few times. He's as eager to learn the results as Pablo is.

I kneel on the floor to give Pablo access to my data port. "I'm ready."

He laughs nervously. "This is so damned weird," he whispers. "I never thought I'd be plugging a tablet into my best friend."

I shrug. "Sorin does it often enough, and I trust you more."

He continues to procrastinate. "How was the integration? Was it…normal?"

"Yeah. And the interface works too. I set it to storage."

He draws a breath, then nods. "Okay. I'll make this quick. I know this is awkward for you."

The cable slides in place. I sense Pablo's scan as he assesses the solar tech's performance. After thirty seconds, he pulls the cable free with a relieved grin.

"I copied the data that I needed, and it works even better than I hoped!"

"Does that mean you'll ace this term, Pab?" I ask as I stand up once more.

"Hell yeah, it does."

The others move toward us, and Daaros says, "I've always known it would work, Pablo. I have faith in your skills." He shifts his gaze to meet mine with a bemused smile. "And the firewall?"

"It activated when I put the armor on," I reply with a shrug. "As for how well it's working, I don't know. You'd have to test it."

He nods and gestures to Pablo. "Your tablet is Botanaari-made. Attempt a remote security scan."

Pablo frowns and glances at me uneasily. I can tell from his expression he doesn't want to do this.

"Hey, it's okay. I've been through worse," I assure him. "A scan is just a scan."

Reluctantly, he nods. "Fine. I just don't like treating you like…a fucking machine. You're not."

"I've come to terms with who and what I am, Pab. I can't change it now, anyway."

"Right." He sighs, then taps his tablet. "Scanning."

Daaros and Sorin peer over his shoulders to read the display. "Perfect," Daaros whispers, while Sorin says, "You really *are* a damned wraith, Kye. Nobody will see you coming while you're wearing that."

Vee crosses their arms with a smirk. "I never thought I'd be jealous of a ZIEG dropout. Damn. I hope you'll consider hiring your friends one day when you're in charge of Daaros' personal security team. I want a piece of this tech."

I share a grin with Vee. "I think I can pull a few strings."

VEE DOMINEAUX

CHAPTER FORTY-ONE

A PARTY FROM HELL

Trin waits on the landing pad for us, hands on hips and left foot tapping impatiently as we file out of our transport shuttle. I'd been looking forward to my brief foray on Cobalt Asteroid until I studied her dour expression. Now, I'm pretty sure something has gone wrong, and I'm silently grateful I insisted on bringing my armor.

She shifts her arms as we approach and folds them in front of her with a terse nod for Sorin. "Have you checked your messages?" she asks him without preamble.

Sorin shakes his head. "I couldn't risk it—as you know. There's better encryption for the feeds here. What happened?"

She eyes me suspiciously, then shifts her focus to Vee with a frown. "Duval happened, that's what. I hope these two are prepared to work security detail at your blasted party. It's attracted too much notice, and someone tipped off Omega Prime. We know they'll be here, but not when."

"I knew it seemed too damned easy," I mutter.

"You see?" Trin demands as we begin to follow her toward the Coalition apartment block. "Even your pet project sensed something was off with your plans, and he doesn't even know half of them."

I bristle at her reference to me, but I keep my mouth shut. This argument is between Trin and Sorin, and while I don't appreciate being labeled as a pet or a project, I can't fault her for using the jab to get her point across.

Sorin holds his hands up in a gesture of surrender. "I only wanted to give our people a chance to celebrate. They deserve that, after everything we've gone through, the losses we've taken—"

"And *I* warned you it was too soon. Planning this event was reckless and stupid." Trin shakes her head in frustration. "It's too late now. Some of your 'guests' have already arrived, as have most of the caterers, bar staff, the deejay... We can't call it off even if we wanted to."

"Then we won't," Sorin replies with a shrug. "Kye offered to help with security for the party before we left Botanaar."

Trin's frown deepens. "If you think *one* cyborg will be sufficient for this, you're dreaming. Get your head out of the clouds and focus."

"I will join Kye," Vee offers. "There are other former ZIEG soldiers on your base. I'll talk with them. We'll have a security team assembled before midnight Standard Time."

Trin's expression softens for a moment as she nods her thanks to Vee. "Good. Speak with me when you've gathered your team. As for you," she rounds on Sorin again, "I hope you know what you're doing. They've extracted the code from Marim, and we believe it's valid. I checked the data myself. Your team is prepping a shuttle now."

Sorin nods. "Good. I'll look over the code before we leave."

"You'd better," Trin snaps. "You've been lax with your oversight lately, and I'm not the only one who has noticed."

She turns on her heel and strides away, leaving us at the entrance to the apartment block. Sorin groans and stares skyward for a time, his expression troubled. Max approaches from behind and lays a hand on the other man's shoulder.

"She's frustrated. Don't let her anger cloud your judgment," Max says solemnly. "And I'll be here to oversee security too. Your last operation will go smoothly, and we'll have Zylar Inc.'s hold on the galaxy dissolved by the end of the week."

Sorin nods once. "You're right, but so is she. I need to focus. I need to do better." He turns to face me. "Are you prepared to fight Omega Prime if they show up?"

"You mean *when*," I reply with a frown. "Yeah, I'm ready. I haven't forgotten that Van Duval had my override codes and refused to release them when you asked."

"They'll be armed with plasma weapons," Vee says. "I'll ask Captain Wax to work security with us. He'll complain, but we need a DFNR-BT series on the team. He's the only one here as far as I'm aware."

I smirk, recalling my only meeting with Warrick Waxman. "Does he still have that ridiculous yellow mohawk?"

Vee snickers. "Nah. He shaved his head since you saw him last and replaced the mohawk with a tattoo. Fashion faux pas aside, we need him."

"I'll leave you to it, then," Sorin says. "I have work to do before my next shuttle leaves."

"Call me if you need anything," Max offers. "Trin and I will make sure your security team is armed better than the damned mercs could ever hope to be."

We watch them leave, and I glance at the collection of armor I carry in my arms, glad I insisted on bringing it. "If Zinn's here, we should ask her to join us too. I don't think she'll have a problem facing her old boss."

"Good idea. Let's find our rooms and suit up, then we'll go on a recruiting spree."

"Why suit up now?" I ask.

Vee grins. "The other cyborgs will want to see your armor for themselves. It's incentive. They help us with this, we help Sorin succeed, and they have a chance to score a suit like yours for themselves one day. But it's all contingent on Sorin's success. Daaros was pretty damned clear on that point."

"That makes a weird kind of sense. Let's go."

When we meet with Trin at midnight in her office above the armory, most of the fire she displayed at our arrival is gone. She's weary, her eyes shadowed and features drawn, her trademark bun in a state of mild disarray. She peers up at us as we enter and forces a tight semblance of a smile.

"I hope you have a team ready for tomorrow," she says.

"We do." Vee takes the only open seat in the room, opposite Trin across her desk, leaving me to stand. "I recruited two dozen people, most former ZIEG like us."

Trin sighs and rubs her eyes for a moment. "Two dozen to monitor what looks to be more than *four hundred*. But you're cyborgs. You have an advantage when it comes to security detail."

"We have three who aren't," Vee replies, "but they're all capable. And Quiara has agreed to watch the security feeds from her office. She'll alert us if she sees anything off."

"It will have to do." Trin shakes her head and stares at the ceiling momentarily. "Damn Sorin. He's always been too quick to call victory. It's why he was captured in his days as the Blue Ghost. It's why I worry so much about this particular event. He isn't here to take the fall, but we know Omega Prime plans to crash his party. Watch this."

She activates the holoscreen above her desk and queues a video to play. Van Duval's scarred countenance leers at us as for several seconds before the ugly merc begins to speak.

"Hey, Ghost. It's been a while since we talked, and I hear you've got a party planned. Too bad not all of your people are as loyal as you think they are. Someone gave me intel, and I know the place and time. I hope you don't mind if I pay a visit. I owe it to you after your stunt with my former second. Fucking Jarek and I have a score to settle. If she's there, make sure your staff isn't squeamish. There will be blood."

I glance at Vee as the video cuts off. "Zinn's on our team…"

"Then make damned sure she's paired with a cyborg at all times," Trin says firmly. "Her mere presence is a liability, and Duval doesn't make idle threats."

"I'll—"

"No," Vee interrupts before I can finish my offer. "Zinn will pair with Captain Wax. He's a DFNR-BT series, remember? You're designed for offense, not defense, no matter what fancy shit Daaros added to your armor. You can't protect her as well as he can."

I don't like it, but they make a fair point. "Fine."

"You'll have my support and Max's as well," Trin adds. "It's the best I can do with Sorin on his way to Megatropolis. Our people tolerate me. They *listen* to him." She rubs a hand across her forehead, then sighs. "Unfortunately, I still have an hour's worth of work to finish before I can sleep. If there's anything else you need, you know how to reach me. Max can show you the armory in the morning. I told him to expect you."

"Thanks," Vee says as they rise from their chair. "We'll deal with Omega Prime—and anyone else they may bring with them."

Trin grimaces. "I hope it's only the mercs we need to worry about, but it's best to be prepared for anything."

I remain silent until we're out of Trin's office, and the door is closed again in our wake. "Do you think Duval will bring reinforcements?"

Vee tilts their head with a frown. "Wouldn't you?"

"Yeah, but who would join them?"

"There are other, smaller enterprises like Omega Prime that would leap at the chance to form an alliance," Vee replies. "And then there's always GISA."

I snort and roll my eyes. "I doubt it."

Vee lifts one finger. "Omega Prime wants revenge on the Coalition, as does GISA. They have the same objective." Vee raises a second finger. "GISA has been known to offer immunity to even the worst offenders if they believe they'll close a high-profile case, and the investigation around Marim's disappearance qualifies." Vee lifts a third finger. "Van Duval has no sense of loyalty or morality to speak of. He doesn't care about past alliances, and he's not above helping GISA if it *also* benefits him."

I grimace. There's more at stake here than I anticipated, and that gnawing sensation of an impending shitstorm grows stronger. "If GISA shows up, what then?"

"We treat it as we would any other mission," Vee replies. "We work for the Coalition now, and it's their people and assets we're paid to protect. If Omega Prime crashes Sorin's party, we'll deal with them. If GISA shows up too, we'll treat them the same."

I rake a hand through my hair and sigh. "Holy shit. After everything I've done, I never thought I'd be planning to defend Sorin's base against fucking GISA. They're... They're supposed to be the defenders of the galaxy. And we're..." I look around the bare corridor helplessly, unable to conjure the words to describe what I'm feeling.

"You still consider them the good guys after what they've done to us?" Vee asks, incredulous. "Think of the damned override codes, Kye. Remember what they sentenced you to on Primordia-1. Maybe GISA wasn't at the forefront of those decisions, but they didn't do anything to prevent them from happening, either."

Ajax's leer flits across my vision for a split second, igniting my rage. "Yeah. You're right. They let it all happen, because we're nothing to them. We were the desperate souls who would do anything for a cure, anything to make our situations better, and they stole our damned lives. And made a profit from it." I cross my arms and scowl ahead. "Fuck it. Let them come. They'll regret it in the end."

Vee eyes me warily. "Just don't do anything stupid. I'm not sure we can arrange a second rescue if you're caught again."

I laugh darkly. "I don't plan on getting caught, Vee. I promised Pablo I'd be back for his wedding, and nothing is going to stop me from being there. Not GISA, not Zylar Inc., and certainly not Van fucking Duval." I pause, considering my next words. "I wouldn't have been caught the first time if you and Luna hadn't been sent to the mainframe. I would have fought anyone else, but not you."

Vee nods. "I didn't understand then, but I do now. I'm with you, Kye. Get some rest tonight. I'll meet you at your apartment in the morning, then we'll go to the armory. Once we talk with Max, I'll call the rest of our crew. Whatever Duval thinks he can do here, we'll show him he's wrong. And for what it's worth, I hope you have the opportunity to bury a fucking plasma bolt in his ugly skull."

My grin is savage. "Don't worry. I'll be ready for it."

Vee chuckles. "Remind me never to piss you off. ZIEG made you a weapon, the Coalition gave you purpose, and Daaros made you a damned wraith. Even without all of your training, I wouldn't want to face you in a serious fight. Duval doesn't know what's coming."

I shrug awkwardly. "I didn't ask for any of it. All I wanted was a chance to *live*."

"Remember that tomorrow night," Vee replies. "Remember why you're here, why you've chosen to fight. Hold onto it, because I think you'll need it to see you through whatever the hell happens."

"Yeah." I shake my head with a groan. "I've never been one for parties, and this one's going to be worse than most."

Vee nods once. "I think it'll be a party from hell."

CHAPTER FORTY-TWO

THE HEAD OF THE SNAKE

**RESISTANCE COALITION HQ
COBALT ASTEROID, GAMMA CEPHEI SYSTEM**

The pulsing beat of the music would have been unbearable without the tuning capabilities of my aural implants, but the bright flashes of the strobe lighting are still giving me a headache. Yeah, I may be a cyborg, but I'm still just as reliant on my vision as any other human.

The tint on my helmet's face shield helps dim the effect, but I still don't like it. And I sure as hell don't understand how Sorin's crew—most of them average humans—can stand it. How are they not all curled up beneath the tables or along the crowded dance floor, screaming in agony from the sensory overload?

My eyes scan the nearby bar, and I have my answer. Alcohol dulls their senses.

"Perimeter check," Vee says over our encrypted security channel.

We were drilled on our responding order prior to the party's onset, and I'm supposed to be the last one to check in. My post is the farthest from the entrance door, between the main bar and the raised dais the deejay occupies. My location is yet another reason why I'm fighting a headache; the bar's patrons shout over the music, and the deejay's amplifiers are pointed directly at them—and me.

A chorus of responses meets Vee's command. The dance floor's clear, the kitchen's fine, the rear exit is clear, the entrance is busy, but Captain Wax assures Vee there isn't anything suspicious yet, both bars are clear…

"Deejay's clear," I state when my turn arrives.

I glance at the woman at the center of the dais, surrounded by holoscreens to augment the strobe lighting and an array of sound equipment I can't identify. She's dressed in skin-tight black leather and matching heels, and her mane of unnaturally vibrant red hair is woven into myriad braids. Piercings glint in the flickering light, lining both ears, her left eyebrow, her chin, and her right nostril. She sways to the rhythms pounding from the amplifiers as she taps her commands into a tablet, then the music shifts to something even more abrasive.

I grimace and turn away, glad she can't see the expression I wear beneath my helmet. I'd only provoke her into making the aural assault worse. I filter out the music entirely and sigh with relief. If only my eyes could do the same.

I walk my circuit from the bar behind the deejay's dais and back again, my eyes scanning the crowd for any sign of Omega Prime. I'm armed with a plasma rifle similar to the one my sister favors, two projectile pistols, a dagger, and all the power my cybernetically-enhanced armor gives me. And despite my complaints about the lighting, it has been sufficient to keep my energy stores at maximum capacity since I arrived. Solar tech is pretty damned amazing.

I check my chronometer and scowl. I've been on security detail for less than two hours, and the party probably won't end for at least another four or five. Duval has plenty of time to make his unwanted entrance, but until he does, I'll be fighting boredom. Pablo's the dancer, not me, and I'm on duty, anyway.

"Call sign check. This is Blaze," Vee says, forcing me to focus.

We use the same order as before, but this time, everyone on the channel speaks up, not just those responsible for their area. Vee will verify each call sign is accounted for at the top of every hour. It keeps us on task, but will also alert us if there's trouble somewhere.

I listen as the others chime in one by one. Zinn is back to using "Pink." Captain Wax has opted for "Tank," a fitting name for what he is. Quiara is "Architect" from her post in the security terminal upstairs. I don't know most of the others Vee recruited, and their call signs hold no significance for me.

"Wraith here," I state when my time comes.

I've opted to use the name Sorin has mentioned a handful of times, since I'm the only cyborg Quiara can't track with her borrowed Botanaari scanner.

And I think I like it. It's a hell of a lot better than Slaughter Bot was, anyway.

I continue my circuit. Another hour passes, more Coalition members and their guests flood into the already packed building, and there's still no sign of Omega Prime. Vee issues another round of checks while the deejay manipulates the lighting to coincide with her latest pulse-thundering track. I don't know if she ramped up the bass since I've tuned out the music, but I can *feel* the steady beat of the music through the floor and the soles of my boots. I'm sure the nearby dancers risk hearing loss.

"Coyote here," a man says over the comms. I think Coyote was the name of one of Max's soldiers, not someone from ZIEG, but I can't remember for sure. "Activity at the rear exit. Request someone with a scanner to confirm IDs."

"Blaze en route," Vee replies. "Need further backup?"

"Not sure," Coyote responds, his tone uneasy.

"Gray, Strafe, head to the exit door just in case."

"Copy that," a woman replies.

"Hey, Blaze," Captain Wax says seconds later. "I have three confirmed Omega Prime assholes at the front entrance. No sign of their leader, but I'll need reinforcements."

There's a pause, then Vee says, "Spider, Ares, Wraith, you're up. Assist Tank as needed."

"Copy that."

I dart through the crowd, using my augmented speed when I'm able, while dodging oblivious dancers and clusters of revelers. My post was the farthest from the entrance, but Vee knows how fast I can move when I want to. I reach Waxman's location before Spider or Ares do and nod to Zinn in silent greeting.

She points to a location beyond the doors. "They haven't tried to come in yet. I'll bet they're waiting for their cue."

"They're going to try breaching both doors at once," Waxman growls.

"Vee has the rear door covered," I reply. "We're ready."

Waxman snorts derisively. "We thought we were ready when they broke into Zylar HQ last year. We weren't. These bastards killed some of our people and abducted you. I want some fucking payback, but they know this base as well as we do. They've been here before."

"Then we shoot first and ask questions later," Zinn says. I can hear the smirk in her tone, though I can't see it behind her tinted face shield. "My former boss doesn't play nice. Why the hell should we?"

We're joined a few seconds later by two cyborgs, who I assume are Ares and Spider. They're both CVRT-BT series like Vee, designed for stealth and light combat, but deadly with any type of weapon. Ares nods to Waxman and crosses his arms, while Spider tilts their head, assessing me.

"So, you're Wraith." The voice that issues from the tall, lanky cyborg is feminine. "It's nice to finally meet you after seeing your face plastered all over GNN for months."

An uneasy laugh escapes my lips. "Um, yeah. That's me."

"Focus," Waxman snaps. "These bastards aren't getting inside on my watch. Ares, I want you to hold position on the right side of the entrance. Spider, you're on the left. Engage camouflage once you're in place. You'll be a nasty surprise if those mercs try anything."

"Roger that," Spider says, resigned.

She disappears from my vision seconds later as she activates her stealth fields, and I breathe a sigh of relief. I don't know why she's interested in me, but now isn't the time to figure it out. I switch to infrared briefly, noting both cyborgs are in position.

"Wraith, you're with me," Waxman growls. "I hope you've learned a few things since our last meeting, because I won't tolerate a fuck up here."

I clench my jaw, instantly pissed, but force a nod. "I'm ready."

He nods to Zinn. "Keep behind me and provide cover fire when I signal. They're starting to move."

I peer past Waxman to the exit. The cluster of mercs has joined the queue for entry, but there are now five of them rather than three. And I recognize the dark-haired man behind them without running a scan. I'll never forget his face as long as I live.

"Shit," I hiss. "That's Jeron Malachi."

Waxman growls an unintelligible curse, then speaks over the security team's comms. "Confirmed ID of Jeron Malachi. Repeat: GISA is on site with Omega Prime."

Vee issues orders for more of our team to gather at both entrances. Van Duval isn't with the group slowly moving toward us, but I know he's here somewhere. The scarred bastard wouldn't miss this for all the credits in the galaxy.

"Confirmed ID of Van Duval nearing rear exit," Coyote says as if echoing my thoughts.

"Classic," Zinn sneers beside me. "He never goes for the main entrance. He lives for the element of 'surprise,' but this time, we knew he was coming."

I move the plasma rifle from my back and brace myself for a bloody fight. I flick off the safety and prime the charges, waiting for Waxman's order. I want Jeron Malachi dead almost as much as I do Van Duval. He's the asshole who ultimately sent me to Primordia-1.

"Take the agent alive if possible," Quiara states. "Max wants to interrogate him."

I growl in frustration. "It'll be easier to end this without risking *our* people if he's eliminated quickly."

"He has intel we can use," Quiara replies evenly. "Take him alive, Wraith. That's an order."

"And Omega Prime?" Waxman asks through clenched teeth.

"Van Duval is the only one of potential value, and Sorin would rather see him gone," she says.

Waxman peers over his shoulder. "Focus on the mercs, kid. I'll handle the agent."

He signals, and the ensuing minutes or seconds—I'm not sure which—become a blur of coordinated chaos.

Ares and Spider converge on the mercs as they step inside the building, taking out one of them before they're aware of the cyborgs' presence. I take aim at the merc in the center as he dodges a blast from Spider's handcannon. I fire at the same moment he's tackled from behind, and my shot misses, hitting the doorframe instead.

Jeron kneels near the merc, who extracts a pistol from within one of his pockets. Waxman charges toward them with a roar as he rips a nanosteel dagger as long as my forearm from its sheath at his waist. I sense more than see Waxman's defensive shields engage, though a faint bluish haze surrounds his armored form, momentarily lost as the deejay's lights flicker toward the red end of the spectrum.

Screams issue from the dancers and drinkers behind us, and I hear the unmistakable sound of projectile gunfire from the rear door. I hope Vee stops Duval more swiftly than we've dealt with our group of invaders.

The merc with Jeron scrambles to his feet as Waxman races toward them, his pistol aimed at the big cyborg's face. I have a clear shot and don't hesitate to fire a second time, even as Jeron shoves the merc to the side. My blast hits the merc's left bicep, incinerating clothing, skin, and tissue on contact. The lower half of his arm falls to the floor, but there is no blood; plasma's good at cauterizing wounds. The merc teeters off-balance and crashes into the wall, where Ares swiftly disarms him.

I shift my focus to the other merc, who has evaded Spider and is now engaged with Zinn. Waxman is trading blows with Jeron, but I ignore their fight for now. Spider's moving into position to help him disable the agent, and he won't need me.

"Fuck," Zinn hisses as I dart past a group of fleeing partiers in an attempt to gain line of sight on her assailant. "Damn you, Vikal! You always were a pain in my ass."

I maneuver around the group in time to see Zinn's assailant backhand her weapon arm. Her pistol flies through the air and is lost within the fleeing crowd.

"I always knew you'd turn traitor," Vikal snarls as he closes the gap between them. "Time to die, bitch."

I engage my speed, and as the world moves in slow motion around me, I know before I crash into the merc's side that I'll be too late.

"ZINN!" I roar at the same time Vikal fires into her chest.

She stumbles backward with a ragged gasp as the butt of my rifle crashes into the merc's helmet with as much force as I can muster. There's a crunch. Vikal collapses, the imprint of the rifle several inches deep in his cracked helmet. I don't know if he's dead, but in my rage, I want to make sure he is.

I drop the rifle and rain punches down on his head in a rhythmic assault that matches the thudding beat from the deejay vibrating through the floor. I lose myself for a time, and only stop when a hand grabs my shoulder from behind.

"Hey, he's dead. Enough." It's Spider. Her tone conveys understanding, but is laced with fear.

I rock back on my heels and shake my head. The merc's helmet is crushed in more places than I can count, his body armor splintered and crumpled in multiple places, the imprint of my gauntleted fists clear amidst the carnage.

I didn't mean to react like this. *Fuck.*

"Zinn?" I ask with a wary glance at Spider.

"She's…" Spider tilts her head and I follow her gaze.

Ares kneels at Zinn's side, his armor splattered with blood. Zinn has removed her helmet, and her face isn't just pale, it's utterly devoid of color. Ares' hands press down over the gunshot wound in her chest. Blood spurts through his fingers as I watch, and I know she doesn't have much time. Vikal aimed for her heart, and her armor clearly wasn't rated to withstand a pointblank shot from a projectile weapon.

"Shit." I'm on my feet before I register my own movement and kneel across from Ares.

"Hey…Metal Man." She sucks in a ragged breath. "Did you…kill him?"

"Yeah." My voice is hollow. Vikal's death hasn't sunk in, and I'm still in shock over what I've done, but it's meaningless if she meets the same fate.

A voice comes over the comms. "Duval is down. I repeat: Duval is down."

"What was that?" Zinn asks.

"Your old boss is dead," I reply as grief sinks its twisted talons into my heart. "Zinn, I—"

"We won," she whispers, smiling inexplicably despite the pain she must be in.

"Blaze," I call over the comm, "Pink's down. We need a medic at the front doors."

Zinn begins to laugh, but it morphs into a cough with her next breath. "Shit. I didn't think it would…hurt this bad. It's too…too late for a medic, Kye. Time to…say hello…to that scarred bastard…in hell."

"No, no, don't."

I look to Ares as he continues to administer what little first aid he can, but he shakes his head. Zinn's fingers curl around his wrists feebly, and she shoves them away with her remaining energy.

More blood spurts from the wound now that the compression no longer keeps it inside. She laughs weakly before growing still, and I know she's gone.

I stand, my vision blurred by tears. I don't know what I intend to do other than make someone pay for her death. Four of the five mercs are dead. The last is shackled awkwardly and huddles against the wall, the stump of his left arm hanging limply at his side. Jeron has been disarmed and stands handcuffed between Spider and Captain Wax, staring at the floor.

My ire sparks as I see him. *He's* the reason Zinn is dead. *He's* responsible for my stay on Primordia-1. And *he's* going to fucking pay.

I storm toward him, determined to end him right here, right now, despite Quiara's order. Waxman knows my mood from my stance alone and steps between me and his captive.

"Stand down," he growls.

"Get out of my fucking way." I shove him hard, but he keeps his feet and repulses some of the blow with his defensive shield.

"I said, stand down."

"No."

I draw back my fist at the same moment a barrel is pressed into the back of my helmet.

"We will subdue you if you force the issue," Ares says from behind me. "Don't make me pull this trigger."

I glare at Waxman but drop my hand to my side, my rage dissipating as swiftly as it arrived. "She's dead. It's that asshole's fault." I deflate and sink to my knees, keeping my eyes focused on the blood-smeared floor.

"Get the agent out of here," Waxman growls.

Spider mutters a reply and moves away, a shackled Jeron Malachi held at gunpoint in front of her. I ignore their departure and continue to stare at the floor as Waxman drops to his knees in front of me.

"I know it's hard to lose a comrade in arms," he says, his tone surprisingly gentle. "But revenge is a shitty way to pay them tribute. It's *never* worth it. Trust me—I know."

"Sorry I hit you," I mumble.

He chuckles. "Had it been anyone else, they'd need to visit Sorin's labs for repairs. Lucky for you, my shields were still active." He claps me on the shoulder. "Come on, we need to help Vee clean this place up. You can start by helping move Pink to the morgue."

My heart stutters painfully at the order, but I nod. I can do this much for her, even if I failed to take down the man ultimately responsible. At least Vikal's dead. So is Van Duval.

The thought doesn't bring the comfort I hoped it would. Instead, it leaves me hollow and cold, adrift in a sea of sorrow as I follow Ares' lead.

I focus on the single bright point of the evening: Without Van Duval, Omega Prime is finished.

It doesn't erase the fact that Zinn Jarek is dead, or that she's the only merc I'll ever consider a friend, but it's something.

We've cut off the head of the snake; it's only a matter of time before the whole organization collapses.

CHAPTER FORTY-THREE

BORN TO FLY

RESISTANCE COALITION HQ
COBALT ASTEROID, GAMMA CEPHEI SYSTEM

After the event center is cleared and cleaned up, I return to my loaned apartment on the other side of the base. Someone has left two new paperbacks on the mat outside my door, but I have no interest in reading tonight. I carry them inside and set them on the room's only table, along with my small arsenal of borrowed weapons, then begin the process of removing my armor.

There's blood on my greaves—Vikal's or Zinn's, maybe both. There's blood on my gauntlets too. I heave a sigh and prime the cleaner bot that crouches in one corner of the room, then stack the various pieces of my armor beside it. The poor, mindless wonder of machinery is going to have a long night.

I move from the tiny sitting room through the bedroom and into the bathroom. A shower is in order. There's no blood on me, and I don't sweat anymore, but I feel dirty all the same. Maybe watching the death of a friend does that to a person. Or maybe it was my hair-trigger reaction to her injury and what I did to Vikal that makes my skin crawl from its contact with imaginary grime.

I start up the shower controls and set it to its highest temperature, hoping I can scald away my guilt and shame.

It doesn't work, but I feel marginally better afterward. I pull on a black t-shirt and matching cargo pants, then rake a hand through my hair. I lack the energy to comb it.

It's two a.m. Galactic Standard Time, I don't want to read, and I'm too restless to sleep. I want to talk to someone, but I know Vee's busy assisting Max with his interrogation, and my only other real friend on the asteroid is dead. But my apartment is equipped with a holoreceiver and an encrypted connection, and I was given the okay to make outgoing calls. I could call Pablo, but he has class in the morning—and if I wake him, I'll be waking Daaros too. That's not a good option.

I settle for calling my sister. She's here on the base, and maybe she's heard something of what happened already.

She picks up on the fourth ping, rubbing sleep from her eyes. I hear a voice murmur something in the background as she struggles to focus on my image.

Shit. She wasn't alone either.

"Kye?" she asks uncertainly.

"Um, sorry. I didn't realize you had company."

She waves a hand dismissively. "It's Tariq. He understands. What's up?"

"I..." I don't know how to begin, and instead focus on Tariq's presence in her temporary apartment. "I didn't realize you were back together."

She smiles and peers over her shoulder briefly. "He was persistent, I'll give him that. But you didn't wake me up to discuss my love life."

I shake my head. "Did you go to the party?"

"No. We opted to stay in. Did something happen?"

"Yeah." I drop my gaze and stare at my hands. "Kels... Zinn's dead."

The grief I've been battling for the past few hours rears up and punches me full force in the gut. I fall apart and hold my head in my hands, refusing to look at the screen.

"Oh, shit. Hang on, little brother. I'll be over in ten minutes."

I hear the screen disconnect, but I'm rooted in place as I begin to sob. Tonight wasn't supposed to end in casualties—not from our side, anyway. And Zinn...

She was a better friend than I gave her credit for. I didn't fully appreciate all that she did for me, taking it for granted instead. I'm a sorry excuse for a friend.

When Kelsey knocks on my door nine minutes later, I don't immediately get up. I'm a wreck and I know it, and I think she'll understand my delay. I gather my waning strength and force myself to answer the door. Tariq's in the hall behind her, suited in his ZIEG-issued combat armor. I frown at him, but he nods in greeting and taps his ear, an indication that he's on duty—or going to be soon. Kelsey pushes past me and waves over her shoulder at Tariq as the door slides closed.

"After your call, he contacted base security to learn what was going on," she says, guiding me to the battered sofa I vacated seconds earlier. "He offered to help with the investigation into how Omega Prime got inside."

I nod absently, glad I don't have to rehash all the details of the party. I'm not sure I have the energy to do so, despite my system's insistence that I'm at ninety-four percent. My cybernetics don't take into account emotional tolls.

"I didn't mean to interrupt your night," I murmur without looking at her.

"If you hadn't, someone else would have," she replies dismissively. "Tariq was on the call list if they needed him. So was I."

"Was?"

"Yeah." She takes my left hand in her right. "I told them I needed to check in on you. Max understood."

I force a strangled laugh. "It's not like that. It's not a relapse, I just… I wanted to talk to someone."

"Then let's talk."

So, we do. I tell her everything, even the grisly part when I lost my shit and raged, taking out every bit of my anger on the fucking merc who shot Zinn. I relay how Captain Wax was forced to intervene, how he stood up to me even though I could have destroyed him if I wanted to. And I admit my guilt, spilling my emotional baggage at her feet like one of last night's partygoers puking up their guts after too many martinis.

But the thing about Kelsey is that she listens when I need her to. She doesn't judge—at least not openly—and when I break down again, she's there to offer comfort. Even when I was trapped on Earth and she was flying around the galaxy on military operations, I knew I could call her any time. She might not have answered right away, but she always called back as soon as she could. I don't know if every older sister is like her, but I'm damned glad she is and that she's mine.

My heart still threatens to crumble when I'm finished, but somehow, I feel better. Grief is a prickly beast.

"I know just what you need now," Kelsey says after a time. "Let's go down to the cantina, and I'll—"

Her words are interrupted by an insistent chime coming from my holoreceiver. I groan aloud and accept the incoming call, certain I know what it's going to entail.

Trin's face fills the screen. I don't think she's managed any sleep since I last spoke with her; the shadows beneath her eyes are deeper than most black holes, and her hair is still in a mild state of disarray.

"I'm glad you're awake," Trin says without a greeting. "We need your help."

"I don't think this is a good time—" Kelsey begins.

Trin cuts her off by holding up one hand. "I don't care what time it is or if it works for the two of you. We've learned the codes Sorin plans to use are compromised. He's walking into a trap, and he's gone radio silent."

I cross my arms. "What can we possibly do from here?"

"Nothing," Trin snaps. "Which is why we need you to go to Megatropolis. You can deliver the correct codes before he kills himself using the wrong ones."

Kelsey stiffens. "You have dozens of former ZIEG soldiers on this base, and you want to ask more of my brother? After everything he's been through because of *you?*"

Trin's expression is steely. "I wouldn't ask it of him if there was a better option. Your brother is the only person here who can slide through security scans undetected."

Kelsey opens her mouth to protest, but I shake my head. "It's fine, Kels. She's right. No one else can do this."

"It's bullshit!" Kelsey snarls. "If he winds up captured a second time, I swear I will hunt every last one of you people down until the Coalition is as dead as fucking Zylar Inc. Do you understand me?"

I bite the inside of my cheek to keep from grinning. I'm glad Kelsey is on my side because she's *terrifying* when she's pissed.

"Your feelings on the matter are noted," Trin says levelly after a moment. "But we don't have much time, and wasting the precious little we do have on a theoretical argument does no one any good." She turns to face me. "Gear up and meet me at landing pad fourteen. I'll have a shuttle waiting for you."

When I nod, Trin disconnects the call. I trudge toward the cleaner bot and my armor; it's mostly finished, though my boots are still in the queue.

"I can't believe she's sending you back to Megatropolis!" Kelsey roars.

"Kels, she's right about the security scans. There's a reason Sorin started referring to me as a wraith."

"I don't care." She begins to pace as I gather my armor and move toward the bedroom. "You've done enough for Sorin's fucking resistance. It's not right that they should ask more of you."

I close the door for privacy and begin the task of stripping, then don my armor. "If Sorin's walking into a trap like she thinks, then everything we've done so far is worthless. My time in Ajax's hell was for nothing if Sorin fails."

She's silent for several seconds, then I hear the distinct sound of a fist slamming into a wall. "If you insist on going, I'm coming too."

I roll my eyes at the absurdity of her statement. "Uh, Kels? Didn't we just discuss the security scans? I'm a wanted fugitive, and you're my sister. You'll be flagged as a threat by association."

"Damn it, Kye! I won't let you do this alone."

I pause to put on my helmet, then push the door open. "You have to, Kels. It's the only way this will work."

She glares at me. "Don't you dare die on me, little brother. I won't be able to live with myself if you do."

She turns away, but not fast enough to hide her frustrated tears. My heart breaks a little more, brittle pieces flaking off and swirling into the void.

I swallow the lump forming in my throat and pull her into a hug. "I'll come back, Kels. I promise."

"And if you don't, I'll haunt you."

I laugh, though the sound is strained. "I don't think that's how haunting works."

"Shut up and let me have this one, Kye."

I know better than to argue when my sister uses that tone. I give her this moment, and when she pushes away, I move toward the table where I left my weapons. She watches silently as I holster my pistols, sheathe my daggers, and secure the rifle over my shoulder.

"You know, I've gone through the same ritual countless times. I never realized how damned hard it is to watch someone else prep for battle not knowing if I'll see them again." She steels herself, then nods. "At least let me walk you to the landing pad."

"Okay."

Trin paces in front of a single-occupant shuttle, an older Zylar Inc. Model Swyfft only large enough to accommodate a pilot and their gear. The interior lights are on, and the engines hum softly in the darkness. I assume this is my shuttle and that I'll be the pilot.

Part of me wants to grin stupidly at the notion that I'll finally be allowed to fly something. I passed all of my simulator tests back on Megatropolis, and I can interface with almost any vessel in the galaxy, provided it has a data access port. The Model Swyfft does, and I have its specs stored in my databanks if I need to do any troubleshooting.

The other part of me recoils at the sight. Trin's sending me to save Sorin's skin without backup. Yeah, I can probably call Luna if things get ugly, but that's an additional risk I'm not sure is worth taking yet.

Trin nods once in greeting, her eyes sliding from mine to Kelsey's while her expression hardens into a disapproving frown. "He's going alone."

"I know." Kelsey crosses her arms. "There's no harm in me seeing him off though."

Trin sighs in exasperation. "Fine. But anything I say in the next few minutes stays between us. If there's a security breach, I'll be eyeing *you*."

"I'm familiar with the drill," Kelsey scoffs. "You said time was short. Don't waste it on a baseless argument."

Trin narrows her eyes, then nods and turns to face me. "Vee is prepping your shuttle. They've agreed to upload the code and an encrypted file for Sorin into your secured databanks before you depart. I... I wasn't comfortable with the procedure. That's typically Sorin's forte."

"Okay," I reply. "I'll have the codes, and I need to get them to Sorin. Where is he, and how much time do I actually have?"

"He plans to infiltrate Zylar HQ at eight p.m. Galactic Standard Time, which gives you approximately twelve hours," she replies. "He'll be in the offices of Diego Sandoval, in the Financial District, until six p.m. If you leave in the next thirty minutes, you should be able to reach him before he leaves. If not, he plans to use the same entrance into Zylar HQ that you used to reach the mainframe. He needs to input the codes from Marim's personal holoterminal on the executive floor. They'll be taking the stairs, if all goes according to plan."

I nod as I process the information. I'll travel directly to the late Diego Sandoval's building; I can access the coordinates from my previous visits. If I miss the window, I'll head to Zylar HQ directly. I can use the same entrance Sorin plans to and sneak up to Marim's office, where I'll wait for him to arrive. I'm not worried about security; they won't see me on their scans—but it makes me think of another question.

"Is the shuttle equipped with an autopilot delivery sequence?"

Trin flashes a rare smile. "Yes. I think I know what you're planning."

"If the security kiosks in orbit think the shuttle is operating without a pilot, I'll have no trouble getting through." I glance at Kelsey, who nods thoughtfully. "They won't know I'm on board."

"Do it," Trin says. "And if you need backup, I've included Luna Zeta's frequency in your data package. She'll do what she can to assist."

"Thanks. I think I'm ready."

Kelsey steps forward to pull me into a fierce embrace. "Don't do anything stupid, little brother. We're counting on you to come back this time."

I chuckle and release her. "I'll be fine, Kels. I can do this."

I turn to face the shuttle as Vee appears in the open doorway. I draw a breath and move forward, determined to see this through, determined to prove to myself and my sister that I *can* succeed in a mission without being captured.

I know my record so far isn't great in that regard, but I won't fail this time. There's too much at stake.

Vee shuffles inside as I enter the shuttle. There's only just enough room for both of us if I sit in the pilot's chair and they stand behind me.

"Trin told me what you need to do," I offer as I scan the tiny ship's controls.

"If you're ready, so am I."

"Yeah. Let's do this."

Vee connects a cable between their tablet and my input jack, and seconds later, the files appear in my system. They disconnect as soon as the transfer is complete, then lay a hand on my shoulder.

"I know you can do this, Kye. Just remember your training. Don't freeze, and keep your temper. A clear mind is your greatest asset."

I nod once, understanding their implication. I can't let my fury overwhelm me, not as I did last night. "I've got this."

"You do. Good luck."

Their hand moves away, and I wait a few seconds for them to exit the shuttle before closing the door. I stare at the console spread before me, go through the routine pre-flight checks, then strap myself into the pilot's chair. Everything is in order.

Pressing my right palm against the shuttle's data port, I interface with its system. I can work faster this way. I enter the command to lift off and guide the shuttle over the surface of Cobalt Asteroid, toward the airlock that will allow me to exit into space.

An eerie calm descends over me as I focus on flying the craft, and I'm able to forget my past, my losses, and my pain for a short time. Despite my genetics, I think I was born to fly.

CHAPTER FORTY-FOUR

MAYBE I'M NOT JUST A FLUKE

MEGATROPOLIS, TRAPPIST-1 SYSTEM

I doze during the ten-hour flight to Megatropolis, but snap awake as my internal chronometer issues a preset wakeup alarm. I had set it to wake me after nine hours, when the programmed flight path through hyperspace begins to decelerate on the outskirts of the TRAPPIST-1 system. I don't want to be caught napping in the pilot's chair when the ship arrives at the security checkpoint outside Megatropolis' fabricated rings.

I don't want to be caught in the pilot's chair at all. I need the security drones and personnel to believe the ship's unoccupied, simply delivering a package to a predetermined destination. My plan is to play dead in the cramped cargo hold.

Checking the shuttle's manifest a final time, I'm satisfied with my work. I'm not as skilled at hacking into and modifying systems as Sorin, but my ZIEG training covered enough that I think it will pass basic scrutiny. It's the best I can do.

I verify the trajectory of the shuttle's path, note that I'm on course, and unstrap myself from the pilot's chair. I curl on my side behind it, tucking my feet back where they won't be visible if someone decides to look through the windshield.

Have I mentioned that I'm taller than most? Yeah, this isn't the most comfortable position, but I've survived a hell of a lot worse.

Now, I wait. The hum from the sublight engines turns off after ten minutes, replaced by the higher-pitched drone of the deceleration thrusters. They fire for thirty minutes, and when I'm just beyond the inner orbit of Megatropolis' closest planetary sibling, then they fall silent as well. The ship coasts for another ten minutes before the final braking sequence initiates.

The console chimes with an incoming message. "Civilian Swyfft shuttle VX9LK2, you are cleared to enter the security queue."

I resist the urge to reconnect with the shuttle's system to verify it sent an automated response. I have to trust that it worked as intended. I'm too damned close to the security kiosk to risk sliding into the pilot's seat again.

The craft eases forward at intervals as it progresses through the queue, and after twenty minutes, it reaches the front. The console chimes as new instructions are given, but this time, they run through the shuttle's automated systems and I hear nothing but the initial sound.

Minutes crawl by. I reach slowly for one of my pistols, certain some bored asshole is going to insist on coming inside to verify the forged manifest. As I ease it free of its holster, the shuttle jets forward.

A bubble of relieved laughter escapes my lips. I'm okay. I'm headed into Megatropolis' space and zooming past the outer rings.

I let a full minute pass before I sit up and climb back into the pilot's chair. I take command and alter the shuttle's flight path to take me directly to the late Diego Sandoval's building in the Financial District. My chronometer indicates I have eighty-three minutes before Sorin's planned departure. It's enough time to reach him and pass on the legitimate codes, provided I don't get stopped by a random security patrol.

The Financial District is cast in evening shadow as I streak through the atmosphere. Lights twinkle from myriad windows and illuminated signs blaze through the growing darkness vying for my attention, while the stars fade above, washed into oblivion by the city-world's rampant light pollution.

I frown and tell myself it's somehow better than what humanity did to Earth, but is it? We're still responsible for destroying a planet's natural beauty, all for the sake of credits.

As I near the abandoned building where Sorin should still be hiding, I take full control of the shuttle and guide it to the landing pad on the roof. There's another shuttle already parked there, a larger commuter model that I'm more accustomed to riding in. As I begin to turn off the engines and cycle the power, I consider my options.

I could walk into the building unannounced, but I might wind up shot before anyone realizes it's *me*. I'm not sure I want to take the risk in case Sorin needs me for something during this final operation. Or I could call him through my private frequency and hope my firewalls are enough to avoid the attention of…well, anyone outside the Coalition. I don't want to give away their location or my own.

I glare at the shuttle's console as seconds tick by. There is only one safe option for Sorin's crew, but it puts me at the mercy of potentially trigger-happy soldiers or fellow cyborgs.

Fuck it.

I check my weapons, then exit the shuttle. Let's hope my gamble pays off and I'm not riddled with plasma rounds before I can say "hello."

I hold my hands up in a gesture of surrender as I cross the rooftop to the door that will lead me to a small atrium and the elevator inside. I didn't think to scan for cameras before exiting my craft, and it's too late to bother with it now. I'm committed for better or worse, and if someone is monitoring the roof, I hope they recognize my armor.

When I'm ten steps from the door, the click indicating a weapon's safety has been taken off sounds behind my head. I freeze and curse myself for the galaxy's biggest dumbass. I should have been using infrared mode. Most of the cyborgs with Sorin are CVRT-BT series. *Shit.*

"You know, I'm getting tired of arresting you, Verex." There's amusement in the tone coupled with a weariness that can only come from someone who has been on watch duty for hours. Maybe days.

"Hey, Luna."

She snorts, shifts into visibility, and moves to block my path. She isn't wearing armor, and I'm glad to see she hasn't changed her rainbow-dyed hair. It suits her.

"Why the hell are you here?" she demands, her pistol still aimed at my throat.

"It's a long story. Short version: Sorin's base was attacked. Trin sent me with intel for Sorin."

Luna frowns, skeptical. "Did she take into account your previous record of getting caught when she sent you here alone?"

"Yeah. She also took into account that my armor lets me through orbital security without detection, and she gave me your private frequency in case I got here too late and needed backup." I pause, then ask, "Can I put my hands down now?"

"No. If Trin really sent you, then call me right now. I'm trying to decide if you're more trouble than you're worth, Verex."

I release an exasperated groan, but follow orders. It's weird calling into someone's head from my own, but she asked for it. She accepts on the first ping.

"Now do you believe me?"

"Fine. Sorin's in the lobby. He's prepping to leave in thirty. Let's go."

I drop my hands to my side as she holsters her weapon, then follow her through the door. The skyscraper's interior is just as forlorn and dusty as it was on my last visit. We enter the elevator, and she jabs at the control panel, clearly frustrated. I'm not sure if I'm the cause or if the elevator is, but when the car begins to descend and she levels a glare at me, I have my answer.

"What did I do?"

She expels a frustrated sigh. "The better question is, what *haven't* you done? Damn it, Kye, after everything you've been through, you should be as far from Megatropolis as you can get. Not all of ZIEG is on Sorin's side here, and we all recognize your damned armor. It was in *our* possession for months."

"Like I said, I only came to deliver the intel. I don't have to get mixed up in…whatever Sorin has planned."

She shakes her head. "You don't get it. Your presence here means you're mixed up in it, whether you planned to be or not. This building's slated for demolition ten minutes after we leave. You can't stay here, and your shuttle's going to be scrap. You'll either have to leave and risk someone pinning the destruction on *you*, which means GISA will be hunting for you *again*, or you'll have to come with us."

"And how were you planning to leave undetected?" I ask irritably.

"Omega Prime dug a tunnel beneath the lobby," Luna replies. "We'll use it to go underneath the street outside and into the sub-basement of their other building two blocks away."

"But why blow up the building? It doesn't make—Oh." I stare at her as I puzzle it out on my own. "It's a distraction."

Her smile is tight. "Yep."

The elevator stops before I can say anything more, and the door slides open. She gestures for me to exit first.

Sorin and a dozen others are clustered in the center of the building's dingy lobby. I recognize Xia, Nate, and Geo from my previous Coalition missions, as well as Chadwick Cleary. My stomach clenches painfully and I grimace. I hope he isn't too pissed off by our last meeting, though he won't remember it directly.

Sorin looks up from his tablet as we walk toward them and frowns. "Kye? We saw the shuttle land, but why—?"

"Trin sent me. It's important."

Chadwick bristles at the sound of my voice. He's armored but carries his helmet under one arm, providing me with an unobstructed view of the snarl that twists his face. Okay, he's still pissed.

"Stand down, Cleary," Luna snaps. "We're on the same team."

"That little fucker was on Titan Base—"

Sorin holds up a hand for silence. "If you want to blame anyone for the memory wipe, blame me. I gave the order."

Chadwick clenches his jaw, but most of the fire leaves his eyes. I owe Sorin one there. I think he was planning to kick my ass—and we don't have time for that.

Sorin turns back to me. "What did Trin learn that she'd risk sending someone here?"

"The codes Marim gave you are compromised," I reply. "Trin sent the real codes and an encrypted file. I don't know what's in the file, but she made it sound important."

Sorin frowns, concern etching his features. "We triple-checked the codes from Marim's interrogation. It doesn't matter. Trin wouldn't have sent you if we weren't in danger of losing the operation. I'll need to extract those files." He glances at Luna. "How much time do we have?"

"Twenty-three minutes." She shoots Chadwick a steely gaze. "I'm going to suit up. Don't make me regret leaving you unattended, Cleary."

He rolls his eyes. "I'll behave, Zeta."

I kneel to allow Sorin access to my neck. He plugs in, removes the files, then disconnects in the span of thirty seconds. He taps and scrolls through his tablet, his frown deepening as time crawls by.

"Trin was right. Marim gave us a false set of codes. I should have let Max interrogate her properly." He grimaces. "We have the real codes now."

"What was in the mysterious file?" Xia asks.

"A transcript from Agent Malachi's interrogation. If we don't pull this off, we'll have GISA crawling all over us, and we all know what that means." His expression crumples as guilt and shame war across his features. "I wish she would have sent *anyone* but you, Kye. I won't see you sent back to Primordia-1. Not because of my blasted mistakes."

I'm grateful I never took my helmet off. Sorin can't see the emotional battle that plays out across my face before I rein it all in with an adjustment to my biochems. I have to stay focused.

"No one else could have passed through orbital security undetected," I remind him in a steady tone, though my voice sounds hollow and distant to my own ears. Maybe I tweaked my system a little too much.

"We can worry about this later if it becomes relevant," Luna says evenly as she strides into the room, fully armored. "We need to leave on time, and someone needs to fill Kye in on the plan before we go."

Her armor looks like a civilian model; it's not the dark blue typically issued to ZIEG soldiers. It has a tan-to-gray camouflage print instead, and the helmet's face shield is tinted as darkly as mine.

"Kye will join my team," Sorin replies. "I can fill him in as we go."

"Will you still need me then?" Chadwick growls.

"I think your cybernetic abilities will complement each other—if you can manage to hold your damned temper," Luna snaps. "I'm responsible for providing a distraction, and my team's in place and ready to go. I won't risk adding him to the mix, not when I'm convinced Patil will show up primed for a fight. As Sorin said, Kye has been through enough."

"And I'm willing to help—" I begin before Sorin cuts me off.

"Luna's team is prepared to face ZIEG's commander," he says wearily. "We all know you're a survivor, but that doesn't mean you need to put yourself directly in the line of fire yet again. Between you and Chad, my team will be safe enough. Just don't kill each other in the process."

"I never wanted to fight him," I snarl. "And the memory wipe was better than the *other* option I was given."

"What option?" Chadwick asks, his tone dangerously low.

Before I can respond, Sorin says, "We couldn't afford to leave witnesses. Duval ordered him to kill you, and it would have been the faster and safer route." He crosses his arms. "Kye refused. If you want to be angry about missing ten minutes of your time, blame me. I told him how to perform the memory wipe."

"Fucking mercs," Chadwick growls. He shakes his head, then slams his helmet in place. "Fine. Maybe I've been pissed at the wrong person this whole time, but if you still have contact with Duval, tell him I'm going to hunt him down and fucking kill him."

"He's dead." The words tumble from my throat, unbidden. "He was part of the GISA raid on the base last night. I think the agent is the only survivor."

"Then Omega Prime's finished," Luna says thoughtfully. "That's one less thing to worry about."

I know I should share her optimism, but the conversation reminds me that Zinn died too. One of my friends was killed in the attack, someone I respected and cared for. I hang my head and stare at the floor. *Damn it all.*

A hand falls on my shoulder, and I look up to find Sorin staring into my face shield. "I know what happened," he says gently. "Max listed the casualties in his report. We'll hold a proper wake when we're done, but I need you to focus now. Can you do that?"

"Yeah. I'm okay."

I'm not, but I can pump more adrenaline into my system to give me the edge I need. One of the unexpected perks of my cybernetics is drowning my grief beneath a tsunami of biochemical compounds—when I'm not too depressed to remember to do it, that is.

"Then let's go," Sorin replies. "It's time."

We move across the lobby to an unmarked door, which might have been used as a janitorial supply closet in the days before Van Duval purchased the building. A trapdoor is set into the tiled floor. Chadwick hauls it open and waits as the others climb down the ladder inside and disappear into darkness. I linger outside until Luna, Sorin, and his crew have gone.

"Go on," Chadwick says. "I'll close the door behind me. You might want night vision down there, at least until we reach the junction."

"Thanks."

I tug on the strap holding my rifle in place to ensure it's secure, then begin to descend. The weak light from the lobby doesn't penetrate more than a few feet into the space, and I switch to night vision not long after. I glance down and note the others have moved away from the ladder's base, another ten feet below my current position. Chadwick climbs onto the ladder as I near the bottom and pauses to latch the trapdoor shut.

Luna takes point, leading the others along an empty tunnel reinforced with nanosteel girders. She sets a rapid pace, and two minutes into our journey, I understand why.

The explosion that rocks the tower rumbles through the earth, concrete, and steel above our heads. A fine rain of dust falls from the tunnel's ceiling to coat our armor, but the tunnel holds.

"That'll be the first charge," Chadwick says from beside me. "Number two should come right about…now."

The second detonation is more powerful than the first, and an invisible shockwave passes through our party. The humans from the Coalition stumble and wave their arms wildly for balance, but we cyborgs keep our feet.

"If I set everything up right, that should have brought the building to its knees," Chadwick says, a measure of pride in his tone.

"You were a demolitions expert before joining ZIEG," Xia says over her shoulder. "There's no 'if' in that statement, Chad."

"Military?" I ask him.

"Yeah. Until I fucked up a job and lost my legs. ZIEG was my ticket to walking again."

I nod silently at the reminder that we all signed that damned contract for a reason. Zylar Inc. coerced us with the promise of a better life… All we had to do was pledge our existence to the corporate overlord. And we did.

We reach the junction a minute later as the third and final explosion rocks through the earth. We're far enough from the epicenter that the blast doesn't affect us this time, but more dust rains from the ceiling.

Tiny lights line one wall of the perpendicular corridor we file into, and I switch back to normal vision. The illumination is dim but more than enough to see by. To our right, a maintenance shaft jets toward the surface, and to our left is another ladder. Luna moves toward the ladder and scurries up to unlatch the trapdoor above.

I remain at the rear of the group with Chadwick until Sorin and his crew have ascended to the building above. He grips my shoulder briefly as I grasp the rungs.

"I'm still pissed, but if what Sorin says is true, I'm alive because of you. I'll get over it eventually."

"How did you know it was me?"

He chuckles. "It's standard procedure for GISA agents to wear body cams. Your strike team disabled the exterior cameras, but not the ones they were wearing. They let me watch the videos after Mat patched me up."

Luna peers down from the hatch above my head. "Hurry the hell up. You two can establish your dominance later."

I snort in response and begin to climb, while Chadwick snickers behind me. "I think we've already established that, Zeta," he calls. "We were just having a friendly chat."

I don't have to see inside her helmet to know she rolls her eyes. "Chat later. We're on the clock."

I emerge a few seconds later into a closet eerily reminiscent of the one we exited the other building through. Sorin and his team are in this building's lobby, staring through the dusty glass windows at the spectacle down the block. A plume of debris is visible between the nearest skyscrapers, rising darkly into Megatropolis' night sky.

"It's impossible to know if the building collapsed completely," Chadwick says from behind me. "Not from here. But I think it'll be enough to keep GISA occupied for a few hours."

"There are already GNN drones overhead," Luna replies. "But we can't stand here and gawk at your handiwork. We need to get the hell out of here."

"Agreed." Sorin turns away from the window with a nod. "We'll be in contact, Luna."

"She's leaving in a separate vehicle to rendezvous with her team," Chadwick says for my benefit.

"We'll enter the building from the same maintenance door we used to reach the mainframe," Sorin adds as he motions for us to follow him across the room to another door. "A few of my people will remain with the shuttle to monitor comms. The rest of us will be taking the stairs up to the executive level."

I nod in understanding. "Trin told me the basics before I left."

"Good. Chad will take point as we move through the building. I want you on rear guard, Kye."

"Copy that."

The door leads to a small parking area behind the building. A white passenger shuttle awaits us, *Megatropolis Free Transit* printed in red along its side.

"You stole a commuter shuttle?" I ask as we begin to climb inside.

Sorin shrugs. "I prefer the term 'commandeer,' but essentially...yes."

Xia laughs. "It's all part of the disguise, Kye, but you were never good at blending in, were you?"

I don't bother to answer. There's no point in denial when both Pablo and Vee have reminded me of the same time and again. I'd undoubtedly be shit when it comes to covert operations, labeled the worst stealth-based cyborg in the galaxy.

Maybe Mat knew what he was doing when he augmented me with the SLTR-BT cybernetics, after all. Maybe I'm not just a fluke of the program as I've long suspected and feared, but one of its successes. I may be terrible at blending in, and I may have made some stupid mistakes, but I am trying to make the galaxy a better place in my own, fumbling way.

If we succeed tonight, I know exactly what I'll do with my promised freedom, something that should have been done generations ago.

CHAPTER FORTY-FIVE

UNVEILING

MEGATROPOLIS, TRAPPIST-1 SYSTEM

There's nothing more terrifying than confronting your past and its demons.

I squeeze my eyes shut and focus on my breathing as the shuttle stops outside the maintenance entrance of Zylar Inc.'s company headquarters. If the Vynaas' cure for my PTSD failed in any way, this is when I'm going to find out. I'll be walking through the same damned door that led me to the AI mainframe and following the same route I was escorted through after my capture.

"Sorin?" I ask, my tone more pitiful than I would have liked.

There are no flashbacks clouding my consciousness and my vitals are steady, but I'm fucking terrified. We can't afford to waste time on one of my episodes.

There's a rustle, then he sits on the bench seat beside me. "I'm here, Kye."

"If I do…anything, you'll stop me, right?"

He chuckles and pats my shoulder. "I won't have to. Your diagnostics came back clean."

"And if the results were in error?" I press. "You'll stop me? You have to."

"I'll do whatever is necessary to ensure this last mission succeeds," he replies glumly. "Even…that."

I know he refers to the suppressor, the only gadget in his possession that can instantly take down a cybernetically-enhanced terror like the one I might become. I hope with every fiber of my being that the Botanaari doctors actually cured me. I can't screw this up.

"Will you be okay?" Chadwick asks warily from somewhere closer to the cockpit.

I draw a breath and release it slowly, then nod. "Yeah. I hope so."

I open my eyes when Sorin rises. He moves to Chadwick's location and whispers to the big cyborg patiently. After a moment, Chadwick nods in understanding. I can feel his eyes on me, and I'm confident he'll intervene if I become a liability. He'll protect Sorin if I lose myself to another waking nightmare.

And Chadwick Cleary doesn't like me, which tilts the odds further in Sorin's favor.

With that assurance, I rise to my feet when the shuttle door slides open and follow the four Coalition members and Chadwick outside. Nate and Xia flank the console at the entrance as Sorin begins to hack into its system. Chadwick motions that I should remain next to the shuttle until we're cleared to enter the building.

I nod, then scan our surroundings. The area is clear. I switch to infrared mode, recalling that Luna surprised me on the rooftop earlier. We're in Zylar Inc. territory now, and Luna believed we'd meet with some ZIEG resistance. I'd like to think I learn from my mistakes.

I unholster both of my pistols and flick the safeties off. I haven't experienced any creeping shadows or the leering face of my former tormentor yet. I want to believe I'm okay, but I require solid proof. And that means walking through the maintenance door Sorin has just opened.

Chadwick takes point, leading with his plasma rifle. I creep slowly from the shuttle toward the entrance, keeping myself between the alley and the Coalition team. Once they're inside, I pivot and race to join them, then secure the door behind us.

Sorin touches one finger to his right ear, then nods. "Geo confirms no alarms were set off. We're clear."

"And Luna?" the woman who calls herself Berry asks. She's built like my sister, the result of years spent in the galactic military, but she smiles more readily. She wears armor plating beneath her Coalition jumpsuit, giving her the illusion of further muscle. A puckered scar mars her forehead, partially hidden by a sweep of auburn hair.

"Luna's in position," Sorin confirms. "We'll proceed as far as floor six, then wait for her signal."

Chadwick begins the ascent. The others follow, and I bring up the rear, staying half a flight down from the others. The stairwell remains quiet. Thankfully, so does my mind.

We reach the landing at floor six and stop at Sorin's signal. Chadwick takes up a post on the stairs a few steps above the landing, then peers at me over the metal railing.

"You doing okay?"

I laugh uneasily. "Yeah. So far, I'm good."

"The Botanaari patched you up, huh?"

"Yeah. And I'm starting to think it worked."

"And I had no doubts it *did*," Sorin cuts in with a pointed glance in my direction.

I shrug and focus on Chadwick. "I wasn't sure. Coming back here…"

"I get it," Chadwick replies. "I still have battles with my own demons. If we survive tonight, maybe I'll apply for the same treatment. I've learned to cope over the years, but sometimes it all comes rushing back in like a black fucking tide."

We fall silent, lost in our own thoughts, while Sorin continues to listen to the comms through his earpiece. I've made it this far. I can make it to the executive level and through any obstacles Zylar Inc. or the ZIEG loyalists throw in our path.

And I sure as hell won't be captured again. I'll go down in a flurry of plasma rounds first.

After almost a minute, rapid footfalls echo through the stairwell from somewhere overhead. Sorin holds up a hand, indicating we should remain in position. Xia and Berry silently edge past Sorin to flank Chadwick on the steps, while Nate unholsters a plasma pistol from his location at Sorin's side. I creep up the final steps to the landing, one pistol trained on the steps below, the other on the steps above.

The footsteps grow louder. Ragged breathing accompanies their passage, punctuated by the occasional sob. Whoever is in the stairwell with us isn't ZIEG. They're alone—and distressed, if the sobbing is any indication. The sounds move nearer until I can hear the scrape of individual soles on the steps and can identify the sobs as feminine.

A petite woman bursts into view, her dark hair disheveled. Makeup and tears run in rivulets down her bronzed face. She skids to a halt and swallows another sob, her brown eyes wide as they survey our group.

"Oh no… There are more of you?" The words spill from her lips as she collapses to her knees and presses her body against the wall. "Please don't kill me. I was only… I'm an accountant. I just want to go home!"

Xia glances at Sorin, who nods once. "Cover me," she hisses at Chadwick.

Xia withdraws a cylinder from one of her pockets, twists off the top, and produces a syringe. "It's a sedative," she says to the cowering woman. "I'm giving you a choice. Let me knock you out for a few hours, and you'll live to go home. Refuse, and…" she gestures to the barrel of Chadwick's rifle, which is aimed with deadly precision at the woman's head.

Another sob wracks the woman's body, but she manages a nod. "Just make it fast. I hate needles."

She turns her head away while Xia jabs the syringe through the thin material of the woman's designer blouse and into her arm. Within seconds, she falls silent and slumps more limply against the wall.

I scan her vitals to make sure, but her breathing and heart rate are both normal. She'll be okay when she wakes up.

Another thirty seconds tick by, then Sorin says, "We're clear. Luna's team is headed to the executive floor now."

"And Patil?" Chadwick asks over his shoulder as he resumes his march up the stairs.

"No sign yet."

I scour the classified sectors of the 'net as we climb, dividing my attention between our rear and my research. I need to know more about Commander Patil, and why they've mentioned him so many times.

His personnel files are more restricted than most. He's former military—no surprise there—and is named as one of ZIEG's founders. His record clearly states he's ruthless, intelligent, and has a history of eliminating targets without sparing them for interrogation. He was only the third human to be augmented according to ZIEG's current standards, and the only one listed as having two distinct sets of cybernetics. He's both a DFNR-BT series and…

"Holy shit."

Sorin shoots me a wary glance, and I grimace inside my helmet.

"Sorry, it's Patil's file."

Chadwick laughs grimly. "Now you know why Luna's so worried about him."

"He underwent a second set of augmentation a few weeks after I was sent to Primordia-1," I continue, unable to stop. "It almost killed him, but now he's defense *and* offense. *Fuck.*"

"But without Botanaari help, he couldn't figure out the science behind your armor," Nate says quietly. "You still have that advantage."

"And as strong as my shields are, plasma still pierces them," Chadwick adds. "Luna has seventy percent of ZIEG on her side. Patil's outnumbered and outgunned."

I don't share his confidence. Patil has my speed and strength, Chadwick's thick skin and shielding ability, and all the training and resources ZIEG has to offer crammed inside his skull. Hell, he probably has access to weapons and tactics the rest of us never did, *and* he's still on Zylar Inc.'s side of the battle. I don't want to know how many corpses he'll leave in his wake before Luna and her crew take him down.

Sorin updates us periodically as we continue the long climb. By the time we reach the skyscraper's middle levels, Luna's team has effectively secured all but the top-most floors of Zylar Inc.'s corporate headquarters. There's fighting in the lobby as Patil calls reinforcements in from ZIEG HQ, but the maintenance stairwell we use remains clear.

We halt outside the door leading onto the executive floor, while Sorin speaks briefly to his crew back on the shuttle. I train my pistols on the stairs below, but all is quiet there. Gunfire can be clearly heard on the other side of the door, accompanied by expletives and screams, periodic crashes, and the unmistakable whine of plasma weapons priming.

I decide to swap the pistols for my rifle before we're given the signal to exit the stairwell.

Sorin disconnects from his call with a sigh. "Luna's people are protecting the maintenance door and our crew in the shuttle. There has been some fighting, but it looks like it's under control now."

Nate's relief is palpable. "That's good. I didn't want to split…"

Sorin nods in understanding. "I know, but with his heart condition, the stairs would have been too much. He'll be fine."

"I'm not sure I can say the same for us," Nate mutters, his voice too low for Sorin to hear.

"This is all going according to plan," Chadwick assures him. "We assumed Patil would be on this level with his most trusted associates."

"How's Luna?" I ask Sorin.

"Busy. They have Patil cornered in the board room." Sorin eyes the door warily. "What we're hearing is the fighting between his subordinates and Luna's. I'm still waiting for our signal."

Something heavy and potentially armored slams into the other side of the door seconds later. Nate dives for cover, dragging Sorin with him. I pivot to aim my rifle at the assailant on the other side, but the door doesn't open. Seconds later, footsteps race away from our location to the counterpoint of projectile weapon fire.

"You should stand to the side," Chadwick advises as Sorin regains his feet. "If a plasma bolt hits that door, some of it *will* get through the nanosteel plating."

Sorin nods and edges away from the door. "I didn't consider that."

Chadwick chuckles dryly. "It's why I'm here."

Two minutes crawl by. The executive level grows eerily silent, and I begin to wonder if we'll be given the all-clear. Sorin stiffens abruptly, pressing one hand against his earpiece as he listens. His expression darkens, then he looks at each of us in turn.

"Patil hasn't been detained yet, but the rest of the floor is clear. Luna thinks she can keep him in the board room while we input the control codes, but it isn't a guarantee. More reinforcements are in the lobby and outside, but Luna believes her team can hold them."

I glance at Chadwick and nod. We've got this.

"It's your call," Chadwick says, "but we may not get a better opportunity."

Sorin visibly steels himself, then glances at the Coalition team. "If we're all on board…"

"Let's go," Nate says, while Xia and Berry both nod.

Sorin taps his earpiece. "We're going in."

Chadwick takes the lead, with Berry on his heels. Nate follows them, his pistol drawn, followed by Sorin. Xia exits the landing, then I take up my place at the rear.

The corridor is in shambles. Bullet holes riddle the walls, office doors hang precariously on protesting hinges, the imprints of armored fists and shoulders marring their surfaces. Half of the overhead lights are dark, their clear shells shattered and cracked. Distant gunfire echoes from somewhere deeper within the maze of offices and corridors as Luna's team continues to battle ZIEG's decorated commander.

Our route takes us closer to the present fighting. Shattered holoscreens rest in corners, overturned desks and cabinets partially block our path, and the walls are adorned with not only more bullet holes, but the warped and bubbled signature of plasma bolts too.

We turn a corner and come face-to-face with a trio in tan-to-gray camouflage armor identical to Luna's. Weapons are aimed and primed on both sides before the leader of the trio holds up a fist. Chadwick does the same an instant later.

"You're verified, all but them," the leader nods in my direction. "Can't get a fucking scan…"

"It's Verex," Chadwick growls impatiently. "You won't get one."

"Copy that. She mentioned he was here." He waves along the corridor, then points to a door near the end. "That's Marim's office. We'll hold the perimeter, but it sounds like trouble's on its way."

"What form?" Sorin asks as we begin to proceed.

The man laughs darkly. "Patil. I don't think they'll keep him contained much longer. Some asshole told him you're here."

I want to ask him how Luna's holding up, but there's no time. We need to get Sorin into Marim's office, upload the codes, and transfer all government functions into his control before Patil arrives.

And I need to focus. My job is to protect Sorin, and I'll be distracted if I learn Luna's injured or worse.

I hate myself for saying it, but sometimes it's better not to know.

Sorin glowers, but moves ahead as Chadwick beckons us forward. We pass two rooms whose doors are missing. Dead or unconscious cyborgs in dark blue ZIEG-issue armor lay in neat rows. Most are adorned with shackles on both wrists and ankles, and all of them display visible signs of recent combat. Some of them will require extensive repairs—if they survive at all.

I avert my gaze and scan the hall for any indication of ZIEG's presence, but I only see more cyborgs in non-standard armor, clustered along strategic points as they guard our corridor. Gunshots ring through the air, nearer than they'd been before. I hope the man we spoke to is right and they're capable of holding the perimeter in the face of Patil's wrath. But if not…

I consider my options. Between Chadwick and me, we *might* possess the strength and skill to take him down. I'll defer to Chadwick's expertise on tactics since my history of unfortunate decisions has landed me in some of the worst shit the galaxy has to offer. And I know he wouldn't trust me to make the right call anyway. I can't blame him.

The last room before Marim's office looks to be a make-shift triage center for Luna's forces. They're as battered as the others, but most of them are awake. I wonder if the ZIEG loyalists—I can't bring myself to call them enemies—were dosed with the same concoction Xia used on the woman in the stairwell. Whatever it is, it's potent if it can overcome a cyborg's enhanced biochemical defenses.

Some of the soldiers in the triage room nod to us in passing, and most offer Sorin a brief salute. If Patil manages to break through the perimeter, we'll have some backup, even if they're wounded. I hope it won't come to that.

Chadwick pauses outside Marim's office and glances at Sorin, who nods. Chadwick kicks the door in viciously, his rifle panning across the empty room twice before he motions that it's safe to enter. He moves aside as the Coalition team files into the room, then crooks a finger at me.

"We'll stay here," he says, pulling the dented door shut. "If Jet's right, the commander's incoming."

Jet must have been the man we spoke to in the hall. I gnaw my lower lip and nod, unsure what to expect if Patil shows up.

"Just tell me what to do," I reply. "I'll follow your lead."

He chuckles. "Good idea. You're still a rookie, no matter what forms of hell you've been through."

He pauses to survey the corridor as a round of projectile gunfire echoes and ricochets from an adjacent hall. "You know what you're capable of," he continues. "I'm built for—"

"Defense, yeah," I cut him off. "I worked with Captain Wax on Sorin's base. I know what he can do. You're the same."

"Okay, good, you do pay attention sometimes." I can hear the amusement in his tone, but it rapidly fades. "Patil was the same until a few months ago, when he opted to have the same augments they gave you added to his system. We'll have to work as a team and hope some of Luna's crew shows up when he does—"

His words are cut off as a bolt of molten plasma streaks through the air from the nearest corridor and embeds itself in the wall. The paint melts and begins to ooze around the impact site. From my vantage point, it looks as if the plasma burned clear through the wall.

"Shit," Chadwick hisses. "There's no time for a lesson in tactics. My advice: If you get a clear shot at Patil's head, take it. I'll shield you as best I can while you do what you were built for. We can't let that asshole through this door."

"I know." I check the rifle and make sure the safety's off. It is. "I didn't come this far just to fail."

Shouts erupt along the adjacent corridor, followed by a rage-induced roar. A spray of bullets hits the wall. Several of the wounded cyborgs exit the triage center, weapons drawn in anticipation. Nods and gestures are exchanged; they'll hold the hallway as long as they can. Chadwick and I will be Sorin's last line of defense.

"How long will it take him to input the codes?" I ask as another roar splits the air.

"Sorin estimated the process will take five minutes to complete," he replies without looking at me. "Patil's almost here."

I run the time calculation while focusing on the corridor ahead. If Sorin started immediately, we have just over four minutes before he's finished. It doesn't sound like much, but when faced with an opponent like Commander Patil, it could be a near-eternity.

But I can do this.

No, I *will* do this. For Sorin, for Pablo and Daaros, for the other cyborgs still threatened by the enforcement of their override codes. For those we've lost, like Zinn.

Commander Patil emerges from the side hall, his armor a mass of scratches and scuffs, but he looks relatively unharmed. He fires back the way he came from as the wounded from the triage center begin to shoot. He moves, almost too fast for my eyes to follow, a blur in ZIEG blue.

All of their shots miss, and he bellows a triumphant roar.

I clench my jaw in determination. He won't win today. Not on my watch.

I flood my system with adrenaline and pour my energy reserves into speed. No one else can match his frenetic pace, but I *can*.

He turns to face the wounded in what should have been a blur, but I can see his every movement with pristine clarity now. I can stop his rampage—I only need a clean shot.

I take aim, tracking him as he whirls through our nearest defenders, striking with his fists as often as he fires his weapons. Some of his targets won't make it, but I can't afford to think about that now.

I narrow my eyes as he pushes a struggling woman effortlessly into the wall and blasts another from close range with his pistol. The second woman falls to the blood-soaked floor and doesn't move, a hole in the center of her tinted face plate. Patil cocks his gun hand back, prepared to punch the woman he's pinned, and in that moment, he gives me the opening I've been waiting for.

I have a clear shot at the side of his head.

His fist begins to fly forward at an impossible speed in the same instant I fire.

Patil's fist grazes the woman's helmet and impacts the wall at the same time my shot hits its mark. There's a brief flare of light as the plasma meets his defensive shield, but it doesn't protect him from the round. He staggers sideways and releases the woman.

Patil falls to his knees, but he's not dead yet. The bastard *should* be; nobody takes a plasma round to the head and survives, not even ZIEG's most elite soldier. The woman stumbles away from the wall, blocking my path.

"Move!" Chadwick bellows as Patil attempts to regain his footing.

She glances over her shoulder with a shake of her head, the last act she performs before the commander grips her neck from behind and snaps it. I don't think that's an injury we're built to survive, but I shove the thought away. There's no time to dwell on it.

Patil turns toward us, murder in his eyes as they glare through his clear face shield. Blood and cauterized tissues are visible in the aftermath of my shot. He begins to charge forward, nimbly avoiding the bodies in the hall as he releases another roar.

There was a time in my life when I would have hesitated, when I would have been rooted in place and frozen by fear. But I can't let this asshole win. Not after everything I've been through.

I take aim and fire. Not once, but twice, both shots striking his face shield. The first burns through the last of his defensive shield and begins to melt the faceplate, leaving molten polymer in its wake. The second vaporizes most of his face.

What seems an eternity later, Chadwick reacts and sprays a round of high-impact bullets at the commander. Most strike his armor and ricochet into the nearby walls, but a few embed themselves into the charred mass that was Patil's head.

The commander falls backwards, adding his corpse to the pile he left in his wake.

As soon as he's down, I drop my rifle and cut myself off from the tide of biochems I poured into my system.

I immediately realize my mistake; I begin to shake and struggle not to vomit inside my helmet. Even though this mission has been a success, I still can't escape my penchant for screwing some part of it up. At least this time, it's a minor miscalculation, one that won't land me with another stint as someone's prisoner.

Chadwick ignores my reaction and stomps forward to unload the rest of his clip into Patil's head. It's overkill, but I no longer care.

I wrench my helmet free as a wave of revulsion roils my stomach into a churning cesspit. My biomechanical organs aren't supposed to react this way, but it's proof the mind is sometimes more powerful than the body, even one as augmented as mine. I retch to the side, but nothing comes up.

"You're okay, Verex," Chadwick says as I lean against the wall and breathe. "Plasma rounds do a number on someone's face, huh? But

I'm glad you were here today, or this whole thing would have been for nothing. He was too damned fast."

"Glad I'm good for something," I reply weakly. "Fuck. I didn't want it to happen like this."

"Nobody did." He shrugs, then bends down to pick up my discarded helmet. "Next time, let your system come back to baseline gradually—you'll feel better. And we can't puke." He places the helmet into my hands, then adds, "You should put this back on, just in case."

I nod, exhaustion creeping into my bones, and pull my helmet back into place. I hope my future as Daaros' bodyguard is less eventful than the past year of my life has been. I don't want to fight anymore. Not like this.

The door to Marim's office opens a minute later. Nate and Xia exit, followed by Berry. I turn around, questions on my tongue, but Nate holds a finger to his lips, seeking silence. Xia points inside the office, where Sorin is seated behind Marim's desk, the holoscreen aglow before him. His trademark blue glasses rest atop his head.

"My name is Sorin Johnston," he begins in a measured tone. "Most of the galaxy knows me as the leader of the Resistance Coalition, and in some corners, I'm known as the Blue Ghost. I am broadcasting from the executive suite in Zylar Inc.'s headquarters."

He pauses to tap on the tablet resting on the desk in front of him. "The document I have just transmitted across the 'net contains detailed information about Zylar Inc.'s assets, including the defunct AI mainframe, public transportation, and the methods they've employed to maintain control of every essential function we rely on as citizens of this galaxy. I believe you will find it a fascinating read. I've made it freely available to everyone with a 'net connection."

"What's he doing?" I whisper.

Nate laughs softly and flashes a grin. "He's unveiling his plans and changing our future for the better. Listen."

So, I do.

EPILOGUE

BOTANAAR, VYNAAS HOME/KEPLER-47 SYSTEM

"I never thought I'd see you wearing an actual suit." Vee grins as they adjust my collar a final time, then stands back to admire their handiwork.

"I feel ridiculous," I complain.

The design of my suit was of Pablo's choosing. It's charcoal gray and tailored for my frame, accompanied by a sky-blue collared shirt, a silvery vest, uncomfortable black shoes, and a matching belt. The suit cost more than I made in my entire career as a scavenger on Earth.

"It's your best friend's wedding," Vee replies. "Even I'm wearing a suit, although it's nowhere near as fancy as yours."

"It's the price of being chosen as Pablo's best man."

My internal chronometer chimes with a reminder that I need to be in the Vynaas' garden in ten minutes. I grimace and point to the door.

"It's time."

Vee grins. "I'll walk with you, then find my seat. Will the audience be split according to who invited us, like human weddings sometimes are?"

"Yeah. Pablo insisted the ceremony blend human and Botanaari rituals. The Vynaas was surprisingly accepting of it."

"The Vynaas isn't half as terrifying as you make him out to be."

I shrug as we enter the guest wing of the compound and are met by Kelsey and Tariq. Yeah, they're still together. Tariq has opted for early retirement, and Kelsey has signed on as part of Sorin's personal security team. Though it keeps her busy most of the time, I've visited my sister more in the six months since Sorin took over than I did in the previous ten years combined.

It's nice—most of the time.

Kelsey beams when she sees me. She's wearing a pantsuit and heels, making her almost as tall as Tariq. "Oh, little brother. Look at you!"

I flush and shoot a pleading glance at Tariq. "Uh, hi, Kels."

"Pablo knows how to outfit people, that's for sure," Kelsey continues, oblivious to my discomfort. She takes the cuff of my jacket between her thumb and forefinger, noting the texture. "Is this actual spider silk?"

My blush deepens. "Yeah…"

Her eyebrows lift at the confirmation. "Damn. He has good taste. *Expensive* taste."

"Kels, your brother needs to head downstairs," Tariq says, finally coming to my rescue. "You can gush over his suit at the reception."

She pulls me into a brief hug, then backs away with a nod. "Of course. Wedding party business."

"I'll talk to you later, Kels."

I breathe a sigh of relief as I extricate myself from my sister. Vee snickers, amused by the exchange.

"I didn't know your sister was interested in fashion."

I roll my eyes. "She usually isn't, unless it involves me."

We make it to the end of the corridor before we're stopped again. Quiara, Nate, and Geo are in the queue for the elevator. Quiara moves away from the two men and bounds toward us, offering a smile to Vee before pulling me into a hug.

"It's good to see you, Kye. How are things on Botanaar?"

"Quiet. I like it."

She smiles. "I'm glad. I wish I could say the same, but since Sorin put me in charge of galactic communications, I've had almost no time for myself. It was a struggle just to make time to come here, but I wouldn't miss this for the world. And no one turns down an invitation from the future Vynaas."

"We'll talk to you at the reception," I promise as the elevator slides open.

"Of course. I want to know everything you and Vee have been up to as part of Daaros' security team." She flashes a grin and steps aside to let us pass.

Nate and Geo follow us into the elevator, but Quiara remains outside. She waves as the doors close and we begin to descend.

"I hear you've talked Daaros into founding a charity organization," Geo says after we exchange greetings.

I smile at that. "Yeah. He knows what life was like for me and Pablo on Earth. He's providing the funding to help other residents get off world, if they want to leave, that is. They get medical treatment, temporary housing, and assistance with school or finding jobs."

I broached the subject with Daaros only two weeks after I left Megatropolis behind, and he readily agreed. Araan has been instrumental in organizing the charity, and he's been tasked with scheduling shuttle tickets and job interviews for those who accept our offer. Vee finds them housing, and I make trips to Earth to promote our work.

We've assisted more than a hundred people so far and receive more requests every day. Going back to Baja Colony or one of the other decrepit settlements that struggle for survival is always painful, but with my cybernetics, I don't have to worry about the toxins, pollution, or radiation. And I'm helping people escape the hell they were born into. I'm helping people like me.

"Careful," Vee warns. "Kye's found a passion more intense than the one he has for his horror novels. He'll talk about this subject forever if you let him."

I laugh but don't deny their claim. "I promised myself I'd go back one day. People shouldn't be forced to live like that because of their genetics, and I want to help."

"And according to our records, you are," Geo replies with a grin. "I oversee the status of charities and nonprofits now, remember?"

The elevator opens and we exit onto the landing. Beyond the glass walls of the corridor, the Vynaas' gardens are in full bloom. The doors are propped open, and Araan stands just beyond in a suit matching mine. He's in conversation with Daaros' brothers, but looks up and waves as we approach. The older of the brothers, Kaalor, holds a tablet in his hands.

"Good, you're here," Iinas says as he beckons me over. "Kaalor was convinced you wouldn't arrive on time."

"We'll talk later," Vee whispers as they slide past, Nate and Geo in their wake.

"I was waylaid by my sister," I reply, eliciting a round of laughter.

"You're here now," Kaalor says with a grin. "I wanted to run through the plan a final time before the ceremony begins. You and Araan will proceed to the front, following the aisle we made in the center at Pablo's request. Araan will stand on the left when facing the audience, and you'll stand on the right."

We both nod. Our parts aren't important to the ceremony until later, but the reminder of placement is welcome.

"Once you're there, remember to smile," Kaalor continues. "Our fathers will follow and take their seats, then Pablo and Daaros will enter riding our fathers' most prized *kiiru*. It is your duty to assist them with the dismount."

"Of course." I smirk, recalling our practice run two days ago. Pablo will need my help with the process, if that was any indication. His attempts at dismounting solo resulted in more bruises than successes.

"Our fathers will then conduct a formal greeting for our guests and a Blessing of the Suns. Afterwards, Taanen Dal'Roaa will lead the *briia* ceremony." Kaalor scans his tablet, then nods. "He'll cue you when it's time to produce the opal settings they'll fit into one another's *diivoraa*."

"You did remember to bring Pablo's setting, didn't you?" Iinas asks me.

"Yeah. It's right here." I pat my jacket pocket, feeling the thumb-sized opal nestled within.

"Good. The last thing we need is a missing setting. Our fathers would be furious," Kaalor says with a shake of his head.

"So would Pablo," I reply with a chuckle. "I won't let him down."

"After the ceremony, our fathers will invite the guests to the reception." Kaalor taps at his tablet and frowns thoughtfully. "The caterers have prepared some of the best Botanaari cuisine, but there are also a number of human items that I'm unfamiliar with. Pablo approved them all, of course."

We're interrupted as a large group exits the elevator. Kelsey and Tariq are among them, along with four other former ZIEG soldiers, Quiara, Trin, Max, and Sorin. We move aside to allow them to pass while we finish our discussion.

Sorin gestures to Trin and Max. They walk ahead, trailed by most of the cyborgs and Quiara, but Kelsey and Tariq remain behind with him. They maintain enough distance to avoid the appearance of eavesdropping, though I know damn well Tariq can hear every word we say.

Sorin's dressed formally, his usually mussed hair combed into some semblance of order, and the blue glasses are nowhere to be seen—though I suspect they're hidden in one of his jacket's pockets. I haven't seen him in person since I left Megatropolis, but I've watched many of his speeches on GNN. He looks tired, but not more so than he did while managing the Coalition.

He offers his hand to me, and we shake. "It's good to see you, Kye."

"Likewise. I'm glad you came."

He smiles, a genuinely happy expression that I've seldom seen from him. "I wouldn't miss it. Daaros has done so much for me over the years, and I know how much Pablo means to you. Besides, the government is efficient enough to run itself for a few days. I have three hundred senators clamoring to make a name for themselves during their terms in office. They want to impress the galaxy, and they only have a few years in which to do it."

I nod, recalling the debate over term limits that GNN reporters fixated on for weeks. Sorin opted to enforce them for the senate as well as their interim chairperson. After four years, anyone currently elected is finished, and a new batch of people will replace them. What they do after their terms are over is up to them.

It's a messy, potentially chaotic system, but the theory is everyone will have a voice via their elected senator. And by limiting their time in office, it ensures no one person gains too much power or influence. There won't be another Zylar Inc. controlling the galaxy. It's too early to know if the new government will succeed, but I'd like to think it will.

And speaking of Zylar Inc., Marim was allowed to retire to one of her estates on the Aloha Moon after Ghost's Revolution, as GNN has decided to call it. She dissolved Zylar Inc. shortly after and sold all of its assets. Daaros bought some of the tech branches, diversifying

VaasTek's considerable portfolio and increasing his personal wealth at least ten-fold. The media *loved* that story.

The paparazzi sometimes capture images of Marim from a distance, often accompanied by the former agent Jeron Malachi. He resigned from GISA after the coup, but I haven't followed the gossip columns enough to learn the details. GISA still exists, though it reports to Max now.

"We can discuss the political situation later," Sorin says. "I won't keep you from your duties as best man."

After Sorin leaves, Kaalor smiles wistfully. "He kept his word to our fathers, at least. The Botanaari have a voice in galactic matters that we were never granted before."

"Sorin keeps his promises," I reply. "He has for us too."

Araan nods. "We still have not thrown a proper party to celebrate the destruction of ZIEG's override codes. We should plan something once the *briia* is finished."

I laugh in response. "You know I'm not one for parties, Araan."

"Ah, but not all cyborgs hate fun," he counters with a grin. "I'm sure your friend Vee would approve."

"They would."

I glance past Daaros' brothers to the guest area, where dozens of white chairs have been placed in precise rows. One of the garden's enormous fountains burbles on one side, while a cadre of musicians sets up on the other. In front of the chairs is a small dais, where my best friend's wedding is set to take place. Trees and flowers of every variety provide a serene backdrop to the scene, while Botanaar's twin suns sparkle in the clear sky overhead.

It's a perfect day for a wedding, a *briia*.

The musicians strike up a soft melody, and Araan glances at me with a knowing smile. "It's time."

"It is. Let's see our best friends married."

We move toward the guest seating area and pause at the rear of the arranged chairs. I glance at Araan, then he takes my arm. It's not so different from the traditional human weddings I've watched on the holovids. But this one is unique. Special. It's Pablo's.

We begin to walk along the center aisle toward the dais as the last of the guests scurry to their seats. The perfume from the garden's blooms is stronger here, but it's a pleasant scent and not overpowering. Araan drops his arm as we reach the front of the assembly, and we both move into position.

The Vynaas and his partner come next, but they don't remain standing as we do. They take their seats in the front row and wait expectantly, garbed in matching white suits trimmed in silver-gray.

The music shifts again, more purposefully this time. I gaze beyond the crowd as a pair of antlered *kiiru* trot forward. Daaros sits atop one, seemingly at home on the enormous beast, while Pablo clutches the reins of the other. Pablo smiles, but there's an undercurrent of fear in his eyes. Even after Araan's lessons, he isn't comfortable with riding. But his *kiiru* matches Daaros' stride for stride as they move toward the dais.

A grin splits my face as Pablo's eyes meet mine.

My best friend, the brilliant engineer who orchestrated his escape from the hell that was our home world, has found his handsome prince. Anyone looking at them can see their future is a bright one.

And I'll be there to share it with them, standing in the background, the wraith determined to protect them as the galaxy rebuilds from Sorin's Revolution.

480

THANK YOU FOR READING WRAITH AND THE REVOLUTION!

If you enjoyed reading this book, please consider leaving a review.

Information about new books and their release dates will be posted on my website (www.ajcalvin.net), as well as shared via my newsletter. If interested, you can subscribe by visiting my website and clicking on the "Subscribe" tab.

ACKNOWLEDGMENTS

If you read the author's note at the beginning of this tale, you already know that Wraith and the Revolution was a long time in the making. Almost thirty years. During that time, it went through so many iterations that I've lost count, and as such, there are probably more people I should thank for assisting with this book than I will remember. Thirty years is a long time, and I'll be the first to admit I'm not always the best at keeping track of people long-term.

I have to mention my brother first, because he is the only person who read the original story (which was then titled The Space Bandits.) Despite the ridiculousness that ensued on the pages of my then-13-year-old self's manuscript, he still found things to like about it. He has always been a supporter of my stories, and without that, there's a good chance I wouldn't be writing as I am today. So thanks, Patrick.

Then there's my husband, who also acts as my sounding board for ideas, a sometimes editor, and is, without a doubt, the biggest supporter of my books. I can honestly say I would never have published *anything* without his encouragement. I have a history of low self-esteem, but he's given me the confidence to pursue—and continue—along this path. If you enjoyed this story, or any of my others, it's because of him. Thank you, Joshua.

There are so many others who have also encouraged me along the way. My parents, who tolerated my "hobby" as a kid, but let me pursue it anyway—even when I went through more notebooks in a school year than should have been reasonable. The handful of close friends that read some of my early stories back in middle school and high school: Vanessa, Erin, Sam, Jessica, and Corey. Those who encouraged me to keep writing through college, even when I opted for a different career path: Nick, Lindsey, and Eric. And then, more recently, the authors I've connected with who gave me the courage to publish *this* book after reading some of my others: L.L. Stephens, Timothy Wolff, C.B. Lansdell, C.J. Daley, E.P. Stavs, Kat Kinney, Ayrton Silva, Diane Youngblood, P.L. Stuart…

I know there are more names that I'm likely forgetting here, but just know that if you've read any of my work and enjoyed it enough to tell me, I appreciate you. Those little words of encouragement now and then are what keep me going. They keep me writing.

For the final copy of this book, I'd also like to thank my editor, Sheena, for wading through this chonky beast and helping me polish it for publication. I'd also like to say a huge thank you to J. Caleb Design for the incredible cover art (for those reading this, yes, that's Megatropolis and its artificial rings on the cover.) And finally, thank you to Samantha of JustMiss Art for the character portraits I was able to include.

ABOUT THE AUTHOR

A.J. Calvin is a science fiction/fantasy novelist hailing from Loveland, Colorado known best for The Caein Legacy and The Relics of War series. By day, she works as a microbiologist, but in her free time she writes. She lives with her husband, a turtle, and a salt water aquarium.

When she is not working or writing, she enjoys scuba diving, hiking, and playing video games.

For more information on the author and news about her writing, please visit her website at www.ajcalvin.net.